SCHOOLING

He McGowan's play, *The Return of Smith*, was staged at Lincoln Ce Living Room series at HERE in 1997. She lives in Providence, Rh land. *Schooling* is her first novel.

'Sim ne of the most special novels I've ever had the chance to read – a thri rystalline novel of adolescent consciousness, a brilliantly unflinching mar of lyricism and erudition, a book which like the best books contains a who gent and unforgettable world. The voice in *Schooling* is intoxicating in it ge – elegantly literary and freshly contemporary, cinematic, playful – a lways flooded with emotion. Really a remarkable achievement.' Jon Lethem

'So rgeous and fluid, so achingly alive, you will remember what it's like to read so ething brand new, as if with her unique sense of language, Heather McGow has managed to crack open the world, like an egg.' Alice Hoffmann

'An rthly, sublime piece of work … completely haunting. I simply loved it.' Azzopardi

'O stonishing. I don't know when I last read a book so quick-minded. It m he conventions of most fiction seem artificial and plodding. This is o azingly fine writer and alert, fresh mind. Schooling is, among other thi the kind of book that makes you redefine what you're writing and reading.' Andrew Greig

SCHOOLING

Heather McGowan

ff

faber and faber

First published in the USA
by Doubleday, a division of Random House, Inc.
First published in the UK in 2001
by Faber and Faber Limited
3 Queen Square London WC1N 3AU
This paperback edition published 2002
Printed in England by Mackays of Chatham plc, Chatham, Kent

A CIP record for this book is available from the British Library

ISBN 0–571–20671–9

2 4 6 8 10 9 7 5 3

SCHOOLING

ONE

I

Did it grieve me to bring the girl. Of course it did. Add to that her
mother just gone and knowing how it is from my own gone young well
of course it grieved me. I said as much to her shooting silences all the
way up to Chittock Leigh. What a fine June day, I kept saying, Mild isn't
it Catrine Catrine to which she always replied, Yes Father. Well, I even-
tually suggested, Let's have some publegs. Just then we passed the Horse
& Trap. Look, *bach*, here's six for me already. Six? she said, Six, what
kind of horse has six legs? Well, I said patiently, What kind of trap is it
without a driver. Maybe it's parked, she said moodily to her shoes. I
pointed to the upcoming pub on her side but when we drew near saw it
was named The Happy Onion. Happy Onion what kind of pub's that, I
said, Onion indeed. Finally rousing herself to speak she said, Well it
could be that your old coachman had his leg shot off in a war. Yes, I said,
And there's no telling the nag isn't a hopalong herself but there are
things you might infer like a publican wanting his emblematic men in full
possession of their limbs and we discussed some if I was a cheating father or simply fatherlike. The White Hart appeared on her side Six! she
shouted and I veered. Six, she repeated thumping the armrest, Six for
me. I laughed. Now who's a cheat, why six may I ask. Because there's
never a white hart without a hunter to shoot it, Father, you have to infer
a hunter. Well I let her have six so we could be neck and neck and she
wouldn't sulk coming to see the new school and there it was before I
knew it up through mist like a liner. Same as it was the very day my own
da brought me though he sprinted away upon arrival whereas we were to

3

tour and have salads with the head. Yes she did go silent again though to her credit never once mewled. We walked through the halls nosing in the dining hall where Brickman used to throw cutlery at innocent backs mine included past the stairs where Hawthorne once told me he loved another boy out through the courtyard to the cricket pitch before it rained. And there it stood glowering across the cultivated green, a bundle of boards, the cricket pavilion. If I was numb until now, well here's where I felt something. The old days, not so bad. Darvish and me having a smoke then walking across to sit on the steps. You could find a form of silence there. It behooved you to take the quiet where you could. Did it smell the same. Why not. Linseed, leather. Sweat. I said, This wasn't such a bad place in my day, Catrine. I replaced a kneepad which had fallen to the floor. I told the story of Mr. Mortimer joining us at dice. I'd related it before. Repetition will make the story myth. She stared out toward School House. I said, I recommend the cricket pavilion as a place for thinking and you'll do plenty of that here among these intelligent minds. She asked, Did Hamey go here, Father and I said, You know very well he did not he was a friend from the old days in Gwydyr. Imagine Hamey at Monstead. What a match that would have been for the old school. No, Hamey left me too. Walking back, such fineness to the old pitch. I kneeled to make a point about the grass. Softer than in Maine, I yelled to drown out my cracking knees, See how all the rain makes their grass soft. On cue, rain began to drop. In the drizzle, I hustled my daughter inside, then swiftly hustled her out again, away from a couple of boys slanting their eyes at us. Grinning louts in cricket whites. Across to the old science labs now a toolshed of some sort. We cleared a patch in the grimy window to spy through. I told her how Prep meant homework, you did it every evening in your classrooms form by form, how Tuck was delectable treats sent from home or bought in town and she'd be given a locker for her swiss rolls and peanut butter, how she'd be assigned a school number we'd sew on her uniform, that Sides was the word for punishing essays which she better not be getting any of. These were important details to get right. No one offers explanations when you

4

begin and asking questions leaves you soft. I described autumn how the trees go their colors, how the walk down the hill to town becomes a golden walk, how she would play tennis and rounders, learn to handle a violin oh how you'll love it here *bach* my daughter my dear how you will flourish among the finest minds in

England. And he jumped back, walking quickly away, for there was Stokes offering slices of ham, tomatoes pale from salad cream. Father and the Head were boys together. After lunch they made for the car his hand on her back propelling her gently waving good-bye to the silent Stokes who stood at the top of the steps worrying the patch he wore over one eye. They would return to London he to work she to watching cricket in the park to attending dog shows to losing her way on buses to solitaire in the cracked-up kitchen. Slamming shut the hired car the school was prehistoric dwindling they circled the drive grinding the gears all the way back. Cutting the hedge-banked corners, Father focused on what awaited, such days would she have, minds to shame Einstein, discovering worlds within words, can you imagine the heritage here this place where I once was how you'll love the old school where they debate so fiercely, they read such books, they marvel at science.

2

They sniff glue. In the alley behind the tudor watch shop where the smells marry, vegetables, piss. Brickie *you stay away from him, you'll see that boy's a bastard* clumsy with the fixative. Bringing up his father's handkerchief to cover mouth and nose. Bastard eyes watering. Speaking thickly through the cloth. Watching her kick away a bottle on the cobbles. Watching her say, How can I hear you through that?

Brickie brings down the handkerchief . . . You're supposed to be looking out, not looking at me.

I told you not to bring her . . . Paul *him too he's even worse* older, fifth form, waits for the glue. Tips of fingers in trouser pockets just the nails. Scarf a concertina around his ears. Looking one way down the alley then the other . . . A yank . . . muttering . . . God help us.

Paul can be your lookout . . . and into the bright street.

Through the village green past the fountain with the rearing horse. As if she needed Paul with his rattlesnake neck always saying Yank. Past the church, its stopped clock. Tea at five-thirty. Half past. Great mattress of white bread to baffle stomachs needing more than a fleck of fish. Jam sandwiches three times a day. Twice. Be fair, there's marmalade in the morning. Which she eats because Father likes marmalade. Past Wenley Smith. Into the Chemist's.

Lavender grannie soaps in crenulated wrappers, shelves of orthopedic devices, plasters. Pumping a solution for eczema. Never warm at Monstead, not like this at least. Never nearly hot. Crossing to linger at the lip display. Behind her a woman curses her child. Salmon to mud with something plummy in the middle range.

The word chutney. Why. Maybe Ploughman's for Tea. Hard roll, cheese and chutney. Fifteen minutes by the clock above the door. Late for chutney. In the mirror she tries FireFire. Hair chaotic, you could say. She didn't pack a brush and why would Father remember. Forgotten pencils, lost hairpins stick her when she lies down at night.

Form a comb with your fingers. Or use a palm to smooth it. Chutney chutney. Might have seen it on the menu outside the dining hall. Posted there to temper appetite. Gilbert never says anything about her wild hair among the jokes he makes. Calling attention to her teeth when they studied calcium, blonde gags when the topic was hydrogen peroxide. As if she didn't have enough problems with hair.

I know things on you . . . Brickie against the counter, cuffs torn . . . What's on your mouth?

Wiping away FireFire.

What's this do? . . . he's picked up a silver tin from the display.

Eyelashes. You have to wet the paint.

Move it . . . knocking her from the mirror spitting in the tin.

What is it you know on me?

Brickie, reflected . . . Something . . . mouth open in concentration painting an eyelash masterpiece . . . You'll find out soon enough.

Hastening over, the clerk What, blustering in misbuttoned smock Do You Think, as if they have personally degraded her commented on her exposed roots You're Doing, with rising indignation With That? Brickie all the while unwavering in his careful application Young Man?

Testing it.

The clerk snatches for the tin but leftover glue has affixed it to Brickie's hand launching the blondish woman into an attack of You public school You think you're the Well I'll tell you Think you can Give it over and Brickie into a dramatically pained Ow You're hurting me That's skin Watch it. Until the woman rips free the mascara with a terrifying smile.

Calm yourself . . . Brickie rubbing his palm, batting thick eyelashes . . . You're hysterical.

Brickie's downturned mouth like that of his trouty father. The ambassador presented Catrine with five dead fish *It's a pleasure to make your acquaintance* so she understood that it was a hand being offered. That she was to shake it. Then the ambassador handed Brickie a handkerchief. Politely indicated nose care.

Brickie and his eyelashes turn to hang elbows against the glass counter . . . You're a snob.

Lend me some money.

What for?

Just lend it to me.

If her hair were wet first she might get a comb through it. What could Brickie possibly know on her. How much did a comb cost. Gilbert was two days away. Bath night tomorrow. Enough time to shampoo.

3

Damp on the washroom ceiling. A spot to make Father say, Atoll of some sort, these curlicues of coral. What will you have, Catrine? More round island. Sicily? Toes add HOT simian dexterity hotter hotter.

7

Draped, she is an atoll. Under water. Quiet. Not for long. A burst, the cubicle door slams open. And she's up in a tidal wave. Maggone at the faucet, cuffs rolled to the shoulder an orderly for the mad, That's Enough Hot, dashing a hand in the water. Why Why must she be so selfish clacking out on selfish (tap shoes? metal on her heels?) self-ishshellfish resounds down the row of cubicles to lukewarm girls in their selfless baths. Selfish mingling with Scrub Yourself Sophie Marsden Not Down There Mind clack clacking down toward Mareka toward Siobhan's obstinate nicotine stains Better Not Be Henna Hathaway clack clack Maggot's prison warden strides Sophie's hanging over the wall now miming scrub scrub now lolling her head Look, I'm Jesus now singing football songs Had a sheep oh and it was good to me. Hearing Sophie's song as she curls sinking deaf, weightless, dead. If Isabelle, no. Once apple trees were their horses. Once rebellions were led across deserts.

4

Mr. Brickman, I can tell, has made steady progress on the copper oxide experiment from last week. In fact something tells me it's become an obsession, *What on earth could be the effect of oxygen on a copper wire* ... Gilbert waist against his lab bench ... That right Brick? Astounded by the possibilities of reactions when a catalyst is added? Lost your appetite, have you? Touch of insomnia? And the odyssey from Tea to Prep, undoubtedly for you it includes cogitating the differences between fluorocarbons and hydrocarbons.

Sir? ... Brickie plays the fool, the boys laugh ... Sorry sir?

But why is Gilbert paying all the attention to damn—her hair is clean. Mostly straight. She arrived early to claim a white lab smock not an ugly green one. Why won't he notice.

In any case ... Gilbert smiles with one side of his mouth ... I'm certain that once again you will awe 3X ... lab coat propped open ...

With your intellect . . . waist cocked between thumb and forefinger . . . Am I right, Mr. Brickman?

Sir.

A game between the two of them and she with washed and smooth hair bleached smock leaning as Gilbert does against a scarred wooden lab bench waiting. Next to her, Vanessa tapes her leaking fountain pen. On her other side, an empty space for Siobhan still smoking her morning cigarette behind the cricket pavilion. Next to Vanessa, Sophie with a finger dug in her ear. And on down the row. All of them waiting standing waiting for the lesson.

He is calling her name.

Yes, sir?

Was that a yawn?

Sir? I don't think so.

You don't know whether you were yawning?

I. I guess I was.

Guess. Yes Americans guess a lot don't they? What is it Evans? Too much bed and not enough sleep, is that it?

And he has made a remark again like the ones about her hips and teeth. Everyone is laughing even Sophie even Vanessa arranging burettes. All of them.

I don't know. Sir.

Dropping his coat and waist, Gilbert has turned away from her, from her foul yawning, from her too much bed, turned to the board with chalk, dismissing her disgusting hair her useless smock.

Vanessa licks a finger to flip a page in her exercise book. Sophie steps back to wink but she was laughing only a moment ago.

Gilbert's bleached collar defines the back of his neck. Hairline. Broad back right arm raised chalking out $2Cu+O^2=To\ see\ you\ oh$.

In the front row Brickie has turned his back to Gilbert. Elbows against the lab bench, he stares at her. She raises her eyebrows. Curls her lip. A catalyst but he won't react. Won't balance the equation. She stares. He stares. Stubborn both. Brickie with his black hair his bastard hair in his eyes leaning as he did at the Chemist's. Upper lip up to no good.

Siobhan slides in past Nessa past Sophie dragging the last and too small lab coat shedding wrappers gold twix and old tests reeking of cigarette smoke ignoring Gilbert's In your own time in your own time.

What did Brickie mean that he knew something on her. She hasn't been in England long enough for trouble.

5

Skipping stones across the dirty pond after school. Sophie and Vanessa come to the other side their four legs casting shadows two and two across her and the water.

Brickie stares at you . . . Sophie. Hands in blazer pockets thumbs out.

No he doesn't.

He does Catrine, I've seen it as well . . . Nessa like a little bell ding ding as well as well.

Do you speak to him?

Sometimes . . . throwing a rock into the pond to see how quickly it will sink . . . He lent me money.

Money? What for?

Sophie . . . Vanessa pulls . . . Let's go in.

Oh go on Nessa, I don't want to.

Why not.

Go by yourself why can't you? . . . Sophie watches her try to skip a stone one not flat enough then back to Nessa . . . I'll be there in a moment.

Halfway to School House, Vanessa stops once and looks back. The sun low, she can't see Nessa's face. Just the pause.

Did you have friends in America?

Used to.

What did Brickie lend you money for? Brickie hates everyone.

They all seem to like him.

That's not the same thing.

No.

They built this dirty hole when my brother was here . . . Sophie kneels down on the other side of the pond . . . People are always falling in trying to jump across.

It seems pretty wide to jump over.

Catrine . . . Sophie folds the hem of her skirt under, watching her fingers do it . . . Someone told me your mother's dead.

Is she?

Raking the dirt for flatter stones . . . You laughed at me in Chemistry.

What? Oh, it wasn't at you particularly. Gilbert's like that to everyone, you'll laugh when he does it to someone else.

Really? . . . *he's like that* taking in Sophie's earnest knees fingers to *everyone* worrying skirt boyish hair . . . To everyone?

At some point.

Another unrooted stone not flat enough to skip . . . I didn't realize.

Don't take it personally.

I don't . . . fingering off dirt off the stone.

Catrine.

Easter. She died last Easter.

Here I've found you flat ones.

You skip them.

I'm hopeless.

Hold it like this, like pinching . . . like a waist held between thumb and forefinger.

What did Brickie—

Why do you think he doesn't like anyone?

I've never thought about it . . . Sophie searches for stones . . . He just doesn't.

Out the back gate lanes switch down around the school fields. One leads to town the town where Brickie lent her money for a comb to straighten her hair for Chemistry for Gilbert for nothing. What are the names of these English plants in lanes banked by hedges hugging the neighboring farms and fields. Littered with horse droppings the frozen ruts trip them as they concentrate on where they are going which is nowhere. Sophie's hands are big as a man's big as Brickie's father's and as she talks she chops the air.

Boys from town pass yelling NUNS for their grey uniforms but whistling at them all the same. In one field grazing cows black and white like the watch shop where Brickie—what was it he had on her?

You seem to do as you're told . . . Sophie pulls her down a hidden path . . . I'd never have thought you'd miss Tea.

I've skipped school before . . . and rolled a tire into traffic slinging a motorcycle . . . I'm not so good . . . a sudden red bird from the trees what kind why doesn't she know the names of birds . . . Isn't it funny that you thought that about me . . . watching the bird fly the man fly . . . That I was some kind of girl you thought you knew but you don't at all.

You probably think you know things about me. That I'm a certain type.

I think you're alright. You ask a lot of questions.

Do I?

See.

Well, you don't ask any at all.

The light cold and orange edges down like it did that day she and Brickie were in the Chemists when he put on makeup and was rude to the woman. Behind a dairy covered with vines beyond the millhouse and a thatched barn past pencils of silos they ramble on with no ideas of destination only the idea that they should not return. Not straightaway. Sophie knows how to sneak into school. They will be alright.

6

The question remains must we all be forced to bear the shenanigans of a few idiotic pranksters . . . Mr. Betts strides the room, turning abruptly on his heel . . . Upon my arrival here this morning I found that someone had left a message for the Head Man informing him I was on my deathbed and would not be teaching 3X's English lesson. Imagine my surprise . . . head to one side . . . To discover I was ill. Can you imagine, and your imagination will be tested this term, that one of your classmates might not be as inclined as the rest of you to study literature . . . another pause for their imaginations to chew on that horror . . . No, 3X, I am afraid this is not how it is to be. We will have our sonnets, we will have our Yeats our Leda our Hamlet with all attendant ghosts and killings and girls got up as boys. What we will not have is pranks or bad manners. So.

Sophie glances back at her. A sly wink.

Five sides each on the matter of poetry . . . Betts holds up a hand against their pain . . . Unless of course, our comedian steps forward.

The shifting stops. She shoves Sophie's chairback. Weakly jointed, it slants into a rhombus.

Well?

A kick at Sophie's seat. Nothing. Another kick. Useless. Sophie will not confess.

So that is how it will be. I'll expect your essays next week. Choose your poison, Yeats, Shakespeare . . . Betts picks up a book.

Low unhappy mutter from the stalls.

Well, what am I to do. Brickman?

It wasn't *me*, sir.

Methinks he doth— . . . Betts interrupts himself . . . I haven't accused you of anything, son. It's your recitation I'm after . . . motioning with a ruler . . . Up up.

Brickie stands. A baroque throat-clearing, then . . . I felt a funeralinmybrainandmourners—

Hold on, Mr. Sack of Potatoes . . . Betts waggles the ruler . . . Shoulders back, head high. Begin again. And when you speak of horses, convince us. You must see them printing their proud hoofs—

But I wasn't, sir. Speaking of horses.

Brickman . . . Betts struggles to compose . . . The sign of mediocrity is a bending towards the literal.

Brickie overthinks that.

Now, continue. I Felt A Funeral.

7

Midnight maybe at least a few hours since Lights Out. What has she woken to mourners the stories of hauntings white lady headless man breathing of the other eight a grunt here Mareka Holland talks in sleep the nine beds the blue bobbled bedspread pulled up so cold she wears wool socks hat beginning of November what awakened her? Moonlight through a slice in the curtains the windows reach up to the ceiling. What's the book where a girl hides behind a curtain on a wide sill. Weary night. Pull your head under the covers to get it hot with breathing. Alone now. Not like in Maine because there was always Isabelle but there was never herself so much as here.

Sophie.

Face deep in her pillow blankets tossed hands folded under stomach Sophie shifts.

Wake up . . . kneeling next to the bed, working out a shoe wedged under her knee.

What are you doing? . . . Sophie quickly awake.

Shh.

Go back to bed, Catrine.

I have a question.

You'll get caught.

Can we go somewhere.

Tell me here what is it.

I'm freezing.

Get in.

In your bed?

Yes. What is it?

I saw something.

A ghost? You saw the—

Something, a shape.

Your mother?

No.

What then?

A ghost of me or something.

Did it have a head? It was the white lady, the—

No. Shove over.

Sophie tries to give her room under a fat duvet brought from Hampstead not school blankets stitched in red *1922*.

Remember I was telling you about my friend in America my friend Isabelle?

Go on.

Once we skipped school . . . they had why had they had it been her idea she remembers it as her idea but maybe it was Isabelle now it seems more like something Isabelle would dream up but she was sure somewhere that it had been her idea . . . And took a bus to a different town any town it didn't matter we wanted to get out . . . with just enough room in the bed that she can lie on her back dropping off the edge a bit and Sophie can lie on her side watching her as she stares straight up at what would be the ceiling if there were light enough to see it . . . We walked up this road . . . curved like an ear . . . It was curved like an ear we walked into the woods and we talked but as we were leaving we found a tire . . . details . . . A grisly tire lodged in the dirt . . . Sophie waits for her to tell it . . . We dug it out. We could see the road down below us.

You pushed it down the hill.

We rolled it into the traffic and we knocked a man off his motorcycle.

Is he dead?

He could be . . . it's close and they can smell each other's breathing . . . I don't know.

You killed him.

Don't tell.

A man.

They will never speak of it again.

A man . . . Sophie's eyes can seem so big . . . It's his ghost you're seeing.

I told you. It's mine.

8

So. Dropped in the middle of a boarding school plot. Pacing the sidelines of a football match. Monstead versus. Who. Something Saxon. Hamping or Felixston. Rounded up to cheer on the fearless Monstead players. Pasty-legged warriors. Pacing one way she passes Simon Puck nose ableed Brickie helping *Tilt Your Head Back* Spenning and Mr. Betts in intellectual collaboration Devon of Art charcoaling ghastly trees Sophie frowning at the boys *What's Wrong with Them* confused *Why Are They Running Like That* Vanessa hypothesizing *I Suppose They Want To Win* Siobhan wincing *Thinking About It Makes My Lungs Hurt* and across the pitch Gilbert applauding the save wreathed by fifth form girls Fi Hammond and the weird sisters. Pacing back she passes Siobhan braiding plaiting Nessa's hair *Some Stupid Saturday This Is* Sophie shouting *You Always Look So Cold Catrine* Devon's trees resemble skeletons unrapt Spenning listening to Betts declare *How I Loathe Mimetic Renderings of Natural* interrupting *Oh That's Good* himself *Pardon* to scribble the wisdom in his blue notebook Spenning nodding ignoring calling *Well Passed, Haynes* Simon throwing his arms *GOAL* in the air forcing a new red trickle from his nose Brickie shoving Puck *Go To The San, Simon* Gilbert sending a wave before she looks away here's Cyclops striding by to survey the troops *Settling Are You?* Yes this is settling Cyclops disappears Brickie's arrived and together they pass Devon dabbling in unlifelike landscapes relating to Betts *Well, the grape got him* gossip à deux Betts sagely informing *A man will burn himself in the same place over and over.* Brickie snorts at that. She stops. They face off. A glare, not without mystery. Behind him, deep in field, Paul Gredville stops to watch them talk. She turns to Brickie, They say you don't like anyone. Is that true. Brickie smiles or could it be the shift of light. Abruptly he mimes smoking a cigarette, grabs Siobhan and disappears.

9

Monday at breakfast Paul in his tight grey leaning down to her . . . Brickie left me in town with glue stuck everywhere. Said he had something to tell you . . . tipping his plate his boiled tomato slipping around the bacon . . . What was it? . . . grease leaking from his fried bread and eggs . . . What did he say . . . so close and even at this time in the morning smelling of cigarettes . . . You'll tell me what it was.

Why would I?

Everyone does.

Doesn't mean I will.

Oh yes . . . the plate right under her nose all she can bear is toast and . . . You will . . . cups from the pitchers of tea and coffee they put out alternating . . . Oh yes . . . tea coffee tea coffee . . . You will . . . snarling sixteen at least if not seventeen Paul the smell of his grease tomatoes curdling her stomach . . . Yank.

Before she has thought not a good idea particularly bad idea she is up to escape the rancid smell but is instead tipping his rank plate eggs tomatoes down Paul bacon down his tight cigarette fried bread saturating his chest hearing as she runs the SMASH of plate his bearish roar the gasps the laughs the trouble she's in.

Out across the cricket field Do Not Step On the Pitch flying to the back lane *howzat* through the trees the shrubbery and out lurching on the furrowed earth. The clear air sings in her ears as she runs scrambling Paul will kill her he must be at least seventeen and no one can protect her from that. How should she know why Brickie stares his pretty mouth black bastard hair why did they act like she should know when she couldn't even tell them what he had on her. Tearing from the dining hall she saw Sophie turn from Vanessa turn with surprise that said she probably couldn't save her from this oh half a bed half a night under a duvet but no protection not from a sixteen-year-old.

The cold air hurts her chest. Walking down a different lane now, one to take her away from school. They will call Father in London to tell him she has flown. *Gone, sir, she's gone.* The teachers won't know why not even Gilbert. Gilbert who apparently shows the same attention to all of them even gobstruck old Siobhan in her too-small smock.

Isabelle would know what to do. Whose idea had it been to roll the tire, she couldn't remember. Isabelle would protect her from Paul.

As she walks, the morning sun a cold ball above, grass at her feet stung with white, the world seems to curl up and away.

Leave the lane for the road to town to find a park or shop. Make friends with the fishmonger, a woman stunk with cats. Forget sleeping nine to a room, Father would find her. *I expected more but I was wrong to.* A car passes then slows. *After all, I was nine when I went.* Brake lights redden. *It was eight years before I saw my father and then a world war between us.* Up ahead, the car pulls to the side. Men kill girls, Isabelle once said. Everyone knows that.

Crashing back into the lane away from killers prying through a hedge faster heart thumping madly for the second time today. Then she hears him. That dry almost high voice EVANS, hears him where the lane meets the road muttering, Oh my shoes were not made for this.

Damn. She goes around the hedge this time.

Raising his eyes from his shoes, What in heaven as she picks leaves from her sweater not smiling pointing at his head, Twigs in your hair as she pulls them out still not smiling asking about a Particular dislike for Monday's lessons as she's straightening her skirt and adjusting her stockings aware he watches the adjusting.

Or are you running away?

Just running.

Well . . . smiling so she'll know know he doesn't pay that kind of attention to the whole class know that he wouldn't watch the adjustment of just anyone's stockings . . . Come on I'll run you back.

Where were you going?

Home. Been up all weekend making sure one of you lot doesn't burn down the assembly hall. Difficult to believe, but I do in fact have a home . . . he falters . . . I didn't mean anything by that, I was trying to be funny. I meant that I spend so much time at Monstead.

Too much. I mean I do—I feel like I spend too much time there.

Doesn't your family come to take you out? . . . opening the car door for her . . . Or are they in America?

No. Neither . . . inside the car warm the seats covered with cream wool . . . Is this from a sheep?

It's fake . . . revolving the key.

Wait. Mr. Gilbert . . . a hand nearly on his to stop it at the crest of the wheel . . . I'm in trouble.

He looks at her hand then her.

She takes away her hand but puts a plea in her eyes not too much not too dramatic but just enough just enough to say your jokes the class laughing a cup of tea not back to school not yet an hour or even half just a small favor.

What trouble he pulls the wheel in the opposite direction of school what sort of trouble is it that has you up and running in the wild. Well Mr. Gilbert she reports smoothing her skirt nicely Have you heard of this boy Gredville in the Fifth this devourer of rodents a night creature well it seems that this dark spirit is out for my head.

Tell me what the trouble is, Catrine.

Turning into a driveway hidden from the road by hedges and a yew. Not what she would have imagined. If she had. A small lopsided house. Covered with ivy.

It's rotting the structure, the roots get in and undermine the mortar

still I do love it . . . his wild mess of a garden not the usual careful English . . . When I have the time I'll get round to weeding . . . leading her
through as he untoggles his duffel, into the heavy-beamed sitting room.

Newspapers tented on the table cups a plate with crusts and jam
dark paintings of streets. Books everywhere. On table speakers chairs
yes on shelves but piled in corners and under the windows.

I should telephone the headmaster, Catrine or they'll have the
hounds out.

He'll make you bring me back.

Perhaps that's the right thing, hum? Oh God . . . Gilbert takes a
sheet of newspaper kneels twisting sections placing one by one in the
fireplace . . . I don't know. I'm not used to these situations. I'm a
Chemistry master not some sort of psychologist. I should take you
back, you must speak to Miss Maggone about unpleasantness. She has
experience in those matters.

Maggone hates Americans.

I'm sure that's not true . . . Gilbert removes books from a stack of
wood selects two logs replaces the books logs go in the fire . . .
Actually that probably is true.

Do you . . . in the chair removing a book *Tropisms* from under
her . . . Hate Americans, Mr. Gilbert?

I don't have anything against Americans . . . standing up peering
into a Toby mug on the mantel then a small box finding matches behind a framed photograph . . . When I mimicked you that time, I
was trying to amuse myself, the class . . . kneeling again striking a
match . . . Sometimes my jokes aren't so funny, I realize that.

Yes crossing her legs then uncrossing finally settling on
crossed . . . What city is that?

Pitiful attempt at Amsterdam . . . worrying the flames blowing
lifting a corner of newspaper . . . Trip I took a year ago. Paintings
don't do it justice.

The fire lit, the room seems to darken as if the light has been
sucked up by the fire, as though the light were O_2.

My mother would have liked those.

Would have?

She died . . . turning to the window because it really does seem darker outside.

Gilbert pauses . . . I'm sorry . . . then continues fussing at the fire.

She liked dark paintings . . . back again . . . She called them democratic.

Democratic, did she.

Why is he puffing away at the fire when he could sit? She has removed the foliage from her hair she should be in a class, English or . . . Do you still paint, Mr. Gilbert?

You sound so sad . . . finally leaving the fire crossing to sit on the sofa across from her with his scar . . . Surely they're not that awful. I paint on weekends sometimes when I'm not on duty.

Paint what?

Catrine.

Sir.

You needn't call me sir in my house we're friends here. I'm glad you like my paintings, I'm glad your mother would have liked them, I can't say anyone from school has ever seen them but—

I like them a lot.

But. Are you warm enough, are you shivering?

I'm fine. But what?

I should put more paper on or another log—

But what?

I feel somewhat awkward that you're here. I know the school wouldn't like it.

You haven't even asked what the trouble is.

Well . . . down at the cushion next to him memorizing the brocade taking his time to say . . . What is it, Catrine?

Stretching out her legs they are long for nearly fourteen she is one of the tallest and that includes boys should she arrange stockings again carefully or simply stretch and say . . . Like I told you before, Mr. Gilbert. Paul wants to kill me.

You know how boys are Catrine they pretend to hate girls but really.

No, I spilled breakfast on him. Humiliation in the dining hall.

Is that all it is.

Did I say humiliation no no I meant to say how that strange heart made his sweater rise and fall, white feathers pulsing as they caked with egg.

I mean good God I thought it was something dreadful something—

It is dreadful.

Gilbert jumps up strides to the window inspects the sky and yes takes waist between forefinger and thumb as he seems to do when thinking or pleased . . . I think it's going to snow . . . smiling back at her then not smiling . . . You weren't even wearing a coat out there.

I do feel slightly sick.

We must get you back.

Please . . . can't help that it comes out so forcefully, bite it down . . . Mr. Gilbert I haven't finished telling you.

But you're ill.

Shifting . . . Maybe I'm just hungry.

Releasing the sky the assessment of snow . . . Hum, I suppose Gredville is wearing your breakfast . . . out into the passage . . . Let's go see what there is. How's toast?

Gilbert's kitchen warm with its Aga stove and old cowhand picture.

Yes I picked that up at a jumble sale does this bread seem alright to you or does that appear to be mold I also bought a complete set of medical dictionaries get yourself a plate from that cabinet published in the seventeen hundreds it's horrifying what they practiced in the name of science in those days.

Taking the plate, blue with a shepherdess on, nodding as he flips her the toast, to butter, of course jam.

Back we go . . . she has the plate, he steers her by the shoulders to the sitting room.

And sitting she could ask what's the upstairs like awkward toast are there fireplaces jam on the corners of her mouth he watches her lick it off.

Catrine, I think we ought to call Headmaster it could snow and who knows what frenzy they're lathering themselves into over your disappearance—

Is it her leaf caught hair or that she is American why can't he let her be why can't he let her stay.

Can't you tell them I'm alright, Mr. Gilbert? That I've fallen asleep in front of the fire, that you think I should sleep for a while because I seem sick or exhausted or something?

Considering her, Gilbert seems fourteen or so with his white scar and his dubious testing of a finger against the table his leaning forward to hear the sound of his voice making that telephone call watching her with uncertain eyebrows waiting to hear it. How a conversation like that would happen how it would go and who would say what.

Paul Gredville, hum?

Sir?

But he is halfway from the room and she knows he is not *like that to everyone.*

Outside the light grows dimmer still. She moves to the window in homage to Gilbert's movement there, testing her hands on hips, waist between forefinger and thumb, observing the garden, wondering at the sky, whether it will bring the snow it warns of, exasperated at the weeds she never got around to pulling, marveling at mortar's submission to ivy, cataloguing repairs. In the recesses of the house the faint chime on noon yet

Do we need a lamp on? . . . from somewhere . . . Catrine?

dark enough for midnight.

9

Most disturbingly, Mr. Stokes had no idea you were missing. He thanked me for my concern said as soon as you were awake I was to deliver you to the San . . . judging by the echo, Gilbert must be standing in the doorway she noticed the roof eaved in the hall . . . It's gross deception I'm taking part in, Catrine. It's a mistake.

I'll go back.

The click of a lamp a pool of light. And he crosses the room to the lamp next to her.

Wait . . . she touches his arm . . . Look at the snow.

Gilbert forsakes his waist to fold his arms. Side by side they watch the white fall. A marvel yet she cannot . . . Have you ever . . . what the hell is she saying when she doesn't know anything.

Hum?

Painted . . . again words again . . . Well have you ever painted a person?

Finally he places yes one hand on his waist holds it turns and leans the other arm and his body against the fogged window behind which the snow floats before which they stand like two decent people in ordinary conversation.

I'm no artist, Catrine. I'm simply amusing myself.

He has forgotten that he has made a mistake that he has lied to Cyclops that she offered to return. He could be thinking of her adjusting stockings he could be thinking of her licking jam she has felt him hold her waist between thumb and forefinger this man on his rounds so purposefully inserting his unclean but could it be shaven in the back hair before her nose to correct her failing experiment to retrieve a hair from her page to hold it up between that celebrated thumb and forefinger, to inquire *Yours?*

Pardon, Mr. Gilbert?

The other paintings . . . again he reaches for the lamp beside her . . . They're stored away somewhere.

Do you still paint? . . . breathing in his faint shampoo . . . What about Chittock Leigh?

As he draws back . . . I suppose I don't find it as glamorous to paint what surrounds me although it can be inspiring here at sunset or even sunrise . . . leaning against the window again . . . But I can't think you're ever up that early.

No remember too much bed and not enough sleep.

Still I go driving sometimes, some weekends. Try to find something.

Look at the two of them leaning against cold windows like old friends chatting about painting and snow and she tonguing her molars to find raspberry seeds from his jam. To review: He has leaned across her to offer up the scent of his hair. He has phoned the headmaster to ensure she will stay. She has eaten his toast and stretched out her legs.

You seem to be avoiding the subject of Mr. Gredville.

Oh . . . the snow quilting the unweeded lawn . . . It's not important.

Him killing you?

I can't think about it now.

Mr. Brickman seems to have taken a fancy to you . . . he watches her reaction she chooses to consider the whitening grass . . . Does he have designs on you?

Under sheets.

You be careful of those lads.

Under striped sheets behind the wardrobe she finds the paintings.

Could it be nearly one o'clock the chimes again although it seems they chimed only seconds ago the unused room dusty . . . Sorry it's a little—I'm just thinking I ought really run you back you ought really go to the San it could be something serious . . . but all the while hefting up the mattress to tuck under the sheet running out to take a pillow from his own bed . . . I will get around to tidying one of these days it's not often I have visitors . . . unfolding blankets drawing the shade. A moment by the window . . . How dark . . . then back to fussing as he did by the fire wiping the bedside table with the sleeve of a robe hanging from the door . . . You'll call for me when you awake, if you need anything. Do you think—should I take you back?

I don't feel well enough . . . kicking off one shoe . . . I mean I just need to sleep I'm homesick I'll be . . . now the other . . . Alright after a nap I'll call you if I need anything besides . . . a small yawn . . . It's snowing your car could get stuck.

Something about homesick, that was the trick, because he softens . . . Some sleep will do wonders.

And she sits on the bed because to get under the covers she might take off her skirt but should she do it here in front of him will her shirt reach down to cover enough.

I'll get you some water . . . Gilbert slips from the room.

Pull the skirt around so the zipper faces front unzip step out. Sweater too why not. Sliding under the covers in stockings and shirt head down on the pillow no surprising pencils. Gilbert's pillow smells of Thursday mornings ten to eleven twenty smells of Argon potassium smells of too much bed and not enough sleep.

Here we are.

Back with a glass of water placing it carefully on the robe-shined table next to her judging the distance. Supine, can she reach it easily if she wakes suddenly dry or parched or needing to quench because she doesn't know what else to do in this Gilbert house in this Gilbert bed.

Don't be homesick . . . looking down at her that noble crease that scar . . . We'll take care of you here.

Suddenly he is stooping is placing hands either side of her shoulders is leaning down is moving toward her so that the smell of him rising from the pillow and the smell of him floating down compresses her as he kisses.

Under striped sheets behind the wardrobe she finds the paintings.

She can't sleep how could she. Leaning. Four of them. She knows they will be of the woman and they are.

It was only a kiss on the cheek but he should have known she wouldn't sleep if he was going to kiss her on the cheek.

She's naked of course. Sprawled, unburdened by covers. Foot hooked by sheet. Body an undulation against the background's creamy hillocks. Demented. No, badly executed shadow by the mouth. Poor lady, lonely without a bottle or bread. Not even a pear for company. And cold, skin an experiment of blues. Gilbert's love of litmus. Portrait of the Acidic Woman. Mixing his palette, Gilbert making light hummingly debating valency, hum might these democratic blues dance together how exactly does matter matter. Amsterdam was better. He should stick to naked cities. The hungry woman with her flesh and bottom and breasts and all of that. Flesh. Staring, mouth caustic. Lying on her side, forehead melting into a fleshy arm. Moaning. Please don't paint me blue again.

Downstairs in adjusted stockings loosened blouse yes and skirt. It happened that she could sleep an hour or so even after being kissed and ferreting out the blue woman. After thinking too much she could still sleep some. Down the stairs hair a thicket the clock chiming it must tell the half hour too it tolls all the God damned time.

Outside the day stays dark, in the kitchen Gilbert folds down a corner of his paper to locate her. At the bottom of the stairs. Pulling hair behind one ear. That's new hair behind the ear where did that come from.

The snow gets on her hair and the coat he has lent. Not his duffel but a wool suit jacket because *I have nothing better*. How soft the notsheep how cold his car how quiet the white around them. In the parking lot behind the San he comes around to open her door . . . You can return it any time what day is it today well perhaps I'll run into you before Thursday . . . hands on her shoulders . . . You shouldn't be homesick you're sure you're alright perhaps we should have left you in bed . . . searchingly as if—

Are you going to kiss me again.

He drops his hands. The white snow and scar. Behind him the school rises up through the weather. Monstead, their castle. His eyes his scar jumping or is it the snow falling between them. Why does he always look at her. What? In his eyes what?

You get some sleep . . . then he turns, slamming into his woolly car so, before she realizes, it is just her and the snow.

IO

DONG Morning assembly in the great hall waiting for masters black capes open like crows eyes still slow still DONG puffy from sleep to file past the statues mustached Giles Dupré Raynes founder in bronze

Apollo a broken Cromwell and Queen Victoria that one just a bust DONG up the aisle between the rows of students standing in carved pews to the first row DONG the row of velvet Simon Puck goggling his eyes fingers reading his scalp for scabs. Morning light through the stained glass above the altar plays on her hand. A yellow circle in the design appears to be a fried egg but is in fact a sun.

Headmaster stands to lead the prayer.

The light stipples Gilbert's bowed head. If no one ever visits clearly the paintings are hidden from himself.

Oh God we have heard with our ears

Yesterday, after the nurse took Catrine's temperature and informed her that there was hardly time for playacting what with students who were actually sick what with winter coming on, she was sent to Tea.

Our fathers have declared unto us

Taking her tray, she received the benediction, pink meat pie wedge, hard-boiled egg staring from its center, noble

noble works that thou did

There were no empty chairs

in the old time

near Sophie or anyone so she had to sit with first years. The younger girls wanted to know about America and she told them. Lies until Brickie passed by on his way to the bread giving her a look that made her go quiet.

World with . . . damn . . . As it was in the beginning

She doesn't try to locate the back of Gilbert's head but it seems to float wherever she looks.

World with . . . damn . . . Is now and ever shall be

Gilbert

World without end.

Headmaster stands . . . You may sit . . . patch over his one eye, three black strings plastered across his globe . . . Later this week we will be lucky enough to hear excerpts from Mr. Spenning's travels in Borneo.

Father on the telephone, Good news But we will continue this morning with Dr. Thorpe's insights Extremely good news On Man's rise from the innocence of brutehood. Man sold their house in Maine. They were to find a new one over the Christmas holidays. Questions of morality arise in A new house where Alternatives are offered of better lives. Did they need a house did they need. Understanding the distinctions between good and evil. What about Conscience. What about Hopes of spiritual ascendance. What about in Maine the day the movers came. Finding that bird's nest with Mother's hair wound in the twigs. No chance of finding something like that in any new house.

It is only after ages fraught with despair . . . Dr. Thorpe mimes despair . . . Hopelessness and grinding . . . his teeth . . . Misery that. Moral law becomes dominant. So *Ariise* . . . Thorpe trills . . . *Ariise* from a bestial to a moral plane of existence.

Across the courtyard with Sophie and Ness. Sophie singing Boring boring boring laddering a scale the sun coloring everything sharply the morning—

Yank . . . he moves in bestial, thin, the height of a man.

They have reached the door to School House. So close. One step up through the heavy oak door four steps down the short corridor to History. Sophie stops singing thunder rattles in the distance voices halt across the tennis courts pupils stop to watch clouds speed across the sun casting the group in shadow then lighting them again. The school cat flashes by. From far off comes the faint sound of a drum.

Look at me.

Well she won't she'll reach for the door past Sophie's protective arm Sophie telling Paul You Bore Us and here's her own voice apologizing no less for spilling on his—

Jumper you mean?

A movement in the shadowed doorway. Brickie steps out. He doesn't register Paul only at her his shifting bastard hair an old tired light in what she can see of his eyes.

Paul leans one shoulder slowly against the wall. Silence. Vanessa gives a little cough. Something has happened between Brickie and Paul.

You saw what she did . . . Paul finally comes away from the wall . . . Leave this.

Why does Gredville plead like that. What does Brickie have on him. Sophie's arm on her back. In this world without end, when does she begin to protect herself.

Brickie pushes back through the door toward History. Watching the door ease closed, Paul snorts, walks away. Then lopes across the courtyard tracking new springbok.

That low tone of distant thunder grows loud and ominous. Louder, louder, it becomes a rattling vibration, resting at the height of an unbearable scream. The noise threatens deafness when suddenly a silver motorcycle appears spinning around the corner of School House. Ploughing through a flowerbed, it roars across the courtyard, heading straight for her and Sophie. At the last minute, the motorcycle jerks to a stop, spraying gravel. A helmeted figure cuts the motor and flicks down the kickstand. Sophie sucks in her breath, starts backing away. The driver's tall, seventeen? Eighteen? He pulls off his helmet. Sophie goes ashen, the dust settles. The boy grins.

Oh . . . Sophie whispers . . . Owen Wharton.

II

Handel floats across the courtyard. Chorus rehearsing The Messiah. We Like Sheep, they profess. We Like Sheep, they baa.

Their adoration of sheep carries down to practice room 9 in the basement of School House. She begins again. Carols against the din of radiators. Deck the wrong note Deck the. The? The halls with—

A shadow falls across her music. She glances up. The boy from the motorcycle is crouching at her window, sliding it open . . . Fa la la la la . . . he jumps into the room.

She splits a reed.

You'd do better to improvise. God that sill's filthy . . . the boy sets down a clipboard, dusts off his hands . . . School's a muckheap. Never play a clarinet sitting down. It constricts the muscles in your throat. Besides, I want your chair.

You can't be in here . . . but she stands.

Can't? Let's make it up as we go along, shall we?

Who are you?

Introductions! . . . he straddles her chair dramatically thunk thunk his boots one either side . . . Owen Wharton, Upper Sixth, taking three A levels including Theatre Arts . . . the boy has odd vowels . . . Passed only four O levels year before last bit embarrassing but consensus was that the Biology questions were absurd . . . is he American . . . I think you'll find I'm intelligent enough for the job.

What job?

Assistance. It's come to my attention that Paul Gredville—

Paul Gredville?

Yes, has made certain threats, certain overtures, if you'll excuse the pun—

I don't need your help.

Oh God. One of those. Something to prove. It's trying, it really is . . . the boy checks his clipboard . . . Let me see . . . Owen leans back, throws open the door . . . Sophie Marsden!

Down the hall, a piano stops playing midscale.

There's a POD . . . warning him . . . Right down the hall, Madame Araigny—

Sophie Marsd—

But Sophie's in the doorway, breathless . . . Yes, Owen.

Tell her . . . and Owen's up and back out the way he came, the window shuddering down behind him.

She turns to Sophie . . . What the hell?

You're not to go out alone. Especially at night.

12

Alone. At night. After Prep's sonnet debacle. Memorizing for Betts. Sad mortality, a Fearful Meditation! Or was it Sad Meditation! Death loop. Follyfield chapel Brinton boys' dorms past the sunken lair of Cyclops. And then French too, the verbs, Araigny's odd vocabulary. Provocation. Insight, what was insight. Enceinte means pregnant. Such a calamitous Prep. Inkfight in the back, a random compass stabbing. Brickie disappeared for twenty minutes and when he returned Annie said, If you're not constipated I'll send you to the Head. But there was no way of proving it. What strong hand can hold his swift foot back? Not Annie's. Eyeglasses at a rake, sweating those tidy diagrams, sharpening, sharpening. Tennis courts. Out by the old swimming pool. La piscine. Or le. Was swimming pool masculine—

YANK out of the darkness like a cat like a life lived under a bush.

A sudden blow. Fearful mortality. She staggers. Elle stagges. It will be done, soon, yes finis.

Bonjour. She doesn't say that because Paul Gredville already has her by the arm beak nearly meeting around an insufficient bicep. Pulling her off the path skinny legs well who can choke down the food here the pink slabs with eyes. Yank he declares Yank he recalls Has anyone ever told you how you sound like you're chewing a brick?

No one had mentioned it.

Didn't you think I was serious when I told you what would happen. Where are you looking do you think someone's going to save you?

No clever answer battered by the smell of his underarm pinned against the tree how the trees go there colors here among the finest chest curves the wrong way concave or convex can he smell her fear or hair washed for Chemistry does he know she has a father or what she ate for tea. Even with his arm down she can smell him worse than that day in breakfast. The night is still there is no one they took the tire dug it out from the worms and dirt held it between them before launching down into the road into the motorcycle into the man flying the man into the bushes into the grass into the hospital. And he is going to teach her some manners is what he is going to do because how would you like bacon here or here or down

Stop it.

Stop what?

How could she not have realized that this is what it would be her with her stupid lab man with hands on blue lady paint a good night ki the motorcycle jerked like it was attached to string he was a helmet in his astronaut back of her head pencils jabbing her at night biting his dirty cigarette palm fingers vague head scraping as he pulls her kinetic against the trunk yelling but there is no one into a bush what kind of bush why doesn't she know bending under her weight their mass his hands slipping under her sweater pressure of his wings against her skirt feathers and hands everywhere over layers of sweater and blazer over her fighting for air ripping kinetic spitting up at him a pathetic mist not the blinding glob she hoped for but suddenly he stops.

Silence. Scrabbling echo held in the trees. Paul lies on his side. Puking? Crying? She backs out of the bush. He presses his face deeper into the dirt but she's

Fuck Brickie.

Hurtling down the path.

Evans.

Her hands white enough to see by. Through the night she runs and

Just one minute.

She is one flight up the marble stairs valleyed in the center when

Catrine Evans.

Yes? . . . not turning smoothing hair yes behind ears go to hell the gesture's her own.

What on earth . . . his voice from outside the Duty Office under the stairs . . . Why the racket?

Not moving . . . Racket, sir?

You sound like an advancing army. Come down here at once.

13

The POD office hardly bigger than the desk it contains. Hooking her heels on the rung. Sitting on her hands. Opposite, a crack in the plaster runs into the calendar and out the other side. Like what. The Seine, a graph. Stocks are up.

Right . . . Gilbert folds his hands . . . Mind telling me what you've been on the losing end of?

She does mind. She has a sonnet to memorize.

Catrine.

I tripped. I fell.

You're lying.

And then he puts his arms around her lightly he touches the wings—

Don't lie to me . . . Gilbert taps his pen on the desk, leaning back in the chair.

You'll tip over.

Perhaps you'd rather tell the Head first thing in the morning. I'm sure Mr. Stokes will be fascin—

Keeled right over, so dark I couldn't—

I'm not interested in stories.

The light fixture overhead is clogged with moths.

Right, first thing after breakfast—

Paul Gredville—

Ah, the boy you threw breakfast on. He's reappeared, has he?

Paul is. Very patriotic. And thought spilling like that was bad manners. It wasn't cricket to waste food. Anti-English, in fact. He shoved me into the bushes. It was nothing. A push. Then he. Ran away.

Don't lie to me, Catrine, I can see it was more than that. I thought we were friends.

So That as Betts would say Is How It Will Be. The POD rooms gets very quiet. Gilbert's chair stops squeaking his pen stops its jittering dance against the table. Even the wind settles. Really, it does.

He tore at my clothes

Gilbert stands up but no room to . . . Aargh . . . so sitting again . . . I'll—

No, no. He stopped.

Of course. Someone appeared. Another boy? Owen Wharton? Or was it a teacher, Spenning, Devon?

No. No one was there . . . this is the truth . . . All of a sudden he rolled over. Rolled into a ball and started. Crying.

He didn't hurt you?

She shakes her head.

Gilbert studies her . . . I don't know whether to believe you.

I'm fine.

Paul Gredville is. A peculiar lad. He's. A bad apple

I wish he'd disappear.

We'll leave the Head to come up with something.

The Head?

Come on, I'll drive you around to the San.

Please don't tell Mr. Stokes. Please.

Gilbert picks up his coat shaking it to assure the jingle of keys.

Mr. Gilbert?

You need to get those cuts seen to.

I saw your paintings . . . her face tight, the scratches swelling . . . The ones you hid.

You should have something put on those scrapes . . . leading her outside.

Why are you always trying to get rid of me.

Come on now . . . opening her door then the back door to throw his duffel on the seat.

Running her hand on the notsheep next to her. Last time she thought it was real.

Slams the door he pushes back the driver's seat then he waits. In the cold car together. She looks where he does at School House the top three floors lit classrooms below dark.

What? . . . why does he say her name like that . . . What, Mr. Gilbert?

You must speak to someone.

I'm talking to you aren't I?

You're not crying.

I don't feel like crying.

Still staring up at the school . . . You're stronger than you realize . . . now down at his hands ready on the steering wheel steering her . . . Some might think you older than you are.

What does that mean?

Hum?

No . . . she won't let him . . . What does that mean?

Gilbert won't answer. After a moment she pushes her head into his shoulder his delicious sweater the two of them like this in his woolly car looking out at the night and school this waist-embracing chemist with hidden paintings and a nearly fourteen American who smells the lab man's warm sweater and through it feels the swallow high in his chest.

14

Well, that didn't go over very well did it?

Startled, she drops her book. It stays there, splayed unnaturally on the ground between them.

Fancied a constitutional? Out wandering the night in the hopes of resolution? Control a Paul Gredville, that the idea? Not what I'd call the plan of a genius . . . Owen stoops for the book, hands it back . . . You don't really think things out, do you?

How does he know.

Catrine Evans . . . amused . . . But I admire ambitious failure.

She blinks. He's still there. The gap between the teeth, toothpick he chews, way he brings up his hand to blow on his wrist.

Scars. Itch sometimes. Do you find that? Scars tingle?

Don't have any.

Ah. No scars. Interesting.

Slowly, she reaches out. They both watch as her finger lightly grazes his arm. Leather's cold.

Can I help you?

Do you even exist?

That's not very polite . . . Owen moves to go . . . I mean, I could ask you the same question.

15

Comprehension last. Madame Araigny knits through the test. The French have Noël. They love to eat Chestnuts. The word for Hubris? Maneuver? Next door, Betts teaches English, his voice sloshes through the classroom wall, a correcting tempest. *Our revels, revels do you hear, now are ended*. The word for Legume. *These our actors, as I foretold you were all spirits*. The word for Pays. Frisson is a thrill, a shudder. *Are melted into air*. The radiator begins to hiss. All bent in study. Questions like Where Was Your Brother Yesterday? There is only one answer, At The Football Match. Askew. Squalor. The Bertillions cluster around the Christmas tree, congratulating each other on A Joyeux Noël. Brickie pulls off his Sweater, blue. This schoolboy here has two Arms and two Legs. In the Summer he will attend the Seaside there will he find Shells, there he likes to eat Mussels. Find a Seahorse! Locate the Ocean! Describe how the smell struck us as we came down the hill toward the dock. The Bertillions notice that Papa is missing. Ou est Papa? In the basement assembling an airplane for Pierre? Sniffing glue? Troubadour. Through the wall Betts *Lucy Trimball, for God's sake, the stress never falls on NOT*. Word for Could Have Taken. Conditional. The salt air used to strike us when we lived in America. Vanessa looks at the clock. Nessa will wear a pretty dress by the Christmas tree and Dance by the Fire for Mummy. Mummy loves Nessa's pretty dress for she sewed it herself. Vanessa chews her pencap Uncle Ian will come home for Christmas back from the RAF he will Waltz there will be Chestnuts. The future of To Spend as in You will spend Christmas dinner snubbing lemon chiffon. Outside the window, a boy's head bobs by, he's wishing he'd been born to the Bertillions with their perfect past and isosceles Christmas tree I wanted better things for you my brother how did it come to this the drugs the wrenched ending to our football matches when did you begin with the anarchy and hair dye how stupid I was never to have noticed. The boy begins to run, late or cold. The word for Hegemony, purple and mimeographed. For Time, Licorice. Madame Araigny glances up from her knitting. Quickly back to the test, Will Spend. Desk gouged with scars, initials. A badly drawn heart. An oval with aspirations. Word for Garden, a hostage of weeds. He made toast for her. Araigny's head comes up, the knitting goes down, Time Is Up. Fini. A wild guess at Insight. *Insignes?* No, failed again.

16

Past Shaftesbury Ave Father spins the combination with one finger tells the cabbie not to take a right can't he see the traffic situation why shouldn't you be educated during school holidays which was not directed at the driver. A different aspect of your education. Certainly record shops are not aspect of any education I've heard of. Didn't we have a lovely supper last night didn't I tell you the stories you love including the ever popular Hamey Eats The Bird the famous How I Did Not Marry Miranda Watson the Barrister's Daughter for I sensed your mother lurked in the world now with all that including the first chicken

I haven't scorched along with some very nice fresh vegetables from your good self you will still insist on pressing your face against that dirty window. No offense my friend to the cab driver. Aren't you lucky to see the finest museums in the world at such a young age.

Drab tea in a shop around the corner from the museum. Four spoons of sugar and often fried bread, yes she has acquired a taste for it. Then up the front steps, hello to the ticket-taker. Through to the second gallery to her favorite painting. A mountain scene, two girls, their Alpine guide. On loan from America. A wattled man, the docent, has a tour group gathered in front of it.

Sensual, self-aware, do you see . . . the guide points . . . As if the figures know they are creations. What a tense scene. Follow the gaze from child to man. And these two figures over here who point to something unseen. Our gaze lingers because we are directed to ponder mysteries.

A man in the tour ponders the mysteries of time.

Any questions?

Yes there are questions, not just Sophie's when she brought Catrine out to the fields of sleeping cows one day after English. After Betts teaching Metaphor. Do you want to sit on the cows? Sophie said. They don't mind. Certainly there are questions. The cows turned once, slowly.

Moving on, my sheep . . . the docent leads his group to Fruit with Fishhead.

Sophie would just stare. You will just stare won't you? A question. Sophie drummed her leather shoes against the cow's massive side. Tattooed the poor cow with its own family. Said Hereford sighed.

An ocean. Turner. Tell me Catrine, Sophie said, Catrine Catrine. Finally she answered, It's like. But then stopped, stumped for analogy. The cow's ears cut her view into three pieces. Indescribable. That's no answer, Sophie shook her head slowly saying in rhythm to her heels against the cowside. No answer at all. Which was true enough.

Here's a painting children love.

A farm, haystacks. In the week before Christmas, Father took her roaming. Scouring the countryside for a house halfway between Chittock Leigh and London. The scenes were identical, eager owner restraining a retriever, issuing practiced belches of delight at the pargeting or stained glass, relating the exciting history of Catholics hidden in the larder. O ye ancient trellis, thy comely mantel. In London they were still eating off a table mapped with the Bosporus, the Nile or whichever geography Father wanted over supper that night, his chicken, her vegetables, their rivers. The brick wall her bedroom gave aspect on was undoubtedly the Great Wall of China or a metaphor. Father had never gone to University so all cracks are rivers to be learned and every cumulus holds a continent.

One night, a pub. Two eaved rooms, a toilet down the hall. They left their bags, the night was thick with fog or was it rain, symbolic weather of some kind. Went downstairs for stew. The bartender's wife set down two plates, then went back to leaning against the bar, watching as they picked around gristle, carefully extracting half-done potatoes. Father saying Be Discreet for Heaven's Sake with his napkin at his lips. When the woman came for their plates, he asked about the town, the environs, the house down the hill. Behind him, two darts players laughed at Father's accent. Or were they laughing from the game, yes, one had nearly pierced his mate's nose with an errant dart.

She went up for her shandy, his Guinness, gauging the brims not to spill on the way back through the crowd. Knowing Father watched. She was no omniscient, but she knew what he was thinking. She sat down, wiped her hands. Picked up a beermat to examine the image of a milkmaid. The town clock tolled eight, nine. They were strangers. Father drew an X in the foam to see if his beer was well drawn. You used to like to do that, he said, draw an X for me. She waited. She watched a man in a rugby shirt try to fix his glasses.

You seem all grown up to me . . . Father looked where she did, at the man . . . In only ten weeks.

I'm the same.

You've gotten so quiet.

I'm the same.

Rabbiting away, a great flood of details. In the old days. Couldn't stop you. What are you saving up for?

Nothing, Father please.

We'll tell our Monstead stories. How about when Treat bolted for Corby looking for adventure. Or, day before Annual Dinner when your Mr. Stokes stole a Christmas pudding from the kitchens. Then there was Peterson who swung through a hatch on a rope that couldn't support his weight. Ended up, all the boys thought me an idiot.

When it was her turn she made up a story about Brickie's mother putting her head in the oven which was supposed to be funny but turned out squalid. Afterwards, in the boxy room upstairs, she listened to the darts players who would not be quelled at half-past but bullied the owner until nearly one.

Oh, you're remembering it all wrong, the guide glares. For God's sake, it was never like that.

Why, Father, was another question driving to the final houses on Christmas Eve. Called away from mince pies, the owners guarded their doorways, refusing anecdotes. Why, she asked again on the way to the restaurant, Father, if we have the money, can't we go back?

They arrived.

Back to America, Father?

Abstraction can increase impact . . . . the guide presents a scene . . . Though one mustn't see abstraction where there is in fact flesh.

A restaurant for Christmas dinner, distorted, abstract. A Savoy or An Emerald. Lost gentility of some kind. Where the lamplight was orange, silver burnished. Unevenly, the strings struck up 'Tis the Season and when the prawns arrived, went Dashing Through the Snow. Sunk low in the red leather banquette, lemon chiffon uneaten before her, she watched elderly couples glide across the parquet. Dances with diagrams. Father ordered port and after a few sips, spirited a bewigged woman around the floor. The apologetic husband tripped on his shoes, she averred discreetly from the man's breath. After a polite while, she excused herself for a powder, leaving Father to foxtrot or jitterbug or lindy.

The eye craves analogies, it's human nature.

Unseen on her return, she leaned against the banquette, hungry for analogy, reviewing the scene around the table. Well it seemed a festive occasion for all. The wife in her slipped wig, Father showing the man her new camera. The man concentrated on the dials, How will your girl ever learn to use it?

She's clever for her age, like I was, Father told him. The wife righted her wig lazily, But a sullen girl, isn't she? Somewhat sullen?

Catrine coughed. Sullenly. They turned.

Moving on then . . . the docent looks at a boy crouched examining the floor, elbows between knees . . . In your own time, Junior.

On the drive home Father turned down the radio, You had no business disappearing like that. None at all. I couldn't think where you'd gone.

Come on, darling . . . the mother extends a hand . . . You'll like the ships.

A different kind of Christmas doesn't seem so long ago . . . she told the dash, touched it, there it was, an oil still life knocked askew by a tree branch . . . Christmas in America.

Father kept his eyes on the dark road where it unlashed before them. Well. The night went on. Now we're in London.

His answer to many questions. In London, Father eats his toast standing as he calls down the corridor, Get a move on, *Cahhtreen*. From swirled blankets, she answers, Please let me sleep. I'll take a tube to the museum this afternoon while having no intention of taking the tube to anywhere but sleep. Father comes to the door then, triangle in hand. I don't know what you get up to all day, but I can at least rest easy you've had an educated morning. Henceforth taxi, briefcase, combination, art because she is a lucky girl, and then the long wait for Father, home at six balancing a tin of something to cook as he shuts the door behind him. To his knowledge, she has never been to the quay, Shepherd's Bush or crossed the bridge on foot. When she said she had seen Lawrence of Arabia at the cinema in Notting Hill, Father said, What, old Larry again? then stopped spooning out rice. Gripping her arms, he sat her down on the plastic chair. Did anyone speak to you because if they did or if they do again I want you to scream your bloody head off. Did they? Yes, she said, yes someone did speak to me, Father, I didn't know I was supposed to scream. Father went very still. Tell me, he said. Tell me. Well, she said and maybe it wasn't so funny, A lady carrying a tray asked wouldn't I like a Cornetto. Father's face took on a look but then he laughed and laughed. You had me there, he said, spooning rice again. You had me. No, don't scream at the concessions. Then he passed her a plate devoid of vegetables, You can look after yourself, I never doubted it.

Cemetery. Unhappy farmer in an overcoat, face covered in boils. Girl with a parasol turning turning.

She seems happy . . . a man in a rumpled suit quickly next to her, cigarette behind his ear . . . Doesn't she? Full of life, this one.

Oh yes. The gallery is empty, Junior and his tour have sailed away. Yes, a cough. She does. She does. New habit that, repeating. From Sophie or.

Dearie me . . . the man glances toward the muffled noise of the tour in the next gallery . . . You've lost your group.

I'm alone.

Ah . . . the man moves to the next painting . . . You're American.

Aust*ri*lian . . . yes, Sydney or Melbourne. Perth perhaps.

Course they don't much like Americans here. Not to worry, you'll blend in soon enough. Pick up the slang, enunciate your *r*'s. I was a boy in Tanzania for two years. You learn to cultivate other voices.

I like my—

Oh, God . . . the man dips his face sharply.

What's the matter? Is there something in your eye?

The man stands before Giotto, cradling his head . . . Ten in the morning, what on earth am I doing?

Looting her pockets for a handkerchief she's never carried. But the man has already appropriated his sleeve in a way that piggies his nose. Vaguely, she returns to the bench but does not sit. An ocean reaches up to the horizon, flat, grey. Analogy for what it's like as seen above.

Sorry . . . he sniffs . . . Not doing so well.

When the man glances up at her, she considers a painting over his shoulder.

Minerva . . . he wipes his eyes . . . Beaut-Beauty.

Beauty's ugly.

Oh no no. It's all in the look . . . the man blinks, sniffs, draws nearer the painting . . . You see the way she regards this soldier. Spirit, the eyes you see. And the soldier. The soldier too seems. Very. Happy . . . the man twitches as if to free his malaise but instead shakes free his cigarette which shoots across the gallery to land at her feet.

What about you? . . . he goes to pick it up . . . You. Happy?

Behind him, the ocean remains unmoved, grey. Above, a speck dot of white, a sail perhaps, difficult to see or is it imagine. Is it imagine when viewing those small dots of color or something you should know.

You don't seem particularly overjoyed.

Minutes until lights out. At the noise, she stopped brushing, hand stilled on the toothbrush. Turned slowly. Maggone stood in the middle of the washroom, hands clasped behind her back. She wanted a word. Silently, the two of them waited for Maggot to find it. A clatter from dorm two. Zuzz of fluorescents. She wouldn't move though the tooth-paste stung. Maggot unspooled her antennae to feel out the situation. We mustn't welter in misfortune, Evans. Sometimes life does not offer us epic proportions. Tapping it out—

Sometimes you simply have to make do.

What an odd thing to say . . . the man sits beside her on the bench.

Deliberately he places the cigarette between them . . . I had a piece of land near Scotland, a cabin for drawing. When it burned to the ground, I stopped, telegram in hand, on my way out the door and I thought, life will forever disappoint. I can't tell you what happy means per se, simply that there are moments when you face yourself and say, I am or No, I am not. Or even, I am destined to remain.

Is that why you're crying, because of Scotland?

Dear me no that happened four years ago. There are other things, adult things.

Are you a politician?

No, not that adult.

They sit for a moment in silence, contemplating the ocean. Abruptly, the man speaks . . . You have your whole life, the marvelous hope of ignorant youth.

Ignorant?

No lines on your face, no worries. Too young for regret. Nothing weighing you, a clean conscience.

Little did he know. A hill, a tire, two girls out of control. A man soaring into the ether. Malice sir I have seen malice for ten.

I regret things.

The man pauses, searching . . . I have—disappointed my wife.

A different guide, a woman with frosted hair, a hipsway, leads a small group into the gallery. Art lovers cluster on folding stools, ready for culture.

The guide opens a book . . . Before we begin. Some perspective on the nude.

That's what I needed . . . the man picks up his cigarette.

Everyone regrets things.

For example?

I killed a man.

The man collects himself. Well it was plausible. True. Who could survive a fall like that. It was a fact. Indisputable. Hadn't she seen the telltale bleeding. It was difficult from the top of that hill but she was sure there was blood all the same.

Right . . . the man breaks the silence . . . Make do, you say. I shall remember that. Have a safe trip back to Sydney.

Perth. It's Perth.

The more easily distracted members of the nude group watch the man shamble past. Guide intoning The Nude. The ocean is flat, one sail, one gull. She could be from Perth. Only the female nude aspires to beauty.

Yes there are questions and strangers will ask them of you in public spaces. You will aspire to beauty, they will march up with a coat folded overarm demanding to know about happiness.

Well, are you, Catrine?

Through the ears of the cow, she watched Sophie lean back on her palms . . . Not for Christmas, no.

I would like to go someday.

It's not what you think. Hot and oranges, oil wells.

I know . . . Sophie stopped drumming her heels . . . I hate England I hate. All this.

All what?

Green. Give me a desert. Enough of Shakespeare. You'd think the man was God.

Catrine's cow began to shift, she touched its bristly hide. I like the desert because it is clean. What did Lawrence mean. Sand is less confusing than shrubbery.

You'd better get off, she wants to stand . . . Sophie slid down her cow's stomach . . . Enough of Monstead, old Betts trying to keep the tragedies straight.

He likes you.

He likes Madame Araigny. We're all exactly the same to Betts . . . Sophie slalomed mines of hardened cowshit . . . Year after year, we're simply different heights, different degrees of poor eyesight.

They made their way across the field, it was after five, trees began to lose their outline.

Something happened to him.

Damn . . . Sophie struggled with the metal latch on a gate . . . What are you talking about?

Betts. Why is he always writing in that notebook? What's he scribbling?

Catrine . . . Sophie looked up from the gate . . . You think too much.

Into the next gallery.

The first guide, wattled, beet-red, stands before a scene of dead animals . . . Decay . . . he whispers . . . You see it in the decadence of the brushstroke, the brutal application, the shock of color.

Another ocean. A girl, bonnet. Valley. Dark as Gilbert's scene. His democratic painting. Amsterdam, he said. Or was it Denmark. In Portland, neither sky nor land was favored one over the other, no God-driven shafts of sunlight or dappled elk, just the rotting passage of time. The day was all wrong, they missed one train, Father failed to meet them. Mother's voice filled the museum as if she were cursing

The rotting passage of time.

They were in Portland to consult a specialist. She was a child then, a believer in daytrips for art. Mother said, Decay can be beautiful, you must forever question your assumption of beauty. No. Mother said, I like to work at a painting. Loudly. Frightening Catrine that she might suddenly blaspheme the lesser Impressionists or mock a bystander's interest in Wyeth. But Mother quietened. They went for lunch as if they were old friends not related, to a French restaurant with no prices and animated snails on one wall. She was allowed small sips of Mother's wine and somewhere near dessert, before, it was before dessert because right afterwards the crème caramel appeared, but before dessert Mother slapped her on the face, hard. Once. Then turning to the waiter, who was setting down dessert, she informed him that crème caramel was the hallmark of inferiority. She had always led Catrine to believe the hallmark of inferiority is lying but it was crème caramel the entire time. The waiter retreated, she looked out the leaded window at one of the oldest buildings in Portland. It had once been a hotel. A dog stood uncertainly in the middle of the street. She didn't raise a hand to her cheek. Outside, a man gripped a baguette. They had never hit her. Mother paid the bill. Mother finished the dregs. Mother had slapped her because Mother was dying.

Stewed tea with Blackened Banana. Across the museum café, the ting of dropped silver. School next week. Return without a house. The chair presses a mondrian into the back of her legs. She drains her tea.

Returning the cup weaving the stark tables past the woman pushing scone crumbs with the edge of her map past Soloman scrubbing newsprint from his fingertips through the swing door up the stairs past the grave guard good morning through the Romans earthenware dominoes Greeks one grand gallery oils second one with red walls sketches last corridor bleached with light. Sculpture Court.

Rodin's hand. Two lovers entwined. Bashful woman on a rock, hands strategically planted, ohmygoodness. Cousin of Gilbert's blue muse. Naked figure of man throwing plate. Girl kneeling for a better view. Man completely naked. Girl a step closer. Light cue and.

Here's a painting children love. Four ruddy schoolboys posed against a swampy backdrop. Flash shoe difficult to. *Hurry the fuck up, Yank*. Mutiny of the odalisques. Hold on. Struggling with the F-stop as the boys marble with the cold, ruining her composition. *Yank hurry the*—suddenly the boys yelp, stumble and scamper away.

She whirls around, letting the camera fall to her side.

A figure stands silhouetted against School House, arms akimbo. Appalled.

You, Evans? You?

Interruption. Trouble. Two days into term two. So this is how it will be. Trouble in the form of Mr. Betts, he of English inflamed with French, the married denying thinning blonde man who, when staring into his Shakespearean ether, sees only Madame Araigny's expressive fingers which, for ambiguous reasons, number only neuf. Trouble is courage taken after months of *Mr. Betts are you alright sir you look a bit peaky shall I fetch Matron?* A Comedy of Errors as the English master,

spying the object of his philandering thoughts on so many lyric afternoons, four emotive fingers of a left hand in midbring of coffee cup to
gentle gallic lips, stiffened his resolve, strode across the staff room and
troubled the Widow Araigny for an afternoon stroll. A choice made to
forsake the usual path in favor of the pastoral route by the old swimming pool. So.

When trouble interrupts on that flat January horizon it does so in
the besotted form of an amateur botanist looking up from nine
adorable French fingers to a scene—

Right out of de Sade . . . Mr. Betts fusty strides . . . Indecent.
Almost, Headmaster I don't even like to but . . . hesitant but not at all
to mention . . . Pornographic I could say.

Yes . . . Cyclops, doubtful . . . That will do I think.

Camera in her lap, finger wrapped with the edge of skirt wiping
the camera lens around and around.

Mr. Betts marches to the window as if to locate decency behind the
curtains . . . Our rules may not explicitly prohibit alfresco nudity, but—

Oh we have seen far worse, Betts. This was hardly catastrophic. I
think perhaps you should return to your Dickens—

Molière it is, Headmaster. Fourth formers.

Yes. And allow me to deal with Miss Evans here.

As you wish . . . at the door Betts spins on his heel struck by the
thought . . . Headmaster, I believe this nasty incident may have unfortunate repercussions for Madame Araigny.

Ahem. I can only implore you then to keep extra counsel on
Madame's health, Mr. Betts. For the good of the school.

Sir . . . a lozenge of light on the carpet and Betts has gone.

Cyclops, inaudible. Then holding out a hand . . . I should think
that lens clean by now.

He takes the camera.

Catrine Catrine . . . a sigh over her his eyepatch his eggshell
three scribbles on his forehead . . . I realize that last term's incident with
the Gredville boy might have its ripples felt in some disagreeable ways—

That had nothing to do with it, Mr. Stokes. They asked me—

And we all want to be liked—

That was not the reason.

But it is not in keeping with the academic code by which you have agreed to abide, by which we all, in order to live harmoniously at Monstead, must agree to abide, to take photographs of your classmates undressed and on the hockey pitch.

He is ridiculing her.

You understand my obligation to ensure this sort of thing does not happen twice.

It was meant to be art.

Cyclops swivels his chair to the window. After a moment . . . Where are you getting these ideas, girl?

Father gave me the camera for Christmas, sir.

So it's Teddy who's responsible.

A joke but answer even more seriously . . . Oh no Mr. Stokes it wasn't *Father's* idea.

Swivels back to her . . . Evans.

Sir, I saw paintings and at the Modern—

When boys do such things you should walk away—

There was a sculpture—

I'm inclined to forgive this brief excursion into your artistic—

I can't really draw but I thought well—

Character, of course a show of remorse should be swiftly under-taken—

I have a camera and art has naked—

Evans. The behavior you have chosen to display is not in keeping with the tenor of Monstead life. Now your father is ahem an old friend, you are a confused little girl and I can only think additional focus on your studies and less focusing of your lens will result in a happier situation all round.

Yes sir.

I have brought your ahem. Incident before the Conduct Committee. Since art appears to be your downfall, I propose an immersion in the sciences. Therefore you will spend an hour before breakfast each morning for the period of one month assisting Miss Dyer from the fifth form in cleaning, sorting and preparing Chemistry materials. Mr. Gilbert specifically requested your help.

Requested her specifically.

Stokes flicks at a blemish on the desk . . . Apparently Miss Dyer is somewhat preoccupied, certain matters at home seem to require her concentration.

Specifically.

Monday morning then at seven o' clock sharp you are to meet Miss Dyer at the chemistry lab. I hope this month will encourage you to see our world in a more scientific light, that you may put some of these foolish notions behind you, leave them behind as child's play and approach the world with the mind of a scientist. Our Mr. Gilbert seems to think you have some real talent in this area and it's not too early to begin bending your thoughts to your A level subjects. Perhaps you will be one of our science girls, Miss Evans, there aren't many, most seeming to prefer English or the dramatic arts, but there's always room for an exception . . . standing moving around the side of his desk . . . I think your father will regard this as fair, don't you?

My father? Please don't tell my father, Mr. Stokes.

Cyclops looks pleased, she has shown panic, a coming unglued. He presses his lips together to convey—what? There are questions, yes there are questions. Silently he nods her toward the door.

A moment outside, listening to the creaks of Cyclops swiveling. A talent for science. Then she bolts down the red stairs out the grand entrance shouldering open the heavy door asked for her specifically front lawn parking lot between the cars of secretaries and cleaners the ones who go home at night to gas fires and attentive pets running across to the patch of trees breaking through them breathing hard through them blurred coming up against the wall to outside.

Can't they take a joke. Rough hand troubling the bricks, like finding like. Face against the cool red. Don't they know how it goes in boarding school stories. Isabelle would not have been discovered. Isabelle. She turns around. Isabelle's face against the cold window. Through the trees, the school's drive encircles a composed lawn. A grid of tidy cars. Give me a desert because it is clean. Isabelle had never taken the cold seat, Isabelle was a girl she once saw opening a door. A voice cried out *Isabelle* that was all the Isabelle she had or knew. Check the tale. Sinking down against the wall. The boys had come for her. Headmaster, leaning back on his swivel chair, coughing into a handkerchief like some victim of tuberculosis, swiping under his eyepatch and reflecting on Nature. Bursar crosses the lawn to her car. Boys will be boys, or bad apples. And Gilbert, hips against lab bench, leaning over, a sidelong appraisal Your Teeth Your Hair You're Disgusting. Bursar shakes a key from its clutch, a breeze picks up, shivering her hem. Bursar shouts You are yourself a bad apple You are yourself wanting knees and forehead sweat mingling hair tangled hands all over. Bursar pulls in her feet and slams the car door shut. Holding his innocent triangle Father will hurry to the phone. Eight two oh three four one? The toast will grow cold as will his fingers where they grip the receiver. Father will say I don't understand, I have just bought a new house and arranged for the piano to sit in the drawing room. No one plays it, no one ever did or maybe the mother did, I can't recall at this moment as you've caught me eating toast on the way out the door, but I will tell you that I wanted the girl to unpack our paintings and roll out the rugs. And you suggesting she's a delinquent of some kind takes me by surprise. Bursar's car disappears through the gate. Father sighs Well, Stokesy, I don't know what to tell you, we only ever had still lifes at our house.

17

Sophie's pulling her down the Avenue after school to show her letters she's been writing to a Dane. As they get to School House, a mattress sails out of a fifth-floor window on the girls' side. Landing in the courtyard, a blue ticking lump.

18

Who can say exactly when Owen Wharton replaces their Thursday-night Preptaker the girl who takes ill or goes missing but there's a fine penmanship out of keeping with his leather jacket. Imagine him as a shadow in the louvered doors to a saloon. Only the saloon is Follyfield number four and it's a cold Thursday night and outside the set, instead of a dusty mainstreet, there's wet green bushes, an iron gate and a distressing lack of tumbleweed.

Owen Wharton, he says setting down a perfect stack of books and that undefinable accent. Welsh? Half a jigger of Scotch? A splash of the States? No questions until half past and I mean none. Therefore no one politely inquires, You a Mick?

When the clock approaches eight Owen puts down his book and blows on his wrist . . . I'm stage-managing the Aristophanes for Percival. Percy's alright outside Latin, when he's not pressing for ablatives, so let's have some volunteers . . . the boy stands, ambles over to the wooden lockers. He wears motorcycle buskins, begins a monologue . . . A play entitled The Birds.

It's black out, the glass reflects an indistinct face.

After all, there seem to be more than a few theatrical types in this classroom . . . Owen raps on the lockers . . . Actors among you.

She turns from the window.

Pay attention. Wouldn't you all like to wear wings? As close to angels as you'll ever get. It's a play where men become birds. A search for a utopia. Doesn't that sound compelling. Mortals, gods, yes it's Greek don't interrupt. About the disaffected, those left out. The birds win you see. If I were Patrick Betts I could point out the resonances I could point out how this is relevant to you brats in your lines of little desks filling your ink pens on the hour tripping to the toilet as many times as possible to avoid learning your history. On the other hand I could leave it for you to learn I could let you actually have a thought on your own which would be novel enough and not unnoble of me. Yes, an escapist play if by escapist we mean the futile attempt by men to escape the anguish of existence. O suffering mankind your lives of twilight, pale generations, you wingless! The fading! Unhappy mortals, shadows in time, flickering dreams but not to worry for there's a wedding at the end, happily ever after and all that.

Shyly, Duncan Peaks raises his hand.

Right, there's one.

Simon Puck stands on his chair, croaks.

There's two, now sit down before you break your skull. Who else will volunteer?

Silence.

Owen leans down to Brickie, plants hands on his desktop . . . You? Wouldn't you like to be a god?

Brickie tips back in his chair . . . Am already.

Legend in your own mind, perhaps . . . a comedian, this Owen . . . But I can provide an audience.

19

A Maggot enters the washroom. The audience consists of a girl at the basin consulting her program for last-minute substitutions.

MAGGONE

So this is what they teach in America, is it? Photographs of boys?

Rudely, the Maggot doesn't wait for a response, but stops downstage for a brief soliloquy before she goes.

MAGGONE

I have longed for a certain warmth since my days in Italy when I took to a boy named Marco. If I had the time now and did not have to rush back down to stalk the row of baths checking that girls scrub behind their ears but nowhere else well I would tell you of this boy named Marco his Vespa skittering chickens in the Piazza Nettuna as we raced for the hills.

Enter the Widow, aknit.

MAGGONE

Do you have Vespas in France, Genevieve?

ARAIGNY

I do not know what they drive now, *les gosses*, for I have not been back in such a time. Twenty years ago Paris made boys like your Marco with difficult lips and questions, hands at their eyebrows and through their hair, I remember a Jean-Pierre, I recall Sebastian, a Luc, Hubert. Heaven knows what has become of them now but I hitched up skirts to reveal showy garters, danced on tables, ran all night.

MAGGONE
(sniffing)

How very Weimar.

DEVON
(entering)

Genevieve, if I had the time now and did not have to rush away to illustrate the finer points of the color wheel, well I would tell you of a boy called Pablo. In the city of Madrid we painted together, he took me under a sheet when it rained well I don't want to tell you at the risk of boasting but he fell for me in broken sentences.

A large hook yanks the art teacher offstage.

ARAIGNY

In Paris I drank alcohol disguised as licorice, cursed hegemony, the status quo, belittled foreign governments for preferring intrusion to insight. I cried Revolution, if you please, let's overthrow the state. I had some youth, some youth was mine.

Oh those days. Dear Marco I penned in the best Italian I had, Dear Marco you must know that until my time in Rome, I had felt the loss of some forgotten beauty.

That sounds poetic, you must read Molière.

Yes, I was nineteen. Please don't interrupt. The loss of some forgotten beauty Marco bedazzler sphinx I think on you in my Sussex bedsit where I eat lentils under a cobweb I can't bring down you are a monument wonder my constant heart you delighted me.

20

At night the boys arrive. Hopping, bowed legs caught by their trousers. Shadows in time. Tripping on the moonlit field, falling but never landing. In his life of twilight, Paul hops too, Y-fronts bright against the dusk. They know she is American, they angle for better light. They are naked, they are nude. She tries to capture their pale generations. Paint a wolf, watch it bite. Betts and Araigny entangled on the hockey pitch, beast with two backs. Real boys in greek surroundings. Mother, an odalisque. Fading. The guide suggests, Use more blue. Have a sense of proportion. Then alarm. Pillow trembling. Difficult to know a dream without the alarm. Stealing through the sleeping dorms. Across the deserted morning to his chemistry lab to lean against the door.

You the brat? . . . shaken awake. A tall girl stands before her, red hair, jagged, lifted by the breeze.

Yes.

Aurora . . . the girl shakes out a ring of keys, shoving Catrine aside with her hip . . . Budge . . . pushing the door open . . . Sometimes I take a quick kip here myself . . . the girl chops on the lights . . . But don't let them catch you.

Cold. Bunsen burners patient under his windows, floor swept clean. Up front, Gilbert's lab bench, cycloned with cleaning powder.

Aurora stops, assesses her. Men's shoes, overtheknee socks, tuck key strung on a chain around the neck, hair. Gently, the girl pulls out the V of Catrine's sweater and drops the key down it.

Better. Nothing pretty about an old key . . . Aurora stops at a dial on the wall, lamenting softly to herself, then she disappears through a doorway in the back of the lab calling out . . . Don't ever expect it to be anything but fucking freezing in here.

What does he think, sitting up here facing them all. Is a question. Second row, third seat across. There she is, directly in his eyeline, unkempt, odd, brunt of his jokes, object—

You American? . . . Aurora reappears cinching a lab coat.

Aust—

I've got nothing to say about them one way or another . . . the lab coat swamps Aurora. Not a student coat, fraying, shrunk with use.

Gilbert's?

Got the flu . . . Aurora shakes out a student coat from a pile, crumples it into a ball and hurls it across the room into Catrine's lap.

I hate the green ones.

Don't wear it then.

Walking over to the sinks, she threads the sash through a slit in one side of the ugly coat.

I used to watch an American show on television . . . Aurora hands her a pair of rubber gloves . . . Did you ever see it? Out in the West. About a cowboy and his friend Kid put those on . . . leaning . . . Pass me that sponge no that one. Kid, the cowboy always said, this is your cleaning sponge, the famous line. Kid, we've got miles to clear before daybreak. You never saw it? The cowboy always fell off his horse. That was the big joke. Everyone was terrified of him but the man couldn't ride to save his life. Do you ride?

I galloped across Arabia on an apple tree I led rebelli—

I do. Or did. He and the Kid could never saddle up in front of anyone. Or they would know he was a crap cowboy . . . Aurora bends to a shelf beneath the lab counter. Out comes a plastic tub crammed with test tubes and beakers . . . Always wear gloves. Dishes've all been rinsed but God knows what chemical's been left on. And we don't want our fingers to wither up and drop off. So, we've got our gloves, we've got our favorite pink sponge . . . Aurora holds it up . . . And if you're wondering where the dishes belong, I'll tell you as we go.

Maybe it was an Australian show.

I know the difference between American and Australian. Kid could ride anything. Once even a buffalo. That's why they were partners, you see. Made up for each other's lapses. That's how it works on television.

I remember now, Miles to clear before daybreak, that was the line.

Don't lie to me, Kid. I can spot it a mile away . . . Aurora pulls back her hair with a damp yellow glove . . . So. Let's have the story. Photographs . . . Aurora waits, holding up her gloved hands in a presurgery position . . . How did you get them to do it?

Well . . . checking the bottom of a petri dish for a prompt stamped in the ceramic . . . My father gave me a camera for Christmas.

Don't look so worried, Kid, you'll give yourself wrinkles.

They came upon me . . . that wasn't right . . . I saw them, I thought I could take a picture . . . was that it then, she thought she was Rembrandt.

Then you asked, s'il vous plaît, might they strip?

Yes. Or I didn't say anything and they just did it. I thought, well. Well, why not.

Why not indeed . . . Aurora strips off her rubber gloves, throws them on the counter . . . That's enough work for one day.

The girl disappears into the storeroom. A moment later she returns holding a brown bottle. Watch me be a scientist, Aurora says rolling her eyes to indicate lunacy. Uncanting the bottle, she slops the chemical onto Gilbert's lab bench.

Isn't that dangerous?

Risk makes it an experiment, Doodle. Aurora snatches the spatula from her astonished hand, What do you think they keep back there? Arsenic? A certain tension creeps in. Please stop, that could hurt him. Aurora uncoils the tube to a bunsen burner and fixes it to the gas line Don't you pay attention? reaching for the lighter. Nothing happens unless you apply heat.

This girl is one loose cannon running back for safety goggles, a real Isabelle this one dragging a stool to stand on, this one could have you with tires down hills and into cars men flying all over the place disfigured, scarred or incapacitated unless the rolling had been her idea after all in the beginning, etc. which has not been established one way or the other but the association in terms of girls, men dead or non and out of control experiments, is simply not a good one for anyone. As Aurora continues to click the lighter oblivious to Catrine pulling out the chopstick holding up her hair the tumbling red meets the burst of flame in a nasty smelt eliciting the yell What Are You Doing Kid I'm On Fire but she keeps forcing the safety goggles on over Aurora's head even as Aurora flaps and beats her off I've Caught Alight, Kid Find the Extinguisher Smother Me Smother Me. Hitting Aurora on the head to squelch her hair but Aurora is laughing and falling can't see past her hair then the bunsen tube catches and drags the fire is falling falling on both of them as they go down down it's all girls and fires fires and girls flying hair obscuring who is who so she is Aurora and Aurora is her slipping on soapy runoff from the dropped sponge slipping and now it's on her the flame and she kicks at it desperately because for some reason they are both snorting with laughter, incapable of stopping any sort of fire Aurora clutching her chest, I'm Suffering Smoke Inhalation and the bunsen rolling rolling I've Got Black Lung rolling laughing rolling down a hill crawling after it over a sponge leaving its wet rectangle on her skirt down down. I'm Dying I'm Dying. The bunsen knuckles against Gilbert's desk, flickering to a rest. Leaps of light cast shadows against the pale wood. Stretching, she twists off the flame. The air changes, the lab cold again. Throat sore from laughing or smoke. Pressing the tuck key against her skin. Slowly she stands.

Aurora remains on the floor in a cross . . . I died in fire, Kid.

I'll Resurrect You she thinks to say later because now there isn't time there's a sharp rapping at the window causing them to jump up in a flurry of caught-in-the-act.

Flash.

They look at each other.

Another flash.

A camera is being held to the window. Another flash. They run over. Brickie. Next to him, Simon Puck, a beak strapped to his nose. Brickie smiles and. Is that a wink.

Who's that boy with the bird?

Brickie saunters back toward School House, swinging a camera, followed closely by Simon.

I don't know. Some bastard.

Is that supposed to be funny? I should teach him who my friends are. Remind him . . . Aurora presses the lighter against her arm, clicks it.

Don't, Aurora.

It only lights gas . . . Aurora considers the lighter . . . I was on fire.

21

Through School House corridors after the Physics she will fail for not understanding angles of light Sophie gushing But Catrine think of the ineffability of particles the sheer ungettability of chaos how disturbing that we are after all nothing more than dust. They continue on, speaking of what lies between milk and milk of magnesia. And what of nothingness? Well says Sophie If you want to speak about death, let's talk about your moth—

Girls!

Too late, a fall of footsteps indicates Betts hot on their heels hallooing their name to reverberate hills.

Girls, may I interrupt your flattery of guitar idols for a moment to touch on matters of substance?

Sophie vaults into the washroom leaving her alone with Betts.

He gauges her . . . I understand that Mr. Gilbert has put you to some use in his chemistry lab.

Yes sir.

Wasn't that thoughtful of him? Even dragged himself to the committee meeting with a horrid case of influenza.

She waits for what Betts has come to say.

Not many would go to such trouble for a disobedient pupil but . . . Betts steps aside to let Puck pass . . . I know that Mr. Gilbert has more patience than most.

She moves to go.

Of course—

What.

Some have it that patience is actually despair dressed as a virtue . . . Betts smiles . . . In the case of Mr. Gilbert, I mean it as a compliment. A true prince. Had he been a witness to the farce, he might feel differently.

A passel of 4Y emerges from a classroom sweeping her up in a lunch-bound frenzy, bearing her down the corridor. What rich comedy you've found for yourself, Betts shouts after her. She finally frees herself by the dining hall. Down the hall, Betts is leaning against the washroom window, ploughing a pen in his blue notebook.

22

Some Notes on Comedy. Beginning with the Unfortunate Predilection for the Literal. These days, so-called *realism* moves us further from truth than a Restoration piece ever did. Or a Farce. Two days ago in the staff room, Gilbert holding court among Stokes and some administrator types. Buffoon, Fool, Clown, Shepherdess. The Hero either misunderstood or out-of-his-element. Contrasts between the rustic & the estate & the pastoral escape where time is the enemy as I broached the coffee urn Gilbert waved his cup toward me in a lavish gesture of chumminess. Mistaken Identity, the Disguise. Patrick, he said with false gaiety, I was about to tell of our conversation last night in the POD room. The staff, huddled around the tea tray like tapirs around a watering hole, were eager to hear as they hoarded their tepid cups to their chests. The Handy Interruption. Turning back to his audience with studied theatrics, Gilbert said, Patrick and I were arguing about Realism. The teachers hung on his Hoax. Abstractly, Genevieve Araigny reached for a biscuit. Coincidence. I stood to one side, fiddling with the blasted ceramic handle on the urn which always sticks. Repetition (often in threes). I refilled my coffee cup. Michael repeated in his whinny, Dramatic Realism. Another weighty pause. *I* was *for* it. They thought that terribly funny. Hoah Hoah. The Surprise of the Inevitable. Stokes laughing so hard tears gushed from his good eye. Percival didn't seem to think it funny and moved away. The Absurd in the Plausible World. Percival knows a fraud. Then Stokes found me watching him. Well I must admit, with some disgust at the way his eye let forth a steady stream of tears. Instead of tragedy's Catharsis we get the Clarification. Stokes wiped away his tears, I believe Michael offered him a handkerchief. Stokes said, By the way Patrick, what is it that has Simon Puck from the 3X wandering around the school with some sort of proboscis attached to his face. A Misunderstanding. Leaving it to me though Percival was standing directly beside me nibbling his Rich Tea like a mouse. Why me, given as I was not the one chosen to direct a school play. Not enough time allotted to address the Play within the Play, that would mean devoting a large portion of my lecture to Shakespeare. Percival, I said as nicely as the situation allowed which wasn't so very nice at all, I think Percival will alert you to the fact that young Puck's become taken with the Aristophanes. I laughed because Stokes did but then he instantly stopped, leaving me laughing alone. A Subtle Melancholia. *Get the beak off that boy*, Stokes said in a steely undertone. With that, he turned back to Gilbert and some story Gilbert was always telling about his father. The comic moment born of self-delusion or cross-purpose. Concluding with the idea that the hero often becomes the villain, the villain emerges as the hero.

23

On Saturday afternoon he finds her by the lily pond.

Catrine Evans . . . he sounds pleased . . . Well hello Evans.

Looking up from her idle kick for flat stones she paints him in the dim light. Crooking back his suit jacket, a jacket once loaned to her, with the same elbowed stance as his lab coat, he stands in front of her. Not as she has seen him these past five weeks, at the fishmarket, Lawrence of Arabia, taking her face in his hands, Some Might Think You Older.

Are you better?

Much recovered . . . Gilbert comes next to her to help assess the pond . . . How were your holidays?

We looked for a house.

I swear I never left my own house it was so cold.

Did you do any painting?

I did not, but I understand you've been making some art of your own.

She says These days I'm turning my mind to science she says I'm supposed to have talent in that area. She's incoherent.

I made an effort to attend the Committee meeting. Some teachers have alarming ideas as to what constitutes fair punishment.

Maggone, right? Wanted to flog me?

Flog? How cynical you are . . . for lack of lab counter, Gilbert bounces on his heels . . . Tell me those photos weren't your idea. You would have chosen a more compelling background than the cricket pavilion.

The light meter wasn't reading . . . kneeling . . . I didn't have the time . . . a dark clot in the water . . . Still, I'd like to see if the pictures came out.

Not likely you'll get the chance.

She looks up to laugh with him, the afternoon sun nice on her face. Gilbert stops bouncing. Takes his hands from his pocket to scoop a rock, settling on his haunches next to her.

Mr. Gilbert . . . she throws a pebble into the pond . . . Did you lie about me being good at Chemistry? Headmaster's about to have me take A levels.

Gilbert finds a cigarette end on the ground . . . You're clever enough . . . he throws it into the pond . . . Don't waste it.

What does that mean.

Whups . . . Gilbert fishes out the cigarette. He gestures with it to the sky and playing fields . . . Monstead's an odd school . . . a fine mist from the sodden filter . . . Very good in some ways . . . noting her wrinkled nose, he sets it down next to him . . . But we're hardly Winchester. Children get lost here. School's falling apart a bit. You must sense that.

The wet cigarette marking a putty sky. Ocher grass burned with winter. Her first day here under the arch Father described Da dropping him in the same spot. *Now it's all falling to bits* Father said but left her anyway.

My father went here.

Your father? Here?

During the war.

Your father lives—

In London.

Yes, you said once I think—

I never said. Where's your father?

Dead. The story of my father's not an interesting one. He died in Clapham. You might know it as the city of fallen idols. Aegeus was a man I hardly knew. Rosie and I were raised by my mother in a shaky hut among grape arbors. I ran there as a boy, playing the lyre. My father was a banished man.

My father was a banished man.

These are the things we have in common.

Picking up another pebble. In the murks of the lily pond, Gilbert's father packs a bag, through the door without looking back.

Daily, wordlessly, my mother boiled roots into nutritious paste. Aegeus mistook her silence for reprimand. He left home because he couldn't put food on our table because there were four of us to face every morning with angry open beaks. If I'm to tell you these things, Catrine, you must promise not to get depressed because it doesn't mean anything anymore. You're not mourning anything real.

Scraping dirt from a knee with the pebble . . . Your father left because of money?

There were many reasons. I had a sister and she died, that's one. Catrine.

What?

You promised.

I didn't.   How did your sister die?

Rosie died of lightning, a bolt to the chest. Cracked her heart. They have a word for it, Leukemia, they say.

You survived.

But Rosie was my father's favorite. And the day Aegeus disappeared he buried a fountain pen and his handkerchief out behind the privy. I was to use them when I was grown. They would save my life.

Betts hurries by, bowed against some hurricane . . . Afternoon! Bit cold to loiter.

Don't worry about us . . . Gilbert waves him on.

How do you get that? Leukemia?

Bad luck I suppose . . . Gilbert turns to her.

Suspect shapes in the lily-clumped water, fishes or frogs.

Years passed. One day while I was at university, the hospital in

Clapham found me. Aegeus had tried to push a woman into the path of a speeding car. Fortunately, she was too fat to be shifted.

A sad story.

You shouldn't be affected so dramatically by things . . . looking out to the sky, Gilbert presses his shoulders to his ears . . . Is it this cold where you're from?

Up at the dun sky . . . Much colder. In Maine where I lived it doesn't stop snowing from about November to March. But you skate and it's—not as wet. Didn't seem as cold.

Well what are you roaming out by a dirty pond for?

They all went away this weekend.

And what will you do when I leave?

Sit by the pond.

Gilbert laughs . . . Well you can't stay out here forever . . . he doesn't think she's too cynical too silly or too affected by things . . . What time is it? Nearly two. I'm signing you out for tea, it's ridiculous on a Saturday to sit by a pond all day.

And the winding roads scroll up school. Toward a new town with new buildings. Where Gilbert leads her down a cobbled street into a courtyard through a large wooden door . . . Watch yourself now this is heavy . . . up a flight of carpeted stairs . . . That's where my favorite tutorial took place . . . down a hallway . . . A brilliant, oh look here . . . stooping to find himself in a long photograph . . . Here's me. Rather handsome don't you think?

A woman passes, swamping them with a particularly noxious perfume. She slows, turns . . . Gil?

They straighten.

Dido . . . flustered, *Gil* kisses this woman on her cheek.

What are you doing here? . . . Dido rocks her ankle back and forth in its heel.

Wandering. Wandering. Decided to show Miss Evans here how handsome I once was.

Coyly . . . Handsome days behind you, are they?

Indeed. I'm a shabby corpse now.

Dido glances down at the papers she cradles . . . You should be here, Gil.

Don't say that, Mr. Gilbert.

I'm happy where I am. Pardon, Catrine? Don't say—?

Corpse. It's not funny.

Sorry. We've been having a little chat, Catrine and I, or rather I've been warbling the hymn, My Dear Departed. We're melancholy.

Now, Dido notices her. Takes her in as if she is a child yes but as if she is suddenly more important as if she sucks up some air in this dim university hallway instead of being the smallest person of the three. Dido, hazy. Harbor lights. No, more like something unfocused. Drunken baubles.

An attempted smile though it is more of a grimace.

Melancholy? You don't seem very melancholy.

The woman confuses, should she argue the point.

I was telling Catrine about my father.

Do you find Gilbert's stories funny, Catrine?

Does she does she . . . Yes?

Doesn't Catrine have lovely hair? . . . Dido remarks . . . Quite the pre-Raphaelite.

More of a Medusa, this one.

Dido laughs.

I left my brush in London. By mistake.

In any case . . . Dido is back to Gilbert . . . There's work for you here. You're needed.

Gilbert puts a hand to the back of his neck . . . Needed. Now I doubt that.

Think about it. I would help you . . . an ill perfume and wafting it too, Dido pats Gilbert's arm . . . I should get back . . . pat pat . . . It seems that Cockett has misplaced a visiting lecturer.

Ah, it's all go, then.

Nice meeting you and gestures of good-bye all around.

Gilbert watches Dido walk to the end of the corridor . . . University life.

Seems boring to me . . . stooping back to the photograph to find him.

Dido . . . he calls.

Now what. The woman stops, turns.

Gilbert shrugs . . . Visit some time.

Dido nods, backing up against the door, pushing through it, waving with her free hand.

Gilbert walks backwards across the bridge pointing . . . That's the old boathouse where many a—debauched night unfolded. Over there you can see a rather famous tree. It was crucial to climb this tree at some point or hum never mind that. You see the precarious building over there, the one on the verge of falling in the river that's the refectory oh and come here . . . he pulls her to him to point . . . Can you see through those trees, that's the spire of the Cathedral. No, we have to go in, it's no good simply seeing it from here. I have to show it to you.

Show her a church will he when he pulls her to him with no thought to how she can smell his shampoo and tweed. Will he tell her what he prays for standing in divine blades of light running a thumb over tallies of the dead. In a pew slide out the prayer stool not to pray but to admire the stunning embroidery never to pray but to kneel hands clasped to feel what it might be like to pray. And if you did if you did pray would she come running would it be back to the old house would it be autumn trying to scrape up leaves before it rained thwarted by gusts of wind would you turn to see her reading at the kitchen window coiling hair around one finger. Had a day like that ever happened in the past.

But questions for outings are Shall we have sandwiches Shall we have bicycles hired from a shop buildings fly by oh trees four skinny roosters in black jackets collages of blue orange past a crowded tea shop on down a hill teeth rattling from the cobbles. This is how her hair comes unbattened This is why she shouts Slow down Pleeease while he's shouting back University museums offer wonderful oh now look out there Catrine you'll do us all some damage. And swinging joyfully off the hired bikes, Look at the fun they're having, she accidentally kicks out the cane of an elderly man. He totters this way two steps. Now that way, three. Breaths held as the bewildered gent sways. At the last moment, the man lurches for the railing and regains his balance.

Good god child you're not safe but they are laughing up the back steps down the hallway into the entryway laughing so hard that the woman selling tickets shushes them but they won't be stopped laughing and laughing because they are friends, Gilbert whispering, She didn't work here when I was a student of course that was a hundred years ago, propelling her by the elbow, Or was it only twelve.

So you're thirty-two or—

Might as well be a hundred.

And into a skylit hall thick with the hush of silence or is it age an old how old statue stretches one hand toward the sky. Questions for outings are bold. Why does Gilbert talk differently in class? Because he feels counterfeit when it comes to imparting wisdom so he borrows a snooty voice from college boys he once knew and gripped by an abundance of feeling for Courbet he takes her hand asking, Don't they seem very much like his own paintings. Well, no. But she chooses a mute nod which is not exactly a lie, more a gesture of preoccupation and directs his attention to a fine painting of a river.

God that's an awful painting don't admire that, it's prudish and nostalgic. Thomas Cole, very boring we don't enjoy his work at all. The exact is never true, hum, no breathing room. Remember that. And furthermore *Gil* wants to be told exactly how they squash artistic enterprise at Monstead. So she provides nightmares of color wheels and fruit displays. And he shudders and can bear to hear no more.

Please resist their inanity . . . he says as he strides away, out of the gallery, through the hallway . . . And I will take you painting. When it's warmer.

Away he goes and she follows in silence because comebacks never occur until later.

24

Translation. I am walking across the courtyard. The sky has darkened and threatens rain. The building before me is large and brown with many windows. A man passes and I ask him the time. What a fine man he is, tall and thin. He wears red socks, evident at the cuff. The man tells me it is half past four, he apologizes for grievances old and those yet to transpire. Then he takes me in his arms and tells me he cannot live without me. Oh he says my God have I longed for you. I need to breathe you in. Don't mind my shirt I have others to spare. You are mine and that is all that matters. We go to a museum, he holds my hand. We walk through the country he lifts me up to watch a flock of birds plunder the sky. Winter ends. We go home.

25

Percival, Latin to the upper forms, Civilization to the younger, sits in the second row using a script to fan his irritation. Next to him, Owen Wharton has his legs slung over the row in front. Onstage two boys appear to be flying but. Difficult to make out. Is that. Are they standing on some sort of

Spying on rehearsal?

Go away.

Brickie squeezes into the hedge next to her. Inside, Owen directs a boy downstage. Simon Puck's beaked and ready in the wings.

Brickie watches Percival make a happy flapping motion . . . It's undignified, it really is.

Then don't watch.

All of a sudden, Owen whips around, staring in their direction.

He can't see us can he? . . . she crouches lower.

Brickie steps away from the window, stubbing his cigarette against the wall. The embers flare in the dark . . . I don't like him.

Owen?

Gilbert. Why'd he stop making fun of you? You're out on the fields taking lewd photographs nearly suspended and if anything Gilbert's—

Well well.

They both jump. Haven't been paying attention. Owen Wharton.

If only my actors were as interested in rehearsal as you two clowns . . . leather creaking as the boy shifts his toothpick . . . Certain I can't tempt you? A small role? Two clever parakeets? Couple of comedic pigeons?

They shake their heads in unison.

Shame. There are incentives of course . . . Owen studies Percival through the glass. Oneself is often found through artistic creation.

We have selves . . . uncertainly, Brickie offers Owen a cigarette.

Owen ignores it . . . Nonsense. To know oneself one must know the other. Student, Hamlet, Vicar. Can you claim that?

Brickie drops his matches. Owen stares at her.

She looks away. Can she. Brickie unbends, clutching the matchbox, cigarette clamped in his teeth. Owen has disappeared.

Mysterious bugger . . . Brickie strikes a match.

What the hell is she doing here.

26

A cricket match was gearing up on the day they came to visit. In the middle of the second over, it would pour, sending boys soggy in their oversized whites under trees to assess the sky, on to make damp havoc in the halls of School House. But before the match, the boys were still listening to weather reports on the radio and Father led her across the pitch where heat rose in faltering swells and the breeze-borne stench of some sort of flower came at them again and again. Father went inside the pavilion turned around once and came out. Walking back he said how the stink of linseed snapped him straight back to the days with Treat and Darvish. Not that I'm into that old boy crap, he said, Won't find me at sixty reliving dorm raids at nine as if the fifty years between were insignificant.

Heard a rumor.

Father is replaced by Aurora Dyer in the pavilion pulling out a cricket bat.

That Fiona Hammond tied you to your bedsprings.

Half-in, half-out, she watches Aurora take a wild swing . . . You look like you're playing golf . . . she turns back to the field, morning.

What do you know about it, Doodle?

Used to watch them in the park last summer.

I'd take care of Fiona, if you wanted me to. As a friend.

Sounds like you plan murder.

Don't be melodramatic. It's not my job to save you. If you've got your cuffs pulled down around your wrists for other reasons, say suicide attempts, that's fair enough. But if Fi Hammond's messing with my friends, you understand, something has to be done. Nothing to do with you, Kid, I have a reputation to protect.

A whistling sound followed by an alarming crash. A stump bounces off her back, bails roll across the floor. She turns.

Aurora, cricket bat on her shoulder . . . Damn.

And together they sit among the spilled wickets looking across the pitch at School House where the boys' side begins to light, window by window.

It's really not that bad, Aurora.

No, it's far worse. Hell's empty, all the devils teach here.

The devil didn't bring her to his university town. The devil didn't hire bicycles.

Someone told me you're friendly with Squeak.

Gilbert? No.

Don't think you've got allies here.

He shook out an ankle so his cuff might avoid the chain.

You're not listening . . . Aurora sticks her with a wicket.

I am listening.

My father has a friend in town. Beatrice. Has me over for tea. Takes me on outings, or we walk her dog through the cemetery. Old enough, but the only one round here who thinks I have a mind. Beatrice, I mean, not the dog.

Other people think you have a mind.

You just said surely, Catrine. *Surely*, exactly as if you were English.

Probably, she had said probably.

In any case, I've been at Monstead since I was eleven and when you're living with teachers they know far too much. They think if you kiss a boy, university's out the window.

Is that what happened to you?

Never mind about me.

Cyclops said matters at home required your concentration.

What did I say? Never mind about me.

Across the pitch, at School House, a boy calls out a window. The smell of breakfast on a breeze. Double art with Devon in the afternoon, Hamlet with Betts this morning and chemistry chemistry—

Kid.

She looks over.

If he thought about you as often as you hope, he wouldn't have time to teach.

What's that supposed to mean.

Want some advice?

Not really.

Don't trust any of them . . . Aurora gets up . . . Including Squeak.

Soft now he comes lo creeping edging over the field pale now permeating now saturating drumroll please for our illumination.

Two armchairs, a table, ironing board, footstool. Hiding in the balcony for a smoke because Sophie found it to be *Too fucking cold for the copse*. They sit side by side, critics, feet up on the railing, appraising the empty set. The crackle of tobacco and Sophie's soft Macbeth Macbeth Macbeth Macbeth Macbeth Macbeth are the only sounds until an off-stage murmur floats up. *As for Jimmy he just speaks a different language from any of us.* Ducking, Sophie makes a production of stabbing the cigarette on 204D. Betts enters stage left, script in hand, crossing to sit in an armchair. *Sweet-stall. It does seem an extraordinary thing for an educated young man to be occupying himself with*. Occupying himself— Occupying *himself* with. *You didn't tell us very much in your letters*— Betts stops. Looks Back in Surprise.

Hello? Who's there?

Gilbert steps out onto the stage thermos in one hand . . . Sorry to intrude, Patrick. I was enraptured by your performance.

Oh, silly fluff really . . . Betts closes the script with his thumb in it . . . Look Back in Anger. Seemed appropriate. That's a joke, sir, nothing to be glum about. They wanted an older type for the Colonel. I volunteered. What the hell. A lark.

Burton played your part, am I wrong? At the Royal Court in the fifties.

Ah no you are wrong on that one. He played Jimmy, I believe . . . Betts kicks a chair gently . . . Have a seat.

Why not. I'm in need of diversion.

Next to her, Sophie lies in a hypotenuse across the balcony steps.

And what are you in need of escape from, Mr. Gilbert? Trying to beat some sense into the lower forms, some, what is it, periodics, elements?

Gilbert nods to a teapot on the table between them . . . That's a prop I presume . . . as he unscrews the thermos . . . Have some of this . . . he pours.

A snorter?

Coffee . . . passing the cup to Betts.

Cheers.

Haven't been sleeping well . . . Gilbert sets down his thermos on the floor . . . Nothing seems to make sense.

Hot milk with golden syrup. Works every time.

Everyone's got an answer.

Has an answer.

That as well.

Running water won't freeze, as they say.

Meaning?

You're thinking too much. What's on your mind?

Well that's the problem isn't it. Not much of anything.

No dead aunties stashed in the attic.

None I'm aware of. Though a peculiar smell drifts down from time to time.

Hoah . . . Betts laughs filtering coffee through his teeth . . . Very good . . . taking down the cup he passes it to Gilbert . . . Wonder if the monsters have finished Prep and are setting about on a rampage yet.

Gilbert leans down to refill. When the light catches his thin nose like that like fire. Teachers bunkered below in their foxhole sharing war, whiskey. Back-home tales. He takes a sip, passes the cup back to Betts.

Thanks . . . sip, brood . . . You're a more patient man than I, aren't you, Gilbert?

Not sure what you mean by that.

Been at Monstead seventeen years. What keeps us here, do you think? When we could be teaching at the university level. Publishing dissertations. Vocations suitable for men of our education. Pedigree. I think of it often. Revisit the circumstances which brought me here. Was it Marjorie? Difficult to recall but for the life of me I can't honestly believe I had a hand in this path.

Is it as bad as that?

Don't you feel it? Brain soggy from disuse. Imagine for a moment we were surrounded by minds like our own. Serious conversation instead of prying beaks off stubborn boys. Leave these schoolchildren to people like Devon.

Women, you mean, sir?

I suppose I do . . . Betts sniffs . . . Is that so awful?

Gilbert places his palm on the teapot beside him as if on the head of a small child . . . I believe, Mr. Betts. That there are ardent minds here. At Monstead.

Perhaps when they first arrived. But encouraged by their more moronic peers, they metamorphose into slugs. When I remember my own days, dialogues I shared with a boy named Mahesh. That was a time. Well, I can't imagine even our sixth formers speak about elevated topics.

That's hardly fair. What about Wharton?

Owen Wharton . . . Betts seeks the answer in the footlights . . . Owen has. Enthusiasm. Reminds me sometimes of Mahesh. He had that. That. Spark. That's all I ask for, a spark. Let us know a light's on somewhere.

There, you see . . . Gilbert leans back . . . They're not all sheep.

Of course Owen has the advantage of only coming to us in the Lower Sixth. Mental paralysis takes more than a year or so to set in.

But you do grant that Wharton has a gift?

Ask me in June.

I find that unbearably pessimistic.

Gilbert, you've been with us what. Four years?

Please don't suggest it's only a matter of time before I begin thinking that way.

I can only give you the benefit of my own experience. Yesterday I had one of them inform me that obliterate meant unable to read or write. I mean . . . Betts reaches for the thermos . . . Don't see me as cantankerous. You make me feel old.

You make me feel naïve.

Tell me this is where you planned to end up. Teaching the same experiments year after year. You wanted your own discoveries. Number one hundred and four on the periodic table, Gilbertium? Working in a lab in California? Before Clara was born, I had my course mapped out, I can tell you. Doctorate at Harvard. Thesis on a French surrealist. But, as they say, Gods laugh at plans. They certainly did in my case.

I didn't have a map. Wasn't so ambitious.

Still, no one could accuse us of not making the best of it.

Don't you find, Mr. Betts, that children can inspire as much as your doctoral candidates?

Mr. Gilbert, I think you are mistaking the pleasure of articulation for inspiration.

No, I find—

But then one's lectures all become the same after the first year or two, easier to do so.

—that their way of looking at the world is not the same as mine.

That's right, theirs usually involves the pub.

Gilbert slowly crosses one leg over the other, a careful finger to his lip . . . Often it is more imaginative, more hopeful. I find some of my pupils more intelligent than adults. Some see possibilities that never occur to me, others have a unique way of phrasing or finding—

Goodness you are a pollyanna aren't you? Perhaps in the old days, thirty, forty years ago when the school was turning out ambassadors,

MPs. Can you imagine a politician coming out of this place now. Like silk from a sow's ear which is a metaphor.

Yes I realize—

And of your pupils, who do you find has, what was it? A unique way of phrasing?

Hum, I.

I see you with that American girl . . . Betts inspects his script . . . I had her read Ophelia when—

Pardon, but she's no Ophelia.

Yes, her accent didn't make for—

I'm certain her accent in no way compromised Shakespeare's poetry.

Such an odd manner, the air of clarity, as if she really sees you as if—

Well, she—

I don't mind telling you it quite unnerves me. Sometimes—

Yes I'd rather you didn't tell me actually.

And those photographs, imagine—

I'm sure those boys had quite a hand in it.

Still she glowers so—the American. It's a disconcerting *knowing*. As if she can see right through one. And so dreary. Why? Do the clouds still hang—

Well, her mother passed away not yet a year ago . . . Gilbert taps the arm of his chair . . . Her father then immediately moved them three thousand miles away.

Still—

No, sir there is no still . . . Gilbert rises sharply . . . The girl . . . pacing . . . The girl has plenty of life in her . . . he snatches the cup from Betts' hand where it approaches his mouth.

I say . . . only the space around his missing tea . . . What are you getting so riled about?

I find your musings quite unsympathetic, quite depressing I must say.

I beg—

No . . . stooping again for his thermos . . . They are the musings of a small mind . . . turning to say, projecting to the balcony . . . And that sir, is not a metaphor.

Exit Mr. Gilbert stage right. Betts sits for a moment hand still shaped for Gilbert's plastic cup. He looks up to the balcony.

On the balcony, Sophie's kicking her to go but she is caught by the lights. More play. Come back Gilbert. Down below, Betts pages through the script, trying to pick up his motivation. Sophie leaves her, slides to the exit, squeak of the door. Betts looks away, looks back.

29

I am not made for England. This finite. Decorous resolve. A grim bearing up. I long for Paris. For an impromptu spirit, a laissez faire. Mahesh says Paris exists only for its possibility, that one should avoid tourism at all costs.

We squabble. Mahesh says it is base and pointless to compare literature to the plastic arts when I simply voiced a preference. Sculpture seems to me more an athletic enterprise than an aesthetic one. Photographs offend, for they imply truth. And painting. How static the tableau of Caravaggio is compared to the life on one page of Flaubert. In reading a book one is never forced to suffer the elbows and umbrellas of outraged mothers or the squalling of their infants. And spinning from gallery to gallery from Rubens to Goya to Degas leaves you at the end of the day with a palimpsest of conflicting style, form and color. An ocular muddle. As you emerge blinking into the sunshine you have nothing more pressing on your mind than the need for a toilet or a sandwich. All that's retained are the four or five reproductions purchased from the museum gift shop which disintegrate in your sweaty palm as you cross the street.

Patch of blue as I crossed the gardens near Fenton with Mahesh. A Wildflower I'd never seen. Made notes to research it in botany books when I returned.

I told Mahesh I will never marry. Nothing can rival freedom. Warm feet can, Mahesh countered, Fat buttocks and soft skin can. The solitary life, I said, Is derided by those who buckle to convention and later regret it. Mahesh said if I am homosexual I should just say so instead of coming across high-minded, etc. I said I simply plan a life without fetters, regardless of man or woman. A life of one's own. Mahesh burst out laughing.

Awake at dawn to a thick white fog softening the quadrangle. A conspiracy of droplets. A cabal of molecules. A form appears between buildings, delving the fog in swaths. Mahesh. Ecstatically I tear across the quad and immediately smack into a bench. Limping, I reach him. It's *Veronica persica*. The blue flower at Fenton. Known as Persian speedwell, I looked it up. Mahesh keeps walking, replies mildly, Patrick, you will lose sight of truth by pursuing it so avidly. *Avidly*. Like a child gorging chocolate.

Hypocrites. They crowd into Mahesh's study to listen to Foster's recital. How he grovels for Mahesh's approval. Watched Mahesh lazily accept cigarettes, compliments from these fickle boys until I couldn't bear the hypocrisy and stared moodily out the window. The rendition was atrocious, beyond reproach. Yet Mahesh clenched his cigarette between his teeth in order to clap vigorously. One imagines the Russians are not such sycophants. As soon as Foster left the room, all the knives came out and one boy fell off the bed he laughed so hard. When we were alone again, I fervently made Mahesh swear he would never give me false praise. He offered to give none instead.

This mind betrays me with interruptions. Desultory thoughts of tennis scores, images of boyhood. Tangents, non sequiturs. I long for a funnel of reasoning, thought spiraling to a critical point. Left instead with this gyre.

Backed out of the Christmas Ball at the last moment. Mahesh asked was it a pair of nice ankles I was frightened of meeting, perhaps a pair attached to shapely legs and so on. I said I was suffering severe insomnia, my head rattled with ideas. Mahesh suggested that rather than take myself so seriously, I try hot milk and syrup. It was after midnight when I heard him on the landing. I threw open the door. Well? Mahesh stopped, leaned himself against the wall and regarded me with a steady gaze of inebriation. Thousands of men have ideas, he said finally, rousing himself from the wall. Most are not important. He began to climb the next flight. I called out, Ideas or Men? He continued walking. I called again, Important ideas or Important men? He didn't answer.

I tell Mahesh that Vermeer was a mathematician, that his paintings are abject studies for perspective. I say it to goad but he simply stares out my window. I know Mahesh finds debate with me tedious. But why must we always talk about paintings, which I loathe, when I could tell him a hundred things about Hamlet.

Mahesh has accepted the role of Claudius. Against my advice. The rehearsals drain him. Today I dragged him in off the landing when I heard him pass by. Why do you never come to see me? Hating how petulant I sounded. Mahesh hovered in the doorway for two minutes then left saying, And what of this solitary life you aim for, Patrick? When he went, I felt an actual stab in my side. Loss for his easy warmth. I like to look across and see him arranged in my window, legs propped against the casement, cutting the window into triangles. I went into my pockets and threw a coin across the room. An auction of lacunae. Art will save you or kill you.

Oxbow. How grubby it is, provincial. The smear of clouds, overheard inanities in the newsagents. Mahesh, virtually disappeared. Paris,

Paris, I mumble mounting the steps to my room. Unlocking the door, I cast about at my drab belongings, four salvaged tea bags drying on the sill, a stack of half-read books. My contribution to literature: dog-ears. Image of myself alone at fifty, sleep fitful due to the niggling inconsistencies of fin de siècle poetry. Here on the threshold, what can possibly come of this. To love is impossible, to articulate, debasing. My own bottomless inadequacy. Literature fails. The novel isn't. Life ebbs.

Easter lunch at Mahesh's parents. Traveling down, a cold dry day. Smoke collected on the horizon. After lunch we took a ramble to shoot rabbits, or foxes, I wasn't clear on which, I didn't plan to shoot anything. I suggested to Mahesh that he join me in Paris. Throw off the shackles of this timetable nation, said I, Escape the dewlapped old guard frowning upon queue-jumpers. I was in full throttle when Mahesh cut me off, Why leave England, Patrick, when you delight so in being miserable? Now, that's hardly fair, I said. We walked in silence for a bit. Finally I attempted a joke. Something wrong with fighting a disposition for indolence? Mahesh shrugged, There's nothing to deplore in a life without literature. Oh no, I contended, There is plenty to deplore. Patrick, he said, his tone cutting, You *do* nothing. Nothing. You conform ideas. You shift this from here to there. And your ideas . . . he trailed off. Mahesh was receiving raves for his Claudius, it appeared to be affecting him for the worse. He strode out in front. I followed, poking the ground with my rifle. So it is better then, I called out, Like you, to parrot? Mahesh stopped violently. Patrick, he said, You should not go to Paris, you should marry. Marriage? I laughed. I think not. A lifetime spent pore to pore? Overhead, a brace of birds burst across the sky. You should take a wife and have a child, he said. Only a man of genius can bear a solitary life. And without further ado, Mahesh turned, brought up his rifle and shot down a mallard.

We spent the night in his boyhood room. I slept on the floor, woke at five, shivering in my bedroll. I watched the sun move a lamp across the ceiling and down one wall. Mahesh slept curled away, feet dropping off the bed. His spine, knuckles against the blanket.

The next day we broke through a thicket of alder, following a stream which snaked across the sparse woodland. Now and again cracks of gunshot reverberated through our valley. Coming upon a clearing where the stream emptied into a pool, we saw that lightning had recently laid waste to several large trees. One alder staggered, caught between his brothers, borne like a drunk. Another spanned the stream, sagging against lichenous rocks, branches splayed. Pinned underwater by one large branch, floating pinkly, was a dead sheep.

She bobbed slightly in the current, jaw contorted in a manic rictus, muzzle pierced by her own mandible. The bone was extraordinarily white, polished by the rushing stream. Foxes had discovered the carcass, the sheep's belly was ripped open. In the fast water, nettles and leaves swept by her moored innards. Oh girl, Mahesh kneeled. He looked up at me. I turned to vomit.

We were silent on the walk back. I knew. Suddenly Mahesh spoke up. Patrick, you will watch your child as it takes its first tottering steps, you will have ample metaphor for a life. You will run to the encyclopedia for the name of the common Cowslip, you will know what it's all for. No, I cried out, seeing the sullen wastrel, changeling in an oily anorak, the disdain, come to me in my decrepitude, mocking my malapropisms. No. I resisted. I began to weep. I had nothing. A full stop. To unfasten my skin, to climb out. But there was no one to climb into. I could offer myself a cup of tea or boot myself into the night. Nothing to do but go back in, unnerved by the temperature. Time to admit I had no intention of removing myself to the shadowed nooks of Paris. I was suckled on Fear and not about to renounce an old friend. I was never a genius. I would take a wife stupider than I so as to have a palliative. Alibi for a life of habit.

We stood, Mahesh and I, looking down on the rude packages of pasture. I had always held England against itself. Come on now, look. A spiral of smoke at the horizon. Landscape. See a forky road cut the fields. There was yellow, green. Pleasure in it. Enough. Let me settle for a gentle obscurity. Constable, Mahesh said, considering me. Yes, I agreed, beaten, Constable.

30

We Like Sheep. Aurora sings Handel up to the lab We Like Sheep, Kid, unlocking the door, We Like Sheep. Singing the way inside Have Gone Astray then not singing saying, Mother says Newmarket This Year so she has to remind Aurora halfway through that she has no idea what Newmarket is, getting out a new sponge tearing at the plastic with her teeth. Aurora winds her hair into a ball, jabs it through with a knitting needle. I stole this from Lucille in the sewing rooms. Looloo. I should have been a better rider, Kid then I would be at Newmarket right now instead of in a chemistry lab then Philippa would be cheering me on wouldn't she? Yes, she says, Philippa would be cheering you on Philippa who is Philippa and Aurora laughs and says, You're a funny girl the way you say things like that God you make me laugh. I told you how she bought me a horse when I was twelve. You know it's my mother. Rinsing, Who has your horse now, Aurora? Nobody, Aurora says, Well God. He had to be shot on account of a stableboy leaving a pitchfork in the wrong place. Aurora fights the faucet. They sacked the boy but shot my horse. Then Aurora gets quiet her hair in that big sad ball. The sound of running water. Too bad they couldn't shoot the boy, she tells Aurora to make her smile. Aurora won't look up. They shoot a horse to put it out of his misery.

Pestles bob in the filled sink. Yesterday they were out on the field watching sports the three of them. Four. Four, because Simon Puck—

Beakboy? . . . asks Aurora.

Yes. Puck is always there.

You know you talk about these friends, Kid . . : Aurora takes a pestle to dry . . . Yet you always seem to be alone.

We were out there the four of us. Sophie wouldn't stop talking about the good the true and the beautiful until Brickie snapped that the wonder was really working his nerves so Sophie shut up and began drawing sulky pyramids in the dirt.

Not much of a yarn so far . . . Aurora's reaching up, stacking dishes.

Silence for a while then Brickie said So these are the golden days I've heard so much about. Sophie dug at her pyramid, Golden seconds more like. Well Brickie was annoyed and Sophie was grumping This too will last, so to rouse good humor yes an effort at levity I shouted To hell with old Stokes that Cyclops I don't need some piece of metal and glass to take snapshots. Indeed said Brickie eyes searching Photos or no he quoted up from under his bastard fringe It's guaranteed we'll haunt each other over the next half century.

He said no such thing . . . Aurora disappears in search of toxins.

In the spin of autumn's tiny helicopters I will see you as you are now though you too will be fifty, seventy, tedious of life, unfit for dreams.

I plan to die at thirty. This from Sophie. I have no use for being my mother the inconsequential worries of

I will be

You won't remember, Catrine.

Will.

When you glance up through a net of trees like these, in that crosshatched American sky you'll find us sprawled under chestnuts watching cricket.

Well it was hockey they ignored and it was too wet to sprawl so they crouched on wooden pallets but who was to argue the more beautiful rendering.

31

So he calls her an original. In his dining room, bringing her to the shut-tered room she never saw the day it snowed the day she leaned in his kitchen doorway as he fussed to make her toast. Says it when he picks up his palette knife says it once more when she sighs from holding her head still for so long. You Are.

Found on a bench looking out at Sunday evening on the cricket pitch back from a weekend at the new house. He said, In early February you were the one I expected to find outside in no coat. What is it you hold against outdoor wear exactly. She smiled. He said, But that is a lovely dress. And she made room for him on the bench sticking out one foot, Father bought me shoes too. Very dashing, pulling his trousers at the knee to sit. Listen to me, he said as she was telling him I don't like wearing dresses so much. Catrine. He had come to the fields to find her, it was no amble to chat about the service, to hear about her weekend away, a reverie for belongings she hadn't seen in nearly a year. Catrine, you should know that Paul's parents phoned the school. He's gone missing. She brought down her cuffs to warm her fingers. Catrine, because he will keep saying her name like that, won't he.

Move your chin up a bit and to the right.

Red? Gilbert's fussing at his palette with burned colors. There's no red here.

Remember what I said? The exact is never true.

As long as he isn't painting her blue. On the bench, she blew on her fingers, It's all my fault. That's not true, he said. But Paul would still be here if it weren't for me. Gilbert thought about this. It's not that simple. Nothing ever was. Gilbert stretched his arm along the bench, Don't worry, parents predict he's squatting with friends in London. Mr. Gilbert, she said then, Did you ever tell what happened that night? He continued to stare at the sorry grass. I made you a promise, he said,

That I would only tell the Head. And then he turned to her with the smile she liked, You must trust me to keep the promises I make.

She twists, someone behind her has spoken.

Gilbert coughs . . . You don't want to come out blurry do you?

Turning back to face him she folds her hands in her lap. He came out of the shop where he was taking shelter from the wind. Screwing up his eyes to make out the sign above the bus driver. This is her father, taking her case although it was tiny and she could manage and he looked like he was carrying a toy there were questions to ask the girl who never left the girl who huddled while the car made heat saying Well the bus stank of cigarettes the whole forty minutes and was late leaving because an old woman was too old to get up the steps in less than half a bloody hour and the lady next to me told me that her boyfriend won't ever take her out at least not and pay for it if I don't throw up it will be a bloody miracle and you know what's funny? What's funny? he said looking right then left, What's funny and don't say bloody. Father, I thought that I haven't been on a bus in so long and how at home I used to take a bus every day. Listen to you rabbiting. Father laughed, She's a rabbiter again driving on toward the Georgian. Behold these barns, stables, ye bungled vegetable garden. A lawn spilling out in swells to the ghosts of rosebushes. A small swimming pool collecting leaves and in its lazy swirl, a branch nudging the dark blot of a dead mole.

I never give people enough neck don't take it personally if there's a touch of quasimodo . . . Gilbert hovers over his palette . . . Slap some green on paper and you've got a landscape, but people, portraits. Impossible. Though it's nice to have an audience.

To admire you?

To pity me. Middlebrow man, his pathetic hobby. Now Courbet, there was a man. Defender of the proletariat, stone breakers, the wrestlers . . . adding water . . . To think the poor man suffered nightmares of school.

Do you have friends there, Father set down the keys on the empty kitchen counter with a bag of rolls bought on the way. Girls you go to the cinema with. Then there was light. In her eye. A sweep of torch, a lady stopped with the tray. Don't Scream At Concessions. They said no to sweets but two minutes later Gilbert was up and down the aisle to buy Maltesers. She watched his return, cuffs short, arms swinging. When he sat down he gave her the box to open as if she were a child. I like to let them dissolve on my tongue, he said as they waited for Cary Grant for *Holiday*. They sat with their dissolving Maltesers sat next to each other waiting and laughing at the students' fashion and it was good. Afterwards, coming out into the Oxbow evening, smoky, vindaloo, it gloomed, they careened down to the carpark. You like it here, he said when she laughed, You like it here where I was a student.

Yes, she said, I have friends, Father, and yes I go to the cinema. My friend is Sophie Marsden, she said, leaving out the part about cows, told Father Aurora Dyer not mentioning the reason for that introduction. It was all in the leaving out though that will have him saying on occasion, You seem different. All grown up. You've gotten so quiet. He thought photographs might help. Let me see the snaps. Oh I am taking photographs, many photographs Father, the kind to write home about but left them at school. I took a photograph of Aurora Dyer laid out on the floor, her hair about her like well like flame. She sounds like she's got some gumption, Father marveled to make her laugh. This Aurora sounds like a funny girl.

What light . . . Gilbert taps the canvas . . . Yes.

Father in the study battering the typewriter behind stacks of papers, Full of moxie that one, because she used to laugh at words like moxie. She went to the window, below were stables and a henhouse. Why do we need so much, Father? Father hunted for an elusive Q. I can't take up all the room in that bedroom. Really? triumphant to find the letter, As untidy as you are? We never had this before, Father and I think, he looked up to see what she thought, I think she would have liked it. Yes, love I'm sure she would have. He wanted to continue typing but didn't. I wish she were here, she said to the glass, I wish she were.

Gilbert gets up . . . What will you do for the Easter holidays? French trip?

Switching from the view of stables, henhouse, back to the metronome of Father's slow finds, I'm going to France, announcing, For Easter. I don't know about that, Father said, glad to be back to his *Q*'s, I don't know about France. What's in France besides French people?

My father said he'd see.

Alright you can relax for a moment, you sound like Cagney . . . Gilbert adjusts the curtain watching to see how the light plays on her . . . I'll be there as a chaperon.

Gilbert in France. A chaperon. There's a surprise. Waving *Le Figaro*, racing across the Pont Neuf. Gilbert tacks back the curtain. The two of them sharing irregular verbs on her bridge in his light. This is what I behold in the brown water of Paris. May I offer a beignet. But she will be lost with Araigny's vocabulary. What scenario requires Obstruct, Desertion, Valor?

Sounds like Madame Araigny has more in mind than cafés . . . Gilbert settles back on his stool . . . Some swordplay perhaps . . . as Gilbert picks up his brush, the curtain pops out the tack and falls across the window again.

Damn . . . Gilbert throws down his brush . . . Have a stretch while I do this.

A china dog on the mantel. Gilbert struggles with the curtain. She picks up a book. Replaces it.

Anything of interest over there?

Not really. I hate books.

Nobody hates books, Catrine.

There's nothing true about a book.

Who said there was?

Then what's the point?

Pleasure, I suppose . . . removing his shoe, Gilbert beats at the tack . . . Seeing. Someone. Else. Suffer.

I read the ending first, see if it's worth beginning.

That doesn't surprise me . . . finished at the window, Gilbert crosses, gives her a little push on the shoulders to sit her down . . . Still, I imagine you prefer dramas.

The wallpaper by his ankle misses the wainscoting by a good inch. You'd think the man would put his art to a useful purpose.

Catrine . . . Gilbert raises his arms to embrace her. No, to grasp the easel. He looks at her, her image, her. Back and Forth. One hand bears a scar. What's the trick they asked Lawrence when he put his hand in the flame. The trick is not minding. Bearing things you never thought you could. Gilbert picks up his brush. And the tack pings out, dropping the curtain across the window again.

For God's sake . . . Gilbert snaps.

She giggles, yes really like a schoolgirl, going so far as to cover her mouth.

Think that's funny, do you?

She goes to him, stretching.

Not yet . . . quickly Gilbert covers her portrait . . . Have a look at this instead.

Over his shoulder, a landscape. Pastures, forked roads. What light. A brook. He laughs he puts his arm around her waist he pulls her to his side.

What do you think?

But what is there to say.

That on his stool he is her height exactly. Exactly right that she can notice paint on his cheek and sleeve much as the dirt colored her uniform that time he saved her from nature pulled her from hedges pulls her to his waist the famous muchheld hip against her hip pointing out something in the painting something about truth. A deep roil in her stomach and chest as he points out MOOD feeling his hand on her waist PERSPECTIVE of new scars the changing COLOR of his brownish eyes. You're not listening, he says without looking and she tells him, No freely not even pretending even laughing. Catrine.

Dropping his hand straightening the painting on the easel which needs no straightening not looking at her. What are you thinking? Might she be bold enough to say I am thinking of a longing. But doesn't that sound dramatic and wouldn't it be just like her to ruin a moment like this. Now the moment has passed. Considered for too long. When he looks, she averts her eyes to the canvas. It is less often that she regrets having spoken without thinking first as Father admonishes than the times she regrets thinking at all.

Gilbert crosses to the door . . . Let's have some tea.

Because there is always tea.

The cold pane looks out on Gilbert's garden. A fence has buckled, sagging in one place. The picture of winter. The pale sun catches a row of thin trees beyond the garden out toward the lane, shearing the last of light into gauze. A motion by the trees, a flash of white. But as she tries to make it out, the window steams with breath. Deer perhaps. Or nothing at all. There are spots that dance on the eyes. Spreading her fingers against the glass. A bee lies caught between the double glazing. Tap tap. Quite dead, bee legs akimbo. A probable suffocation. An example of not knowing. Overcome by the view.

In the kitchen he clinks at the cups in the cinema she sat next to him in the dark her world without end their knees up on the seat in front his smell his shaven way laughing as she took her coat around her like a smock then not laughing to say Do you want mine too Oh frozen one Oh arctic muse I am colder colder even than that.

Do we want biscuits . . . he calls from the kitchen.

And she felt his breath on her as he turned to say a word or two and it was warm.

Or are we watching our figures?

Sunday, in the darkening, Gilbert's teeth trailed as he stood. It's getting late and I'm on duty. They left the bench, walked toward School House. She took a leaf from a bush they passed, cracking it in her hand. He said, I'd like to paint you I'd like to—Is it that you feel sorry for me? she asked, Is that what it is? Gilbert stopped short,

Pardon? That you do these things with me, letting her leaf drop to the ground. I like your company, he said. Is it on account of my mother or that people think I'm dirty or—Stop, he said and walked up the three steps to the heavy wooden door. Then he turned, looking down on her he said, It's not so complicated. Certainly not pity.

Gilbert comes in backwards, carrying a tray.

Ear against the window. No one else has him. Not like this, backwards and domestic.

Setting the tray on a table by the window . . . Toast and honey.

I never had so much bread in my life.

We'll show restraint, save the biscuits as an incentive.

I can hear the ocean. I thought only shells do that.

It's trapped air.

Behind him, the light makes golden squares against the door. He will be the one to swap oceans for air.

Gilbert glances up from buttering . . . You're shivering.

Butter knife still in hand, Gilbert disappears. She can hear him opening a door down the hall. He reappears holding a sweater, tosses it to her.

Thank you . . . the sweater reaches her knees. Metallic smell of the lab mixed with something boiled.

And Sunday evening you were out by the playing fields without a coat. What on earth were you up to?

Thinking.

A radical act at Monstead. What were you thinking about?

The service . . . she reaches across—

Hold on . . . Gilbert takes her wrist, briskly rolls up one cuff, now the other . . . So, you like the evening service? I find them stuffy.

I like the building. Ever since that day. When you brought me to your university.

Not religion then, so much as architecture.

We never went to church in Maine.

You prayed at home? Folded hands, bright halo, kneeling by your bedside?

I don't believe in God.

I see. Neither God nor books. What do you believe in?

Toast.

He surveys the piece in his own hand . . . Well, there's honor in that.

Do you pray, Mr. Gilbert?

With you lot? Just to make it through the day.

Seriously.

Seriously . . . Gilbert stretches out his legs and crosses them at the ankle . . . I have faith.

In religion?

In people. Mushy things I'd rather not go into.

You won't tell me what you have faith in?

Perhaps it's not faith at all, hum. Perhaps it's superstition.

She reaches for the sugar. Gilbert watches as she dissolves a large spoonful in her tea. She only takes two.

I get the feeling you've never simply sat down and cried.

A knocking.

Why would I do that?

Well your mother died for one, you live in an entirely different country, you don't see your father very much.

A knocking at the window.

I saw my father over Christmas.

Don't deflect the real question by addressing an ancillary one.

A KNOCKING AT THE WINDOW.

Catrine, did your mother tell you not to cry for her?

There it is, the knock. They both jolt, she slops some tea on the carpet. A comic moment. A woman outside, leans against the window forming binoculars with her hands.

Dido . . . Gilbert jumps to his feet, exits.

From the dining room, theme and variations on the battle of precipitation. The back door opening. The aria, I rang the bell. Dido sniffing from the cold air, coat removal movement.

I saw a figure in your lane with brambles in his hair. I've never laughed so hard.

Did you walk?

I did I did. Oh . . . at the sight of Catrine, Dido stops abruptly in the doorway, looks back at Gilbert . . . You have a guest.

Come in come in . . . Gilbert steers her in . . . You remember Catrine from Oxbow. Let me get you a cup.

After ensuring Catrine notices that Dido notices that Catrine is wearing Gilbert's sweater, Dido enters the parlor setting. She glides directly to Gilbert's easel.

Not bad . . . then she lifts the landscape, flicking her eyes from the portrait to Catrine to the portrait.

I'm not allowed to see it yet.

No cheating . . . Gilbert, in with a straight-backed chair.

Dido lets the paper fall . . . I saw Patrick Betts yesterday.

Did you.

A colleague of yours, isn't he?

Yes yes. What are you learning, Catrine?

Hamlet.

There, Hamlet, you see.

He was at college giving a lecture.

Was he . . . Gilbert picks up the teapot . . . Come and sit down, Dido.

Dido walks over but leans against the chairback . . . On Dostoyevsky.

Really. The Russians, hum? Well, there's no end to the man's range. What did he speak about, The Idiot?

It was intelligent, slightly crusty. He doesn't keep up. Which you have to if you're—

Sit down, Dido, for God's sake.

Betts seems bright to me.

Really . . . Gilbert gets up.

What do you think, Catrine?

She looks to Gilbert for the answer.

I'll get another cup . . . exit Gilbert.

Dido goes to the window . . . I love Gilbert's house. A pretty little orchard he has out here.

But you want him to move to Oxbow.

Dido leans against the sill.

Don't you?

Gil has many gifts. A superb teacher. He would make a popular lecturer with the university crowd.

He's popular at Monstead.

Is he? . . . Dido regards her carefully . . . Yes, I imagine he is.

Imagine what? . . . Gilbert sets down a cup, goes out again.

The woman steals Gilbert's chair, calling . . . I'm hearing how your students adore you.

Gilbert returns with a package of biscuits . . . Not true. They never laugh at my jokes. And they have horrible names for me.

What do they call him, Catrine . . . Dido leans forward, shooting Gilbert a prankish glance . . . Tell me.

Can't remember.

Catrine won't go in for public humiliation. She's moral, this one.

Ah . . . Dido moves back . . . Too bad for me.

I'm not.

Nothing wrong with being moral . . . Gilbert shakes biscuits onto a plate, sits down.

Sounds boring.

Yes, or judgmental. Not living and let live . . . Dido sips her tea . . . Or let living? How does that go, I'm all confused.

Catrine's very direct . . . Gilbert offers Dido a biscuit, fiddling with the props, hamming it up with sugar tongs and slices of lemon.

Is she?

Here's a girl who says what she thinks. Most of the time well some of the time. Actually, now that I think about it, never. But she's. Virtuous though somewhat.

There's trapped air inside her teacup.

Cynical. A follower of the Greeks. Diogenes, perhaps.

Dido takes a thoughtful bite . . . A philosophical American, you say.

That's right.

Diogenes. Interesting. What about Aristotle?

Oh, Catrine's most certainly a Peripatetic.

Her cue, she stands.

Sounds complicated.

At the same time there's a touch of the dramatic, a real Punchinello. I see a future love of Ionesco, Pirandello, even a fascination with some of—

Once—

Our comedies, Restoration, parody.

She cannot make herself heard.

On the other hand, I wouldn't rule out tragedy—

I killed a man.

Gilbert swallows.

Back in America.

Silence. The distant sound of a dog barking. Slowly, Gilbert puts down his cup.

So you're a fugitive? From justice?

It was an accident.

Dido looks up over her biscuit, skinny eyebrows hooked in pleasure . . . Tell us what happened.

I was on a hill. I stood on a hill with my friend—

I love a good tale . . . Dido draws her feet up under her.

My friend Isabelle and traffic rushed below us . . . she looks from Dido to Gilbert . . . You don't believe me.

Don't stop now!

Isabelle was my friend, she wanted to get away from school. I went with her. We took a bus out. Out to a town we'd never been to. Climbed up a hill . . . adjectives . . . A big hill. Down below there was traffic. That's how I remember it . . . she falters, can't help it . . . But I'm no good. I made it up.

No no it's true . . . Dido cries, leaning forward . . . I don't believe you made it up. Anyway, it doesn't matter. Don't stop.

Did you really kill him, Catrine . . . Gilbert says to Dido . . . Or did you just want to?

Did he do something to you?

I didn't know him. He was some man on a motorcycle. Besides, it's a story.

Outside, the patch of white does not reappear. In the painting a gull a sail edelweiss a shirt something you should know or open for interpretation. The bee kicked out against death, on his back Good God If only I could right myself. And tomorrow he will still be dead and they will continue with hot drinks. You expect radios to stop playing, the world to mark an end.

You have a dead bee here.

He raps on the door and she lets him in her hair wet from the accident. It is after she splashes tea down her front after she washes up and after Dido takes her leave. Gilbert comes into the bathroom comes in sits on the toilet seat takes her wrists. She examines his thumbs he tells her he was married to Dido. Knocking, he says Alright in there? as she struggles into her wet T-shirt still wet from the splashing. They are kissing in the corridor, she hears the sound of sucking. Gilbert says Let's open this a bit for the steam and squeezes past to push open the tiny window turning he watches her attempting to hang towels in a manner suggesting they have not been used. He says You might not be familiar in America but those are supposed to get wet. Out in the corridor he raps on the door Are you in there? And as she is saying I Am Familiar he is taking her hands saying Dido was my wife behind him the bowl of soap features five shellshaped that one on the top more the shape of something melted. Cheese maybe. Are you angry with me?

She looks at him sitting on the toilet seat wearing his half-day sweater with the sleeves pushed up tells him No. She hears him treading upstairs. Folding a newspaper. In the kitchen. He ignores the soap she melted he takes her hands both her hands in his two much larger teacup-warmed hands on the back of one his scar a larger dash than the one above his mouth. Likely burned by a brush with lab bench the deadly cocktails of Aurora Dyer. Wet hair drips dampen her T-shirt. Plosh on his forearm. Pulls her so they are knee to knee he says Dido and I were married. He considers her with his fourteen-year-old look, she should have brushed her teeth. I wanted you to know that. Why? Because his thumbs rest on the back of her hands. A squeeze he drops them he goes to the kitchen.

32

Gilbert's Fiat speeds back to Monstead after some shepherd's pie of his own devising. And more on fathers. How he drove to the hospital and sat a long time staring at his King who watched a point of light in a dark room. In the corridor sat a mother, purse on lap, hands on purse like a little begging dog while Gilbert's father proclaimed Attica a bloody Babylon, saw chimeras tangled in antennae. Finally Aegeus, skin milky cloudy something at the bottom had been disturbed, left the fishing show. Ah, Theseus, a hand to my forehead to read the forecast as behind him on the screen men struggled to bring up a bass. Theseus, have we long been separated. I was a gawky thin trousers too big at the waist as well as too short wardrobe of a boy spending all his time inside. Back and forth I paced in my ill-fitting clothes. Told him I had never found his pen, that I had failed to slay that old bastard Androgeus who always worked Father's nerves something terrible. The message here, Catrine, is very clear. One will always fail one's father. His poker partner Benny from down the hall interrupted, came in to gawp at The Son. Then, as is its wont, time dribbled away. Mother was describing the lettuces when my father slipped into his coma. What a commotion. Doctors rushing to plug him into a socket. Benny helping himself to the suddenly useless playing cards. We waited. I had never known my father, now he was a machine that could breathe, pump blood, boil you a cup of water.

Mr. Gilbert—

A fly gloating on his marble shoulder—

Mr. Gilbert, can you watch the road please, you're making me nervous.

Rarely seen a car on this stretch. And I've driven it countless times.

Anyway, I couldn't bear his static eyes.

From around a corner banked by hedges flies a tire. Four. A car. Low and yellow. Roaring past.

Silence. A bird somewhere close. Sounding like inside the car.

Triumph . . . she picks at her knee . . . Wasn't it?

Driving like the devil. Never seen anything like it.

Gilbert's Fiat begins the final ascent up the hill to school.

So, now you can boast that you know a man who killed his father. Mercy killing. That's how I sleep at night.

Mercy or good manners.

A siren. Gilbert pulls the Fiat to the side of the road to let a fire engine pass, lights blazing. They crest the hill. Gilbert pulls into Monstead's back driveway. Slams on the brakes. Out across the playing fields, thick billows of smoke roll up to the sky. Three fire engines circle the cricket pavilion. Water gusts in sheets. Figures spill from School House running to hem the playing fields. The pavilion, Father's favorite place. Someone's bowled a googly alright, a shooter a yorker for now it is on fire.

33

The stage is set for catastrophe. Backstage, a wooden machine on wheels falls over and nearly crushes Duncan Peaks. Meanwhile, onstage, Percival paces. He strikes the boards with yellow chalk marks.

Confers with Spenning, he of History, who has come to the project out of his great love for all things needing lists. The men unfurl an architectural rendering. Inigo Jones and his assistant Capability Brown huddling over it. A weighty decision, where a lone tree will stand.

You! . . . Spenning startles a ginger girl . . . Move that . . . he points to a prop left behind from the previous rehearsal.

Owen Wharton strides across the stage to relieve the staggering girl of *Anger*'s ironing board. Simon Puck helps. For whither wanders Owen, there goes Puck.

Wharton . . . Percival uses a loud whisper . . . Wharton.

But Owen is gathering strewn newspaper, now unbending to notice her in row GG, now waving a friendly newspapery hello. Shy Percival tugs Wharton's upraised leather sleeve. Wharton Wharton. Tall Owen motioning instruction to offstage Pucklet. Mr. Latin & Civilizations hanging from Owen's sleeve tugging tugging. Oh it's all happening in the theatre.

Simon appears, roosting in the seat next to her. The two of them are ready for fun.

Percival pulls Owen into the audience, his whisper carrying . . . Duncan Peaks Flubbing his Real Hash of the Bloody imbecile.

Meanwhile, as they say, Duncan Peaks has collapsed on the stage steps, head in hands.

Owen throws his feet over the chairback of row B ignoring Percival's disapproving tap . . . Let's hear it, Peaks.

An alarming silence.

If you can't remember your lines, Duncan . . . Owen continues . . . We'll have to replace you. Is that what you really want? Just Try To Remember and you will.

It's a lot of lines . . . the boy delivers.

Your parents will be there, Peaks . . . onstage, Spenning fights to be heard over the ginger girl's violent hammering . . . Stand up and try again.

Duncan stands . . . If the Birds are older—

Hold on . . . Spenning marches over, plans armpitted. He takes Duncan's shoulders, forcing them back.

Sir . . . Owen tries to calm the man . . . He'll get the hang of it.

If the birds are older—

Project, son. Take it to the balcony.

If the Birds are older than earth and therefore older than gods, then the birds are the heirs of the world. For. For . . . Duncan stutters, appalled . . . For—

For the oldest always inherits . . . Spenning throws the sketches at Owen . . . Do something.

34

Burning lingers in the air. Blackened sausages at Tea, smoky Prep, startled awake in the arms of guardians.

Gripped by the challenge of fitting his entire lesson notes onto the blackboard, Dr. Thorpe stands on a chair, a scribbling madman. In the rows behind him, Duncan cradles his head sobbing softly, Simon Puck is tapping his beak experimentally against his desk. Minter and Mareka are well into the semifinals of a compass dig. Forearms are the day's battlefields and their desks are bloody and bloodier.

Sophie's miserable, Bohr's son won't answer her letters. Does Catrine think she offended by not mentioning the Nobel win.

Not necessarily, contemplating Mareka carving a bold *S* at her elbow, Not unless he's an egomaniac.

Red river from the compass dig curls across the floor. Licking chair legs as it edges toward Dr. Thorpe.

Sophie pulls up her feet, Next time I'll write a compliment.

Satisfied with the beginnings of his cramped composition, Thorpe steps down heavily from the chair. Splish. He regards his shoes. The floor is scarlet. He glances up. 3X stares back, angel faces glazed, strafed blue by enemy inkfire. Or in the case of blubbing Peaks, water-glutted and red. Minter has his compass raised. Puck stops pecking.

Carefully, Dr. Thorpe sets the piece of chalk on his desk, folds his arms.

What is it? Don't you want to learn?

They don't know the answer.

35

After hockey before tea, Aurora comes looking. In the changing rooms. Yes, exactly like in the boarding school books, steamy, white undergarments, pink-cheeked after a trouncing at hockey, they crowd in various states of dress and undress as the script suggests though Daphne misreads the directions and enters in a swimsuit. That was so like Daphne. Meanwhile, Vanessa is wondering whether given the opportunity, Catrine would or would not kiss Greg who is Indian. Buttoning her shirt, Greg has the annoying habit of always jiggling is it possible that he can remain still long enough to kiss a girl, but Nessa is sounding views on it from her stepmother and they are half-dressed when here's Aurora cold from outside with a nonregulation scarf tight around her head saying, It's freezing, Kid. Saying I need you, closing Catrine's locker to see better, trapping her fingers in the door, Meet me in the cloakroom.

Sitting on the bench in the cloakroom below the coat hooks, Aurora holds up a hand to warn about splinters. Then she feels around in the pocket of a coat hanging overhead, takes out a roll of mints and pops one in her mouth. Thanks for coming, Kid.

Tripping on a boot, catching herself on a hook, she falls on the slatted bench beside Aurora, Well, I'm hungry, tetchy, ankle throbbing, Will it take long? Aurora focuses on the mints, Sorry Doodle, can't agitate a man on a full stomach, but she peels back the wrapper into a furl and passes her a mint, Extra Strong.

Aurora, she says and boldly too, Aurora? Silence but for the steady hiss of heat from hot water pipes lashing the cloakroom ceiling. Outside the door, boys rage up the steps to Tea. Aurora assesses her thumb for splinters reappeared, Well, Kid, she says finally, looking up at Catrine. I did it.

What? Getting up from the bench, she crosses to the other side of the cloakroom. No, Aurora. You didn't. Aurora rolls her eyes, Of course I did. Can't you foresee anything?

Why? Why would you do that? It was a good place. What did they speak of that day she sat half-in half-out the pavilion. Aurora takes the mint from her mouth, I tell you, I didn't think it would go up like that.

Silence. Then Aurora throws down the roll of Extra Strong saying, I don't know why I did it, Kid, just to see.

More silence. Aurora gets up, The pavilion was a fire hazard. A building that can shoot up in flames like that. Finally she speaks, It was here for fifty years. Since my father. It survived war. Aurora moves the mint to the back of her teeth, Not my war, Kid.

Now Aurora walks no saunters to the other side of the cloakroom. Standing on a bench, she takes hold of the rack overhead, leaning forward until just her toes remain on the wood. This is good for stretching out your back, she says, hair jagging down. Aurora, please. Dropping off, Aurora goes deeper into the room, disappearing behind a line of coats. She follows. Aurora? A shuffle. Are you crying? A pause. Wanted more sweets. Aurora sits with her back against the wall, scraping the floor with a key or coin, We had some fun in the lab, Kid, Aurora watches her hand scrape scrape, Remember the bunsen? God I laughed.

She remains standing, she pulls on a hook, she says, It's Prep soon, since there's no chance of food anymore. Aurora takes out a watch with no strap, Ten minutes. My father gave this to me. It's worth quite a bit of money. Apparently. Made by a famous company, Aurora holds up the watch as if trying to read a message on the face, Swiss I should think. The Swiss are good at watches. Aurora? Aren't they, Aurora says, Aren't the Swiss good at that? Aurora, you said I could help you. Very precise people. Went there on holiday two years ago. Germans as well. Mechanical. Her stomach pitches with hunger. My father showed me how to take apart a car engine once. But then he couldn't put it back together again. Philippa was furious at that. You know, *Mummy*. And she says, because it didn't seem as if Aurora can be stopped, Where is your father? Ended up paying a man to fix it for him. Probably a German or Swiss—What do you mean where's my father? At home. With my mother. No, wait. I can tell you exactly. Finger to the watch face as if to still the minute, Aurora says, Six o'clock. Reading the newspaper. Thumb in his drink, not on the glass mind, but in it to make sure the level's the same, that no one's creeping up behind him and siphoning it off. Since it's winter, Philippa will be watching the fire. If it were spring or summer, she'd watch the garden. Her job is to say, Is it? How dreadful? whenever he reads out some news even though she read the paper before he came home. Daddy would like to watch television but won't watch before he eats supper because that's common. Aurora, I have to go. Aurora puts away her watch, Well, that's how they are.

They walk to the door, Aurora hands her an envelope. A scrawl, *BEATRICE. 14 Marvelle Road.* Aurora, in the doorway, staring from the window of a moving train watching Catrine flash by, her last hope village. Aurora, she says, It will be alright. A bad lie. Aurora glances down the hallway. Well, she says, Miles to clear and all that.

36

Cue our crone, speedily from the wings. Quicker, quicker, quick—Alright, hold everything. Who the hell's on makeup? Edward? Come on, son, she's ugly enough, but we need the grimness played up a bit, take into account all those nights of gin and misery. Give her a rheumy touch of yellow around the eyes, there's a boy. Now, Maggone, a slope to your step, if you please, remember your motivation. Remorse simmered over the years to a stew of Evil. And who's going to suffer for it? That's right, now go again. Beautiful. Right, the girl enters downstage Left. Bit faster, there you go, on the way to bed. Let's try that again, swifter, crone, swifter girl. Maggot, think Terrier After a Rat. *Rrrr.* Exactly. No, no, by the wrist, take the girl in a pincergrip by the wrist. Better. As you're dragging her back to your maggotflat, ignore that the girl's slipping in her slippers. Perfect. Little less innocence on the part of the girl. Don't overdo it, she's not a naïf. Cue Sophie, appalled, excellent, excellent. Once in the flat, remember that the girl hasn't been in the maggotflat since she was a new girl when the maggot confused her with a girl named Mary sat her down with a cup of water and rules about pocket money and things to be sewn. In that scene, when the girl finally spoke Maggot improvised nicely, shot her eyebrows dancing past her hairline, wonderful, suggested that the shock of the foul new world in her very sitting room was enough to send her to the gin right then and there. More of that sort of impro, if you like. And the girl needs to remember how that moment felt, though it looks like you're having trouble enough with the script. Hang on. A blue dressing gown? Who's the lunkhead on wardrobe? Sorry, that's right, supposed to be all wrong, a gift from the father, gorgeous gorgeous. Excellent choice, it really is a dreadful blue. And is it actually *furry*? God, that's fantastic, you'll have them howling in the galleries. Quiet please. Maggot, you're hamming up the scold a bit, this isn't the Christmas pantomime, take it down a notch. Line, please? HOW WELL DO YOU KNOW AURORA DYER. And again, more forcefully, you're implicating the girl in arson. Steady on, no need to deafen us, we're right here. Don't repeat it four times, three's quite enough. Nothing from the girl, this is all taking her by surprise. Tad more sullen, that's it, you can't help it, it's in your nature. HORSEPLAY ON THE HOCKEY PITCH AND shuffle those papers, Maggot, yes as if they catalogue the girl's crimes. Roll in authority like a pig in muck, good good. Of course, the real shocker is the ending line, GREDVILLE'S EXPULSION, EVANS, WASN'T THAT YOU? A long pause. Even longer. We're shocked by the impact of the Chemistry teacher's perfidy. He swore he was trustworthy, but he's told the girl's archenemy. The girl, hello? Don't drift off into your slippers, this is a delicate moment for you. You're to walk up the two flights to bed. Silently. And in that walk, we want to feel the sleepless night awaiting, how you'll churn in your bed's horsehair dip thinking how horse is my valley not dreaming wondering will Gilbert make fun of you in the morning will he mock the savagery of wet hair you couldn't tame in the night will he look at you down that roman nose will he say why won't your experiments do what they should, hum. Will you even sleep at all.

37

The animal we looked at today was the pig we could see how the masseter muscle worked on an omnivore, the pig. The pig has salivary glands on either sides of the jaw, it also rolls the food to the back of his mouth to go down the esophagus. The epiglottis of this pig will close when the pig swallows food. This stops his food from going down the windpipe of the pig which could choke him otherwise. The actual stomach digests two things. The stomach of the pig will contract and expand accordingly. It is a reservoir. We looked at the pig.

38

The first recorded history of the town is far too boring for me to go into here, needless to say the good stuff begins with my arrival in nineteen and well before the war in any case and yes the second one don't be cheeky. I will say one thing about the school the Monster on the hill, it provides stories hm well some would say gossip but I was always told that gossip is for the frivolous and if I enjoy it well does that mean I can't also enjoy enjoy enjoy—

Shakespeare?

Shakespeare. Right because if I set my mind to it I'd be as sharp as any of them. Sharper now mind your step and give an old lady a pull up. There we are. Didn't realize this place was so close did you. But then the train's half of it. I love the train. There's excitement there you go Tolstoy yes have you read that one where she jumps in front of it oh that's a good one Yes I can enjoy the classics Tolstoy I can and still have time for a gossip. To take the edge off. I suppose they're not going to let you come anywhere like this are they I suppose it's this they'd call frivolous if they knew. I know you're indulging an old woman I'm not going to try to buy you a balloon or cotton floss ooh what a black look what a vocabulary she's got in those eyes Roger when they don't even have cotton floss on National Trust grounds anyway. Now over there turn around is Penford castle. See it. Turn back. That's for a different day. Personally I would rather go to the zoo but that's what London's for. So we'll make our way down that treacherous path over there buy our tickets then across that narrow lane and that's where we find them. Palm. Orangery. Succulent. Tropical and if we don't get carried away we'll have time for them all.

There has been frost. Making their way down the path, the two of them and Roger banging against her legs as she leads the way, Bea's old hand like a claw on the back of her neck for support. The other hand bound in Roger's leash. A small slip, Bea could snap her neck.

I don't have any children myself. They talk too much and I like to be the one doing the talking. Then again . . . Beatrice takes a tighter grip . . . Your Monster provided all the children I ever needed. Though . . . Bea pulls on Catrine to slow her, horse commands . . . Those boys were snobbier children than I would have raised. That was in the days before girls as you can imagine a more peaceful time. Oh if you could have seen them in the old days with their weak hearts and weaker Latin all over the map on account of the parents. When all they wanted was mothering without smothering not that I'm maternal which is a word I've always despised. They came for tea . . . Bea squeezes her neck as if to say I'll have you know.

At the ticket stand, Bea narrows her eyes at the sign . . . Take this.

It says . . . holding the leash out woodenly, stepping around a truckling Roger . . . It says, Children Under Twelve Half Price.

Bea tucks her glasses over each ear, blinks at the sign . . . Children Under Twelve Half Price. Well . . . Bea regards her over the glasses . . . What do you think of that?

Unzipping her money belt . . . I'm thirteen.

Bea places her hand on Catrine's . . . Put your money away.

A girl in the Comprehensive uniform and an oily anorak leans against a parked van, watching her idly.

Clara . . . a squat woman approaches the girl, counting change . . . Dad's parking. He said you're to have fun . . . she shakes her daughter's shoulder, the notes flutter to the ground . . . *We're* to have fun.

The girl bends down to pick up the money. Silently she hands it back to her mother.

Well it's better than the dentist . . . the woman pushes the girl toward the path.

Bea balances her grip on the counter, searching through it . . . Two please . . . to the woman . . . Two *adults* . . . sliding the money across coin by coin.

Bea hands her a ticket . . . This is where we leave Roger . . . Bea ties the lead to a post by the counter . . . Digs up my own garden enough as it is.

Her dog has worried eyebrows.

Will he be warm enough?

Bea looks up from her tying . . . He's a dog.

I don't really know about dogs.

Never coddle a dog. Come on come on . . . Bea bringing her close to say . . . What did I tell you about maternal? Poor dog, not a bone in my body.

Across gravel to the narrow path snaking toward Palm House, turning sideways every few moments to let the leavers by.

Palm House was built by a man named Stewart who wanted to be Capability Brown but wasn't. You can see . . . Bea points up to the rafters where birds dart . . . It's no Kew.

Hexagons form a glass firmament. Birds dash against the panes, forgetting, over and over again. Plants, trees in shaggy tangles. From somewhere the tinny echo of running water. An infinite nutshell. The smell of earth as well as cold potatoes for some reason. They pass a small fountain, flowers with sharp leaves.

This morning Mareka gave her an extra garter to control her hair and she paid homage to Aurora. Hair in a big ball, she could hardly think her fingers trembling as she wound it through the night he came to her with scars and fathers his way of looking reluctant almost pained when she speaks eyes taking her in twice first his painting then on the easel keeping still as requested providing an expression he can hang in the drawing room. Trust me. Over his palette. Coffee at breakfast, because she wouldn't go refill the tea not with her hair like that not in front of everyone. Coffee had her heart pounding in her throat when she ran to find him. There he was shambling down the Avenue toward the lab after Prayers. Mr. Gilbert, her nose began to run too, long ago she lost her gloves. Come over here, he said with that pained look, To the lily pond for a moment. What on earth is having you babble in foreign languages I need a translator for, hum? To calm herself, she fixed on the pond. There was the day he told her about Rosie but also said You mustn't be affected by things. Well, Catrine, he said as she looked into the dirty water, What's the new drama? If I might have the cast of characters, supporting parts, etcetera. She came out and said it yes right there before Music. You told, turning it into a question, Did you? He made a spooling motion with his hand, I told——? And it all unwound in too many details the tartan you told you told the smell of gin you told slipping in slippers and finally Paul Gredville. After all you said you wouldn't tell you said. To trust you. Then his face changed from smiling down on her as if she was the morning's amusement to something over her left shoulder. She turned, there was Madame Araigny struggling with the wind and Betts dropping some books. Let's chat before Tea, he said, I'm away all afternoon. Before Tea in the library, he said. Meet me there. She went one way around the pond and he the other. Catrine, he said. She looked up. Rest easy, now, I didn't tell. She smiled or grimaced. Whichever. He put his hands in his pockets, Rest easy. As she walked away he called out, and it carried across the pond, I like your hair like that.

Tropical, which is next door and hotter, we save for last. It was designed by Stewart but finished by his brother after he perished in a boating accident. And you can tell the difference in a heartbeat . . . Bea takes her hand . . . We'll begin with trees then onto the flowers that eat grown men.

Please. Trying to loosen Bea's grasp from her waxy skin and cracked fingers. Please let go.

Come come . . . Bea grips her tighter, leads her along a cobbled path between rows of flowering bushes . . . Not yet . . . calling over her shoulder, palm hooding her eyes . . . Save the best for last.

A man and a woman holding hands with a child pass. They waltz to yield, a hand-holders traffic jam.

And . . . Bea squeezes her hand, pointing up.

Dazzled for a moment, standing below a green sky, the water, hand held fast in Bea's warm palm.

A Norfolk island pine and they fit it in a house.

Leaning back to take in the entire tree.

Set this in your mind so the day you're wedged in the back room with some uninvited guest you can fold your hands in your lap, nod pleasantly and replay it, the smell of this tree, these four pebbles in their little square.

I have a bad memory.

About what?

No, a faulty memory. I can't recall—

Dates and battles? Irregular verbs?

The past . . . pine crowning at the roof . . . I won't be able to remember the smell of this.

Practice. My advice—

I don't remember advice either . . . reaching out for a pebble.

Bea presses her lips into a thin line . . . I don't think you should remove that, faulty memory aside.

My father says I do things without considering the consequences . . . she replaces the pebble.

Well I think considering the consequences sounds very boring. A tame life, indeed. What if flies considered consequences? There wouldn't be any carnivorous plants. Would you prefer to be mundane or to have the colors of a Venus flytrap?

As noted previously, they come to you armed with overcoats and questions, demanding answers you are content without.

Well?

I'd prefer not to be eaten.

Yes . . . Bea scrapes her lip with her teeth . . . That image doesn't quite hold. Still, we remember what we choose to remember . . . Bea walks away . . . You'll learn all about the unconscious in the Sixth form . . . using Aurora's crumpled envelope to point . . . Orchids.

Leaning forward to draw breath over the soft folded flower. Not England but rivieras boats villas the names for things in Mediterranean countries. Something unfolds yes something cocooned tight in her throat beats upwards. Garden. Rake leaned against a door. Loud laugh, the clink of silver from the tea shop the bubble of a universe the jar of an experiment two children huzzing and Bea saying—

Sixth form's safe for Freud. Psychology will only give you nightmares at this age.

What's the point, memories aren't real.

Who said they were? . . . Bea takes out a handkerchief, snorts into it then stuffs it up her sleeve . . . And if nostalgia replaces truth, at least we have nostalgia.

But if your memories are changed by other people's stories, then it's not even your own nostalgia.

Bea faces her . . . What on earth do you take comfort in, child?

I take comfort . . . rubbing a petal between two fingers . . . In mushy things.

Careful, now, they bite. I'm waiting for a proper answer. Do they let you get away with avoiding questions up on the hill?

I take comfort—

I've the feeling you're going to quote me something. You have answers of your own, do you?

Who is this woman.

Hold people hostage with your silences, I imagine . . . finally Bea turns away . . . Off to the Orangery or we'll miss our train.

39

He is standing at the library window creating her in every passing pupil. And when she will not be drawn in Hazel or Diandra he suffers the night she had. Troubles with Maggot sleepless night. He presses a foot against the window seat Mareka pulls away the curtain to sit on the sill he pulls out books touches spines notes how grey clothes form a shadowed jumble on her wooden chair. Moneybelt over rungs tuck key who did they belong to some girl who believed in Amsterdam. He begins to feel the night. Mareka brushing her hair sparking in the dark room. Drowsy black saucers under his eyes. A hand against the card catalogue to steady himself. Will you ever come. A spin of the globe. God if she would only lift him up. Truant muse pressing his forehead against the glass.

40

Never liked orchids myself. They always seem obvious. Still, they're expensive enough. Isn't it odd . . . Bea stops abruptly . . . How flowers can alternately smell of life or of decay. Can sicken or sweeten, depending. Nothing more brutal than the smell of dead flowers, including, and as a nurse I can attest, a dead person. But then there were lots of delays with medicine during those weeks. Oh how a war will focus though and I can tell you your predecessors up on the hill learned a thing or two when they went west. I had letters from them little lord muckety getting mucky on his hands and knees in the victory garden that's the sort of empathy that destroyed the upper classes after the war having their lessons in what all, barns and pig stalls and falling into the Welsh river and through it all the undying nationalism. Mr. Mortimer, Stokes. That's the sort of blindness, blind faith, that saves you in the end. Look at this darling bridge would that we could walk across it but it's decorative only my sweet. Hurry hurry. Are you prepared for an increase in temperature and a jolt back in history . . . out the glasshouse . . . Tropical as always we save for last so hot in there like a bath in there. A quick trip through the Orangery which is boring in the winter but we must be methodical and onto the Succulents. There's nothing not to like about the Succulents although I won't say it again nothing compares to the Tropical which is like—

A hot bath.

A hot bath, I'm repeating myself. There you see, Roger doesn't mind that sort of repetition. It's all philosophy to à dog . . . Bea has dropped her hand in favor of propelling her by the small of the back through the Orangery . . . Keep your hands off the lemons.

Past fuchsia and citrus trees, out the back and along the path into another small glasshouse. The Succulents.

Bea again in the small of her back . . . Something disturbing about a cactus in England though I'm told there's palm trees in Cornwall which I have my doubts about. When I get back to Marvelle road after a day in the glasshouses, I feel I've been to Morocco.

What's Morocco like?

Morocco's far away and mysterious and since I've never been that's all I meant by that. So, Agaves. Nothing for fifteen or twenty years while they build up their reserves, then boom, a huge stem seven meters shoots out bearing hundreds of brilliant flowers . . . Bea points . . . Silence, then boom. The very effort exhausts it to death. But worth it don't you think, see the photos?

A placard bearing the proof of twenty middling years, one grand moment, then death. A tweedy man in nineteen sixty-three standing next to the stem for a comparison of size.

What an ugly . . . Bea folds her arms . . . Why choose such an ugly cap on that particular day?

Down the way, a cactus bearing red flowers.

Crown of thorns . . . Bea unwraps a qualitystreet . . . Want one?

I don't eat sweets.

They move to the living stones, camouflaged Succulents.

I shouldn't . . . Bea looks at the chocolate as if they have an arrangement. Then she eats it . . . Why are you here?

My father came to Monstead when he was young.

Perhaps I knew him perhaps he came for tea to mock me in French.

Evans . . . lightly pressing both palms against the quills of a cactus . . . His name is Teddy Evans.

A flicker across Bea's face, something in the eyes.

Did you know him? Bea?

Prickly pear . . . Bea points, smiling . . . I think. What about your mother, is she with him?

No. She's . . . words again words . . . Deceased.

There, I knew it was something. Those dark looks you give don't come from nowhere. What a pity. We've all got death in the family. You know what I was during the war?

114

Nurse.

A nurse. So I know a few things about people and their conditions. Course, you haven't had half your arm shot away. But that's easier damage . . . Bea contemplates pebbles which are really plants . . . Your mother's dead, then. Well don't set any fires about it. If I were different, I'd be up the hill in two minutes, have a word with Armand Stokes. But I know my place . . . Bea scrapes at her lip with her teeth as if it is a struggle to know it.

What will happen to Aurora?

Oh, yes, change of topic, good idea. Aurora's parents will take her to a place where others are paid to pay attention to your children.

They shot her horse.

I'm sure they had their reasons . . . Bea steers her out of the Succulents now off the crowded path now briskly across the sharp lawn sidestepping the Do Not Step On The Grass sign for That Do Not Pertain to Us and on toward Tropical which you will remember is hot as a bath.

41

God how he sweats. Globe stopped in Tonga and he's overdressed for the occasion. Tooshort cuffs don't provide enough ventilation. Sweat coats the skull he holds causing it to slip from his hand. Yorick crashes to the floor bounces once rolls to join dust under a bookcase. Gilbert throws himself to the windowseat gazing dreamily up under the mosquito netting out at palms lining the Avenue searching for her among children listing to lessons bearing schoolbooks on their heads.

A wave of heat reduces Bea to a coughing fit as they enter, spectacles off, hanky conjured from sleeve to tend to tearing eyes.

The house is thick with leaves, the heat indeed a bath. They move sluggishly, navigating a thick clump of ferns, stopping before a large fern with fronds like antlers.

So your father was at Monstead during the war.

Yes . . . absorbed with the staghorn of the genus *Platycerium*. An epiphyte.

Parasite of the plant world. Or is that symbiosis I don't know. You might. Are you . . . Bea pushes at her glasses . . . Good at the sciences?

Not plants.

Ah . . . Bea looks out the window, back toward the ticket booth . . . What sorts of stories does your father tell you about his days at Monstead?

Boarding school stories. Stealing cake, swinging through the roof on a rope, arson.

Doesn't that sound thrilling. Nothing else?

He never talks about evacuation.

Not to fear it was mostly peeling vegetables by the sounds of it. Oh I had the letters from Wales. Dear Bea how we miss your fire and your garibaldis. Well I barely came home in those days. I was on nights at hospital. After the war I never wanted to see any of them from the Monster. These days, they pass on their way to town.

Did you know Cyclops back then?

Cyclops? How cruel you are. To call people names like that. God but children are cruel.

Betts rose like a misanthropic moon. *God you make me laugh when you tell stories like that* Aurora would have said *What happened next?* Betts edged over the craggy hillscape of English primers through a mist of chalkdust for it was the end of English and I was waiting for Sophie who told me she needed to fill her pen but did in fact appear to be stealing something from a duffel bag under the lockers. *Go on* Aurora would clamor *Go on Go on.* Betts bent down for a dropped board eraser, then up he popped like a character in a comedy. *And what did you do, Kid?* Well, to divert attention from Sophie's law-breaking, I concocted a question on rhyme. Betts balanced himself to standing—*Well Diverted* Aurora always interrupted stories *Well done*—inadvertently smacking the board eraser on the desk and in the process giving himself a coughing fit. Evans, he told me, You're not as bad as you might be at the English Language. Now, I had a friend in university by the name of Mahesh and though he was not born in this country, he had the finest command of English I had privilege to hear. What I mean, at this point Betts was trying to get the chalkdust off his suit, By this anecdote is that some day you too might speak as well as Mahesh. *He didn't say that.* Yes, he did, then ended the speech by saying, Perhaps we are not divided by a common language after all. *That* Aurora would be pouring a compound down the drain *Is fucking hilarious, Kid, a comedian is our Bettsy. Then what?* We left him looking up the quote in a book. To see who said it originally. *Isn't that just like old Betts* Aurora would say *To steal the words of another.* Aurora always had a comeback.

Betts blinked then as if he had not just said It Could Be That You're Not Such A Heathen After All. And she left, pulled along by Sophie. They were late for break, all the bread might be taken but Sophie wanted to stop by the tennis courts to spin out the stolen yoyo in a great vortex. I need bread, she told Sophie. Come on. Sophie untangled the string, Go on then. Well there was little point to bread without Sophie's vegetable paste so she stayed. Sophie spun out the yoyo, up it sailed up up and there was Simon Puck in the fork of a tree watching them with beaky curiosity. Owl-boy, Sophie said, annoyed the yoyo would not go in a perfect circle.

Nearly conked by the yoyo, Brickie arrived. Said Leave Simon to his trees and birds stop this playing at children you won't have anyone believing these parts you assume, that revels with round plastic disks keep you amused. Puck flew. Sophie went in for bread. Brickie stood with the red globe in his hand. Man delights not me he told it. Brickie reeled her in. Don't forget our unfinished business, Yank. Sounds from Break in the background the rising bliss for bread, vegetable paste, application thereon. I'm here to trouble you he said. Puck walked by the arch with a flat piece of bread, exceedingly large it looked. It's a ploy she said A ploy for suspense. Brickie shrugged, walked away. And Sophie spun out with slices of dry bread they dented with their thumbs then ate.

42

In the center of the Tropical glasshouse, through ferns and a thick set of climbers, a rectangle of water bears figments of reeds, papyrus. A tall boy sits on a bench, feet propped against the pool.

Scraping through the plants, she comes out next to him. Owen Wharton continues staring at the water, arms folded. Hunching under the ferns, she waits. Owen takes his hand from his pocket, blows on his wrist.

Mareka said you got those scars from a knife fight in New York City.

I'm not American, don't think that.

No, but half-something.

From the other side of the pool a woman's voice rings across the water, the Comprehensive mother arguing with a hidden person. *Are you ashamed of us?*

Owen reaches out for a stick, trailing an oldsweat dankness as he does.

My friend left her dog tied up outside. Now she's afraid he's frozen to death.

Owen's face is flushed from the heat. A fern droops above him, resting gently on his hair. Owen reaches up, breaks it off then looks at the attenuated branch in his hand . . . Shouldn't have done that I suppose. Disturb the ecosystem . . . he points the plant at her . . . I saw Aurora Dyer leave in a black car.

Aurora burned the pavilion to the ground.

Hmm. A stupid hut . . . Owen sucks on the fern, studying the various trees under the globe . . . Look at this little world in here.

The cricket pavilion was there a long time. Almost fifty years.

What does it matter . . . preoccupied with thoughts of his enclosure . . . They take things so seriously at school.

Aurora should have known what would happen.

She never doubted it.

Staring at his shoes running a leaf's serrated edge against her fingertips Aurora's hair uncoiling over a box of swan vesta there was no history for her it was only in the end result trying again and again for gain in the damp air.

So, Evans, you didn't audition for The Birds. I expected to see you there.

I don't like to act.

It's good fun to make a dance of the unpalatable.

Rather be Stage Manager.

Need training for that. And you don't know enough . . . Owen points his foot to a tree opposite . . . That's a coffee tree . . . he considers his shoe this way and that, sets it down . . . Which of your parents is Welsh?

Father.

So your mother's the American.

Was the American.

Your moth—

Wharton!

They both start. Mr. Betts comes thrashing through the greenery.

Careful sir . . . Owen holds out a hand protectively . . . There's water.

Sweating, Betts extracts a piece of bark from his sweater . . . Thought I might find you here. Caught sight of you from over there, the sugarcane . . . looking up from his extraction, he nods . . . Evans.

Betts discreetly tamps his brow with one sleeve. She moves to sit on the low wall. Trails her fingers in the water. Stalks and reeds lie in thick crosses.

Thank you . . . Betts takes her place with a sigh . . . How's Hamlet?

Nearly done.

Good good we'll be talking about the Polonius surprise tomorrow so you'll you'll . . . something catches his attention across the glasshouse.

You said you were looking for me, sir? . . . Owen takes his feet off the wall one at a time.

Without ceremony. Wednesday afternoon. What else am I to do . . . Betts waves a hand dismissively . . . Family's about. Was driving by and thought. Wanted to sound you out on a theory of mine . . . turning to his coat he takes out some folded papers damp with heat.

Went well did it?

I'm beholden to you, Wharton, as always. I think you're right, the place to pay attention is the fear of water . . . Betts taps on his pages . . . Alienation.

Across the pool, Bea appears between two banana plants, waving both hands.

Betts glances up from his notes . . . Why is that dreadful woman signaling aircraft?

Beatrice tells her she knew it, that Roger was halfway through a container of discarded yoghurt and looked none too pleased at the disturbance how dairy disagrees with him and how I'll pay for leaving him so long but mostly Bea says again and again Like a Bath Like a Bath. When they leave for the train, after plants, cocoa and pineapple, the peaked-hat woman and her comprehensive daughter stand in the parking lot with Mr. Betts, blue notebook pressed to his chest.

43

Now here's a surprise. Off the train with Beatrice into Chittock Leigh's darkening afternoon. Twenty minutes to get to the library where Gilbert waits, spinning a globe with one hand, petrified skull in the other.

Yanking Roger out of traffic Bea is saying Chemistry is saying Aurora told me you were helping in the lab that a Mr. Gilbert arranged it as an alternative to God knows what, the cane I should think. And she is telling Bea how Monstead's heydays are past that the cane has been abolished she is stepping back from the kerb to avoid the dog. Bea muttering How progressive how up-to-date indeed. So you may be a Science Girl what with all that work in the lab.

Well the air is blackening it seems every atom of it and Bea is allowing Roger to conduct her arm to unheard music, the cars along Station street scoot along agreeably and for the sake of variety two buses pass, then a moped. Merrily in a singsong way not really listening to herself she is saying I might be a Science Girl I might very well be a girl with those kinds of abilities.

I never trust that sort of singling out myself . . . Bea's arm detached, it belongs to Roger.

Pardon?

So long as you don't believe you're the only one.

And Bea suddenly wants her day in court so the expression goes saying, As I get older I find I like people less, I find that people disappoint that—

Not everyone disappoints—

That I am ready to die, enough alread—

It's not a choice when you die, so go to Hell. Well, it sounds very much like shouting though it could be the wind or a polite attempt to make herself heard over traffic. What type of person would choose something like not living. She seems to be walking yelling back at Bea. And people, some that is, when they go. Leave Things Behind.

Spinning out away behind her Bea calling Wait love Don't be angry Visit me again. The sky goes a grey dark rain hovering transoms lighting she's down the street and up the hill. Running past guild hall that stupid shop that sells nothing nearly knocking over a perfect child. Heathens on the run. Past the lit windows of a house no one there People Can Disappoint well she could go on and die then the old crone though she should stop saying that or will end up in hell burning through the gate the corridor they are lining up for Tea mother boys pushing past Araigny knitting something toasty for Mr. Betts flying up the steps into the common room ending at the slatted window seats folded over breathing hard. Breathing hard and nothing else.

44

Crossroads don't exist except in mythology don't be taken in by those who would have you believe. An eye has no resolve of its own. An eye is not a thing unto itself like bear or chicken you see it is attached by an optical nerve to an object called brain or the old grey matter. An eye cannot be set upon the world to make its fortune. It needs constant attention and cannot simply be left to fend for itself. I ask you, have you ever seen an eye at a junction, stick over one shoulder, red handkerchief knotted at the end? Or in a lorry headed south for winter? Be sensible, an eye has no thumb so how can it hitch? You cannot attribute to an eye any sort of independence. Think of the optical nerve as a sort of highway. Along that highway to the eye comes a message from your brain. The message might read Blink. It might read Wink or Stare. The brain is the decision-maker here. The brain is in charge. In this way, if an eye wants to cry, a brain must give permission first.

The Stranger. Of Mice and Men. Not there by the science labs nor hurrying past the lily pond rushing because he's late. Timon of Athens. Dictionary. GILBERT a centimeter-gram-second electromagnetic force. GILBERT islands lie in the South Pacific. One Gilbert lies in England. Perdition. Peregrine, a swift. Please. Surrender. Time passes.

An hour spent staring out the library window. The dusty curtains frame a proscenium arch opening onto tennis courts, Avenue, Follyfield. Now even the atlas remains answerless to questions of absence. Desertion. Beached on a remote archipelago of western Kiribati, no ship in the distant pacific. No rescue, no flag. Bairiki. Birkenebeu. Once protectorates, now independent. Only one Gilbert island remains colonized.

You wait with the others by the new parking lot. They go in Fords they vont dans Peugeots. You wait. One by one they disperse. That small group under the tree. Two of you left. Now just you sitting on the cold stone steps at the front of School House, the ones only visitors use. Joyce Tebazalwa who never leaves walks past she says They will never come for you they will leave you here for the vultures for your carrion to get picked clean. You light a cigarette consider her through the smoke Joyce you say Joyce I am here enjoying the snap of February air would you mind leaving me to my thoughts on reincarnation which if you don't mind me saying from the looks of your marks on the last Human Studies test might be a subject which could benefit from your application. But she ignores that sits down. You say How do you stand the cold here. A quiet girl but she replies The cold's the least of it. If you had a cigarette you would grind the butt underfoot. You ask Is your family in Uganda still and she says No London if you sit on cold steps like that you get piles I heard it from the radio. When she leaves Owen passes he tells you he sees your underthings you say it is on purpose but stand anyway to avoid piles. Then he's here he's here the car it's here and you run toward it and he doesn't know where to stop you don't know where to stop running You're late you're late I've been waiting my whole damn life to which he replies Have you noticed the first words out of your mouth are so often curses but he's laughing because he knows he's late that you can't wait to get the hell out of there. The large loop of the driveway and as you drive past the path to the boys' end you pass him. He your betrayer. There he is. He of Chemistry stooping in his long grey coat with a slash at the back the coat you think turns him into a funeral director he sees you and his hand goes up he smiles raises it halfway sheepishly halfway up it could be that his arm ends its journey by his shoulder a hearty wave a halloooo but you've turned away. He deserted you. For four days this school this town and certainly that teacher will not exist. You go on. How's the flat Father how's London how's the table with the crack the alley behind where I once saw a rat. Serviceable it's serviceable but I prefer Felmar where you can take riding lessons during the summer where we can learn the names of plants and paint your room any number of colors not including that horrible purple you once craved in Maine. How are your courses how are your lessons. I am learning so much about what to expect. I have discovered religion in the form of Prayers how faith comes in all colors that one can have faith in people in mushy things as well as in God. I have learned that in Oxbow you can spend debauched nights I have learned that Cary Grant started off English not American I have learned that the English recipe for punctuality often involves simply not arriving at all. Goodness that doesn't sound very reliable, who was that who tortured you in such a manner. Oh Father he is a man with a smell to his neck he is a man with a voice like a caught gate he has made me tea and hired us bicycles to find art but apparently he's like that to everyone. What else what else. A girl burned down a pavilion she got the idea from looking at me. My proximity sets fires. Don't worry Father not in a car. Look at the sky I don't want it to rain look at that house what is that sign why does the road fork like that. What else have I learned. England didn't need our help to win the war. Discipline is for our own good. Live by the sword die by the sword. This too shall pass. Maggone tolling her bell every morning as we wake in wool hats and gloves. Dorm full of the same cold girls over and over. We dress. Oh Father how can I be lonely when I am never alone. Breakfast did you know you can eat a boiled tomato for breakfast and sometimes fish. Key cold on my chest warming with the day as we gather for prayers as we say As it was in the beginning, is now, and ever shall be: world without end. Then lessons single ones Maths, English are in the morning double ones Art, Biology are in the afternoon. Well I'd be hard-pressed to choose a favorite but it has been discovered I don't mind saying that I Am A Science Girl. Chemistry you ask well it used to be my favorite but now I am not sure. They call me untidy they call me petulant. I tell them my manner looks insubordinate but isn't. I know I know I can't stop talking. What will we plant in the garden there's the trip to France at Easter where does this road go. Did you see that tree it looked like Churchill the clouds are so low it might rain. What about France they say it is an opportunity Madame Araigny says language improves when faced with necessity. Like needing a croissant she did she said that very thing. When you were a boy did that shop Wenley-Smith exist did they sell day-olds in a paper bag twisted into pig's ears you get three bad ones like eccles cake and always a good one maybe eclair. What about Frank's they have granny smith and cox orange pippins was the river there did the cemetery spill out graves like a shook-out cloth did you ever know a woman living on Marvelle road I met a girl with a bit of blue crayon stuck under her skin. There's a play about birds they rehearse every night. I watch them try to remember no no I have enough words to rehearse. There's a boy here who stares his hair needs cutting he torments me with held information. I know I'm rabbiting I like to rabbit. Blathering then I can't hold it in I'm like a river Father I'm burbling I'm not shouting I'm not well I opened the window I wasn't sure you could hear. Is that better. The bus I took didn't come this way. Father did you hear about the president the American one shot in the back outside a restaurant. A teacher told us before history and everyone cheered. No not me. I wondered if I were shot would they clap like that. But it's about nuclear weapons which they hate over here. The sun slips behind a cloud I can see that it was never out looks like clouds from here on in. Fi short for Fiona knows knots her father's a sailor. Reef half-hitch cat's paw. Just for a minute just for a minute. I am rolling it up I am can't you see. I was going to stick out my tongue to pant like a dog. I wanted to suck down the clouds so it wouldn't rain thought I might stick out my hand to test for the drops. But I won't I won't I'm rolling it up. What else can I give you tall tales of the man in the funeral coat stopping me when I ran away finding me in the bushes and taking me home. He put me to bed with a kiss to the forehead he set water where I could reach it if parched. I found paintings of nudes blue with cold.

And when I came down for coffee for tea he said why not stay here forever. He said you seem so at home here and that bed suits you so well why not stay until you grow old. Well I refused I was beginning to miss school already I'm sorry I said it's fishfingers for tea I'm sorry I said I believe Prep requires my attention. He was devastated for he wanted my company. He made up for it though, painting my portrait in the light of a dull day. I like him Father I like him but he disappoints me why didn't he come to the library when he said he would was he nuzzling the blue lady or Dido from Oxbow. Was it after a night of too much bed and not enough sleep. I know it's so obvious the reason I hate the reason which is that it didn't really matter. I saw a turkey under that bridge I swear a peacock or something. Have you heard of an American show where the lead cowboy can't ride horses. He has a sidekick. I need a sidekick. Remember Aurora that girl with moxie I met her every morning last month to wash up the lab no it wasn't a punishment Father it was reward for being named Science Girl. Her hair hung jagged, but she gave up. Why didn't he come. I thought he was my friend. I tell him about my life. I swear it was a turkey I swear it. How should I know why it's under a bridge. But you can't expect the reciprocal from those who are like that to everyone. What, Father? A dog a dog. I don't know if I even like dogs they sniff you all the time and Father I would only see it about four times a year. Maybe we can rent one for the summer. That woman in town well her dog Roger you can never get it off your leg. Father will you think about France can we discuss it some time promise you haven't dismissed the idea. There's a castle there's a swan. I thought today Father I thought today as I waited on the steps about Hinduism. In a class called Human Studies yes very well we had some tests. Can you only be reincarnated if you believe in reincarnation. Why are you laughing. Well I'm only saying there's no way to know. Why didn't he come Father I have to make myself not care I have to turn it off like a switch. He promised he would only tell the Head because it was in my best interests to tell the Head. Maggone gunned me down I had no warning. It was him it was him I know it was him. He never showed. I know I know a broken record. Can't we have it down for five minutes it hasn't been ten Father it's only been three. I'm going to be sick. I feel it rising in my throat. Make him come next time Father I'm trying so hard not to care and he looks at me like he's both known me all my life and never seen me before. I'm a stranger to him I'm something else to him I'm someone he confided stories of kings and rosies. He failed his father at a young age. Have I failed you Father? Well it very nearly breaks my heart to hear you say that Catrine Evans. Fidgeting with your socks rolling and cranking the window like Ford were paying you to test it and now you're out with questions of failure, true or non. Father please your eyes on the road please Father you know how nervous cars make me. Failed in what way when you're the cleverest girl in the world. The world without end? The solar system let's have the planets too. Would I say to a girl who failed me Let's paint your room let's unpack more books we'll look at the stars or is it too cloudy. Tomorrow we'll go on an outing we'll go to a film one of our epics would I say those things to a child how can you speak of failure like that. Father. Did she say anything to you Father before she went say for you not to do something. Like smoking you mean? Something else? No she didn't ask for anything else. Did she ever ask you not to think on her. No pet she never said that. The cows are lying down. You never failed us. You never did. Father. You know child have you ever stopped to think why it might be you ask me these questions in cars and cars only. Father. I steel myself Yes? Did you ever want a son did you ever think your chances were gone when she couldn't have more children. Now you were the only child I ever wanted handful enough and what exactly do they teach at that school Difficult Questions for Faraway Parents is it? Father. Yes. Sometimes I want to be more than one child for you both son and daughter. Truckdriver, horn. And who is it needs some raggedy boys with their football and their mud their wanting attention and new trainers. Out at all hours and wrecking the car. I remember how I was to my father when I took that job with the barrister. Romancing Miranda though I knew no more about it than I'd seen in films. My father at home learning to read. I was callous I was uncaring I put some blame on him that I couldn't go to university with the

Monstead boys. We had no money I was a terror I drank to avoid it I worked for an Englishman I thought I might marry his daughter. Do you think I'd want a son like I was. How miserable I would have been married to Miranda Watson who actually despised me. Took another seventeen years but your mother had pity for a stupid boy. Tell me Father tell me when you met Mother tell me how she saved you. Now there's a story you're surely bored by. Then tell the story when Hamey put the bird in his mouth. Tell about what the woman said when she came back in the room and saw yellow feathers coming out his mouth. Tell me the dress Mother was wearing when you saw her in London. The way she dropped her drink and what that man said when you wanted to punch him. Was she very elegant was her father so disappointed you could read it in his eyes. Her father was the kind of man with olives in his drinks her father held the gentlemen entranced with stories of his business. The year was nineteen hundred and sixty wasn't it Father or sixty-three and you took Mother out on the landing you said she was the woman you planned to marry. She looked like she had diamonds in her hair but they were paste and the light caught them and her eyes and you felt raggedy. You see why would I want a son like my boyself. And you danced the whole night and with her mother as well so you seemed friendly and since they were American they weren't as rude about your accent as the English for you could have been Dutch or South African or Nordic. Yes and your mother's idea of wooing was to take out those infernal letters from her purse and read them to me so I would understand what real love was. Some Henry and Catherine. I said you said I don't need letters to tell me how to love. Yes and when she went away again I wrote her I wanted to be you see I wanted to be every bit as good as her letters but you know it yourself I'm better in person. On paper what tries to say something comes out as nothing. She loved your letters Father she loved them she told me that she loved them that they were silly and sad. Well she came back so I suppose. She flew and she hated flying and London. Enough of this why do you want to hear the same thing over and over. Do you think Mother ever wanted a secret or to speak without practicing. To go through a day without saying It's a word it's a word I swear to you it's a word. If there were a train back Mother would be on that platform looking down the tunnel watch herself walking up the weedy drive to stare in the windows but there's nothing there it's all gone the paintings the piano. You'll see them soon in Felmar where you'll paint your room any color but purple. Mother thought what if I am strange. Stranger why do you speak without moving your mouth. Can we be sure you even have a mouth. You perpetually state but never inquire for when you query your voice does not rise to indicate a query. And the familiarity you assume well that must go baby with bathwater. This is not your American. Get hold of yourself pull yourself together. Mother says I am trying to pull myself together I have no mouth I have no voice. Give me rituals to stave off the sameness butter rubbed behind an ear leaf in my underwear secrets that are mine and mine only. Patterns no one else can find. A path from this class to the next some order to words touch my left ear As it was in the beginning one knee against the other And our mouth shall shew forth thy praise. No one can take it from me no body knows. Are we there are we nearly I don't have it done only a thread please Father I can't breathe from the heater. Promise my leaves the box next to my bed where I keep strings and a button the four folded pages in my prayerbook amulets to ward off desertion. The film we saw it together Father they couldn't get home they built a tunnel but ended up in enemy camp. How to avoid tunneling the wrong way and how to understand north in the dark. Four days four days and back for evening chapel on Sunday. I'll shine my shoes so I won't remember the feeling of leaving your voice our things Felmar Maine what difference does it make I am left alone Sunday evening. The weekend I visited the new house for the first time I returned full of memories or images that pass for memories I saw him after the service he came looking for me I'm certain of it I was wearing the new shoes he called them dashing he said I was dramatic but in a way that indicated he liked the dramatic. But now that doesn't seem possible Father it seems I invented his smile his taking humor from me or finding some kind of pleasure in my company he stood there in the gloaming in the courtyard I had a leaf in my hand torn from a bush cracking it

I smelled it he said Come to a matinee he said I like your company he said there were reasons that were not as complicated as pity I think about it again I go over it in my mind the situation the light the shadows beginning to creep down School House the nearness of him the snap of that leaf his words like water he wanted to spend time with me he wanted my company I'm trying to think Try To Remember review every situation which might have provoked his absence Father make it go away I don't want to be alone stop this stop such persistent absence.

47

No one turns when she comes in. Dorm 3. Minuscule suitcase clocking her knee. Smell. Forgotten after four was it only four days at the new house. No valley in the Felmar bed. Could sleep curled but didn't. Hitching the case onto the hospital bobbled valley. Click click. Bureau, chair, uniform. Wrapped in blankets on a deck chair by the pool watching the drift of winter debris, turning when Father brought sandwiches. Father saying, All you need is a mink stole for you look very Port Out Starboard Home. Very QE2, putting down his sandwich to swab the deck. The mustard and the laughing made her nose hurt made her nearly say it Father. Father. Click. Now the clatter, the calling out, Mareka's clothes humped on the bed. And seeing him swab the deck like that well what was the point. O Towel hook, O Number, O Tuck Key. Back to the room, unzip, let it fall. Is it worse he asked than not coming at all. She waited, passenger with folded hands. Listened to him set her suitcase on the backseat. Is it worse Father, no it is not worse. Buckled, she sat up and wished for a boater. She would set it very straight on her head, striped band parallel to the ground. A boater would keep her chin from a petulant downward tilt. She would never allow it to be jaunty like those in boarding school books, framing a face made frantic by cheer. Monstead did not require hats. Imagine Aurora Dyer in a boater. That was a good one. It all snapped back on the drive, the names, the throng. On the way they spoke of traffic of other cars and Father's business.

48

A fight breaks out. Sophie's pulling her toward School House after Prep and they hear the scream as the boy goes out the window. They stop, look back at Follyfield. The lamp outside lights up the brick wall. The boy lies folded into the spare rose-bushes.

49

It wasn't your fault . . . leaning back on the theatre steps, Owen Wharton addresses the air.

What wasn't my fault?

Who's that? . . . Betts cranes around the arched doorway.

Oh.

Catrine Evans from 3X . . . Owen consults the script resting in his lap . . . Sir, it's We were all to blame in our different ways.

Yes yes I have it, Wharton.

We were Up by the laundry *all to blame* Stokes plucks a burr from his sock *in our different ways* supporting his weight *in our strange but different ways* with a hand placed on Simon Puck's head.

Owen gets to his feet . . . Page sixty-six . . . he tosses the script to her . . . Evans will help you learn your lines, sir. Got dramatic blood, this one.

The theatre door swings open, releasing birdcalls. Percival serpentines his mousy head around the door . . . We need you here, Owen.

Betts (glumly) . . . Seems you've enough burdens of pageantry, Owen, without me adding to them. Don't let me keep you.

The Colonel's an old plant, Mr. Betts . . . Owen pulls Percival back inside . . . Don't forget India, don't forget the Maharajah.

The door shuts behind them, caging the birds again.

Betts sighs. Then, crustily . . . Perhaps you and I were the most to blame.

You and I.

Give it some effort, girl.

YOU AND I!

Don't shout . . . Betts squints up. She does not shade his light.

You and I?

I think you may take after me a little, my dear. You like to sit on the fence because it's comfortable and more peaceful.

Sitting on the fence!

Tell me, my dear. Where did it go. The spontaneity, the poetry of bruises.

No, sir, the line is still mine—

Apricot beauty, soliloquy of wristhairs, an unfaltering tenderness despite the delicious efforts at toughskin. Tell me.

In spite of all the humiliating scenes and threats! What did you—

Is there hope of a reawakening?

Your line will be about the letters, sir. Remember, the telegram, you're confused because of having to drive up so suddenly.

Can't I quit this . . . Betts sinks deeper into the step . . . You know what I mean, you with your selfish sorrow. Your body's been donated to Science. To French, to Art. Tell me . . . he hisses . . . Is there any getting out?

Bonjour . . . Araigny steps into the thin margin of green next to them.

Genevieve! . . . Betts brightens . . . What a pleasant surprise.

Humbly, Araigny drops a stitch . . . I wanted to thank you, Patrick. Mr. Stokes tells me you agreed to serve as a chaperon on our Easter trip.

Indeed. Aix marks the spot and assorted bad puns. Of course, I've been to France before with my. Marjorie. I. Can't say I boast any sort of fluency . . . he notices her fidgeting with *Anger* . . . Not like our Evans, I'm certain.

Madame throws her a sorrowful look. Let us hope the girl does indeed prevail at Science.

She holds out the play.

Araigny purls, liply, Frenchly . . . *Mais bon*, I won't interrupt your studies.

No, no . . . Betts leaps up, snatching the script . . . You're not interrupting, not at all.

Exeunt teachers of French and English. She goes to the window.

And for the Greeks, Percival pointing at a first year, whahooing with his hands, winging them out. In the aisle, pacing between seats, Duncan Peaks, hand to temple, lips moving then stopping. He pulls out a script, checks, lips move again.

Brickie. Beside her at the window hair in his eyes and that.

I had a cake. In a shape. She told me I could be an actor.

Don't be an actor.

The Ambassador was away on business. He came to Monstead when he was a boy. Thither at the arch where old boys once stood, our fathers, Ambassador, Evans, the crumbling not crumbling in those days. Without regard to the two of us. No taller than that in grey shorts and all those days up ahead including war. My father. Puck walks by eating a meringue, beak pushed up to his forehead. My father Brickie says has never done anything out of the ordinary. The Practice of Insipidity my mother calls it icing another cake. When I was seven Brickie goes on When I was seven she stuck her head in the oven. After that she's never stopped baking. That must make sense to someone. Not to me.

No, not to me.

The Ambassador led the campaign against admitting girls. Thought Monstead would lose its ranking once they came. Thought it would make the school frivolous. But they needed the money.

Frivolous? We have fires here in our very own fields.

That's not war.

What do you know of war? Do you know the difference between mercy and good manners?

You are not Lawrence, Evans, this is not your Arabia.

There are other wars.

You mean Us v. Them? The Still-Hope-For v. the Not-Much-Left? The Jaded v. well, the Jaded.

Yes, the daily battles. Tea v. Coffee, Socks v. Stockings, to tell or not.

Never tell.

I don't.

I saw you the day you visited. You remember, I was wearing cricket whites, standing outside the cloakroom with Paul Gredville. You were being led by your father.

Trees turn their colors, the walk to school becomes a golden walk.

Wearing those ugly dungarees and dirty trainers. Your own clothes. Like it was that easy.

What are you talking about.

You were yourself then. More than you could ever be once you got here.

I'm still—

No, they've squashed you. Look at your shoes. Boy shoes.

New shoes from Father. They turn toward Brinton, leaving rehearsals.

Did your father ever say anything to you about his time here? . . . Brickie divines the ground with a stick.

He talked about the raids.

Dorm or air?

Both. Told me about blacking out windows, stealing food.

They sit, backs against the wall.

From a distance, Sophie calls out . . . What are you two doing out here in the fog?

Brickie watches her walk toward them . . . You know . . . he taps the stick . . . It doesn't matter . . . tap tap . . . What I have on you, it's nothing really.

All along it was nothing?

Brickie looks down to her fingers marking his sleeve. She removes her hand. He raises his eyes. It's about our fathers. Our—

Aren't you cold? . . . Sophie stands in front of them, hands on hips . . . I just got back . . . she turns to the pavilion, the efforts to re-build . . . What a mess.

They all look at the ashes.

Some loon that girl was . . . Sophie slides down the wall to sit . . . She used to fuck boys from town. What's a sinew?

Aurora was alright.

Inelastic fibrous cord . . . Brickie pulls at the short winter grass.

Maggot said my face is a miscarriage of sinew.

Singed grid in the grass, the remains of the cricket pavilion.

I heard they're arranging something for us something for the trauma, an outing.

Trauma? . . . Brickie spits out a blade of grass . . . For a fire.

Au contraire, we have suffered. It was a terrible waste of. Of. Of wood.

Brickie laughs.

Brickie's going to be an actor . . . leaning across to tell Sophie.

No one wants to pay attention to you, Brickie

They might. I have the looks for it.

No you don't.

Do I? . . . he turns to Catrine.

Not really.

Oh. Well it wasn't my idea.

Only child . . . Sophie says . . . Typical.

There might have been more. She had miscarriages . . . Brickie says . . . One in Africa while the Ambassador played bowls. He came home just after. How was he to know.

Did she tell you that?

No . . . Brickie throws the stick . . . I found out.

Hello.

Gilbert stands before them. Brickie's stick has landed on his foot. Warily they greet him. Lovely out he suggests. Yes yes they agree. On the cold side. Have you been monitoring the work of our builders? That's right. Gilbert regards the lack of progress and the three of them,

I suppose there's more going on than meets the eye. Yes yes they are in harmony. More than meets the eye. He points to her. May I have a word?

She stands. Sophie's eyes drain of blue. Brickie's absorbed in his fingernails. Silently some might say sullenly she gets up and follows Gilbert across the playing fields toward School House. Past Araigny at the old swimming pool petting Tripod tangling him in yarn together mourning lost limbs and digits past Simon Puck brooding on a low wall past Betts scribbling in his notebook composing his sad comedies.

50

Marjorie on the beach that time we went to France. Pregnant, she stretched out among the pebbles, her great white stomach, a hill. The view behind it, the sloppy village of Gordes or Grasse, something. I couldn't bring myself to stroke her belly though she wanted me to feel the child kick. She fell asleep, I covered her shoulders as they began to freckle. When Marjorie woke, pebbles clung to her thighs. She had slept for an hour or so. I watched her wake as I reclined in a deck chair. It was nineteen sixty-five. I contrived a disguise of the typical Englishman on holiday, though I chose not to wear a knotted handkerchief on my head. I leaned forward as Marjorie blinked against the sun. Flicked a few pebbles from her derriere. I allowed my hand to linger on her thigh then dropped it to her knee. It was the magnificent haunch of a beast. She carried my child. We roasted to the color of aubergine and were shrill when we voiced our desire for ices and citroën pressé. At the seaside bistro, Marjorie giggled on cheap wine. I ordered tartare and pronounced the meat badly while ordering and bad when it came. We were the English on holiday. I propelled Marjorie's bulk through insouciant villages where tributes to our countrymen, blistering and obtuse, were sold on swivel stands outside the shops. We strolled. We ate small tubs of pink paste, fish roe, leaving smears on our shirts and bags. We were silent. Nary a topic in common. I thought about Zola, Molière. From time to time Marjorie offered a remark on the discrepancies between here and there, the lack of courtesy in the chemist's. I forwarded the concept of cultural differences. Her eyes glazed. The day came to an end in a town square. Pallid horses moved lethargically around a track, nodding to the cheers of three or four sordid Frenchmen. There they went, the horses, around and around. After a bit, I turned and stood with my back against the fence. I was not immune to the notion of a controlling metaphor. I watched the Frenchmen eat their tubs of pink roe in one assured swipe, with bread or fingers. Was I always happiest a spectator. One man reminded me of Mahesh, had the same sleepy eyes. Our final year. Marjorie and I returned from the horses dusty and tired. Marjorie's sandals had caused her to bleed between the toes. With Dettol, I wiped away the track, the French with their innate knowledge of how to eat roe. We wanted the restaurant where they would speak to us in English, a form of transportation devised for tourists. Pony with some sort of fringe. The next morning we would pack our suitcases in silence, drive to the airport where I would overtip or undertip the driver. We were not French, we did not know how to eat roe. We were the middle class and the middle class English and I was a married man with a child on the way. It was some years later when Clara first began to speak, that I got up from my armchair and walked away. Out of that cloying heat and stubborn domesticity. Yanking the door behind me, I escaped into the hope of evening. Through the streets I went, exalted! I would never go back. In the shedding light I ran, on and on, intoxicated by the merest doorstep. To the train station. And there on the point of collapse, I stood, hands on knees, managing breaths. Please, I said forcing the man behind the counter to cup one hand behind his ear. Please. The racks of schedules, pamphlets swam. I had something to say beyond expression. Help me. I needed to tell this employee of British Rail. A one-way ticket, yes. It was that I wanted. I straightened to catch my breath. My hand went to my money. One Way Single. An hour later, I returned home, drenched. I took up my place by the window. My book remained where I'd left it, on the table, facedown, as in flight. Brontë. Trust a Brontë to have you running through wet streets. Marjorie had noticed nothing. She continued to fold in the kitchen listening to the radio.

51

In the POD office, Gilbert throws his gloves to the desk, himself to the chair and begins the opening chords to the apology sequence. Catrine, about last week, our arrangement to meet in the library. Somewhere near the top of his head where the wall slips down behind it, a grey circle as if a ball has been bounced there repeatedly. That or Poland. The strings prepare for a bridge to contrition. There's absolutely no, looking for, Excuse for it, a pen, I apologize. Glissando, I'm terribly terribly sorry. Quietly now in preparation for a final crescendo, Gilbert sets down the pen, picks up the gloves. Brown shoes heavy one plus one on the floor, set there. They have squashed her, she once wore. She once wore. Looking up, she pulls back her hair to see him clearly.

They have a name for you. Behind your back.

Gilbert bites at his lip.

Squeak, they call you.

Noises off. Conversation at the bottom of the stairs rises and falls, resounding in the well. My mother was quite ill. Gilbert searches for quality in the fingers of a glove. I was called away. Urgently. Had to wait by the phone. She says, Ill she was ill you had to wait by the phone? She does not say A Familiar Enough Tale. He says, Yes nearly dying rheumatism or typhoid a fever of sorts, cancer malaria a host of ills I wouldn't wish on my worst enemy. How could I have left you waiting in the library, the girl who hates books. What was I thinking to do such a thing, he says. Alright, she says getting up, Alright. Enough already. Or something to that effect. And he—

Wait.

Bends his head to her sleeve. Folds her sweater at the cuff. He

138

glances up, oh god the grin that grips her heart . . . I never told Miss Maggone about Paul hurting you, Catrine. It must have been Mr. Stokes who betrayed us.

Think. This tweed reach to halt the abrupt exit his attempt to righten the situation along with her cuff. Gaze into his eyes. Deeply, that's right. Now compare this moment to a composition. Landscape of courtyard, brown tree, empty field. In the foreground there's the rough outline of a dictionary. Recall, four days ago, an empty library. Four days ago—

Forgive me for not sending a messenger.

She stands up.

Forgive me, Punch.

In the doorway, she turns, he smiles. He knows.

What are we drawing?

Buildings.

52

The way it's constructed, Catrine. Up from earth, not down from heaven, church or non. We're after truth, remember. See this, we may be in for an early spring. In this pale yellow, in those leaves. The crocus I saw on the way home yester—why are you laughing?

Crocus. Sounds so dainty.

I'm planning to undo all that Miss Miss *Devon* . . . spitting . . . Has wreaked. So you can stop reveling . . . lifting his leg to brush out a pebble from the step . . . In mediocrity. In plebeian ideas of daintiness and the expectations of what teachers should speak of, crocuses or or anvils. When I ask what color's this and you say Green, don't laugh that's exactly how you said it, Green, well I put it to you, what about loden? What about teal or jonquil? Where the hell's barium? And what of our friends turquoise and celadon? Are you planning to exclude them from the garden party? . . . Gilbert wipes color from his brush . . . I beg of you, do not get mired in dull dull Green. Green is a downward slope to nowhere . . . he begins to replace the handkerchief in his pocket.

There's paint on that.

Gilbert folds the handkerchief, places it between them on the step.

What does plebeian mean? . . . blowing on her fingers, winter still, crocuses or non.

What now?

You said I had plebeian ideas.

Nonsense. Perhaps I said there was a danger of forming them, when listening to the likes of a Miss Devon. Common, it means common. Originating from the common people of Rome . . . he holds out his hand for the cutting board which serves as her easel . . . Let's go inside Harrington.

He sets off down the path checking for her over his shoulder shaking the doctor's bag to settle their art supplies . . . because art needs housecalls . . . holding it up pointing to the stickers, CND, SWS . . . Don't tell, they'll call me Marxist. I think I told you about falling into this river.

Yes, yes he's said it all before.

A middle-class teenager has ideas about universities, punting and the like. Not easy to push a boat with a pole . . . over a weedy bridge . . . I won't mention Monet as we cross this, I refuse to be ridiculed by a twelve—

Thirteen—

Yes, year old. Punchinello's subtle insults . . . prissily . . . I admire crocuses—

That's not my voice.

Almost out and out calling me sentimental. So I think I've been insulted enough for one day.

He insults himself.

I'm sure I'm complicit, now look up.

They have come to the end of the riverbank the end of their

jaunt the end of Gilbert's rabbiting as Father would say. Father would have no patience. Might I trouble you, friend, for more matter, less art.

Gilbert sets the doctor's case down at his feet, working out the groove left in his palm. Noticing that she watches him, he mouths *up* dropping his hand to point.

And there it is, a green no, luteous dome in the sky. Here's his sentimentality his mushiness, curled up over the trees and Oxbow chimneys. Harrington. The weather has turned, sun back under the roof of clouds, sky forming a low dome above. Gilbert telling her about the roof, burbling the chemistry of rain. Why it makes copper go this shade of. Jade. Standing next to her no not in tweed today half holiday Wednesday after all so wearing his duffel light around him gold because a chemistry teacher in a grey town turns wool that color. He shifts, she looks back to the roof. Why bother with copper if it just turns. Turns. That color.

Into the echo of Harrington's marble entranceway where a desk encircles a knotty tree. White paint in her hair. Gilbert pulls her past the bald man surveying her over bifocals, Gilbert nodding *this is usual, thirteen-year-old girls with white caked hair in your marble library* then pointing up again . . . Fresco.

Painted in the dome, angels and deer. A bearded man . . . God?

St. Francis. Here's his wife, Lady poverty.

Around the desk and man, with his bag under arm, his hand on her shoulder, Gilbert leads her up a flight of stairs. Into a dingy common room of burn-dotted armchairs. He stops in a smoky plebeian corner to buy them coffee from a machine.

Always say a prayer for these, they can be quite vicious. One exploded on me in a bus station once . . . he buys a penguin too . . . Does chocolate count as sweets which I know you don't eat?

No . . . she tells him . . . Those are more like cookies . . . knowing this will amuse him which it does smiling as he rattles the knob for a second biscuit.

Handing her the cup and . . . Watch it that's hot, red or blue?

Blue . . . penguin he leads them back out to the corridor . . . It's illegal to take refreshments from the lounge so hurry . . . past doorways of smoked glass apologetic . . . I revert to student behavior whenever I return.

Gilbert opens an unmarked door to a small room overlooking the entrance. A balcony. Or is it a mezzanine is it a shelf is it a ledge. Potted ferns on either end of a glossy bench. She sits down. Far below, the serious man belted by his desk. Head, a portable dome.

Gilbert sets his coffee on the bench next to her . . . Regarding symmetry, the line of the doorway . . . his hands dart as they assign . . . Those windows, the ornate frame of that door. See the way this window behaves? Let's discuss measure. Let's learn about perspective. Let's discover how to translate what you see instead of what you know.

I'm not very good at perspective.

Stooping to his doctor's bag from paying art a housecall the white domed light bleaching his face . . . Yes . . . a certain press to his lips . . . Quite.

Caught on the balcony well above the serious round desk but some ways below St. Francis with his trouble & strife Gilbert pulling out protractors and pencils in a manner which suggests humming although he is not his concentrated air oblivious to her and her coffee sipping her taking care not to let blouse or mouth stain brown her wanting in an idle way to throw something over the edge to watch its descent to measure speed distance velocity she could stay here like this with Gilbert moving so surely next to her in his pullover a bitter smell to him he has no classes to teach so no baths to take on Wednesdays could stay like this for some time with him about to give her some perspective which she hasn't yet decided if she really wants.

They sit together, looking down. Cutting board and easel propped side by side against the balustrade. Ready to sketch. Gilbert shows her how to break perception into boxes. Draws a grid on her paper says

This might seem boring but you've no idea how useful it will be in the long run.

And he smiles down at her. Gilbert has his own grids the lines bracketing his mouth eyebrows a horizon the axis of nose around which his whole face can turn and sometimes her stomach flips around it too. I'm going to draw the ceiling she says lying back on the bench to face the dome so that when the door swings open when Gilbert flicks around with a surprised *hello* she has a very strange perspective an askew you could say perspective of the door angled away the man's body much larger at the bottom than the top a matter of what one knows versus what one sees a matter of comparing the body atilt in the doorway beyond her bent knees and tented skirt to the doorway itself framing him.

Struggling up, there's no way to delicately drape her skirt clutching her cutting board to her chest knowing even as she's doing it that her blouse will become imprinted with his soft horizons.

Mr. Gilbert. Evans? . . . Mr. Betts, hair frowsy, as if they've called him and he came running . . . Good heavens.

Patrick . . . Gilbert puts down his drawing paper a strained smile a strain to the way he puts the notebook down on the bench between them marking a divider a boundary a border she is right the way over there I, on the other hand, am here. In his *Patrick* a sort of startled amused lift to his eyebrows a standing a curl to his hands dropped to his sides. She is watching him not Mr. Betts but following Gilbert's lead she gets up too stooping to collect their penguin foil and coffee cups standing helplessly not knowing how to not draw attention to their rule-breaking litter.

Well this is a coincidence. Advanced tutorials, is it?

Of an artistic nature, Mr. Betts, rather than a scientific one.

An artistic nature . . . Betts takes in Mr. Gilbert from the shoes up . . . I'm confused.

I was showing Evans the structure of Harrington here, perhaps you recall from your own University days, Patrick, how beautifully this building exemplifies certain notions of architecture, form, construction. Yes hum so I was showing Evans, who has taken some interest in technical drawing, how to site along an axis, etc. Formulate theories of plane—

Isn't Technical Drawing usually a Fourth form subject?

Well yes. Technically . . . a strange whinny . . . Still if we were always to follow the school's pace one wouldn't know who ran the country until one had reached the Lower Sixth. Studied politics. Difficult to shut out the outside world. It always intrudes . . . Gilbert watches his toe touch a leg of the bench . . . I find.

The outside world, that's true enough.

Silently, Gilbert raises his eyes to the intrusion in the doorway.

Well, what a fun day you're having. And you are altruistic as always, Mr. Gilbert. Not many would give their time on a day off.

That's why we teach, isn't it Patrick, to give of ourselves?

So it is, Mr. Gilbert *obscure latin* as they say.

And you Mr.—

I was down in the green room, Harrington has a marvelously well-preserved collection of rare moths.

So you're a weekend lepidopterist?

Doesn't that sound rude . . . Betts snickers . . . No, more of an amateur botanist. I was sent up to speak to . . . groping for the name in his hair . . . A Mr. Powell. Any idea? Records room or some such. I'm a bit lost.

Down on the left two doors. Actually it's marked Records.

Well I shouldn't have any trouble then. I look forward to seeing the results of a day spent in such academic vein . . . Betts turns in the doorway . . . What fun . . . he says it to Gilbert rather than to her in fact the two of them have not looked once at her standing by the balustrade litter in hand.

The men stand motionless, staring. Then Betts laughs abruptly . . . Off I go . . . he leaves with a slam.

Slowly slowly Gilbert sits down on the bench staring at the just shut door his shoulders round his back to her. She sets their coffee cups down, plants them in the potted fern. Keeping the foil to squeeze into a ball.

I flashed him.

What's that?

Mr. Betts. My skirt was kind of up—the way I was sitting and—

I see.

Squeezing squeezing, the foil scoring her palm . . . He already thinks I'm pornographic.

Does he? . . . Gilbert trails his hand along the bench beside him, no doubt measuring the fit of door to frame, factoring the ingress degree of cold air. Finally he swivels one hundred and eighty degrees to face her. And the lines of the background drop away.

Is that grid helping? I could show you the way tangents work. Degrees of distortion. It might help. Then again it might just confuse you.

Gilbert leans forward leaning not his drawing paper but chin on hands against the railing. She sits next to him foil in a ball leans her elbows looks where he does. Below them a woman at the desk, terrier snuffling her ankles, hectors *There's never been any trouble about it before. Are you new? Where did you come from?*

She wants to bring her dog into the library.

Yes.

That man won't let her.

No. How insignificant things can seem, hum . . . Gilbert turns to look at her, resting his cheek on his hand . . . From a height.

Facing him, her face pressed against her own hands, the perspective is mostly elbow, sleeve, fingers. Then Gilbert. Sharp-nosed. Eyes wide, pupils making small shuttering movements. Beyond Gilbert, the white walls of Harrington. Betts, he wouldn't look at her disarrayed across the bench. First photographs, now this.

Mr. Gilbert, are you allowed to sign me out on half days?

Of course . . . sitting up . . . What's on your front?

She pulls at her shirt . . . Your grid.

For some reason her nose is running. And he pulls out his handkerchief but as she is blowing they realize it is the one with paint so he has to root through his doctor's bag to find the antidote another handkerchief to wet and take the paint off her nose. Finally it appears Gilbert has forgotten about Betts bursting in on them on their Wednesday on their balcony. Finally they are alone again even the woman with her dog and the librarian's agitated baldness remain far below as much a fresco as the deer above just Gilbert and her Gilbert saying, Even some on your eyelash, concentrating on the motes thereon although that paint has been there the entire time to remind her out the corner of one eye that she is the kind of girl who gets things all over herself.

You mustn't let Mr. Betts disturb you. After all nothing in the school rules forbids a master taking a pupil out drawing or even for tea in his or her home.

No I've never read anything like that.

Especially a foreign student who cannot visit his or her parents as often as the others, a pupil such as that risks feeling homesick, lonely. Surely it's only charitable to ensure that a foreign student won't feel isolated in our country. In fact I almost think I've seen something in the guidelines encouraging that sort of thoughtfulness among the staff.

When I asked if you felt sorry for me, you said no.

And I meant no . . . Gilbert pulls back resting his elbows on the railing . . . I suppose you imagine I have endless amounts of spare time. That I'm bringing Joyce Tebazalwa off to paint the old bridge by the river, owning up to a sentimental affection for Courbet. Or that Minter and I discuss symmetry and angles in eighteenth-century buildings over tea. Is that what you think?

There is nothing really to say to that but at least she can know next time Sophie says *He's like that to everyone* can say, No he's not like that to everyone, I'm different. Not that she would of course. Not that she would say that. Not that it's in the school rules not to say that, it's just not the kind of thing you say.

He still looks at her . . . Is it?

No.

No . . . he stretches across her to pick up the doctor's bag a T square . . . Don't make a scene, then. Let's go home.

53

But first he stops at Penford because she spots the spire from the road and begs not to go back yet. We can have tea there's always tea and I've been to the gardens. First he says No. Then he says No again. Finally he reverses, one arm around her seat.

Jumping in place as he locks up the car in the sudden rain Hurry up hurry up to which he says, We really have to see about your core temperature huffing as they hustle from the carpark in the drizzle. I want to see the castle, she says, I want to see it, a child repeating herself.

Foul.

Disgusting . . . she has part of the sandwich in her mouth still laughing but trying, after all she has charcoal on her front, paint in her hair and likely still some left on her nose, let's try not to have the bread fall from your mouth. This is not some slapstick.

Dreadful.

Please don't make that face, Mr. Gilbert.

What this one?

Don't. I'll be sick.

Good God girl not here. They'll behead us. What's funny about my face? Don't eat that sandwich to spare my feelings. I think this scone . . . throwing it down, it bounces . . . Has been around since the place was built . . . consulting the menu . . . Fourteen eighty-two.

Same heat system from then as well.

He laughs, fangish, flicking his eyes up at her, hazel they call that, the color of.

In Penford's grand hallway, Gilbert follows her to a picture framed in ornate gilt curlicues . . . Here's an epic of the art world. A reproduction of the *Martyrdom of St. Lieven*. He was a bishop, set upon and killed by these robbers. But first they cut out his tongue and fed it to their dogs for lunch. There it is in those tongs.

The bearded man a saint the ecstatic tongue a slice of ham. They are near the window the rain has stopped she is about to say something American possibly embarrassing for it has been a long day what with Betts the rain stale scones in the old stall and brownish ham in his sandwich a roil to her belly which could be love or bad food. She has felt adrift like this before both hot and damp.

He's answering, Don't be ridiculous. Of course it's not the last time I'll sign you out, leaning his shoulder against the old window with its buckled glass a microscope looking out to the stable teahouse the town down the hill. His skin in the western fading light like paper a sheen tired together at the end of the party.

Gilbert takes a step a slack to his knees as if to make out something behind a tree a sort of cary grant manner of coat through akimbo arm, After all, do you think I want an end to stale sandwiches? You went home for Break let's speak about that, he says or does it come of her own accord memory can be like that math equations then the hen-house door in Felmar fixed with laces. Barefoot in the garden after a brief encounter studying the house four lit windows ceramic lamp by the television. Mother never let her watch in a dark room it is hard on the eyes. Father's inadequate light rounded over his desk as he made cramped notation. No dog no company nobody to unexpectedly pass in front of the kitchen window no neighbor returning some bowl. The grass was sopping pyjama bottoms clung to her leg she might have riled herself into a tornado of fever. Gilbert still amutter because her thoughts come quicker than this. No one to find her a fright in the garden haunted statue galatea come to life. Inside poorly lit a father. Father in a name sewn into school clothes one hot night in a London hotel when the flat next door had a grease fire. Father in sellotape in set square in geometry. Your father

Pottering around on his amateur botany Wednesday like the old hen he

Was a smoker when I met him hair all over never met a comb he liked Lucky Strike his appendage a gangle of limbs thin as spaghetti straddling up to the bar staring at my hairpins those aren't real his idea of a pickup can you imagine pulling me out against traffic to say he would never take no for an answer that was your father head hung over the railing of the liner while

Nothing's changing

I stomped inside with girls from Brooklyn quickstepping into New York Harbor then up the seaboard stopping and starting into restrooms in Rhode Island for more Royal Crown the red peanuts I loved Connecticut night in a cabin stepping onto a mingy porch wrapped in a mingy towel where the badgered sky tested clouds zzzsshhh the distant highway sweet night my life opening me releasing me he is your father it was it was

Where do you go when you leave me like that, Catrine Evans?

And before she knows what exactly sliding her arms through his studying what exactly around his waist and he recoils a step but she has her face firmly against his cardigan chest musty daytrip.

54

The drama begins one evening in a courtyard behind an old mansion obviously used for some other purposes, a school or somesuch. It is a ghostly night. Swaths of fog make it difficult to see clearly. A figure emerges. A young man in a raincoat. He approaches a waiting girl.

BOYISH MAN

What ho, young girl. I think I know who you expect to see.

GIRL

Perhaps you do not know me as you think you might.

The boy ignores her and checks his watch.

She should be here by now.

GIRL

I want to be a delighted girl not delightful, you understand, but a girl with some perspective. He took me to a balcony to teach it. He said I will tell you how to translate what you see instead of what you know. Well I see a girl who does not know. I cannot find the pleasure in order they urge me to take. Cursed with an untidy mind. Once Sophie Marsden took me away across the back fields to a place of lying cows. We can sit on them she said. And though I did not believe, though I was afraid, I sat on one. In the thin sun, we sat each on our own cow while Sophie spoke of her brother's achievements and I thought, I know what kind of girl I am. But ever after I have not found it.

SLINGS & ARROWS OF OWEN WHARTON

I can only laugh at you, your petulance, when I think of what has befallen me. Why I have rough hard stories, enough for two lives. You stand here before me in your rumpled knees as if I should pity you. I prefer your tales, your wandering, to bleatings on evil house matrons, long days, forsaken comfort. You are here to learn, not to love. Although you may learn not to love, which is another thing entirely.

GIRL

I don't believe in your scars. They are more likely from pencil wounds, perhaps even self-inflicted ones, than cuts from a knife.

BOY-MAN

Recognize your own scars, leave me to mine.

Cue dead mother. Nothing. The boyish stage manager crosses and peers into the wings. A silence ensues. A silence which says Look, where the hell's the dead

mother? We've all paid quite a bit of money and if she doesn't appear soon we're
going home.

GIRL

At home, the home I had that is, another home from this one, not that
this is not any kind of—

THE SAME BOY

This is not a home yet you eat here, jam sandwiches, thrice a day.
You sleep here, bundled in your logic of scarves and mittens. Tell me
you do not learn here, that you do not have at least one friend and two
enemies. Do you not hunch over the toilet in the girls' washroom, afraid
to touch the cold seat, rubbing waxed paper to take the edges out?
There's the rub, a fistful of toilet paper. This is as much a home as any
I've seen.

GIRL

We wanted horses but only had trees. We never named them, that
would have been foolish, we rode out fields, our hair flaming back,
nothing kept us, not fathers or dinners we were—

YOU KNOW WHO

Yes, bored.

GIRL

I was going to say that we were different then.

WHO ELSE

We?

GIRL

I mean me, for I never had a friend named Isabelle.

You chose to leave her, this Isabelle, for you make your own decisions.

GIRL

(sadly)

I have done it to myself.

YES YES

I arrived from somewhere else, time passes, they forget you have a different voice. Once I saw you in the corridor on my way to swim, you looked like you were hardly here, I pressed the back of my hand to your face to keep you with us. Say, I am I am I am.

GIRL

Take me for a buffoon?

PARTING LINE MAKE IT A GOOD ONE

Girl, I won't take you at all.

Now it is the next day. Here is our heroine after an uneasy night of sleep, after all she has been confronted with the idea of her own complicity, but let's not get so trapped in false notions of time, look at this morning, look at this day. April already, crocuses spotted by those who love nature. The girl is leaving breakfast.

Out steps a TALL BOY.

GIRL

They told me you had left for the city. I took you for dead.

GREDVILLE

I'm not so easy to kill, I am not a man on a motorcycle, yes that one back in Maine. Admit that you dreamed I would die the night I held you to a tree. Do you think you have that sort of magic, to wish a man gone and là it is so?

WHARTON'S BACK
(consults script)

You've been phased out, Gredville. Get thee hence.

GREDVILLE

But I'm not really ready to leave yet.

WHARTON

You've served your purpose, now vamoose.

Annoyed, the boy crosses to exit.

WHARTON AGAIN

Did you see the ghost back there?

Gredville shakes his head.

WHARTON

These absences are intolerable.

As Gredville goes, a DIFFERENT BOY, one with bastard eyes steps out from a doorway.

BRICK

I believe you accentuate your differences in order to draw clear distinction between yourself and us. You are more American here than you ever were in Maine.

GIRL

Your round vowels and looped cadence betray Americans well have I known.

BRICK

(in a snide aside)

She has yet to understand we are all one.

A CROW flies on.

PUCK

Words can make wings. Words raise a man out of himself.

WHARTON

Wrong play, lad.

Exit crow.

BRICK

When you stood on that hill and the highway, yes I said highway not motorway, rushed beneath you, you knew then, though you would not admit it, that this would be your last chance. Your American hair matted from lying in the leaves with Isabelle. You wanted to keep her. You had to have something, you no longer shared horses. Here was your last chance, you had to make use of it. What would it be? Something grand, something unforgettable.

GIRL

It wasn't like that.

BRICK

You want to believe that Isabelle remembers, that she too remains bound by the tire tale. But Isabelle never gave it a second thought. The man, the motorcycle, the hill, the terror, it all disappeared with your flight here.

WHARTON

What an American day it is, a year ago, April, mother gone, what have you to lose, why not push heavy objects down down into the innocent.

Oh blame the moon for wayward thought, or too much sugar from the cigarettes. Isabelle Isabelle. Moving on to skirts, to real horses, fielding comments regarding her legs, she no longer has use for bridled trees. You need some other way of holding on. Find the tire stashed under leaves, it waits for you. Go on, no innovation this, the wheel, after all. A matter of history. Oh it feels so good, the cool damp rubber, it has the weight you long for. But you would rather fly down that hill yourself. Ah, the tire goes for you, the man burps up and sails like you knew he would if you ever let yourself finish an idea to its logical conclusion. And now. You won't let it go. You see the tire where it isn't, coming around corners, in your sleep. It is not there, American girl. Nothing is. Which frightens you more. She's gone. You left her in America. No tire, not even four, will bring her to you.

GIRL

I can see the flamenco dancers kept in her mirror and the way—

WHARTON

Oh, enough on this Isabelle already. She botched the auditions.

GIRL

Then tell me about my father.

A BRICK

You are not the first to compare his hand to a trout. Do you ever think back to a time when all you knew of this country was the word *sweets*.

GIRL

My father. My father. You sat next to me, we leaned against Brinton you told me you feared for me, my shoes. First you said you had nothing on me. Then you looked out to Sophie sailing over the horizon and revealed, Our fathers.

IAGO

A common theme, the death of fathers.

WHARTON

Gredville!

Rebuked, the villain scuttles offstage.

Wharton throws an arm around the Brick.

WHARTON

Watch her turn from you to see the laundry harridans share cigarettes, what a hash they make of it, the trickery, there is art to lighting matches in the wind, an art they do not have, but stay, no matter, look at this girl and her delight in the wind, sun, in the morning cast to the brickwork there, how red it glows. She is not hurried to anywhere, yet you tremble on the balls of your feet, appear ready to flee at any moment. When you do, will you name it she who walks away?

BRICK

What do you find so interesting in those biddies?

GIRL

Look how they enjoy the wind. Although it feels cold to us out here, to them, after a night by the presses, it must refresh. I lived in America in a town where summer lasted, where children baked in cars as they waited for mothers. We seldom wore shoes even on the hot tar, even riding bicycles—stay, I barely have it. But I remember the library where we watched films. How the seats were six lines of six. Books to be shelved lay piled against the walls. I remember seeing them as I surfaced from worlds of chariots and trenches. The books were talismanic in their ordinariness. You are just a girl in a library, they suggested. Did I think I lived an epic life? Did I think consequences restricted to celluloid?

If I may just interject here.

No.

I had a similar experience myself. Dislocation. Upon my return from a place with the marvelous name of Wittenberg (pronounce that *w* as a *v* if you will), I learned of my father's death at the hand of my uncle. I was home but nothing was the same, for my mother married my father's murderer, yes my uncle one and the same. Mother indulged her new husband something terrible and began affecting a certain giggle that new brides acquire but really is quite unfortunate in a woman over thirty. Now hold on, there's a point, I'm getting to it. There I am, back *des vacances*, Father? Dead. Mother? Giggling. Uncle? Dad.

Our fathers are quite well.

It's the mothers we have a problem holding on to.

I have a mother near London. When I went home at break she made me a marzipan cake. In the shape of something, rabbit or train.

Oh, well then, shall I kill myself, yes or no. As I was saying in regards to dislocation, to say the least, you can imagine coming home for the holidays and finding not only is your father dead but perhaps your uncle (now dad) had a suspect hand in that translation.

I told her I was too old for cakes in shapes. She said the Ambassador might take us to Denmark as part of his job.

HAMLET

Denmark's so dreary. What about Mexico?

BRICK

I thought how much easier it had been in junior school, when I could tell her about sports, she loved my re-creations of important matches, hockey, cricket, tennis. I was on all the teams.

WHARTON

(throwing down script)

I can't keep up with this.

GIRL

You played cricket. I was off the boat, touring. You leaned outside the door to the day scholars' cloakroom, though to me it was just a door. You wore cricket whites stained with red, I must have wondered had you bled or picked cherries for I did not know then the color of a cricket ball, nor a bowler's propensity for rubbing it against his his—

WHARTON

Pullover? Jumper?

BRICK

I developed a hacking cough from cigarettes. I couldn't run as quickly and subsequently lost my place on the team. Not that I cared. Who would play simply to have subject for a mother?

GIRL

You made my father nervous. You stared out from under your hair. You had the eyes of a bastard, cold, hard and black as wells.

You spoke to your mother of lessons you had never studied, it was the cover of a book you glanced at in WH Smith's while you waited for the train. You improvised stories, conceived friends you don't have, tales your teachers never told you.

BRICK

I didn't want to disappoint.

HAMLET

You knew you already had.

GIRL

They've gone in, the women who smoked in the sun. What I miss most is anticipation.

HAMLET

To extrapolate?

GIRL

To want.

BRICK

I was in a chemist's shop in autumn. A salesclerk was working there, she had brassy hair and a nature to match. She wanted me to act differently. I couldn't help her, for it was my nature as a schoolboy to act so, hers as a salesclerk to act là. I followed you, of course I did. I wanted your. Attention.

WHARTON

You're jumping to the conclusion. She has nothing yet to give you.

Enter OPHELIA, late for breakfast, hair still wet.

Oh for God's sake. You can't just pop up out of context.

OPHELIA

The boy wants your reflection. He watches you take your books from the small wooden locker, notice you are missing one, one you have need of at that very moment. You walk to the rubbish, the radiator, the inkwell, the empty lockers below the window to find where they have stashed it. For, no matter how often you fail or how acutely you display disinterest, you reveal an ugly sort of fascination for your studies. This must be punished. Lo, you find the book underneath an old football bag that's remained unmoved for weeks. You walk to your desk. You open the lid because you like the smell of wood. There's nothing inside but pencil shavings. You wait for the Preptaker it's six oh three. You wait for the Preptaker it's six oh five. At the sound in the doorway, you turn. You see him watching, how you stare at one another. You will turn first because that is how it has to happen.

HAMLET

Wait a minute, there are times I turn first.

OPHELIA

You will go to fill your pen more times than necessary. Once you need the blotter, now the ink didn't take. You have a cartridge pen. Why not use that? What do you think will happen if she sees you shamble past?

HAMLET

I don't expect anything to happen, it's a force outside myself that propels me. I have no way of stopping it.

GIRL

When we returned to London I thought of him again. At night I stitched my A lines into I lines because I saw that is how they are here.

My bedroom in London, in the flat I call the plastic flat, looked onto a cobblestone street. I hated that street for its age. I don't know how to sew, my fingers soon were cramped and pricked. I looked out the window, I stuck my fingers in my mouth for relief. Down the street, a figure huddled against the night. I thought of him then, this boy against the doorjamb. I do not know why, nor how memory works. That night I slept in my jumper, I called it a sweater. I wanted the creases out, wanted it rumpled. That's how I had seen the others.

OPHELIA

If you think on this boy so much, farewell to university.

Enter FOOL, in his hurried but vague manner.

FOOL

We all know you here as the cynical girl, the American girl. We were told you were coming, our men were instructed to watch for you on the cliffs, to report back when they saw your blue and red mast tip the horizon. They said we would be visited by a host of plagues. We knew you would bring this on us. Around you, a boy meets the dangerous city, a girl burns our history to the ground. Clearly these incidents cannot be separated one from the next when you stand at the center.

HAMLET

Tell me, girl, why did you think on me that night you sewed?

FOOL

Oh now, look you. Such unspeakable acts has this American done. Her brutish manner, her brooding. I know that the memory of her mother may yet be green, yet since her arrival, something rots here. There is a room at Monstead where her deeds unravel. I tell how I find her loping across the hockey pitch, slavering at the zips of older boys. They laugh, I think it less than funny. Pornography runs deep in this one's veins. I have not yet reported finding *les amants surpris*, the girl recumbent, provocative, on the balcony of Harrington with our own master of science. But look you, it is not only I who notices her seductive ways.

GIRL

I thought only that you stared.

OPHELIA

Girl, let your interest in these matters fade. If only we had burned it together, watched the hockey bibs blacken to ash. Remember Maggot, her pinched face handing them out before a game, red or blue. Never to wear bibs again, imagine.

FOOL

I tell you when I saw her, a girl that age, burlesquing on fields where our innocent play their hockey, inciting those boys, it unsettled my stomach. If the parents of Hopkins, Trethorn or Stevens witnessed the perversion I endured, our doors would be closed today.

Enter the MAGGOT, slick body bound in sweaters.

THE MAGGOT

It's the edges that want taking off. There's some way of breaking her.

BRICK

You have already in the shoes she wears.

THE MAGGOT

I gated you once with Sophie Marsden. You were on your way to lunch after Cookery, after failing quiche lorraines. Running, you took shelter from the rain under a piece of dirty plastic. The plastic shifted, slopping dirty water over the two of you. Ill met under the arch, I punished you to remind you to behave like ladies.

I hoped it was too late for that.

THE MAGGOT

You think I am contrary, rank, maddening. The phlegmatic crone who wishes only to vex her girls. I am plebeian, spinster, dried and unreasonable. No tears, no joy. Certainly, no smile has crossed my face in fourteen years. How odd am I with my gin to be mocked, my underlit flat and overfed fish. Has she ever been found out of antique skirt and cardigan these twenty seasons or off school property? Think you she has a home save our school? And which would make me more abhorrent?

BRICK

There are more things in heaven and earth than are dreamed of in your philosophy.

THE MAGGOT

On bath night, three weeks or so after you arrived, I came in from doing a turn around the grounds where the night smelled sweet and young. I expected your dorm-mates to provoke, but strangely, they were docile. There was a sense of lightness, was it me or the evening. I was a girl, visiting Marco, seeing a fresco for the first time. In the washroom I checked down the row of baths. A quarter hour later I checked again. I opened your stall, you floated underwater. There in the river, your narrow naked body shivered like a leaf. You did not know I watched from the door. On the wall, your dressing gown hung, draped from a hook, it was blue and all wrong. Next to the grate, your slippers waited one by the other. Tartan slippers. Tartan. I was overwhelmed by a feeling of fondness and grief. I wanted to rip you from the water, to clutch you against my chest. I wished for words. Words. Which words would fresco our washroom ceiling. None could.

OPHELIA

So you closed her door.

THE MAGGOT

I said nothing.

OPHELIA

Then you betrayed Marco.

THE MAGGOT

Yes, yes. That's right, I did. My god, I always have!

WHARTON

Pipe down, Maggot, this isn't your epiphany.

THE MAGGOT

Sorry.

FOOL

Tell me girl, your thoughts and wishes, bend they toward France?

GIRL

France. When the list goes up, curiously my name will not appear.

FOOL

Yes, you think you will away to France but—oh dear. Have you not
your father's leave?

GIRL

What's this? You have a plot, Fool?

FOOL

No plot. I simply indicate to dear Polonius how your marks suffer, that
focus is needed, not diversion at the Easter holiday. Sorry, look you
frowningly? I only want you better than you are.

GIRL

My father denies me France because of you?

WHARTON
(shuffling papers)
I'm losing all sense of order, have we reached that bit?

FOOL

Last autumn, on the yearly outing to the natural history museum, I watched the girl. Where others gaped at displays of constructed bears and wolves, this one wandered churlish and ill tempered. As if for her the whole class should be contracted in one dark brow of woe.

GIRL

Well, I had no cause to think the Fool might act differently.

FOOL

My intents are not wicked but charitable.

CROCONIUS happens past on his way to a town meeting.

CROCONIUS

What a crowd have we here. Is there circus in town?

WHARTON

Late on the entrance as always. Take guidance from the Fool who always makes a timely entrée.

FOOL

What ho, the hero arrives, the girl's partner in foolishness. Think me not deceived. I have eyes. I see. The balcony remains fresh for me.

BRICK

The man with the hand dashed by white. So different now in our lessons. Once your terrible jokes and snooty voice were directed as much at the girl as your other pupils. But in a trice they ceased, you leave her be. Now when you look on her I see something change in your eyes, in the creases by your mouth.

FOOL

Then I am not alone in my suspicions.

GIRL

His terrible jokes remain, I assure you.

POLONIUS

(from behind a screen)

He drives you away from school to reveal our English nature on Wednesday and Saturday afternoons. He indicates which trees own sap, which label as coniferous and those you won't find in America. He tells you no horses galloped through the new world, lists which animals hibernate, which die, then forgets which of these befalls a fly. He charms, wheedles, adores. Finds reason to touch you, the better to beguile. Outside the classroom, you fall for his pedagogy. Table manners, the elegance with which he opens doors his deference to your opinions on trivial matters. Sandwiches? Curtains? Applications of philosophy? Habits of the domesticated cat? He wins you with humor and diplomacy and attention. Yet he remains as helpless without you as you without him. Green girl, do you believe such slyness? Tell me you do not.

Wharton pulls down the screen. Paul Gredville looks up meekly.

WHARTON

For God's sake, Gredville. Have some self-respect.

GREDVILLE

Alright, I'm going.

And he does.

GIRL

In happy time, will it all come clear.

BRICK

You need awareness, I beseech you. This man has motivations. Find it in the stars, in their trains of fire. Look out, see it in the hills, bread, the locomotion of clouds.

CROCONIUS

Perhaps you should not be out in the hard morning. You lack outdoor wear. The air bites shrewdly.

FOOL

Your good beauties cause this girl's wildness.

CROCONIUS

Come now, is she not an American girl? Do we not as masters have our pupils' happy hearts at stake? I have taken the girl to tea in my home. I have made her the pie of our shepherds, I have shown her paintings and the men who made them. I have whispered in her hair. How she moves me as she tramps away in her big men's shoes, her queer way of walking as though one ankle has need for the other's assurance.

A BATTLE-AX on her way to market hears the ruckus and listens in.

BATTLE-AX

Like you I offered warmth, greenery, a respite from the bleak. My dog had reservations, for the girl had a peevish nature and often shot him dark looks. Dog, quoth I, this girl has need of our good charity. To the gardens we went, a conciliatory tour. Perhaps I should have been more certain with her. I could have revealed why I call that school Monster. I am old, you won't listen. Leaving me forced to talk to a dog. When I was a girl, I was beaten like a rug. When I was older I knew a man, he came to me with his right eye shot out. He should have been conscripted, fighting, what was he doing, a cyclops in my hospital, where was his eye? Other men were glad to tell their stories, this one stayed resolute, mute. I changed his dressing twice a day. The eye let go slowly, weeping as it went. I held the man at night, he wept for the right side of the world. Daffodils ate antelope, the sea turned to butter, yellow martlets lost in bricked chimneys. He was allergic to morphine, we had nothing else.

CROCONIUS

I hoped to be the one upon whose shoulder she cried. I hoped to see her through all forms moods shapes of grief. I have been tender, I have been kind. Reproachful? I'm afraid so. And equally, have I caused her distress. My mother was ill, I had little choice but to wait by the phone. I am naïve enough to believe sir, that I have also caused her a small form of happiness, a laugh for a painted handkerchief, bad weather, stale cake, Courbet. You brick, you hunch, you frown, sulk beneath your beetling brow. You threaten her and lose your books. How can this serve her?

BRICK

I am not duplicitous.

CROCONIUS

Then you call me so.

OPHELIA

If you had listened to me those times in the lab. Make friends not from here, you heard me advise it. These difficulties would not happen upon you now.

FOOL

A pleasant walk after lunch does much for my digestion. I like the vista of the playing fields, the open expanse undulates behind the changing rooms like a woman's form. The progress of the new pavilion certainly attracts my interest. Here's a day, no different from any Monstead day. A survey of the cricket pavilion. But you are there already, perhaps like me you chose to forgo the baked ham. You stand on the field, your gaze to the grass. Lo, our hero arrives muffled in his scotch scarf. Do you think you can remain unnoticed in the middle of a field? We have a headmaster who, had he both eyes could not see what is so plain to me. I desired only pleasant ambles. Why then am I treated to such intimacies between the two of you. The girl smiles up, one hand at her locks. Even from my distance, I can see you have remarked on it. What have you said, that her hair pleases you? That you long to touch it, whisper in it, to kiss it? Her gesture offers too much. I can tell you that hair is not a suitable subject for any staff member save to give instructions on restraint.

CROCONIUS

How do I convince you as to the nature of my heart?

GIRL

At *Holiday* he sat so close I could sense the short soft hairs on the back of his neck, his cunning profile in the dim light as the sellers of ice and sweets moved through the empty aisles. There weren't many of us. It was a matinée and the girls were desperate to sell, they came up again and again and each time he smiled, not his real smile, the fangish one, he saves that for me when we two are alone, but a nice-enough grin. The girls retreated, he turned back, listened to me or finished his thoughts. In the black-and-white world, our cinema, our Oxbow, I needed only his unwashed smell and the idea of his neck.

CROCONIUS

We are friends, I pretend nothing else.

BATTLE-AX

I stood before orchids, prattling on about I know not what, the glasshouse reeled, I saw you fading before me. I knew from your scowl, your care with my dog, your hesitant way of disturbing memory, that you had no mother. She's deceased you said but I knew already that danger lurked.

GIRL

Danger?

BATTLE-AX

Let me say, your arsenal needs constitute more than a crafty way with a tire.

GIRL

I saw a painting. Perhaps I was the bishop of St. Lieven.

HAMLET

My father was a king.

The group threatens to be late for assembly. Here is the ELDER rushing past on his way to provide moral guidance for troubled minds.

ELDER

What have we here?

HAMLET

My father.

ELDER

Speak, my son.

HAMLET

My father would have died, no matter that I eased him to his end. I spoke to you of that, the day we returned from Oxbow. You see I always tell my confidences in cars, you pull them from me. I never mean to. But suddenly I find myself wanting to talk about my mother with her plans for lettuce. Rosie came to my father in his final moments. My father shouted Benny, What's it all for? And from down the hall, Benny responded with the name of his favorite bitter. My hand stays on the wheel where I know you watch it slashed with white and wonder how it came to be slashed with white. If I could keep you out for a week of stale cake I would not bore you with tales of my mother waiting on Father's last day wanting lettuces. Bringing photos of an old dog they had with a bad leg. It wheeled itself on a contraption Father made. And more, of a skiing holiday in France, the first car. When Mother came in, she pulled up a chair and for an hour we heard stories of that dog on wheels, and the one before that, which had legs.

ELDER

Ariiise ye, from the innocence of brutehood.

GIRL

Give me back my epic life.

BRICK

I had a stupid need for conkers. I waited for him as I always did on the steps to the boy's changing room, thinking about conkers, how I never played anymore, the games I played at junior school, well I've dwelled on that already. I waited for him as I often did on Tuesdays, he had physics, we would walk to lunch together. You hadn't been there very long, we had been in town together, the three of us and he asked about you. He wanted to know why I had brought you the day we sniffed glue. He called you that name, the one we all do. Two girls had tied you up under your bed, he thought that terribly funny. A bird in the dirt turned to us with bright eyes as we passed. I said to him I wish you didn't find some things funny. He said But imagine her lashed to her bed like that, unable to get away. They were tearing off ivy, three men on ladders. One dropped a bit of yellow tin, it brushed my ear as we walked inside. Into School House. He said Come in here for a moment and brought me into the cloakroom. A first year was trying to hang his coat, we pushed him out. He said I don't like you around her. I said I fancy, he said You don't, I said Listen, he said No. I said You aren't hearing me, I won't leave her, I won't do as you say. He said Leave I said he said Fuck off I said Don't he said Fuck I said I love.

OPHELIA

Why did I burn down the pavilion if not for this? You are a Science Girl, you still have chance for university.

GIRL

Am I a Science Girl? Or did he say that to protect me, I don't know.

OPHELIA

So the burning was in vain. Remember the bunsen flames. Think that you joined me as I crossed the field, the lighter atwitch in my hand. I knew not what I did. Hard light from the pyres of padding and bibs, the smell of burning plastic jolting me awake. The flames moved to eat netting draped on a shelf. Standing in the doorway, the fire grew hotter and hotter at my back. I did not know what I was nor where I should have been, for there were only the two of us, myself and the pavilion. Our arrangement was clear. Gladly will I suffer for you that you may leave your mark.

ELDER
(sourly)

No better than a beast.

GIRL

In Maine I did not think Is this a school? Is this any sort of voice to have? What way is this of weather or plants? How it was in Maine was simply how it was.

ELDER

Now you are a girl who thinks too much.

GIRL

I would return to days before a balcony, photographs, a tire. Days before questions.

ELDER

You are American, they have difficulties discerning right from wrong. It is their moral code which does not translate.

CROCONIUS

She has an eye.

WHARTON

An I?

CROCONIUS

A gift. Her art will serve her well, save her perhaps.

GIRL

In London, a hidden woman revealed herself. Hello, she said, This is a museum, a place where we have bodies. Look at me, my smart brown suit and shoes that clack behind my hidden door. I have you already fooled and the art hasn't yet begun. Here I am, delirious in my skin. My nerves own my body, she said, Which I can temper and abate at will. Hello I said I am a cynical science girl, atoms disturb me. I am full of blood, bile and enzymes. Goodness, she said, You are harmonious. Oh, I said, I did not know. Come with me, said she, I will take you to a place where outline does not exist. I do not want to go there, I said, Even to a place of abstraction, even to a place where the real is exact. Well, she said, You will never be a blue lady if that's your attitude. You have not yet made it behind the wardrobe where real art is kept and until that time you'd do well to listen to your elders and, if you need reminding, well your betters too. I said, because I was proud, I have a head with individual character. She didn't like that much, saying, When you are naked you are ideal, that is if you are a true nude. If you insist on owning all this character on your head or in your face well so be it, but you will never be a study. Character compromises, dear girl. Yes, I said, I know, but I don't care if I never end up behind the wardrobe. I don't mind telling you I was close to tears. For abstractly, I am still rewarding. Oh no, she said, That's not true at all and if you continue to speak in that tone of voice you will never be analogous.

TWO

I

Grey fog settles on the tracks. The wind picks up, swinging the sign Chittock Leigh Chittock Leigh. A rattling from down the platform is not the sign but a fourth former at the vending machine. A day Father drove her to Euston himself. Took the morning off work, bought her the ticket, pressing it into her palm as if she weren't the same girl who'd spent the summer caroming around the new city with a tube map, no lunch, cinema schedule. To the perfume counter at Selfridge's, the market, a warren of stalls selling old pewter teapots and military overcoats. Lawrence of Arabia twice, Wuthering Heights, A Brief Encounter which takes place much of it on a train platform. As well as in a café like Bishop's where she bought her fried egg sandwiches where the man took the woman's hand between the salt and pepper shakers. Gilbert walks across the platform to Darton at the machine. A possible word of caution regarding exploding refreshments and Gilbert moves Darton back to the group. When Father disappeared to buy her ticket she watched a man kiss a woman on the mouth. She left lipstick on him. There was always kissing in train stations. Spenning doesn't watch Thorpe draw a map for him in the air, he's checking checking and again his list. Tempton, Thaxted, Williams, Woodward. Betts stares blankly into space. On the balcony or the mezzanine knees tented her skirt. Had he said something out loud. I watch you. A screech. Betts turns, Thorpe brings down his hands, the map disappears. Conductor nods, whistles again. Off to the side Brickie has one hand at the back of his knee Puck in his beak says the night will never end. We are all in this together. And it will go on and on. Father said, Never wander near the park or Kings road where there is a dark element. Meaning the loitering roosters, rollies clamped between yellow fingers. Even the girls had vicious hair and one smashed a man's camera when he took a picture. Down the platform, Gilbert looks up over his ushering fourth formers, smiles or maybe it's a grimace. Behind her, Dr. Thorpe, If you please ladies, plural because Fi Hammond is rushing up from finding her yellow pullover forgotten at the ticket counter. Dr. Thorpe, bull's breath out his nose, Miss Hammond, fourth formers are down in the next carriage with Mr. Gilbert and Miss Devon and that not being a regulation jumper let me not catch you wearing it. Fi runs toward Gilbert, ankles flying up in white dashes. And Gilbert, watching her over the heads of his group, switches to Fi as she gets closer. That's perspective for you. Can't be helped. Thorpe's voice in her ear, Up we go. If she resists he will bring up Thomas à Becket or Augustine because something in her behavior or the consequences to it will have resonance for the man. Oh, reaching for the handrail can Gilbert see her own white socks. Oh, pinkish from schoolwash. Oh, in a fake way as if it is A Brief Encounter, Pardon Me, Dr. Thorpe I Was Lost in Thought. Turning at the top of the steps to watch Thorpe raise his thumb to signal Devon or Gilbert or the stationmaster or himself.

Vanessa next to Sophie. Opposite, a choice. Girl who sweats or Brickie. Swaying, the train has begun, and here's Spenning shuffling papers staring Well Sit Down Then, Girl. She has to go with the stink or risk Flirt.

Three parts to this excursion and you'd do well to listen today so that tomorrow's essay questions don't induce suicide pacts. Of equal weight will be Mr. Betts' comments before and after Tartuffe this afternoon. Now, we are inclined to think of Bath as a Roman town, however it did not come into prominence until—

The train picks up. Rattles out of town. They are leaving. Past the cemetery police station ugly house another and another four fields flash past a country road parallels a moment man on a bike barking dog field field field. Nessa has a bit of paper, Sophie draws on it, they laugh. And laugh. Helpless, Nessa leans forward against her knees. Sophie glances up at her, she has been seeing Maine in Sophie's shoulder. Smile, sheepish. Turning, a farmhouse. Behind it, cows humped in hills. It will rain. Cold hands. In her lap, nails cut straight across. Patches of eczema. Stop it, Catrine, that's disgusting. Out the window, a red mini drives up a hill. I'm not doing anything, Ness. The mini arrives at the farmhouse, she steps out, takes down the scarf she wears to protect her hair from the wind. Inside he watches a football match, can hear it in the background. Father, yes love. Father. I have a question, Yes love oh go go run man you've legs of con-oh. Crete. Father. I'm listening *bach*, Damer's a fool is all. What's on your mind? Easter, Father. France. Remember, the school has a trip there. Silence. Offside, crowd roars. Penalty, he says and she hears the television snap off. A trip to France is it. I want you near at Easter, Easter marks a year. But Father, pushing at the coin return, Father the trip's after Easter, only for a week, and there's four weeks of holiday, Father. Daddy. Da. Holiday not vacation as if Holiday will push the balance to yes. We'll take the ferry. Hovercraft or something. Papa. The cart rolls by.

Orange squash, penguins, hard rolls. She goes to Spenning, right in his ear, Going to the lav, Mr. Spenning. Lav. Who says Lav. Waiting at the far end of his fourth form carriage. Palms flat against the metal, bottom against her hands, she watches him come to her. His hip catches on a seat, an embarrassed smile, up the aisle to her, hand over hand, light flashing on his face and off again as he passes windows, making his way to her for she has news she has to tell him and tell him now, Father said Yes.

On the platform BATH. Betts with his list and hair, the kerfuffle of it. Striking coach drivers have spoiled everything and who if not he will see to it that no one's limbs get amputated via train, veering toward apoplexy when Gilbert and Devon's fourth form group mingle with his third formers hissing, Mr. Gilbert sir if you would just

Give A Hand, because Gilbert is showing Simon Puck his trick with a coin.

You can't blame her for not writing anymore . . . Sophie catches up . . . Your friend. In America.

Isabelle? . . . below them, Bath spreads, clammy and white. Who said anything about it.

Three thousand miles, Catrine. It's like dying.

We were never really friends.

You were. You had her letters. Last term. I saw them.

But there have been no letters from Isabelle. Biro-trenched onionskin. Carefree divots. No blue sails have arrived for her at Monstead. No untidy pages bearing those hurdles, the American *r*. Flagged pinkie over cream tea, Catrine? Pinafores? A Governess? Latin?

Georgian . . . Spenning has them puffing up a hill toward the main square. At the back, *Bringing Up the Rear, Mr. Spenning*, Betts entertains with a story about a monk who fell in love with a swan and jumped into the river though that was a rare sort of occurrence even in the twelfth century.

Thank you, Mr. Betts. The river you are currently passing over harbors an unusual breed of and Brickie next to her saying Araigny's finger was cut off by a nazi when she was four.

That's horrible.

Well there are horrible things.

And apropos of nothing, certainly not nazis, she laughs. They are fueled by freedom, the twenty-six of them, outside school they are ordinary human beings reveling in company. Chosen company. She has invited Brickie, Simon Puck, Sophie and Ness to join her for a tour in the country. And driving down in headscarves and mittens, wicker basket on the backseat, they toast each other and the paucity of traffic, spouting little stories that end with a joke or someone made to appear foolish or in her case, trailing off into silence as the original reason for the story suddenly proves elusive. Giddy with the idea of an outside world, of beings not limited to eleven through seventeen, but inhabited by small creatures, midgets, well infants they call them, and wily pensioners, jaws clicking as they maul the biscuits. Spenning's paleolithic spurts will not moor them. For they have emerged blinking into a world not Chittock Leigh, not half-day Wednesday when half the town shuts up. But a workweek, a real town almost a city actually. Caught up. Carried away. Impulsive. One of them will act outside the domain Pupil. A noble act for another, a decent one for his friend. Yes, they will treat and be treated as citizens.

Abruptly, she stops. Someone smacks into her. She steps aside and Simon Puck shoots past, undenting his beak, scowling.

Tell me, Brickie, what you have on me. I know it's about our fathers, when they were boys at Monstead.

You don't have the courage to hear it.

I do. I have done things. Survived things.

There's blood involved.

What's blood to me? Nothing. I've seen blood, houses laid waste. Tell me.

I'll think about it . . . Brickie in a fine turn. He tears down the hill, catching up to the Dodo.

The Ambassador at twelve or fifteen, hurling cutlery at the scholarship boys. Miniature Father at nine, eleven. There were photographs, Mother brought them out when he was away. In Wales, standing behind his father's house, shovel in one hand. His mother had already sailed for America. Not so long afterwards he was at Monstead and the Ambassador was teasing him with fat fingers saying I've got something on you and. Father being led up a hill by his mother was another. Mother taking her fingernail to get the pages apart. That's why your father chose me, I reminded him of his mother, though no man wants to think that. Mildewed album. Yes, it was my accent he fell for.

Cry of a gull. Down the riverbank, fourth formers sketch the river house. Devon circulates, arms crossed. Her voice trailing up, You're *really* moving towards something. The lurid color is Fi Hammond in her illegal jumper *really* moving. From her vantage she can see Gilbert.

Gilbert taking Fi's sketchbook, Gilbert leaning down, kissing Fi on the mouth. Putting one hand on a yellow shoulder.

Waiting for the loo are you? Yes, her hands cold against the metal. Will you enjoy Bath and he put his hands in his pockets and swayed with the rhythm of the train as if he too waited for the loo although as far as she knew neither of them had checked to see if the latch read vacant or occupied. Have you been avoiding me but as he said it he looked up the train toward the third form compartment toward Betts so it was clear who was avoiding whom. No, I'm not, I'm not avoiding you. Patchy hands cold against the metal wall. I spoke with my father last night, he's sending the permission slip. Gilbert looked puzzled. The door swung open, a boy came out. Go and sit down, Gilbert said for no reason. What do you mean permission? Posting it, his signature, the check, so I can go to France. Oh, he said, That's wonderful news.

They will have sufficient vocabulary, nine fingers will ensure it. On down the riverbank taking out notebooks brown for geography. Dirt clods sellotaped to a page, a flowering grass found in Chittock Leigh, stages of sediment, contours, cross section of a rock. A fresh page for flint, for Bath.

Over a bridge. The town whitewashed, the smell of ocean. Seaside. Four buildings form a square. A man in the doorway of dry-cleaning presses two fingers to his temple. Baskets of colored eggs in the windows, streamers. A year, a year Easter day. Her pen has bled, the taste of ink. Never get through a day without blue somewhere, blouse, arms. She is wasting away they said and it was a waste. The smell of car fumes, gasoline. Dr. Thorpe talking about carriages. On his pause for breath, Spenning quickly interjects a note on mesolithic hunters. When Mother was wheeled into the library on a cot, Father put away the photographs for good. They are sentimental. But he didn't know she kept the vintage letters, Dear Catherine Dear Henry. They think you will die from the pain of it. Or is it you who thought that. If it were something you could refuse. Thank you, no.

Vanessa holds out a can of Lilt. The group behind her, their straggled height of hair, brown, yellow, black. Brickie, Joyce. The treeline in the square, the roofs. This town a hospital all white and straight as a sheet. Drinking down the effervescence the pineapple sweetness a remedy.

A day by the ocean when Isabelle told her they wouldn't be girls again. Smelled like this. Like salt. Tasted of salt.

You'll go back, I expect . . . Nessa reaches for the drink.

Their fingers overlap. No, Ness, there's nothing for me in America.

Sophie appears slapping a rolled-up magazine into her palm, What'd I miss, shoving it between her knees to take Nessa's notebook.

And they move on. All so fraught one moment, the next nothing. Deflated, then expectant. The excitement of possibilities, of accidents and fortune, alternate and collide, drumming a pulse above her ear. Through the streets. They could rebel.

In the park, Spenning passes out lunches, the sun crawls out. Figures on the Lawn. Gilbert on a Bench, lunch beside him, face raised to the blank sky. Even those few minutes in the hot corridor he kept glancing over her shoulder to sight Mr. Betts.

A tap. Simon Puck alerting her to a spot where the grey balds in her knee. Sophie is dismantling her sandwich, revealing its sordid inlay. Butter webbed to cheese.

Sophie, stop . . . Nessa, easily disgusted . . . It's like open heart surgery.

Brickie shifts, picks up his leaning hand, looks at it. Buttercup pressed to his palm. Immersed, black hair a curtain, sandwich balanced on his knee.

Suddenly, a packed lunch lands on the grass between them. Betts, pulling off his jacket.

So you are to be our hero, Brickman. Congratulations.

Nessa and Sophie stare . . . Brickie?

He's peeling the flower off his palm.

And how are you finding Mr. Percival's direction? I had the opportunity to stop by your last rehearsal. Your director is certainly taking a number of liberties with the translation. Aristophanes must be a dervish in his grave . . . Betts pours a cup of dark syrup from his thermos . . . I was asked to operate the machine but I'm already engaged in some theatrics. I'd prefer a lighter role, still . . . Betts knocks back the coffee . . . What do you think, Brickman, are we victims of vanity? This thirst for applause, is it only ego gratification or is there more to it?

Peaks couldn't remember his lines, sir and Owen Wharton threatened me—

Could it be that our own lives offer so few opportunities for noble action?

She stands, brushing grass from her skirt.

Betts squints up to place her against the sun . . . Back at half past, Evans. And don't find trouble.

A stuffed rabbit plays a tune on bagpipes. Through the shop window, the muffled strains of Auld Lang Syne. A short man appears by her side, smelling of attic. No, smelling of mothballs. Mothballs in a closet full of dresses useless in Maine a closet full of shoes.

Well that's hardly an Easter tune . . . he raps on the window, encouraging the rabbit to come to its senses.

One day in London she rode double deckers from Knightsbridge to Deptford. Back to Notting Hill. Hammersmith, Chiswick, Richmond, Twickenham. Sat up top, in front, chin on hands. Watching waiting women spot the bus, the small glad twitch when it came into view.

The man appears inside the shop pointing out the rabbit's deficiencies to a salesclerk.

The landscape changed, became green, then grey again. It was the beginning of a feeling she never had in America.

Gilbert finds her on the steps to the library, looking at a parking lot . . . Nice view.

I'd like to go to Greece someday.

I thought we were off to France . . . he sits next to her.

Greece is white and clean like this, don't you think?

Supposedly Athens is filthy. Rabid cats, begging children—

Rome then.

Are you enjoying the Romans?

She looks at her shoes, in them, Arabia. I like the desert because it is clean. To have a battery of horses at your command.

A motorcycle pulls into the parking lot across from them.

Gilbert nudges her . . . Why so quiet? Trouble with the Romans?

No more than usual.

I saw you watching that funny rabbit in the shop.

A short man came up next to me and I looked at him, and I thought this man has a head flat enough for chess.

That's very funny.

It's not funny. It's cruel. It's Easter and.

And what?

Mr. Stokes said when I look at him it's like being caught in crosshairs. Maggone called me petulant. I had to look it up. She asked why it is that I can't take delight in things.

That's absurd. If you could see the way your face lights up when you speak of the lepers in Ben Hur. You take delight.

Not the right way, not like the others.

With a naïveté you mean, delight in—

I'm a cynic you said.

I was warning you. It's boring not to trust people.

If you always think they have motivations, you mean?

Exactly . . . Gilbert fans out his fingers . . . I'm getting dishwater hands now that you don't wash up in the lab anymore . . . he reaches for her hands . . . Did yours survive?

She tries to pull away. They grapple. He wins. For a moment he considers her ravaged palm, the skin hard and cracking. Blooms of dried blood.

What is it?

Eczema. From the weather changing.

Hum, has it changed? . . . he touches the ropeburn marking her wrist . . . And this, also eczema?

Yes.

Lightly outlining the patch of paler skin on her palm where it frills at the base of the thumb. He looks at her, they are close, huddled over her hand as if over a rare object . . . It looks painful. Don't you have medication?

Bergamot. Borne on a breeze.

Mr. Gilbert.

Gilbert puts down her hand. Fi Hammond stands before them in her yellow pullover, hands on hips.

Mr. Betts sent me to find you.

Gilbert stands . . . Did he. Well, here I am . . . brushing off his trousers . . . I'll do some research on your eczema, Evans. There must be a solution.

Spenning rushes up as they approach . . . Madame Araigny has arrived as has the Wharton boy . . . Spenning is sweating, almost shouting, a vaudeville of the scatty academic . . . They are collecting lunches, in a few moments Madame will be available to speak with your group about Tartuffe, Mr. Gilbert.

I don't know if we're ready for that yet.

Yes well when you are when you are . . . Spenning looks down at his tie, scratches at a spot then looks up at her . . . Rest and rust, Evans. Go join the others.

Moving away, back against a wall to look up up at the fan vaulting Thorpe at the Abbey orating *We must harken back to a time when a king had the sort of power* the scalloped effect. At the low end, very small. For all Thorpe's thundering Prayers, zeal steadily forcing one strand of hair over his forehead dooming him to spend his lecture taming it by hand or breath, for all his rabid hymn singing, Thorpe is exhausted. They are saintless, they have failed him *I beg you to imagine this nave* the words come again and again her ear against the shell his words lapping. That day after chapel. Finger tracing the wall behind her, the old stone. That is a lovely dress, he said. It was striped and together they looked out over the fields, cricket, hockey. She brought down her cuffs to warm her hands. She wanted things but it was enough that he was there next to her, that she knew about Rosie and he admired her new shoes from Father. An evening breeze delivered the smell of grass and was it for having just seen Father that weekend or was it the grassy smell stirring in her, England, a giving in. Gilbert's hand tapping the back of the bench, a gladness for him, the evening and looking toward Follyfield, Brinton, the age of it all. Liking the shape made by the outline of School House and chapel. The smoothness of the banister in her hand on the way up to bed. Gilbert's tapping hand kept tapping and the wind kept stirring the smell of grass, the landscape stayed the same but she saw the piano and railed against it all.

2

On the way to the Roman baths, she stops by a tree, hand against the bark to steady herself. They will think she's been at the glue. To feel Bath bark, here she is, in Bath. And she will try, yes she will. Overhead, a tremendous whoosh. Running out from the park, she stumbles into the square. Above, a flock of swans fills the sky, a great feather bed soaring above Bath, erasing the blue.

3

On the way to the Roman baths, Betts and Owen Wharton catch up, smelling of smoke and coffee.

Catrine Evans . . . Betts asserts . . . I imagine one doesn't find this sort of thing in your country.

Not any more.

Owen stops to pet a dog tied to a lamppost.

Don't agitate it, lad . . . Betts shakes his head . . . It'll garrote it-self. I've seen it happen.

Owen leaves the dog. They continue on.

Actually it was an anecdote about a rabbit tied to a car. Child left it there a minute . . . Betts makes a face . . . That's the thing about children, what is, simply is. Don't yet have a polished sense of logic, of—

Hypothesis? . . . Owen smells his hand.

Foresight. A notion of What if. A child will think, if a car's parked, why would it move?

Inability to extrapolate.

Precisely. You see it in the first formers, no detachment . . . Betts tears a leaf from a bush, absently tests it with his teeth . . . Poor bunny kept up as long as it could.

No doubt it avoided a certain death by myxomatosis.

There you go . . . Betts throws down the leaf . . . There's the bright side, Wharton.

I don't like dogs . . . she says quickly to rid the bloody rabbit im-age . . . They seem. Pointless.

They stare. The wrong thing to say.

Don't they?

Betts smiles indulgently . . . Everything has a point in your world does it?

They protect you. Keep you company . . . Owen looks over her head to confirm it with Betts . . . They lead the blind.

I'm not talking about the blind.

What about pastries? Art? Not much point in most things if you follow that logic. Music, theatre. Dogs for dogs' sake, after all . . . Betts walks faster . . . Don't tell Shakespeare what's pointless.

Yes, but you don't have to feed him. Or smell his breath. Have him on your leg all the time needing to go out.

Betts stops . . . You're right. Shakespeare is marvelously well be-

haved. You only take him out on your terms. There's an essay for you . . .
Betts looks over at Owen.

For Royal College.

Well, perhaps not Royal College.

And they laugh like old friends and talk about some lecture series
and she falls into the role of mute dog-hater. They will dissect her afterwards, Fancy saying there was no point to dogs. There's a girl with
no detachment. A third former mind you, not one of the younger ones,
but old enough to know about consequences.

I heard about a kid, a kid in America . . . interrupting their lecture
projections . . . Who dropped a—a bowling ball off a—a bridge to see
what would happen. Onto a car.

Ah . . . Betts looks confused.

In terms of detachment . . . switching between them to see if they
understand . . . What you were talking about before, the rabbit. You
see, the boy couldn't understand that a person might be hurt. Because,
like you said, he had no foresight.

What happened to the man in the car?

The man in the car . . . she picks at her hand . . . The man in the
car ran off the road. And. They didn't see what happened next.

They?

He, I mean. The boy. Never knew if the driver was hurt . . . again they
look at her oddly . . . It happened to a friend of mine. A personal friend.

Well, personally . . . Betts picks up, Owen still watches her . . . I
think it's a problem of early attachment. Some children are too reliant
on parents to make decisions for them. Especially moral ones. A boy
drops a bowling ball because he has had no previous experience making decisions. Everything laid out before him, tea, bed, mummy with a
dishcloth tied about the waist. Put that boy in the service, see what
happens when he has a revolver pointed to his head.

An odd silence. Then old Betts is off and running on ex-pats, T. S.
Eliot's book of cats after all she is American, does she agree that poetry is in fact an escape from emotion rather than a headlong hurtle to-

ward it. And while she's turning that conundrum over, Owen's getting pebbles caught in his treads. Finally they leave him stooping to scrape them out with a twig.

Upon reaching the baths she is the first to see the group, Araigny, Devon, Spenning, and most interesting of all far more fascinating than the English teacher's fondness for poetry or Wharton's for pebbles, or even Spenning cantering up in slow motion to ask if Betts wants to lecture next and where is Thorpe or should he himself talk about the baths for he can't find his notes, what is equally interesting is the sight of Gilbert, jaunty, one knee bent, foot on the railing, leaning forward, smiling down, pointing out something to Fi Hammond who sights along his outstretched arm much as she herself has done on more than one occasion.

Old Spenning . . . Owen arrives . . . The man's a gibbon . . . pulling her to sit on the wall next to him.

She reaches into her blazer for cigarettes.

What's this? . . . Owen snatches the pack, launching it behind him . . . Smoking's not in your character. I'll have to have a word with Sophie Marsden.

Simon Puck lands under a nearby tree, staring beadily at them. Owen waves him away. . . . What are you seeking there in the dust, Evans? America?

No.

Then what are you up to?

Pebbles by his boots make the head of a man.

Careful of inventions . . . Owen glances over his shoulder at Gilbert . . . They'll invent you back.

You don't know what I'm thinking.

Let's play a game. It's called Hazard a Guess. What's the date I think to myself. Hmm, what could it be. Hmmhmm. Now here's a coincidence, looks like we're coming up on Easter, and lo the girl goes gloomy. Why might the clouds hang on her so? What do we recall happening at Easter besides the resurrection of old whatsit.

She stands.

Owen yanks her back down . . . Resurrection doesn't sound right. What else could it be, let me think, just a minute, it's right on the tip of my—

Owen, please.

I've got it!

Don't.

I've suddenly remembered what happened at Easter exactly one year ago.

Shut up shut up.

Your moth—

She turns, Betts, Araigny, someone.

Sorry, *bach*. No one interrupts me . . . Owen grins . . . Wouldn't dare. Easter month. Your mother died at Easter, am I right?

What's that, Evans, say something?

A fear. Fearful meditation. Sad mortality.

Well now, you see, that's Shakespeare you're quoting. And in fact, I'm asking *you*. Give yourself the speech for it, Catrine. Suit the word to the action and the action to the word, if you will.

I can't.

Surely you know what must happen if you don't. Why make yourself go through it.

I can't hypothesize.

For god's sake, you're not a rabbit lashed to a car.

I can't.

Open your eyes.

But she's fallen asleep in the forest. She will wake with rabbit ears.

4

A man from the town appears wearing a peaked cap emblazoned with a crest.

Our resident expert . . . Spenning jabs him as if the man too is mesolithic . . . Mr. Reggio.

They all watch the man describe the baths, rounding his eyes though it soon becomes clear that the alarm is in fact impediment. The man organizes them into a line to drink stinky water from paper thimbles. Araigny wrinkling her nose in a petite French moue. Fi Hammond. The girl is clean you have to say that. White socks to an exact length and short so no need of constant hitching. The water tastes deliciously bad. White shirt tucked into skirt, yellow pullover draped over her shoulders as if after eggwater she might well engage in a set of tennis. Shiny hair girl, bergamot lass.

Guaranteed to cure any illness, after all it was rumored beneficial for Leprosy . . . pop-eyed Reggio circulates, refilling cups.

Like a garden party . . . Gilbert says it right into her ear, coming up behind her.

She starts.

We were interrupted earlier.

Sipping, she studies him silently over her tipped cup, taking in his long nervous fingers strumming the railing, the other hand grasping, that's right, his waist, one knee thrust out to show he is relaxed, the sort of young master capable of joking with his students, of not taking it all too seriously. He smiles at her, she takes away the cup, looks into it. Listens to the song, Another outing, To paint this time, Somewhere with nicer food.

Don't tell me that if it's not true, Mr. Gilbert.

She watches him run a hand through his hair as he walks away. Don't let go. In Howlands, struggling for portraits, the sound of his sleeve as he reached for the light. She can't. Can't seem to hold on.

Three steps away, Gilbert swings around . . . You like those lads in leather do you? Wharton, I mean. Best stay away from him. Another Paul Gredville if you ask me . . . Gilbert crumples his cup . . . Wednesday then.

At the interval. Brickie and Owen in lobby consultation. The filing in. The squeezing past knees. The unsettled. Audience of rustle audience of toffee offerings and assessing Bath fashion. Yellow winter wear in the gallery. Bad hat in the second row. Man down front rehearsing the cough he's excercised nicely during Act 3. Chime. And a sharp dig between the wings.

You're hurting me.

Brickie, on the edge of his seat jabs her again . . . If you're desperate to know, eyebrows jerking each jab, I'll give you a quest.

Quest? Another chime, imminent theatrics.

On the other hand, if you don't want to know—

I do I do want to know.

Do you have it in you?

Yes. I accept. Any quest.

Noise in the back of his throat, skeptic ocean.

I have done things, Brickie. I have gone against their rules. Led men across deserts.

Shh . . . this from some Mareka, Daphne.

Brick—

It might kill you.

Nothing here could.

Alright, his mouth by her ear breath tickling . . . The way you'll know at last is.

Their lights fade, Brickie's voice drops.

The way you'll know at last is.

Drumroll.

Found in.

Cleante and Tartuffe step onto the stage beauty-marked and powdered.

Number 26.

They're all talking about it. This is the time to tell you bluntly After school when our English Tutor is earning and ensuring the affections of a certain coquette, steal into his office. Up the door through the stairs. Disturb the papers flooding his desk, rummage in books piled thereon *shhhh* old man's compiling a new history of Monstead says the actor or Brickie *pardon the offense* one or the other *sacrifice your resentment* finally putting all those scribbles to use. In the office of Monsieur Betts is where you will discover the ghastly tale of yore I mean your father. *Unjustly accused.* If you fail, Evans, if you fail you are just a girl who cannot read between the lines then you *Lose glory* deserve not to know *shhh* neither what your father did nor how it is that an apple never falls far from its tree.

6

They prepare to return to Chittock Leigh, for the hypocrite has been flushed out, the lover tested and found sincere.

And here he is. In the shabby cloakroom, extricating his coat from a pile of duffels.

Mr. Gilbert?

He turns . . . Ah, Diogenes. Searching the streets for an honest man?

Do you like her?

Sorry, what's the question?

Fi Hammond . . . outside, the sound of a cheer . . . Whether you like her.

Fiona out there, Fiona taking her chemistry O level, that Fiona?

Another cheer, Puck's voice clear above the others.

Whatever it is, come out and say it. You burst in here like your hair was on fire.

I didn't.

Do I *like* her, I think the question was. Let me see. Fi Hammond seems intelligent enough. Has always displayed respect for the science. Seems to do her Prep. Has always been courteous. Has never, to my knowledge, tampered with the levels of dangerous chemicals while entrusted with the upkeep of the chemistry lab.

What can she say to that.

All in all, I would say that Fi Hammond is quite likable.

You had your hand on her back. Maybe she's not sure about your motivations.

Which are?

Pressing a finger against the window, watching the tip of it whiten . . . I don't know.

The school rules are quite clear. I suggest you go back and review them . . . Gilbert's tone changes, becomes serious.

He turns back to his coat. When she is inches from the door, sullen inches, Gilbert calls . . . Wait.

She stops.

Come back.

She does.

I have a gift . . . pulling out a square of cloth, he hands it to her . . . My handkerchief from our day in Oxbow. Paint won't come out. It's an accidental canvas.

Greens she tried to rename.

Don't scrutinize it, not much good at the abstract stuff.

She folds the handkerchief into tidy squares.

A tug. He has hold of her hair. Pulls it gently . . . What goes through this mind at such warped speed, funny Punchinello? I'm going to conduct a study. Something to make my fortune, hum? . . . winding the theory in his fingers her hair . . . Oh . . . letting go . . . Was that unkind? I was trying for a joke.

Sometimes you're funny.

Halting by the window, he registers the comment, face changing from a big intake of breath to a stunned expression involving his chin . . .

Sometimes? . . . folding arms . . . Well how often would you say? . . . down his nose at her . . . If you were forced to estimate?

What is he talking about.

What's the number? Come on, you've done it in maths, percentages. I've seen it.

Mr. Gilbert—

No, no. I'm fascinated . . . folded arms forming channels in his sweater . . . What's the percentage of my success?

Seventy—

Seventy?

Eight.

Seventy-eight. Not so bad. And yours . . . he does the math . . . Ninety-one.

That's high.

Yes. But I'll have to try harder or make fewer jokes.

Maybe I miscalculated.

You seemed quite sure.

I wavered a bit.

It came out very absolute. Seventy-eight. There was no questioning it at the time.

But now I'm remembering some things you said in Oxbow that were pretty funny.

As a scientist, hindsight is not your friend. As a scientist, you must back up your data before going public with it.

But. You were standing there like that. Waiting. I was pressured.

Ah . . . crossing . . . You'll be better prepared next time . . . over his shoulder . . . To stand the pressure . . . at the door . . . I've given you a Gilbert original. And you can rest assured that however promising a student Fi Hammond proves to be, she doesn't own art like that.

Paint thick in spots. Doesn't have him, is that what he means, Fi doesn't have him. Gilbert opens the door. Pulls on his jacket, shirt creasing as he shrugs it over his shoulders. She runs to the window to watch him walk.

Outside, Owen is leaning against the building, bored, arms folded. The doors swing open. Here comes Gilbert pulling at his sleeve as he jogs down the steps. As he passes Owen, Gilbert stumbles, lurching forward abruptly. She lurches with him, bumping her forehead against the glass. Awkwardly, Gilbert manages to catch himself on the railing. He looks at Owen in disbelief. Owen takes out his toothpick, throws it to the ground and walks away. Gilbert runs his hand through his hair. But she saw. Owen's foot flick out.

7

Back at school, Pythagoras proves to be the final unraveling of Duncan Peaks. The Maths teacher has disappeared in the night, baby, cough turned fatal, no one is certain. Spenning stands at the front of the room holding a ruler in one hand. Rulers go with mathematics, this he knows. Sophie goes to the blackboard. Mr. Spenning, we are onto triangles, scribbling out $a =$ Mr. Spenning, sir, $b^2 + c^2$. We have moved onto the stupidity of the Obtuse, the sagacity of the Acute. Gently, Sophie takes the ruler away from him, We are done with metrics, sir. But Spenning, frozen and paling, stares at the back of the classroom. Sophie looks up, her eyes widen. One by one they turn. Duncan Peaks lies in the corner of the classroom wrapped around an abacus, shucking the beads, rocking himself.

8

Boys had differently shaped heads in the nineteen forties. Square back then. Boys crossing hockey sticks, half-men in tennis whites. Trophies. Classical music dribbles down the corridor from the short part of the L. Photograph after photograph. Red carpet. Courage. Lawrence in all that sand. Contending with the breath of camels and poisoned spiders in his blankets. 26. A swan and a beckon. She pushes open the door. The office is empty.

9

Four days ago I asked for your replies to Hitch's letters. Today I hold before me seven pages of quasi–William Butler rip-offs from Chambers in the Third. Apparently this pitiful sheaf comprises your concern for overseas friends greeting death. You boys recall the meaning of the word comrade, don't you? Yes, well, think about what it's like for your old friends now in aeroplanes, now staring down the wrong end of a Howitzer. These are boys with whom you once sat around a fire, boys who once advised you in your quotidian schoolday struggles. These same boys dare I say friends are today huddled in trenches, barbaric and confused. And you think you suffer you with your lessons in temporary classrooms. Yes perhaps they once housed farm animals but Western Literature will not be diminished by the faint trace of pig. Need I remind you what's happening across our river? Your fathers are dying. Where the devil do you think poetry will get the O.M starving in a trench? Darvish, Treat. Give our boys incentive, feed a boy's soul with school stories, boost him with tales of less haunted days. Set it down, set it down. If a schoolgirl in the second half of our century steals through these secrets won't she want our history? Shattered eardrums! Lost fathers! Banished children! Alright, alright, so I digress. Brickman, I asked you to signal when I began repeating myself. Assembly notes. 15/3/47 I have been informed that older boys have been beating out the younger for their share of the squish. Any boy caught doing so will lose games privileges for a week. It tries my patience it really does. We will not behave like castaways during our time in this Welsh hell. A word concerning the *frisson* which took place in the science laboratories yesterday. Not very amusing, it nearly set fire to the dormitories above. Boys doing science will remember that Tangley and Duke are housed overhead so wash the vegetables carefully don't run on wet floors please remember delousing at four remember your FATHERS ARE DYING. Wash your hands. Please. Please. Vegetables are not bootscrapers. Please, your letters to Hitch in Italian trenches please, a warm word for Stokes who recuperates in Sussex please remember our masters departed in service, M. Drake, Dr. Bovart, S. E. Powers and R. C. Farthing-Smith in your prayers in our dirty nights. Don't forget India, don't forget the Maharajah. Remember V. Banks his gypsy moth a dark dart in the flaming skies of Africa, he was a target, boys. Your fathers are targets, YOUR FATHERS ARE CRYING. And our beloved D. E. McGraw, shot down over France. Bad luck. We will miss them all. But, Negland, dear Negland, who only returned to Monstead last month, has already led the cricket elevens to our biggest victory streak ever adding a win over Cheltenham to those over Monmouth and Bromsgrove. Round of applause. Word of warning to those engaged in private wars. Tangley and Duke have formed an alliance and last night undertook an ambitious raid on Conwell via the vegetable passage. Do you understand that your friends will die do you understand that if this is what passes for strategy, we might as well rip off the bedsheets and surrender before Prep. No. This is not how it will be. We will not have scattershot attacks. Boys will first present tactics to Prefects. You will calculate risks. You will project casualties. Yes, this includes midnight feasts, dorm raids, ratcheting a child to his bedsprings. Each act of arbitrary ostracization, all your works of torture. Boys will be men about the whole thing or see me. What would Hitch think had he witnessed the scene I came across last night while making the rounds of houses. These blubbers youknowwhoyouare will take yourselves suitably to task via self-mutilation, suicide attempts or psychiatric disorders in your mundane futures. I won't have boys thinking of their fathers I won't have namby-pambys longing for Sussex and the dear departed you will pull yourselves together you will you will try to remember

Remember what?

She spins, pages float to the floor.

A quest, Yank, didn't I say quest? Don't waste time . . . Brickie picks up a book from Betts' desk . . . You're pathetic. Do I have to show you?

She gathers up the spilled papers, replaces them on a desk covered with letters, notes, bits of bark. Two red berries. Still life of Apple Core, slantingly cubist Sandwich Crusts on Foil.

What's his story?

Who, Betts?

He's unhappy.

Aren't they all . . . Brickie flips pages distractedly.

Brass ashtray in the shape of a palm. Offering Greek coins, string. Catarrh pastilles. Cuff link. Jade dot. Clipping a young cuff as he raced across the Oxbow quad. To his wedding. Marjorie in white. Smooth to the touch. She zips the delicious dot into her moneybelt. Sifting letters on his desk. Yellowing *Dear fellows   Much encouraged to know the school's behind me on this lark, not like on that mad canoe down   If the gerries ever   In an airlift with an O.M. Hughes several weeks back   Used to snore through Latin with Berger   Send over more Monsteadians, not many are used to these conditions*

Brickie outlined at the window, Certain it was this one bastard eyes scanning dark eyes dark

Brick—

Shut up, Yank.

Yes, dark Heart. A black chapel gown hangs behind the door, deflated crow. Brickie still at the window. Unhooking the gown, the slippery black of chapel, collar sheened to purple by his hairoil *and the betrayal of mind betrays me* his sleeves hang long past her hands *I run across the quadrangle I delve the fog I am*

Not as bad as you might be at the English Language.

Brickie looks up . . . Idiot.

Grim reaper.

He tips the book toward her, pointing to a photograph.

Stokes?

Yes . . . Brickie says . . . And he's got both his eyes. But down here's the good bit. Your father—

A noise. Shadow in the doorway. They freeze. Betts. He looms, he enters.

Quickly, she slips off the gown, kicking it into a shadow.

Well, he says, well well what have we here a pile of mischief the American girl the boy from London in places where they should not be rifling through the belongings of a teacher. And my notes do they amuse? Or do they mean so little as to mean nothing? Am I simply another figure knocking about, lost to a better past, meting out the old grey matter in this blighted setting?

Betts walks to the window, holds his hands to the radiator beneath it . . . Out there's where you two belong, isn't it? Isn't there some hockey some rugger—

Don't play rugby here sir, on account of—

Don't patronize me, Brickman, I know there's no rugby here and there hasn't been for years . . . Betts considers the playing fields, quietly . . . There was a time before girls. We were a serious school then.

Zipped at her waist, his round cuff link presses the point. The three of them stare below at figures in grey zagging purposefully around the field. The window rattles. Cue thunk of ball, a solitary shout.

Betts turns . . . Why are you going through my possessions as if they're trifles?

Sir, she asked about her father. I meant to show her the book where—

Brickman, do you intend to make absolutely nothing of yourself? Is that your objective?

Brickie shrugs.

Don't the two of you have enough to do don't I for one give you enough Prep have you revised for the test on Monday? Do you know the meaning of the words Husbandry, Capitulate or Thews? For you

clearly understand Defile, and you have provided ample definition of
the word Sully . . . Betts leans back on the radiator, the window behind
him rations light . . . Ten sides. Both of you. On the subject of history.
You seem to share a fondness for it.

Ten sides, sir, not really fair.

You're absolutely right, Brickman. Let's make it fifteen.

IO

Détente?

Stop for a moment.

A relaxing of tension between rivals.

I have to open the window.

Thews? It's freezing.

Sit on the radiator then.

It burns. Thews?

Don't flash me, Yank I've no interest in your underthings.

Muscular power or strength.

I knew that one. Tell me—

Desist?

About Paul.

Desist, Brickie.

I won't.

Husbandry?

Don't care.

Indolence will—

Why did you go out that night?

We have insular lives here, that being. What night?

Drop the sham. I know what happened last term.

How would you know?

I can keep a secret. But I have a theory, that being a speculation or
assumption—

A proclivity toward—

That you wanted Paul to attack you.

Wanted? Maudlin?

Did you?

Calumny, that being—

Damaging talk about another. Answer me.

Don't be stupid. The consequences seemed—

Abstract?

Yes, muddy.

Actually, it's Without Reference To A Specific Instance.

I thought I had to do it or I would always hear him, think about him.

It was your own despair you went for.   What are you doing?

Radiator's hot. Desultory?

I give up.

Disconnected, random. Oligarchy?

Obstinacy, no routine, no idea.

Ruling by a very few.

Betts, for example.

Exactly. Sully?

To rifle through the belongings of another? To mar or defile part of the school's heritage?

I wouldn't put that on the test.

Might, to watch him detonate.

It's time that you Clarify, Brickie, that is inform.

But you failed to find it.

And this is where you tell me.

What now?

Yes.

Say you can't do it alone.

I can't do it alone.

But you don't really believe that.

I would have found out.

Not without trouble. Don't believe me? Then you haven't really seen trouble. If I have to tell you, well, it's a matter of our background yes history a matter of trouble encountered years ago in black and white.

Go on.

Certain?

Yes.

If you're ready for the blood, the scene of us revising vocabulary in Follyfield 4 dissolves to show a boy—

TELL ME.

Stokes has one eye.

Yes, yes.

Your father took the other.

Go to hell.

There was a gun—

Prevaricator. Mendacious—

Ambassador saw it all.

He was wrong. A case of mistaken identity.

Why didn't Cyclops go to Wales? He was in hospital, bleeding out his eye.

My father did not shoot Mr. Stokes.

Come back, I haven't finished. I am undone, arrested, partial.

Partial to insanity.

Your father, mine, Stokes, Chambers, an accidental meeting on the playing fields. The night, you see, the night was dense with fog—

Day, Brickie. It must have been day.

Day, then. How about evening?

Alright, evening.

It was grey as coal that evening years ago when the boys met over by the copse, a winter evening wherein the moon—

Not full.

It's my story. Half a moon was beginning to rise, an early moon, so the effect was the ending of a stormy day, half a pellucid moon oh shut up, a *thinnish* moon then, not giving enough light for say, silhouettes. Armand Stokes, seventeen, kneels to grind out his cigarette in the damp ground.

Cyclops doesn't smoke.

Well he did back then. Anyway, he's been waiting for Teddy Evans. Stokes has sent Mercury to fetch the lad. There he comes, young Evans on the horizon.

Horizon?

Stokesy's butting out his CIGARETTE, we see the moon gleam off the silver—

Gleam?

—of a trigger.

It's not dark.

Horror, for a rifle—

How could it gleam in the evening?

Shut up.

Well, get it right.

Doesn't matter. Stokesy's got a rifle and Teddy's by his side. Evans, Stokes says, It's like this. I'm seventeen and about to be conscripted and this is a matter not about courage or the country's honor let's not question whether or not I'm crapping myself about going over what I want you to do is take this and shoot me in the leg make me that is render me incapable of going over. Teddy Evans, hair wild, manner insubordinate—

Brick—

—begins to walk away. Oh no, he says, a moral lad he, I will have nowt to do with this.

Nowt?

Well he says something with a Welsh flair and begins legging it over the field. Without thinking it through, young Stokes, the same Stokes now our Head and spiritual leader, hefts the rifle up to his shoulder. But what's this, up from behind a knoll, Ambassador and Chambers back from a smoke. Against the backdrop of the school, what do they see. Your father. Stokes with a gun aimed at him. Then. *Boom*.

Cyclops shot my father?

It's true. And the bullet. Speeding through the air toward your father, the bullet checks the angle Stokes has given it. Angle of a man with unsteady aim. The bullet peels away and strikes a lawn roller leaning against the cricket pavilion. Bullet ricochets off the metal. Heads straight back whence it came. Hello. No time for Stokes to think or duck. The bullet bows, Pardon me, may I have that eye?

Stokes aimed for my father—

Blood everywhere. I should think. Spattered, dripping.

It's a bad story, Brickie.

Your father had a fondness for the old pavilion?

I never told him it burned down.

Well, Stokes didn't serve, so his plan worked. Cost him, though.

Half the world. Fool.

But imagine, and your imagination's being tested, old Cyclops as a crack shot. Boom. No Father, no you.

I I

There was a dog and birds. Gwydyr in winter like an apple. That cold. Or the smell reminded me.

Hamey, you left me too.

I drank with Americans on the train back. They'd give you as many cigarettes as you wanted. Reason enough to immigrate. I taught them songs. I had songs, you just had to ask. Dirge. Latin. Hymn. Drinking songs. I had learned a few at Monstead.

And before I walked back that muddy track home to where my father waited with his unreading eyes, I stopped by The Plough. A man remembered me and bought me a drink. Cheapskates faked amnesia. I couldn't understand what people were singing. Fell off my stool after not too long. Sprained or twisted my knee and could barely manage the door alone. A woman with yellow hair offered me her arm, then her home. Thought I'd better convalesce, bear myself up for the re-union with Da. The lady was about forty, or so she seemed at seven-teen and four pints. She may have been younger. She may have been twenty-five or eight. Edna. Edith. It's not the passage of time playing tricks on my memory, for it is sharper now than ever, in fact I clearly recall that I couldn't remember her name the next morning. She had a parakeet and I was reminded of the time my friend Hamey Rhys-Jones-Llwelyn ate a woman's bird. This one was blue, named Popeye. I pressed my face against the cage to measure my mouth against it. I was never the type for a grand gesture, eating birds. Legends. Mam had legends, from her days of drinking and a handbag she had with fur on it. Thick suede or. Like a little dog. She called it Rudolph. Telling Da, I've got Rudy, clutching the rank mat to her chest as she went to meet Mrs. O'Brien who was Irish but had a cousin who lived in America. It was always America she wanted back to. During the course of the night Mam'd forget where she was and set the bag down in a thickening puddle of stout or vinegar or piss. Rudy. There were stories Rudy got up and barked, saved Mam from falling in the river. But I'm no good at writing it. Words have never been friends. Mam an American living in Wales saying her *a*'s wrong until the day she left. I went to school a Welsh-American, served time in England, then to the border for the war. I don't know which words belong where. I confuse dystopia with dyspepsia. And whereas I suppose one might result in the other, these mistakes won't take you far in academic circles. I never know if I'm being understood. I check myself even when I'm making sense, amalgamation amalgamation is that what I really mean?

When I woke up in the bed of Edith or Edna, there was nothing to tell me how we had spent the night. Conjugally or not. I assumed it was because she had the bread under the grill and sausages half un-wrapped as I bolted out the back. Had it been a year later, I would have stayed for the sausages.

Da unstuck himself from the Bible to cut me some bread. The house was as I'd left it eight years earlier. He said I had English vowels. That's enough to curb your hunger. Said he wished he had written more which was unusual in that he couldn't write. We sat down. I had a few Do you remembers . . . ? I knew Da was pretending he did. I made some up for a test. At those he laughed the hardest. It was difficult to understand how he fared during my years away. And the war. That is if he even knew about it. I'm not one to make my own father out to be simple. Avoidance. I prefer that term. There was no one to say that Da had not moved from in front of the fire, first wood, then gas, the years I'd been at Monstead. And there was no one to say he hadn't been enjoying the company of an Edith or Edna all this while.

He didn't remember Rudolph. I knew it was somewhere in the house. She would have taken only the best things back to America, the dress she came in, her mousecloth shoes. Not a dirty Welsh dogbag answering to Rudolph. But the house was too small to hide it. You always found what you were looking for in Gwydyr. No one had a house big enough for secrets.

She would have a big white place of secrets in America.

Da couldn't cook, I had to help him even with breakfast. I would have asked, what have you been living on these years? But he might have answered, I haven't been at all. I've said it before, I'm no good at writing it.

Would ya marry me?

I left the sausages to blacken around the edges. But I let Da tell me how he wanted the eggs. That's all the same to me, he said. I told him I hear you, though I didn't know what exactly was the same as what. Home. Holding my words on the tongue a moment to fuzzy them. Instead of what I found at Monstead, to spit words out pearls. Or turds.

Would ya marry me, I said inside my head again and again. Was it a song I'd heard over the radio, on the bus. I don't know. It was a refrain stuck in my head. Would ya marry me? I proposed to myself, something I put to the trees while I smoked. Please do.

You know Latin now do you, Teddy? Da said. Yes. Well then, he said, You can read the Bible to me because I haven't been able to these years your mother's been gone and I didn't say your Bible's English. I said, That I will, Da. But I was prone, forgive me I was seventeen, returning to a place I might have outgrown, I was prone to inserting short diatribes against religion, if you can measure it against philosophy, I said, And I think you can. Does God exist? I was seventeen.

Would ya.

My speech couldn't find itself again, once you've heard yourself a foreigner, your voice stays strange.

If I was in The Plough telling stories, thinking I was home again, suddenly a fellow would turn quiet. Scotch is it? But if he knew me from being a child, it would be, You've spent too long away, Shed. And the ensuing sport would be to relate favorite English atrocities. Who can blame us, you always need a goat to send into the woods. Take the attention off yourself.

The war was over.

I was seventeen.

On my way back to Edna's I stopped to rip up hawkweed, tethering the stalks with a bootlace. Just because a woman has yellow hair and took advantage of you without too much provocation on your part, there was no call to walk away with her toast under the grill, the sausages half unwrapped. There was an obligation for the politeness your mother brought you up with at least until the age of nine when she departed for her home country of America to find the man she really loved, the man married to a woman who was not she and the man himself she really loved, not your father. There was a need for that kind of consideration.

Would ya. Would ya.

Don't need rumors haunting you on your first visit home. Rumors you left some woman with uncooked toast. That won't do, as Mr. Mortimer used to say. No no no boy, that won't do at all.

She came outside, standing at the top of the stairs. Hello I said, waiting on a name until I was certain. What do you want? in her dressing gown and a pair of boots, hair all triangles. I felt a sudden fondness, her hair rebelled in the night the same as mine. Did she have similar difficulties taming it in the morning? I would ask over tea, while she grilled breakfast. Sausages I hadn't stayed for. Toast. Homemade jams, certainly. Marmalade if I was lucky. Morning. I held the flowers to one side. But then, I dared not move, there was such a black look on Effie's face. Granted it was early, for the visit was an idea which gripped me upon shaving, a ritual I had not undertaken, it should be noted—for fear of painting an inauthentic portrait—since my arrival home. I was more inclined to spend an hour attacking breakfast and, depending on how I felt about the day, questions of man's ascent or descent. But this particular morning I had risen early, as much out of guilt as any sense of propriety, for my father was still working at the age of fifty-two, and over the shaving bowl, I was struck by the necessity of a call, an apologetic call on Miss Effie. So there I stood at the bottom of the steps in the early morning, charmed by her crooked hair. The black look remained. It took some minutes to digest that the great muddy boots she had slipped into undoubtedly belonged to a man. And by the looks of it, a man two and a half times my size.

Placing the flowers softly on the lower step, I said, I'm sorry I was in such an awful rush the other morning. Please forgive me. I curbed neither inflection nor vocabulary. Effie said not a word, slamming the door behind her, but as I turned I heard from inside the house a great guttural sound. The window flew open, well I say flew but what with the damp winter just past, the condensation required some effort on her part. When Edna finally managed to heave up the window, she bailed out her reddened face and screamed, Fucking English prick English prick English prick.

I was seventeen.

I needed Rudolph. Woof woof. That would make her laugh. Though perhaps not the man in there with her. Not him.

It hadn't been such a bad war for Da. I knew it when Jack and Gregor came over to have a look at me. They were glad to see Da still had some relations to speak of.

And we're glad to have you back Sheddie, though you're all caught up with your stupidself and speak like them.

I asked about the war but they turned to England and people they knew who'd died.

There's a job for apprentice at the surveyors', Jack said, I saw it yesterday on a card in the window.

I said, Is there. I didn't mean to stay in Gwydyr. Do you know this lady Edna, or Effie it is with bright hair hanging around The Plough? Athea? Jack said, That was quick. And Gregor laughed and laughed and finally shut up and got pale and started to cough. Athea, then.

She's a sister of Thomas who drowned off the coast a few years back who played football for England. Did she follow you home, Shed? Did she say, how does it go now, he looked over at Gregor but Gregor was looking at a china dog Da kept on the mantel. Turning back, Jack said, Did she say, You're troubled and go mournful at the eyes?

I stood by the one window in the front room, the same window I used to watch Da set off from every morning, away to work while I stayed wrapped in my blanket lighting cigarettes for Mam with the lamplighter matches. Athea, then. I can't remember a thing about her, I told Jack. But it came to me, yes yes I could recall her saying exactly that, that for all her yellow hair and wayward lip color and the nervous wobble to her heels, it was the recognition which made me follow Athea that night. She knew it was no good feeling troubled at home when all along you thought trouble came from being a stranger.

I turned to Jack. Where's this surveyors' then?

The office had the sweet rot of a rich man dying in a cabinet. He was English of course, as if I needed more associations. I couldn't help my vowels coming out thin for him. Would you marry me? With the sound of the el. He drove me to the Algernon in Cardiff where these past years the English sipped brandies on the veranda and waited for the war to pass. I never expected to find anything like you in Gwydyr, he said driving up on the curb accidentally. I didn't mention that, in terms of first impressions, it might be best to avoid hitting the biddies in their cardigan shawls and horsy teeth. But first impressions are never that if you belong to the club.

Watty had white hair in his ears. He was a better driver after two drinks, a worse one after three. At the hotel bar he bought me a brandy. I would have preferred gin. I tried to impress him by what I knew of surveying, only he turned out to be a barrister. I had never been inside the Algernon, having only been to Cardiff twice in my life. The lounge was dimly lit and smelled of cigars. I thought the lack of light might be related to the war just over, blackouts, conservation of resources. But it was dark for the biddies. Shadows are kinder on age.

I'm taking you on, Watty said. As my apprentice. Apprentice made it sound more like bricklaying which I appreciated. Though I also hated the reason for his charity. I was the closest thing he'd find to English in Gwydyr. Old Watty ate peanuts, cracking them open with his teeth. I'd have rather seen open heart surgery than watch that man's stained teeth grasp the dimpled shell and peel it back like the skin of a banana.

I chose instead to watch two biddies play cribbage in front of the fire. They argued and the bigger of the two looked on the verge of throttling the slighter one. When I glanced back, Watty had finished disassembling the nuts and was now intent on some personal housecleaning. Finger edging up his nostril. Shell detritus trembled on his upper lip. I coughed, excused my drifting attention with a witty remark about the two ladies, and looking back at them, wondered the extent to which Watty would next take his diligent hygiene. I had another brandy, he disgusted me less. There was a daughter who remained in England. She was only twenty although he must have been close to seventy. Her mother, he bent to find a peanut in the carpet, we lost in childbirth. Ah, I said. My standard response to nonstandard remarks. Watty found his peanut and again I politely looked away.

The biddies did not spar as I hoped they might. Though I like to think that when we left, shawls were tossed aside and fists were raised. Watty drove back to Gwydyr with all the windows down. His hair wavered in the night breeze and snowed dandruff on his collar. I was reminded of a Rembrandt, a man in overcoat with thinning hair. Mr. Mortimer had the coasters.

Watty saved old flowers smashed between the covers of romantic books, poetry. Shakespeare. He pressed me to talk with him about Hamlet. I wouldn't. Among the shelves of papers and files I deposited apple cores and pits of chewed-up paper in hidden corners. I would come across them days later, disgusted to realize that I had more in common with the old man than I might have liked. Only a matter of time before I was forcing brandy on a young idealist, skin of a peanut dancing on my lip, finger dug up my nose. Only time.

The bell above the door tranged. Thinking it was a client, I ignored it. Gwydyr was in a fever about the new barrister, all wanting to sue neighbors for the horse getting out and eating their carrots, or for libel which previously went by the name entertainment. Months since the end of war, enemies were scarce.

Trang. There she was. I loved her. I could have given her some free legal advice her in her long legs and clutch. Hat like a clam. I'd have advised. Well nothing.

Miranda, Watty doddered up, some piece of lunch stuck to his face. Oh, you're the daughter, said I, making mental note to talk with him about Hamlet then if that was what the old man wanted. You're English, she remarked over Watty's shoulder as she was hugged. No. You sound it, she said. That's a sore subject, Watty warned. I was thinking that the Barrister should drive us all over to the Algernon, buy a round of brandies and I could seduce his daughter under his very own eye. And then I was paralyzed.

Watty dropped into his swivel chair. He could spend a full day in it, only getting up for the lavatory and I am not certain even then. Chewing paper in my secret aisles, I would hear a terrific noise and look up to see the Barrister rolling madly toward me, propelling himself forward with his heels as he shouted, Where's the good brain God gave you and find that damn notice. It was only by the grace of said God that the plane of the floor was as true as it was. Any dip in the grain and old Watty would have pitched himself through one of the plateglass windows in front or tipped backwards into a pile of collecting hairballs coughed up by the dying tabby he refused to put out of my misery.

Miranda. I leaned against Watty's desk for support, my legs buckling in agony. I looked up at her, attempting a sort of apologetic yet at the same time charming smile, one clearly indicating, Legs! Who can help the devils! But from the alarm she registered, I leered like a madman. Miranda. Dark and lovely on reliable legs, she reduced me.

Sit down, my darling, Watty said, oblivious. Darling was too much. A nonsensical torrent blurted forth. I lunged to the storage room to collect myself. Leaning miserably against the cold brick, I had the striking thought that a body is not simply vehicle for a brain, but contributes, rightly or wrongly, for better or worse, to some kind of whole. I was disturbed by this—I don't think I can call it anything less than a revelation—for I had invested heavily in cogitation to the exclusion of even an elementary understanding of physiology. I was in no mood to be overtaken by systems I could not fathom, never mind control. I had neglected my biology studies and now I was paying the price.

The bricks were cool. I was content in the back room. I certainly took no guilt at shirking, after all, it was Watty's fault I had been reduced to such a state. I felt better. I had read of hot flashes though I had understood them to be confined to women. I became confident that I had suffered a momentary instability. The day was hot, and it suddenly occurred to me that it was after four and I had not eaten lunch. There were reasons for my collapse. I kissed a brick, I don't know why.

I gathered myself to reenter the front room, quickly trawling for thoughts not sexual or deviant. This was more difficult than it seemed. I was seventeen, and in my experience, attempts to avoid a subject usually compelled it, my mind being somewhat contrary by nature. I tried to chase down an innocent boyhood memory.

I had begged my father to take me fishing for perhaps a year when he finally succumbed. The fishing sites in Gwydyr were limited, though as a six-year-old I believed I could catch a trout in rainwater if I set my mind on it. We left at dawn. I made us black bread and ham sandwiches, there was not much to eat that year and the meat was an extravagance. I packed the food on top of our rain gear, jumpers and a tin of worms I had spent three days digging out of the garden. Upon our arrival at the fishing spot, I don't know how it happened, did I heave out the gear in my excitement to get to the worms? Was I cold? Anxious for a jumper? All I remember was the slow arc the worm tin carved in the air as the sandwiches flew up over the water. They're still good, I cried, lunging down the bank toward the river. No. Da held me back with one arm, the other crooked around our rods. Please Da, they can dry out. But we could see the bread was already beginning to sog and drift into pieces. And the sun was not strong enough. We stayed to fish. This was my first memory, an uneasiness as I waited for dinner hour to approach, for Da to begin shifting as his hunger mounted, unable to resist—and who could blame him—throwing me a glance or two as he tasted our lost sandwiches. The restorative powers of this memory on my legs and breathing were not great.

The back room smelled of coal though it was too damp to store a lump. A funny trick a mind can play when senses won't collaborate. It smells of coal, says your nose. Yet it's damp, replies your skin. Then cognition chimes in, What would coal be doing in the storeroom, addlepate? Time moved forward. My legs were legs again and I was becoming less agitated and more irritated. Who was this woman, alright, creation then. Even if she was Watty's daughter, what right did she have to come barging into a place of business dressed as she was with legs in stockings and a skirt, a skirt that. Well how did she sit down? Yes the more thought I gave it, the more I was appalled by the lack of respect I had been shown. It was an affront. Without further ado, I charged back into the front office, my legs serving me well on this occasion.

She was leaning forward, I shall never forget it. In emphasis or reiteration, difficult to tell. As if the Barrister were the most charming person on the globe. Head at an angle as if she hoped that Watty might release another nugget as compelling as the last. This, when after three weeks I could tell you that old Watty's antics on the office furniture was about as fascinating as it got. Emerging from the memory of my father, my distressed self at six, I wondered had I ever looked at my father as Miranda was looking at hers, with such kind indulgence?

Don't be shy, Watty said with a fart. Then she turned, killing me. She had hair in waves. Don't ask me to describe the style, I'm no good. But I know it shone. Well for God's sake, the lamp was directly above her, I'm not a sentimentalist. Her eyes, a sort of green. Did she want me to join the two of them, I couldn't tell. Her knee was bent, right over left. Soft. Curved like a comma. I began a sentence I wanted parsed.

There's the files to——file, I said intelligently. Language, as I've mentioned, not my strong suit.

Well those can wait, it was she who said it not Watty, from whom I took my orders. We must get to know each other, she continued. My father's been telling me how helpful you've been.

I struck a pose, yes I admit it. Braggadocio. Hands casually in pockets, back against the wall. In truth, of course, it was for support, out of deference to the buckle in my knees. Ah, I said. As I've mentioned, my reply to the beguiling. She was a vision, but then I'm prone to exaggeration. I waited for something intelligent to surface, but only the banal swam up. Have you come from London? How long are you planning to stay? It was more interview than conversation. Feeling myself beginning to slide down the wall, I directed my hands from their home in my pockets to a fingertips-bent, one hand against the wall support, a position I had seen Mr. Mortimer take up when in the deepest contemplation. That eased the situation for the time being and we chatted amiably with the Barrister interjecting from time to time but mercifully resisting any temptations for snot excavation. In such a case, I would not have known which way to look. The idea of giving Miranda a glance she might interpret as judgment of her father, the pain that might cause her, was enough to bring on a finger cramp. I managed to balance myself to a standing position, vigorously rubbing my hands but furrowing my brow in an air of erudition to suggest that finger massage was the sort of distracted habit found in genius.

She knew a boy I had known at Monstead, an insufferable lout in my opinion but I agreed with her assessment that he held England's hope for political reform or some insanity. He was two years older than me, closer her age than mine and I found myself jealously speculating as to the nature of their relations. According to Miranda, in the years since leaving school, Brickman had established himself as indispensable to some member of the government. Sycophant, no doubt, to some sausage wreaking havoc on the working class.

There's a rumor, she leaned closer to convey a secret, I bent to hear it but she adjusted her shoe, That Brickman was affiliated with the Resistance.

At this I snorted. Yes, snorted. The *French* Resistance I asked, or the Prefect resistance to not enough sugar? I couldn't help myself. In truth what I remembered best about Brickman was his penchant for taking cutlery between thumb and forefinger, targeting the back of a junior's head and unleashing said weapon with the vicious flick of a Japanese throwing star. He and his cohorts gained much amusement from it. Having been a victim to this torture myself, I know a fellow can not easily forget the shock of impalement while engaged in a mildly pleasant activity, refilling a jug of tea or stooping to address a classmate. Though it must be added, if one were not the target, it was fairly amusing to see a fellow's face quickly fall. But the notion that Brickman led or was involved in any worthwhile organization was ludicrous. Really, did old Brickman aim forks through knotholes as Poles quivered beneath the floorboards. Oh anyone is capable of changing I suppose.

In order to deflate the Resistance comment, I gave an inquisitive lift to my eyebrow, a sort of Good old Brickman How is the Old Boy expression. At this point in the game, I had no friend in integrity. Deftly I maneuvered the conversation to the nature of her involvement with Brickman. She imparted that it was innocent. I would have had trouble seeing them together, Brickman appraising a fork over a meal in a French restaurant. But I was glad to hear it directly.

Well I should let you blabla, said she, gibberish about getting back to work while she had errands to finish. Your father took me to the Algernon once, I mentioned. It was lovely there. An invitation so obvious I blushed.

Back in the storeroom the sloppily mortared bricks gave no answers. In her absence. Why hadn't the bricklayer troweled better. It would trouble me always.

Da and I were eating when she came by the house. I had purchased a chicken on the way home, and we sat at the table attempting potatoes that were stones near the middle. With cooking, timing is all. At the knock, Da went out for the door, Gregor often came by when he gauged we'd be at supper. I heard her voice. Gregor's never sounded like glass. A piece of chicken went down the wrong way and a bone caught in my windpipe. I could have died. I was more concerned with humiliation. I jumped up, gasping for air. Throwing my midsection against the sink dislodged the bone. They came in. Mr. Watson's daughter, Da repeated. I leaned back against the sink sending a prayer to my legs. She took my chair and Da pushed over the step he used for the taller cabinets. I perched.

We spoke, I don't remember much of it. I recall Da saying I can't imagine how my son landed that job with your father, Teddy never was one for numbers. I didn't know what to do with that. A father mistakes his child for himself. You see it all the time. I scraped at something on my trousers, well nothing. You could see Da was impressed by Miranda, though not so happy over her nationality. After an awkward silence while Da finished his chicken and ate around the potato centers, he shooed us into the front room. Go on now, tying a cloth around his waist for the dishes.

It was still too light for a lamp. Miranda picked up the china dog and barked at me.

Yes.

Replacing it, she said, Are you a good cook?

My timing's still wrong, I said and blushed for the phrase seemed to take on a different meaning.

She told me she had instructed her father to bring us to the Algernon the following Sunday. Then we spoke about Brickman, it seemed he was to be our common subject. I contrived ways to tell her about myself. I was seventeen, forgive me for needing to convey more than I wanted to hear.

Last night I had a dream, I said. Miranda said nothing, so I continued. I dreamed I was a girl. I dreamed I had long hair and wore slippers. I sat at a table full of strangers, at the head of which a woman sang the most beautiful aria. As I was listening I accidentally scraped a boy's foot with my ankle. The whole table turned to stare at me, disgusted. Flirt, they shouted, Flirt. These strangers frightened me but I could not explain myself. Then the singer leaned down to me and said, He told me about you. What? I begged to hear it, What did he say? Oh, the singer whispered, He said, Oh, the simple allowance of the girl.

Baffled, Miranda shifted her attention to the window.

I attempted clarification. Being a girl is the same as a boy. It struck me as I spoke that this was a wholly unsuitable topic of conversation so early in our acquaintance. I tried again. Or that I know what it's like to be a girl.

Do you?

The remark humbled me which it was intended to. Well of course not. Still, I thought perhaps I did. It might have been a time to return to Brickman, I could think of several cryptic ways to imply his stupidity while appearing congenial.

And what is it like to be a girl, then Ted?

Well I couldn't say I knew exactly.

I'm simply trying to understand which part of the dream made you feel this way. Was it having long hair?

A trap was being set, I knew it. Caution was called for. There was the Algernon the following evening, my father in the kitchen with the dishes and a dish towel slung around his waist, there was no chance I was going to fuck this up. Not if I could help it. At the same time, I've mentioned before, I was seventeen. Opinionated. A difficult trait to mask.

I should go I suppose, she stood. I have to make my way back before dark. It was the invitation I came to extend.

I walked her down our lane. It's this, I said. In my dream I felt they could tell me what I was. Brushing that horrible boy's ankle was a mistake, yet their opinions were formed. On the other hand when the appraisal was flattering, I was happy to accept. The simple allowance of the girl. Why should it make me so happy?

I can't say I understand, she said. I was sorry I had ever brought up the dream at all. Did she think I was peculiar, homosexual or taken to wearing ladies underpants? It was a lot to bear.

We stood at the end of the lane where the hedges ended and the road began. I would walk her another mile to her door but while we were still hidden, I stopped. A lozenge of white throat lay abandoned by the drape of her scarf. Without thinking, I drew the lapels of her coat to cover it. My hands frighteningly near her breasts. You'll contract a cold with that exposed, said I. She thanked me, we were silent the rest of the way.

There were more biddies than before. Eavesdropping, Watty established that some type of gymkhana had taken place with horses and the lot. Men passed by with trousers that bagged at the knee, jodhpurs they were called, and high shiny boots favored by the fascists. Wives, well women too ugly to be mistresses, absently tapped their thighs with riding crops as if urging themselves on. To what.

Spending. The Algernon was used to this type of event. In autumn they held hunts, sausages called it population control, a favor to the farmers because the foxes ate their chickens. You knew some plaid-clad banger would vomit up this profundity. As if in that case the farmers wouldn't mind a swarm of inbred hounds chased by twenty-five alcoholics on the brink of a coronary destroying their land in order to give one geriatric fox a nervous breakdown. Not that I cared one way or the other.

You wonder what it was like here during the war, quoth the Barrister. Whether anything was different.

Actually I was wondering whether I would be obliged to suffer more brandies or whether with Miranda present to accompany her father to brandyland, I might be granted a reprieve of the gin and tonic variety.

I should imagine not as much as we'd think, Miranda said.

I had no idea what they were discussing. I had my head in the menu. How long since I had tasted Yorkshire pudding a dish which, with my timing difficulties, I could never venture to cook. Monstead made a nice Yorkshire pudd. Chewy in the center. There were not many superior dishes from the school cooks but it behooved you to notice when they did something well and you had to hand it to them on the Yorkshire pudding. I made my contribution to the conversation on this topic.

There was a quiet.

Teddy, Miranda said. We're speaking of politics.

Politics. I could see I was to be unfavorably compared to Brickman. Ah yes, I responded but food is always political isn't it?

The waiter penguined up before I was forced to further expound on this theory. And the Barrister, being kinder than his daughter, ordered us all Sunday lunch.

Before the first round arrived, I had successfully avoided brandy, ordering instead a very political gin and tonic although now I think perhaps that was a lady's drink, no matter, I planned to impress both

Miranda and her father. The B knew me well enough from the working hours we spent together. Yet I felt hardly knew me at all. At the office I was surly (seventeen), my mind cloudy. No amount of tea could awaken me from the sludgery of forms.

So I seized the chance. When the penguin came, I aimed toward conviviality, raising my drink and toasting. I couldn't find much the three of us had in common but finally, my arm beginning to shake from holding the glass straight out, it came to me. To politics, I said. And good old Brickman, hoping I wouldn't choke on the gin or the lie.

Mine was not a mind content with Yorkshire pudding. I deliberated on Miranda, our history together. I had, on the first occasion, suffered a paralytic fit, and on the second, given her pause as to the question of my mental health. Add to that the portrait of an ignoramus I was halfway through painting.

Rifle through, old man. Rifle through. What would Mortimer say. There were refined topics for conversation, I was familiar enough with Shakespeare for God's sake. They weren't to know I read him on the toilet. Mr. Mortimer had a genius for bringing people out. Opening up the conversation, getting a man to tell what he might not bring up himself for fear of appearing a swellhead. I missed the old man. The gin was making its way to a sentimental bit. Blazing a trail to where the scratchy music sounded glorious, the fox hunt was romantic. The beginning of alcohol was always the best. A few more and I'd have drunk too much or not enough. Difficult to gauge. Good times at school, times you remember only while having a gin and tonic surrounded by horsy sausages. You never knew it at the time. No no. At the time you felt you were in a cage. Misunderstood. Preyed upon. But you were connected, three hundred like you, though at the time they seemed so different. At the time it was miserable. I wouldn't go back. Not I at sixty reliving dorm raids at nine as if fifty years had been insignificant in comparison. Get a hold of yourself those who say school days were the best days. Pathetic. But Mr. Mortimer and the four of us. Once Stokes was gone. Lawn roller, the copse, it was only one evening out of eight years.

Darvish, God rest him. Treat and Hawthorne. Working at their father's banks by now. It was all laid out for them. In the trajectory from table to mouth I toasted the four of us. Five including Mortimer. He would find another group. There was nothing special about us. Of course he was going to make you feel special. But he was like the others, glad to see the back of you. Remember him laughing so he convulsed. Over one of your stories, too. How was he going to find that in a new group. We were unique. Treat copping an American accent for the redhead at Corby. Until she knew he wasn't enlisted. Selling his coat on the bypass because he couldn't get back before chapel.

The gin and tonic was sweet and effervescent. A warm evening in June. A girl content with her own mind. All most attractive. I was sitting but the gin made me feel qualified for standing. It wouldn't do to be reduced every time to nerves and paralysis. No no boy that won't do at all. I must bear up. For a start, I was not some innocent. There was drunken seduction in my past. Who initiated it was unimportant. I had woken to a woman's hair in my mouth, her back curved into my belly. Yes it's true for a while I couldn't remember her name. And perhaps I did follow her home for reasons that transpired to be other than what they were, but we do the best with the information we're given at the time. Miranda, well she wouldn't be getting just any seventeen-year-old. I knew my way around.

The food.

I looked where she pointed. On the table, a polished shank of meat. Yes.

And is that for all three of us, I asked about the Yorkshire pudding. I had by now spent some time in my head, but Yorkshire pudding had its own significance. Perhaps I should have excused my drifting attention. There are hierarchies, they change as you age but they're there all the same.

You *are* hungry.

I was in a state is what I was. Miranda pudding Miranda pudding.

Watty tilted a bowl of peas, scooping with a wide flat spoon. He's a growing boy.

I could have eaten the plate it came on. But I was careful not to chew too enthusiastically. At one point I affected a sort of sidechew. I saw a sausage across the room doing it. Talking, even drinking, with the nonchewing side of his mouth. Economical. But I was not accomplished enough for that.

Miranda asked was I to be a barrister like her father.

He could be an actor, Prospero said. The old man wanted me to join the local dramatics group doing All's Well.

Not I.

Go to the auditions. For the merchants. As an Englishman, we need participation.

I didn't say I'm not English, I don't have to prove myself a part of anything, so audition yourself you old sausage. I didn't say I don't need to be up on stage for Shakespeare when I have him in the toilet. I said, I won't wear stockings. I get easily chilled. If they make me wear them, I'll end up in bed for three weeks. It happened the last time I went out improperly dressed. It's something to consider. You haven't suffered our spring months. They'll kill a man.

Shakespeare isn't always done in stockings. Miranda slivered her beef. You'd expect her to take the old man's side.

I can't act.

I don't know if it was because she had taken a liking to my new way of chewing or the prospect of seeing me in stockings, but Miranda invited me to a Shakespeare in Cardiff two nights following. So I could get a feel for the acting and words.

Didn't say what I'd rather get a feel for, said alright.

We left Watty dribbling happily by the fire. If the cribbage biddies found him in their spot they'd have something to say about it.

On the Algernon's veranda yes veranda she pulled up my hand to protect the wind from her cigarette.

Miranda on the Veranda, I said.

Father doesn't like me to smoke.

I like to see a woman smoke. My mother smoked. Then I had an attack of coughing. I was always putting my foot in it like that.

Makes your clothes reek. She puffed at the cigarette. You'd make my father very happy by doing this drama. It's important for him to feel a part of things.

I told her I didn't know why the Barrister loved Wales. I said it seemed stupid to love things you knew nothing about.

Well he had a friend, she said.

Was he a singing rugby playing coal miner, I inquired.

No.

I needed to calm down. You didn't want to get me started. I had an American mother, for God's sake. And how was I to know Watty's friend was shot down over Germany? There were always those stories of lives being saved. Watty was one of them, by this Welsh friend. It was too much for me, with the Yorkshire and all. I sat down on a potted plant which I mistook for a bench.

You're a funny boy, she said through her smoke.

Did she mean humorous or insane. Her expression indicated she was enjoying whichever it was.

Oh Miranda, said I.

You'll help my father then? Between her slender fingers, the cigarette was helpless. And I was caught. Her hair in the moonlight, what torture it is to describe when you have no range of language. I understood Hamey then, the hunger that has a boy put a bird in his mouth. Miranda, I said as I stood, for the planter was cold. If you told me you'd have me in tights I would find some tonight.

She blew out some smoke, a little through her nose. I'm not sure what you mean by that.

And I said it I said it without thinking without considering the consequences I went with the collaboration of my mouth, teeth and tongue, the syllables they wanted to make I heard myself say as I'd been asking myself these three days, only now aloud I said Miranda, Would ya marry me?

I was seventeen.

And it was seventeen more before I asked again. I found her sitting in the corner at a dance with diamonds in her hair, the American Girl. Well they were only paste, I saw it when I took her in my arms for a waltz and later, on a balcony, when I told her she was the woman I planned to marry.

For when you're seventeen, it's forgivable not to know your own mind, to confuse Shakespeare with desire, to end up wearing tights to gain a lady's love. Then to spend three weeks laid up in bed with a fever which no amount of contrition makes right.

How can you know it.

She wore them in her hair again on our first outing. A man came up to her while I was on the toilet. Well, I said on my return, If you don't mind, this woman is being entertained.

Well, the man said to make fun of my voice. Well, he said to her, *Whooo*'s this then? The American Girl wouldn't answer. So the man turned to me, What's your name?

My name, I said taking the girl by the arm, My name is for my friends, and leading her out towards the lights of Trafalgar through traffic and into the park, I confessed I had stolen the line from Lawrence of Arabia, I told her I had no money and might never have money, I would go to America if that was what she wanted but I couldn't leave her not her nor here not in London for she made me laugh, she read books and kissed me and had such a neck.

12

Owen paces the stage tapping a pencil against his forearm. Down on one knee, Percival is proposing to Brickie who has wire wings fixed to his back.

Find Basileia . . . Percy turns to Owen . . . We'll go with the wedding dance one more time.

From a tree, Simon watches her take a seat in the audience.

You're not dancing? . . . a voice in her ear, Betts . . . I'm surprised . . . he sits down, closing his notebook . . . I took you for a dramatic type.

Can't sing.

I wager you have quite a voice. I'd like to hear it having read your sides. A Welsh father, biddies at their cribbage. Very humorous. I suspect you almost enjoy writing. What will discourage you from trespassing in the future, may I ask? Nevermind, I was entertained. Perhaps stories will be your forté, Evans. To write, one only needs a pen. Of course, by pen I mean enclosure.

Onstage, Brickie takes the hand of a reluctant girl Liz Estrada or somesuch he leads her through two columns of second-years. The girls sing . . . Phonéya is that far country—

A fair imagination you have, Evans.

From the stage . . . They plough the fields there with their tongues and sow and reap as well.

And you'll settle here yet. You have friends? Your own age I mean.

Sophie Marsden.

Owen strides across the stage . . . Hold on a minute.

The girls stop singing. Owen tells Brickie something which makes him laugh. The boy has a nice laugh, give him that.

Wharton reminds me of an old Oxbow friend . . . Betts stamps his foot . . . Pins and needles this is not how I would direct this scene. Tree should be farther downstage. And someone explain why those girls are dressed in every color of the rainbow. Still, who's interested in my opinion.

Where's your friend now?

Mahesh? . . . Betts chews on his pencap . . . Everywhere you turn. Grinning down from advertisements, on television. Changed his name to act in films. The chicanery of moving images, hardly a career for a grown man.

Maybe it's not an audience he needs, but company.

Company of actors?

The girls sing again . . . They plough the fields there with their tongues—

Just company.

Betts coughs, holding up his notebook to shield the spray.

Onstage, marrying the girl in golden furbelows, Brickie trips. Betts jots a note.

NO

I saw you, he says as they hunker through another field perspiring up the pastoral meadow path the chit of random birds and a thickness in the air as last night's rain bakes mud. Doctor's bag bucking her side, thewy, she insisted on carrying it. I saw you. Gilbert stops, easels against one shoulder. The sun aglint off his unwashed hair. Peaks and divots. Holding open a gate. From the balcony. You were down below, cozy in the audience with Mr. Betts. What were you two cronies discussing?

Doctor's bag scrapes her knee as she passes through the gate.

Perhaps the English master was praising your vocabulary . . . Gilbert latches it behind them . . . Whatever it was, you were certainly intrigued.

Mr. Betts said I had a fair imagination. He said I'd settle here yet.

Gilbert snorts . . . How thoughtful.

Once Betts told me I might not be so bad at the English language . . . she stops to take off her sweater.

Distractedly, Gilbert catches her shirt as it inches past her navel . . . And who asked his opinion?

She pulls her arms from the sleeves, balls up the sweater. Gilbert still has her by the shirttail.

Mr. Gilbert.

Sorry . . . he lets go.

Kneeling to shove her sweater into the doctor's bag, she looks up at him. Profiled against the muddy background, he has the nose of an explorer, the worry of a new world.

They continue on.

Mr. Gilbert, did you know that the word allude and the word ludicrous both come from *lud*, the Latin word for play?

Is that right, well what thrilling lessons are to be found in English, hum? But today's lesson is in painting not etymology, not vocabulary, which I leave to your friend and mine Sir Patrick Betts.

Gilbert stops on a rise too slight to name Hill. A proposed landscape. All I see is mudscape, she calls. From the shade of a lone tree. All I see is brown, Mr. Gilbert, so he will look up from unlegging an easel. But Gilbert continues to unleg, saying, Monochromatic. Shades of the same color. Etymologically speaking, since you love language so, from the Greek *mono* meaning single, *chroma* meaning color. Well it seems dull to me, she says. Insipid. A hand at his eyebrow to find her against the light. Insipid, Punchinello? Insipid? Walking to her. For her. Her very own.

They met by the rearing horse, he came for her in the Fiat, window scrolled to half-mast. They drove with wind buffeting inside the car. An anomaly, a day like this in April, do you know what anomaly means? His cuffed elbow on the door frame where the window wasn't, poking out easily as if it has been summer their entire history instead of today being a Deviation From the Norm, a day it might reach twenty. That being a celsius account.

Insipid, you say? But he smiles as he walks toward her.

In London, eighty degrees sent the English into bewildered fannings of newspapers. Damp missionaries stranded on the Bloomsbury veldt. Undone by heat. How well Gilbert handles an upswing in degrees remains to be seen. Shirt rolled to an easy forearm boded well. But careful examination revealed many errors. Points lost for black socks.

Drab, you think? . . . he reaches her . . . Will you stay under that tree? Ignore the landscape I've taken such pains to provide? . . . Gilbert takes the bag from her . . . Come on, you can take heart from your great love, Thomas Cole and his Drab River School.

She never said she loved Cole. Or had she. Perhaps she had. He arranges the paints, fanning out the tubes. Who does she love. A question that.

At Christmas I saw a landscape I liked . . . taking the paintbrush Gilbert holds out to her . . . A postcard. They were having a picnic, men with pipes, a lady in a necklace.

Picnic? You mean *Déjeuner sur l'herbe*? That's . . . a dry cough . . . Not what I would call a landscape. Certainly information to keep from Mr. Betts. He'll fear a restaging of it on the hockey pitch.

They snicker together because they are both anti-Betts because shrubs and greenery doth not a landscape make. Not when there's nudity involved.

A swell of wind shimmies the new leaves. A thin line of yellow to her paper, snaggling it for a leaf. What about this Dido, does the teacher love her still. A query to which old Gilbert hems, hums and improvises an artful analogy. Different sorts of loves. The foreground and background of ardor, Manet's peaches versus his leaves. Platonic, romantic, the fuzzy line between. Does she understand. Well not really, but why did the teacher move his love from a peach in the foreground to a leaf in the back. Well, he says shyly these questions are highly irregular, but I found that my wife was herself after all, not the person I fashioned to love.

Oh. And silently they paint together in their brown landscape quiet together. Side by side in their worlds considering who they love sharply in a foreground sort of way and who are the blurry ones, the victims of perspective.

In the center of the canvas she has the beginning of a trunk, from the bottom up this time instead of the usual top down, so she has learned one thing. Although, it strikes her now that the most important features should appear slyly to one side.

My tree's smack in the middle and very bad to boot.

Gilbert's head jerks up . . . To boot? You sound so English saying that.

He is tricking her.

What's the matter?

I don't want to sound like you.

But I've been making a concerted effort not to sound so affected.

No, the snooty voice is funny. In fact, I give you eighty-two percent for it.

Has there been another panel? Where was I when that convened . . . Gilbert flicks something from his paper . . . Had I known, I would have trotted out some superior puns.

Puns aren't funny.

Good to know. Still, eighty-two percent is not ninety-one. Though you have the challenge of not falling.

I won't fall.

Gilbert acts glum, mutters *hubris* and *youth* so much *promise* so little *compromise*. She laughs at his show, the poor moron left in shadows. Wait, you're laughing, he says, That's worth an eighty-four, eighty-three at the very least which only makes her laugh harder. Eighty-five, eighty-six, he continues. Stop, she sobers, taking her landscape off the easel, I'm the judge.

Gilbert watches her set the painting on a patch of dry mud. She steps back to let him see.

My, my . . . he evaluates . . . Wild tree. And yellow. You're a secret Fauvist, a—

Faux vista?

Fauvist. From the French, meaning wild beast. Meaning emotional exuberance, vivid color, unconventional form over the more traditional civilized lines.

Then Gilbert sets down the paintbrush he's been using to describe the air because in trying to reposition her easel she's getting ludicrously tangled in its legs. Hold on, Hercules, he says walking over. Yes he does own too short trousers, bad socks and a limited hairwashing routine but Gilbert also owns strong hands that trick fleshheating chemicals hands which are at present moving her easel to the north, precisioning new watercolor paper carefully, tacking sheet to easel. Her hands would leave the paper furling and smudged. Upper right bottom left like hospital corners the sheet of paper a bedsheet. White shirt. Laundry smell with an unwashed Wednesday souring—

You smell nice, Mr. Gilbert.

He looks down at her, sweeps her paper with the side of his hand, then moves away, back to his own easel. Dropping down next to the doctor's bag to find a better brush.

Didn't mean to say it aloud. Dipping her brush in the water cup. A wrong thing to say. Wet brush aloft, surveying the uneasy land, uncivilized, a wild beast, she will choose caesious, orpiment, grege. Consider. Consider the words first. Gilbert never goes quiet. Has never simply left her to the stutter of birds. If this were a play he would stride over, he would do something dramatic or exit. Drama doesn't bear silence. Or is that exactly what it bears. Silence to feel what are the actors feeling. In a play, they would have better background than this. Hillocks on their way to rocky mountains, edelweiss, a tricky brook. And there would be other characters. Stock hardy types found in all trustworthy British dramas. Morally upright in an unself-conscious way, not secretive or So You Might Think, undemanding and useful. The plot would not involve painting which when it comes right down to it is dull as mud to watch. No, the plot would expose a secret or two, held out to a thrilling conclusion, inevitable but at the same time surprising. A revelation concerning the hero. A transformation involving the villain. Instead, they are lodged in mud and Gilbert will not act as rehearsed.

Suddenly he's here holding a clean palette. Quietly . . . For you.

She turns to say—but he flinches, a stab in his eyes. A fleeting look, something. Fear? He gives her the plastic disc. She would have preferred a wooden palette with a hole for the thumb. Shoulders hunched, Gilbert walks back through the stubble to his own easel.

Silence. They paint.

Memlinc.

She looks up.

Gilbert, absorbed, painting, a surmising nose scratch . . . Memlinc was a Flemish painter. From the Flanders school which is a region we now recognize as Belgium. You remember. France's attempt to control the cloth-producing towns of Flanders led to the Hundred Years war.

French flags festooned the list's border. *Allons-nous en Provence!* announced the jovial title. The details were admirable. Apparently the weather in Southern France can be unpredictable. Who knew that hovercrafts usually depart on time? It seemed a meeting of participants would be held one night next week. This meticulous information, for the organizers had done their jobs scrupulously, was followed by a list of participants. Brickman, Craven, Curran and there it was. Or rather, wasn't. A surprising omission between Eggles and Finch.

Gilbert glances up . . . We won't have any fun in France without you.

Valor, Bucket, Foretold. Armed with Araigny's vocabulary, they will only have words like Grief but will really know Grief if they ever need a Toilet. On the other hand, she knows the word for sandwich. And more than one type.

Now, van der Neer, well, I attempted homage once . . . Gilbert's shirttail's out, fingers grasping waist, he dabs paint idly as if waiting for a bus . . . You've seen the results in Howlands. You said your mother liked dark paintings, didn't you?

She rinses her brush. A cloud moves back, *tada*, the sun.

Catrine?

She squeegees out excess water.

It gets boring, you know.

What does?

The constant deflection.

The chemistry teacher walks briskly downstage. Hold on, the follow spot can't keep up. He sets down his folding stool and takes the girl's hands. All very deliberately. Silence. His rolled-up sleeves, the greasy hair, paint on his fingertips like a child. A long moment. They stare at each other. The audience grows restless, shuffles programs. Above, a caw of bird spills down, away.

I asked you a question about your mother.

The sun catches his scar, his nose becomes a blade.

Don't ignore me.

Mr. Betts says Never Capitulate.

Patrick Betts, need I remind you, IS NOT HERE. And what the hell does that mean? Surely Mr. Betts did not intend . . . Gilbert sighs, there's no other word for it . . . Well who knows what he intended . . . taking her hands to his forehead, Gilbert cools himself after his exertion to make her tell, then drops them. It's not good, he murmurs and returns to his easel.

Propped before her, a yellow effort, incomplete, the underbelly of a rock. Fabrication, because the exact is never true. She chooses violet. Gilbert grumpily clanks his brush against the water bottle.

Violet grass violet tree . . . My mother wouldn't have liked the Fauvists.

Don't talk about her to appease me . . . still grumpy.

She would have thought all that color was ugly.

You're inventing . . . brushing the air . . . Invent away.

My mother didn't—

Doesn't matter . . . and grumpier still . . . It's all invention to circumvent feeling.

That's not true. My mother would have hated those painters.

Gilbert yawns.

She didn't like a muddle—

A muddle? *Muddle?* . . . Gilbert's yawn turns into a snort . . . I can't say I've ever heard an American say that. Muddle!

Stop.

You'll be as snooty as me in no time.

I said stop it.

Why, what's wrong with sounding English?

You're not funny for one.

Gilbert stops laughing . . . What is it? . . . he walks over, kneels next to her tiny canvas chair.

For some reason her hands cover her ears like a child cusped on tantrum. Paintbrush held in fist, sticking in her hair. Oh no oh no not now.

At her height exactly, he appraises her, eyes flecked with hazel which could be a slogan for some type of chocolate. Muddle. How could she have been so stupid.

Hold on a minute . . . Gilbert wipes her cheekbone with his thumb . . . Is this The Crying Scene?

Go to hell.

Gilbert is not taking the position he should, the sympathetic character employed hitherto. He stands, wet ovals mark his knees. Takes the bridge of her nose between thumb and forefinger.

Stand up.

No.

Pulling her Never to his chest Capitulate what is his white shirt like pressing to a sheet so clean a handkerchief. Gilbert wraps his arms around her.

I won't cry for you . . . struggling . . . I'm not a Punchinello not your—

He has her so tight wrapping his arms a vice advice It's not a betrayal to sound like us platitudes he's platonizing her taking her up so tightly his shoulders and back prepared to bear her weight and she she no.

He is saying Your mother said you were not to cry for her, I knew it the very first time we met. And then he cries, yes yes it is Gilbert who sobs, sobs delicious in her hair, webbing it with snot and sympathy. What is he to Evans or Evans to him that he should cry for her.

He's dropped her at the rearing horse, given her hand an extra squeeze and she's up the hill toward school. Is it any accident that a word like Muddle proves distressing.

Wha—she screams, a monstrous phoenix floats up from behind a letterbox.

The bird goggles its eyes.

Simon. Go away. Wander elsewhere. In the road for example.

She increases her speed up the hill. Gilbert pressed her hand he. Simon matches her pace. She tries stopping abruptly. Skillfully, Puck dodges, avoiding collision.

Go find Owen, why don't you.

Simon raises his beak.

She begins to run.

Mostly you try not to perform as expected.

She doesn't have the stamina. Simon catches up.

But out it came beyond your control.

What are you talking about.

Explanations about libraries crème caramel canned vegetables how you were never supposed to eat them. Paintbrush gripped in your fist and Gilbert saying let it go let it go not about the paintbrush, not profound in his I knows because he shares a horror of unfresh beans but because once he had a sister yes fatherless they starved sharing false adagios in the parlor.

You don't know anything about it, Simon Puck.

This is the way with sisters and mothers. They are never considerate of those they leave.

Think I listen to some beakboy.

Your mouth brutal against his neck nonsensical you've heard of it possession when the blabbing overtakes you couldn't register your knees you ended at him ended with breath at his collar will end up making rude guttural noises in the scared dark verses you want if you could only remember the words.

I never mewled about my mother.

How you love his collar—

She never had

the back of his neck.

Really, the boy has lost his mind.

You want into his skin bloodstream want him osmotically. What a child he must think you heavy at his shoulders soggying his shirt with your foolish sorrows.

Gilbert's—

Your someone to talk to your epic version your vergil your anomaly.

Pigeon-brain. Your head's in the sand, ostrich.

Slung against him, a man with motivations, you thought about white spaces left when the paintings came off the wall those old letters she was always reading Dear Catherine Dear Henry Love Catherine Love Henry reading all about those separated married to other lovers. She cried didn't she? Cried for love.

Yes.

Finally you let yourself lean amewl against his chest he murmured above he was a conch. In his chest you found the ocean.

14

Mountains. A desolate wilderness. The background contains a single tree and the sheer rock face of a cliff. They enter in stages of exhaustion. A difficult journey. Not much longer. Here is Brickie, trustworthy Athenian, a crow hooked on his arm. Another boy a Stuart or Adam with a magpie. Nervous first years porter luggage. Brickie is fine, eyes casting about with annoyance, projecting to his audience, straight to her it seems.

I'll be damned if I know where we are.

Do you suppose we could find our way back home? . . . Adam stumbles . . . Hell.

That's where we're headed alright . . . Brickie sighs . . . That's where we're headed.

The seats are filled with masters, Stokes' arms folded and smiling, casting his one good eye now and then to Bea who strums her fingers glad for an outing, yes everyone's here, handsome Duncan Peaks resident amnesiac, even old Araigny who has stopped knitting for once but perhaps in order to cast Betts reproachful glances as he pets the wifely hand claiming his knee.

Onstage, lights play on Brickie's black hair, he has them in his thrall.

Oh what a plan the race of birds could launch! Listen to me and power untold is yours.

And here is Simon Puck center stage. Beak dirty from so many days, battered but no matter for he has gold and green wings, he dances.

O Treachery O Treason to betray us so.

It will be his grandest moment.

Puck shrieks . . . These men are spies, their lives are lies, so kill without regret.

Brickie cowers but is still strong.

Neither shall the misty mountains, nor the foaming fountains save them from our beaks.

Anon, Dr. Thorpe emerges as a prophet and Spenning is a lawyer shouting, Tis wings! Tis wings I crave!

Lo let them present Fi Hammond rolling in strung up on a machine propelled by those photogenic boys from the hockey pitch. Trouser clad, they bring her forward. And descending on this marvelous contraption, no doubt she tied the knots herself, Fiona is a messenger from the gods, shaking her fist with useless petulance.

My father Zeus sent me down to say the Olympian gods desire a sacrifice.

Brickie and Adam laugh, they turn their backs on her.

Fiona tries again . . . Mankind must slaughter sheep on holy hearths, and fill their streets with smoke.

Brickie quotes . . . Men are to worship birds not gods anymore. Now, go singe some youngsters with your lechery won't you?

Dido across the aisle laughs like a donkey. Betts turns to shush. Owen is missing, in the wings, perhaps. The play continues. A truce, a feast. Brickie splendidly gowned, newly winged reaches out his hand to the girl . . . Oh my lovely oh my sweet take my wings in your shining hands let me lift you lift you above the sky and soar beside you through the buoyant air.

Puck flies . . . Noblest of the gods on high!

Applause.

THREE

I

Here it comes, a turning comment on pennies or the radio. Outside the land flashes past the yellowgreen you will know as jonquil tinge to the upper leaves though they travel down down leaving what little they have known. And remarkably, he is silent. Not to know she has his art in her prim hands. Handkerchief. Mappula. On the way. Father said, An honor it is to be chosen. Join these classes your Mr. Gilbert holds down south. That a teacher has it you show such promise you're to stay with his very own family. After Easter lunch, roaming to show what they could do with the Felmar potting shed, convert it to something for her delight. Painting studio. Didn't it amaze him, Father, for her to resound so in both chemistry and art. Talents seemingly opposed in nature. Painting trees to resemble lemons hardly qualifies for an accomplished eye. Surely. Yes, surely. Yet all of a sudden, private tutorials, studios. But what does she know really, about talent. Perhaps yellow signals genius as it can signal caution. Hazard ahead. Pure hands, a triangle around his art. Give Way. Hands scored by old eczema now clearing. Hands capable of a *Déjeuner* perhaps or *Martyrdom*. After all, you can't assume she knows a thing. Juddering to avoid a sweater in the road. Arms up as if hailing. Come back Come back. Not knowing you never can. That's the thing about sweaters, they lack a fundamental understanding. How did it go. That old sweet song. Fingertips against hipbones. Falling into a patch of lab bench sun. Leaning to give her cream for the eczema. Refrain something like. Stay.

What's the matter?

Pardon?

You keep checking the rearview mirror.

Do I? Careful driving. You'll take— Why are you turning around, I said it was nothing.

Because it's not nothing. It's something. What is it?

It's odd.

What is?

I swear I saw a car. First back at the petrol station. And again just now.

Why is that odd.

It's not. You're right. It's not odd. A coincidence.

Gilbert's forward cranes and squinting herald spectacles in two years. Neck, a hooked concentration to phrases of oil, dashboard warnings of kidney-shaped lights, road waltzing car, ONE two three four, who leads whom. Hurtle toward our destination. Note quantities of gasoline, conditions of weather, overtaking escorts blinds flapped against a weak sun. Soon to be asked A penny for them for which a lie will be composed to avoid the obvious Why it is your trousers don't hit your shoes. Nearly as bad as You Smell Nice. Which we have seen earlier won't do at all. Hands folded on lap in a way to set Maggone agurgle with delight. Lapped, hands clasp portable art, a Gilbert original on her heavy skirt. A sober value, an unknown fiber. Flannel? Wool? Father insisted on good impressions, not jeans. Breeding. Overtheknee socks gripped by elastic matron garters which will imbed. Not good girl tights. That sag between thighs. Not knee socks. Father says they are for Catholics. At the wrists of handkerchief-held hands, her new red cardigan's ribbed cuffs. At wristbone. Patiently awaiting a delicate wedge of tissue or art. Should the need for nose care or art appreciation ar*iii*se. A sleeve not impolitely accordioned halfway to forearm, the result of an overheated harassment by dangerous escorts. Not like some we could mention. No. Here's a lady, says Miss Maggone. Indeed, a marchioness, replies Madame Araigny. Although it is generally accepted in these circles that Miss Maggone would not know a lady if a lady bit her on the forehead. But a generous Marxist allows the proles their opinions. The anomaly in this case are the shoes, they must be addressed if we are doing a complete survey which it seems we are. She mentioned that Brickie once equated her shoes with Monstead's excellence at Squashing, in the hopes that Gilbert might have some light to shed on this peculiar analogy. Ignoring her plea for illumination, he looked shoeward to comment, Those are quite a pair. Where's the lad you robbed them from? Did you have to kill him? And, It looks like you could do some squashing of your own with those. The conversation rapidly deteriorated from there, without her once resorting to what would have been a fair, one might say provoked, comment in the comeback department along the lines of certain inadequacies in ratio: trouser cuff to socks. And was that something found only in Marxists because she has seen the misguided on streets, both in Chittock Leigh and Oxbow and if this is a way to recognize that breed she'd like to know about it. On the other hand it remains equally likely that the lopsided ratio is a gene born in British men of all types, dormant or recessive, Marxist or otherwise.

2

Car horns, pauses, unheard replies to misunderstood questions. She wakes with donkey's ears, dreaming she is dreaming.

3

You're awake. Were you warm enough?
  Is this yours?
  You wore that once before, don't you remember?
  The day I ran away.
  You came out from the bushes like a maligned Puck.

You let me sleep then too.

Yes and I loaned you that. It was snowing. Here it is April, not much warmer.

This is how it is with best friends tearing away from school, from it all. They ask amusing questions to make each other laugh. For example. Who is the woman in his blue paintings? But this makes Gilbert stop laughing. What bolt of clarity struck her while she slept, hum? He becomes peevish, Aren't I here with you? It took some finagling to extricate myself from France. Then, relenting or inventing, one or the other, he admits, The paintings are a composite. I signed up for a course, painted from the model. She was—a girl from town. Then he wonders, Is this harangue actually retribution for his library absence? If so, she has forgotten the second half of the forgiving principle. That could be true. Forgetting is something at which she excels. She prepares to list things forgotten, the woman who watched her sleep, a library fit for dying. This exchange.

Does my coat need a wash?

What?

You appear to be sniffing it rather suspiciously.

It smells like you.

That's alarming. Should I be alarmed? What's that like?

It's like. Chemistry.

What a relief. And here, I feared I might smell like Physics or heaven forbid the dreaded English.

I told you that once, that you smelled nice. The day we painted mud. You gave me a horrible look.

Did I? Perhaps I didn't hear you correctly. Perhaps I thought you said, You have lice. Or, You suffice. Although I quite like that. Yes. You suffice.

Are you saying that to me?

No. You more than suffice. You. Saturate.

Sugar water.

Yes, delicious.

And you. Are anomalous.

Thank you very much.

That was pretty funny about the sugar H two O. You can go up to an eighty-six for that, Mr. Gilbert.

Most generous.

4

You sure chips will do? I don't think we'll find anything else. Here, I vinegared these without thinking.

I like vinegar.

Sit up on the hood. Still warm.

Need more salt.

They've packed up and gone I'm afraid. I had trouble getting these off them. Swap with me. There's plenty of salt on mine.

Do you want to sit up here too?

I'm fine standing thank you. Need to stretch a bit. How I love this time of day, evening. Look at that sky. How purple it is.

A Fauvist sky. Mr. Gilbert? What's wrong?

Sometimes I regret. It's. I don't want you ever to be sad. I mean you know I thought you should cry but at the same time I don't know. I. Want to help.

You do help.

Sometimes when we're having fun, we're joking, I worry. That we're not serious enough. I should be more somber, perhaps.

You're somber enough.

I appreciate that.

Why can't we make up our own way of doing things?

Yes. Why not, indeed. It's just us here after all. Away from the Council on Proper Behavior.

Away from everything.

Going somewhere very far.

South by southwest.

Yes. It was just a thought. I needed your advice. This is nice, this cardigan. Rare to see you out of school uniform. And your eczema's cleared up? Here? And here?

I showed you.

Yes. You also smell nice.

Like vinegar you mean.

Much nicer.

That's good.

You have some salt, here on your lip.

Do I.

Give me this.

But I'm not finished.

Finish eating in the car.

Okay.

Catrine?

Yes?

You are my sugar water Fauvist.

Taste more like salt.

Catrine?

Yes.

Look at me. I do

I know.

And you. How do you feel about me?

I have to tell you something.

Tell me.

It won't change your opinion of me?

No accusation of pornography has.

This is different.

Hum?

On a different scale.

How so.

There was a man. In Maine.

Ah. I think I understand.

He had a motorcycle.

Should I be jealous?

I don't think so. He was driving along a highway. I stood at the top of a hill with my friend Isabelle.

This sounds familiar.

There was a tire, we dug it out from the dirt. It made sense to, we did it without thinking first without thinking of the consequences as if we weren't ourselves at all but watched two other girls. We pushed that foul tire and it rolled. Rolled down the hill. When it hit him, the motorcycle, the man, he snapped up and flew. We killed him.   I did.

5

And last night it was the moth. Caroming off the unworkable lantern. For show only, like the bellow pump hanging in the kitchen. Banging and fluttering til she swept it away into the corridor banging herself against a low stool in the process.

They are come, as Vicar would say, to the second of four hills. Gilbert keeping up his prompting commentary a Buck Up Not Much Longer singsong voice. Yelling back chummishly to the vicar's German exchange student, Follow The Leader, Piers. Two Three Four. The vicar suffers asthma, if they walk too fast he'll keel over blue. Mrs. Ingle has Gilbert by the arm, guidance for the tricky parts though she clutches him closely enough on the flataway.

They have been friends, Vicar and Mrs. Ingle, since primary school, Vicar mentioned it to Catrine on the drive when it was just the two of them in his Deux Chevaux. What a dutiful son, Mr. Gilbert was, how often he's visited his mother in the years since Giddy arrived in Newquay. And these painting trips, well aren't many so thoughtful nowaday, the vicar said. It took her a while to understand that the vicar contrives accents for comic effect.

Thérèse hums a jingle from television. The vicar would rather hymn, yesterday he tried but even Gilbert got stuck on the middle verse. Thérèse has a mother from France, after fifteen years still won't speak English even in the shops.

I had a friend once, her mother was French. But from Canada.

The French in Canada when they say yes, sound like ducks.

Piers stops against a stile to light a cigarette . . . Sorry . . . preventing them from crossing to the final field . . . I'll die in another moment for waiting.

Whah . . . Thérèse quacks . . . You see, a duck.

Is that how they say it, really?

You speak French then? . . . Piers says it to his cigarette which has caught a raindrop from the branch overhead.

Do you really need that, son? . . . Gilbert has Ingle through one arm, doctor's bag on his other.

Ce paysage, il te plaît?

If we are to have enough time—

We should wait for the vicar, though, correct? . . . Piers, to Gilbert.

Oh well yes of course.

So you can say—? . . . now back to Thérèse.

Je m'appelle—

Well that will come in handy in—

I know French.

Do you? . . . Piers turns to her, exhales . . . And what can you say?

Right, here's the vicar, put that out now, hum lad.

I can say—

Come along, Evans—

Nous verrons ce que nous verrons.

Piers raises an eyebrow . . . Oh, les clichés? *Oui, les chiens aboient, la caravane passe.*

Ah your poor parents, misguidedly under the impression it's English you're here learning . . . the vicar puffing, a catch-up red . . . Sounds like French to me. Don't let them think I had a hand in it.

Piers stubs his cigarette . . . A moment or two of French with two pretty ladies—

Children . . . Ingle, over the children's heads. Thérèse sticks out her tongue.

—is something I think even my father would approve of. English skills be damned.

Well your English is excellent.

Bowing . . . Madame Boucher.

I won't blush for you, Herr Piers if that's your game.

Game? Do I have one?

You seem to.

Herr Gilbert, do you hear this? How my character has come under attack.

Ingle turns, unhooks herself from Gilbert to face the four of them straggling through the last field, they slow to watch the smoothing of her maroon smock. Mrs. Inred a better name for her because a customer likes to buy a nice chop or two without entering an abattoir and nothing hides blood like a nice deep red, nothing I have yet to find. That smoothing a kind of reminder Why I Wear Red as if to say it could be your blood ends up here next if you don't mind your games. Inred turns back. Gilbert has not waited.

When did he become this expedition leader, Everest, walking stick and outdoorsy deep breathing. Finally a glance. He blinks, then turns to climb up on the fence to address them. Waiting for the others, Piers again lighting a cigarette. Behind Gilbert, bored cows. Some lie, others stand. Newquay undulates beyond. Piers struggles to keep his match lit to the strains of Inred telling the vicar about breeding capons. Thérèse whines about the cold. And still he won't look at her.

Oh to hell . . . Piers rolls the cigarette sucking to catch it lighted.

Right then, on our second day, Cows. We'll begin by—Evans?

Sir?

You looked as though you had a question.

No.

Right. As you know, by the end of the week we'll be painting, but first, an introduction to form. Sketch rapidly, abandon any desire for perfection. Let's hope our friends here will provide you with some interesting poses. Off you go, I want to hear those sketch pages turning, turning. Ideally you'll have used up your entire sketchbook by the time we make our way back this afternoon. However since I know you to be a thrifty lot, not naturally inclined to wild abandon, I'll be happy if you have ten or twelve sketches to show me. Vicar, Mrs. Ingle, I know you both well enough to emphasize the following. It is the cows I'm interested in, the *cows*. We may progress to sheep when we begin painting, the wool will make for a useful lesson in monochromatics and subtlety . . . a fleeting look . . . Which some of us have studied in the past. But for today, Vicar, Lucy . . . stretching out his mouth as if they are deaf and lipread only . . . COWS. Don't get caught up in some tree that takes your fancy in the deep background, or spend hours obsessing on three weeds at your feet. I'm looking for speed, risk, versatility. I want you to draw from intuition. Draw not from your mind, but from your hand. This is a lesson in trust, hum. Trust your hand's eye. Imagining that your hand has sight will bypass that which so often gets in the way of art, of so many things—the brain. But I—I'm getting away from myself. Any questions? Vicar?

So as I understand it, Mr. Gilbert. We are to sketch these cows with our conté crayons or our charcoals or even a 2B or 4B—

Yes yes—

—and to do so at a rapid, *intuitive* pace. As if they were models.

They are your models, Vicar.

Well, not—

Any other questions? Let's stay this side of the fence posts shall we, in case one of our friends divulges a set of horns.

Vicar unshrugs his rucksack and mumbles to Mrs. Ingle. Cigarette pressed between lips, the ever-smoking Piers bends to untie a portfolio of fine German papers.

Do you remember . . . Inred hails Vicar . . . John, that time in Truro?

You mean . . . Vicar's fastidious pencil points . . . The time with the man who wouldn't let go his butter knife.

Evans?

That's the one. Not sure why I came across that, still—

Sir?

One never knows what's brought up at any given moment . . . Vicar takes his pencil between his teeth to smudge.

You're managing?

Well the fence. It's at the wrong height.

Ah I see what you mean . . . Gilbert regards Thérèse who has raised herself up by standing on the paint case. The others ably balance their drawing pads as she and Gilbert did on the balcony that day in Oxbow. But the fencing hits her smack against the neck.

Sit . . . without warning, with a smell of smoke and sweat, Piers takes her under arm and around waist and hoists her up.

Hold on . . . Gilbert puts out a hand—

If any lunatic cow begins to charge, I'll pull you off . . . Piers hands her up the dropped newsprint and pencil case . . . On my honor . . . a wink.

Thérèse eyes her.

I'm fine . . . turning to tell Gilbert . . . Up here.

If you fall—

I won't . . . back to her fresh paper and charcoal because what is it she wants really. Percentages, the two of them in a dirty landscape.

Coming into his mother's house last night, mother over a solitary cup of earl grey a pool of lamp in a clean clean kitchen, Oh Michael.

For that was his name after Squeak as she was Catrine after Punchinello, after My Sugar Water Fauvist. How her stomach pitched to hear his name like that. As if she had said it herself in the dreary corridor leading to that bright kitchen. But there was his mother, like him around the eyes and in the jaw. Not in the nose, which must be re-gal legacy. Gilbert kissed his mother lightly on the top of her head as she stood to say, I didn't hear the front door but then it could have been me dozing a bit, hm. And who's this? said about Catrine in a third per-son way. Was she expected to answer? But Gilbert moved his hand to his mother's shoulder, This is the American girl, Giddy. He called his mother that. Giddy.

After ten and Giddy makes hot milk and toast for them. Gilbert takes her to the third floor of the narrow house where the ceiling slopes. The bed tight with a white counterpane. Will this do for you? he places her small suitcase down by a chair as if the case contains glass. She nods yes. You have pyjamas, he seems confused, this will be the night of the moth. Yes. He sits on the bed. An intricate design carved into the headboard, acorn atop each post. Turned away, she faces the head of the bed, this is the American girl pushing a finger into the groove where the stem meets. Finally he speaks. This used to be my cousin's bed. Not Rosie's? No, I don't know what happened to her bed. Perhaps it broke. Perhaps it was discarded. When she turns back, he is watching his hand run against the quilt. Won't look up. They call this moquette, he tells his hand. Oh, she says. Then after a moment, Who does? Here's the silence, this, the night of the moth. Downstairs Mrs. Gilbert washing out one two three cups. Catrine? Mr. Gilbert? What is it? This. What a funny word that is, moquette. Catrine? It sounds like. The night. You tell me Mr. Gilbert, what it is. Then his hand roughly in her hair and she takes it, draws his hand down against her face and presses her cheek into his palm. The night of the moth.

When Gilbert leaves, it takes a year for the door to close behind him. In his attempt to shut the door silently. For a year she watches the light in the stairwell outline the back of his neck, the strange position of his arm stretched out behind him, shoulder. It could be that she is an artist after all, for her thoughts are of the difficulties of depiction, capturing that kind of foreshortening, darks, the greys, the browns of shadow, creases mapping his journeyed shirt. What a challenge to show discrepancy in similar colors. When it is all about shade. In the Felmar potting shed this summer she can try that cleft of corridor, Gilbert's closing, closing.

He leaves, Giddy's tidying noises have long since ceased. Cold feet, square they are, a line of toes, taking out the nightgown Father gave her for this trip. Pyjamas are better, gowns coil up to trap you at night. Lacy neck scratches. Anne Boleyn, does Father think. Lace makes a lovely nest for a guillotined head. Bloody on a doily. Ouch says the head. Henry the eighth, drumstick big as a man's arm. Reaching for the lamp, the house quiet, before the moth. Painting tomorrow, drawing at least. Which is familiar.

Before walking out to examine the light, or today, over the fields to draw cows, before meeting the others, Thérèse, Piers, bloody Mrs. I., it is different. Evident at breakfast, well, evident enough the night before in that leaving, his good-night, his door-closing, the family jawbone. Evident, as if that isn't enough, which it is, in the breakfast kedgeree and bread Gilbert cuts too thickly to go down the toaster. Coming down to the smell of fish and rice, Giddy's fuss. Gilbert hovering with his tongs, general debate on the dimensions of toast, much ado about the freshness of milk. In the chaos, neck bloody, well blotchy from lace, tired from the moth, making her way through practically the entire pot of tea. It will have her jittery on the cliffs.

Dreaming still? Gilbert sets new, thin toast before her. Behind him, Giddy. Trying for that good girl look, concentrating on butter application. Butter so cold it rips her toast. Hide the tearing. With jam or lemon curd. But there's only foul marmalade for disguise. Gilbert's hair in greasy morning clutches, a hand on her back as he pours more tea.

Catrine.

Inred leans against the fence looking up at her.

I've been watching you. You have an innate sense of light. Do you know what innate means? Or intuition?

Did she. Well, what did the woman think it had been all along.

I notice where you choose to shade, where you take more care, where you dash off a detail. It's intuitive . . . propping her badcow against a hip, Inred turns to a clean sheet . . . Perhaps if I align myself with you, the cows will stay still for me.

Vicar pulls at his muffler . . . They're well aware of how you see them, Lucy. As so much a pound.

You cut up their families . . . she agrees with Vicar.

But you like a nice beefburger yourself sometimes, am I right?

No, where I go to school they're more like cowpats.

Dear me. Too dry. The trick is . . . Inred surveys the cow in front of her . . . Half a chopped onion mixed into the meat.

I prefer shepherd's pie . . . looking over at him. No sign Gilbert has any sense of hearing.

Well, it seems I was making excuses, the cows are quite still but my drawings are even worse.

The woman reminds her of someone.

Do I, pet? Who's that then?

A lady in the town where I go to school. Beatrice her name is, she has a dog named Roger . . . shading a cow with an innate sense of light . . . She's wise. Very wise.

And your family? In England with you?

The big cow turns to look, Well? . . . In a village north of London.

Gilbert stops by . . . Are we all relinquishing our brains?

You must like to visit them there.

He speaks to Piers . . . Don't be so nervous son, the mistakes interest me . . . on to Thérèse, guiding Thérèse's hand as he once guided hers.

Yes, I like visiting a lot.

Understand, Thérèse, feel. You're not positive where your hand will go, that's the sense we're after, hum. Lost control.

Mr. Gilbert . . . Inred displays her work . . . If I lose any more control I'm liable to have the law out.

Gilbert chuckles, no other word for it, even old Inred looks surprised . . . That's exactly what I'm looking for, Lucy.

Always preferred sheep myself . . . Inred wipes her hands on her front, it is her common gesture.

I prefer sheep too . . . looking cow hand cow hand, then trying for that lost control Gilbert so loves, cow cow cow letting her hand go Free the hand from the tyranny of the brain Let go let go.

You have the most extraordinary hair . . . Inred stays focused on the cows, pencil moving madly as if her hand has no obligation to her body . . . Like wild tentacles. How on earth does your mother manage it? But then you're a boarder. I forgot. You're staring at me as if I've lost my mind.

Yes, I'm a boarder. I don't know how she manages . . . back to the field of cows.

Clips. She used to pull it back with clips. The metal slides drew the hair off her forehead like a set of theatrical curtains only her hair was too heavy, the play was always over before she reached the bus stop.

We all have our crosses to bear . . . Inred pushes a finger into the dense bundle piled on her head . . . As you can see.

Giddy has what they call strawberry hair. When they arrived that night, the night of their arrival the end of the drive the night of the moth, Giddy sat at the kitchen table with a cup in front of her, solitaire and a straight back, hair splayed out across that straightness in a way that was immediately apparent as an unusual way. And to be sure, in the morning all that strawberry was wound into submission. More straw than berry. That night, yes the night of the you know what, while Gilbert prattled, taking coats and mufflers, too many movements for the task at hand, describing unnecessary descriptions, weather con-

ditions, missing signs and was the haddock slightly off or was he indulging his hypochondriac vein the one he really tries to suppress and,
Oh how good it is to see you again can I make you another cup and
what about you Catrine, waltzing around the room, bouncing off walls
like one of his famous electrons. In the midst of Gilbert's bouncing
and cheer, she and Giddy silently sizing each other. The conclusion being something along the lines for both of them of *I see you exactly*. So,
Giddy said, You are this Catrine. She did not continue with the I've
heard so much about line, but it was implied or perhaps that was only
an American saying, it is difficult to remember sometimes. Yes. Sit
down and let my son make you something hot to drink. Was there a
something in that *My* Son or was it only her imagination, the disrep-
utable one. Yes, Catrine, it doesn't have to be tea, love would you prefer cocoa? Cocoa, yes please, Mr. Gilbert. She said it quickly so no
one, although since there was only Giddy that really meant Giddy,
would for one moment sense anything unusual. For instance, the use of
the word love like that, like Love. Yes, casual. Odd, not only in that
Gilbert has never said it before, not only in that it was clear that if old
Giddy were not sitting right there, Love would not have been uttered,
but odd how Love like that, inserted in a cocoa query in the kitchen,
meant nothing. Less than silence. And he having just kissed her on the
car like he did. So she looked at her hands and at Giddy's hair and pro-
jected that it would be restrained the next time she saw her. That being
the following morning at breakfast at kedgeree and too thick toast.
And so it was.

When I was a girl . . . Inred has been speaking this entire time.

And when Gilbert went to telephone Vicar to ensure the old Deux
Chevaux was up and running and could safely transport certain members of the party, she and Giddy sat in silence over the remains of egg
and fish. When it came right down to it Giddy was one of the least
giddy people she had ever met. He says, my son does, that you're a natural. Oh, I'm not so good really but he teaches me. I was sorry to hear
about your mother. She could hear Gilbert at the phone in the corridor

outside the kitchen hear his abrupt Good-bye. He saved her. Or he didn't, one or the other. We're off then, he said one hand at his stomach still preoccupied with the previous night's haddock. And Giddy with her tight hair scraped back, stood to fuss about sandwiches Gilbert assured her they didn't need.

But you have hair to write home about, don't you . . . Inred sketches furiously . . . I'll tell you another secret, a woman I know lives toward the bay has quite a problem with hair loss. It's a constant amazement, how you decay. The horrors I could relate. For example, when you wake in the morning, your face holds the night's grooves, the wrinkles of your pillow. Imagine the elasticity in your skin . . . fingersnap . . . Gone.

Lucy . . . Vicar in passing . . . What tales are you frightening the poor child with?

Still, you've nothing to fear you're—

Fourteen.

Goodness, I was never fourteen. Another thing, light. I can no longer read in sixty watts. It's got to be a hundred these days. Subtleties of light are lost to you as you age.

Lucy, many artists painted so-called subtleties well into their eighties and nineties.

Vicar, this is girl chat now.

Well, I never realized girl chat meant decay.

Inred leans, confidentially . . . Men don't understand. Another—

I'm not sure I do.

I should hope not, at fourteen. I'm not referring to the obvious creaks and groans, the arthritic bores, no, it's the nuances that devastate. I mean I can tell you I see the other end of the spectrum, death-wise. Not a lot of room to couch it in my line. Death holds no secrets to a butcher. I've spent my life with muscles and organs.

Organs? . . . Gilbert in passing, no doubt on his way to scold Piers for precious sketching . . . I have this sensation, Lucy . . . pushing at his stomach . . . Anything you can diagnose?

Careful, she might treat you as she would a cow . . . Vicar chops at his throat.

Watch that she doesn't take a cleaver to me, will you?

Very funny . . . Inred rests her savage pencil on top of the fence . . . Do you want my help, Mr. Gilbert?

Yes please . . . hand still on stomach he's been walking around like napoleon since this morning.

Let's have a look . . . Inred takes his face in her hands looks deep into his eyes . . . Umhm . . . pulls down one eyelid then the next . . . Umhm . . . places the back of her hand to his forehead . . . Umhm . . . pinches his wrist between her forefinger and thumb . . . Eat anything peculiar this morning?

Well it's been since yesterday.

Now is the time to consider meandering cows, or watch Piers, note whether or not he has, after so many warnings, finally managed to revoke his German propensity for perfection in favor of an abandoned sense of the line. What could be the point of harking back to yesterday's supper, half of which still rests on Gilbert's handbrake, the other half of which proved so provocative.

It's certainly not food poisoning.

I had this haddock, surely that must—

No no . . . Vicar weighs in . . . Food poisoning happens immediately or not at all.

And you're not feverish.

Now he glances at her and where the hell is she supposed to look.

Hum . . . Gilbert's hand absently traces light circles on his coat.

Shall we get you back to the village? . . . Inred drifts back to drawing.

Probably my imagination . . . Gilbert watches Inred return, moves to the vicar . . . Not much in the way of sympathy from the ladies. I'll turn to you, Vicar.

Don't go giving me anything contagious, Mr. Gilbert. I've no interest in sharing your discomfort, though I'll listen to your other woes.

A short prayer for me or somesuch.

Butcher pencils a tree . . . Good thing you're not a ruminant, you'd suffer four times the pain.

Well I could offer you Timothy, *Drink no longer water, but use a little wine for thy stomach's sake—*

None on me, Vicar—

—and thine often infirmities.

—though the idea's not a bad one.

Piers appears . . . I have some brandy in my flask.

I can't condone shots of liquor in a cow field, Piers, this is a family outing.

Your often infirmities.

What's that, Catrine? Ah yes, my often infirmities. Often delusions would be more like it. Those are some saucy cattle you've down on the page, Vicar.

Mr. Gilbert, you know my limitations.

Gilbert meets her eye . . . No such thing as limitations. Isn't that right, Miss Evans?

So you say.

Right . . . Gilbert watches Thérèse . . . Take your pencil like this, forefinger along the top. That way it's more difficult to make a precious mark.

Finished rearranging Thérèse, Gilbert glances over. Peripherally he is hers always.

Now he is beside her, squeezing next to Inred, taking her paper, leaning against the same fence that cuts her thighs.

This line is strong, this one here . . . the top of his head, his nose as he speculates on the drawing . . . Are you comfortable up there? . . . Gilbert glances at her, he does that, those quick birdy movements.

For now.

How are you coming Mrs. Ingle? Cows behaving?

It's a different sort of drawing, Mr. Gilbert.

Good good . . . Gilbert pulls himself up on the fence, whispers . . . Can't bear you taller than me . . . swinging his legs around as he says . . . That's what we're after, Lucy . . . reaching for her sketch-book . . . May I see?

Several cows, four sheets of intuitive pencil marks, an innate understanding of light, all products of a relinquished brain. She has talent for losing control.

Gilbert's chin pressed into thought . . . Interesting, what do you make of this?

I changed my mind and began to draw something else.

Excellent . . . he turns the page. Silence. His eyes move away from the drawing to his hand where it grips her book.

That's you.

I see.

You got in my eyeline when you went over to the vicar, so I drew—

Well it's remarkably unlike me.

It's a lot like you, you're leaning against the fence, see and your hair—

You choose to turn your back on all this . . . in a wave of his hand, Gilbert gathers the landscape, cows . . . In order to sketch some hideous teacher.

I liked that tree behind you . . . watching a moody cow contemplate the horizon . . . Besides, you're not.

What?

Hideous.

And these points on my head, those would be my horns? Am I devil or bull?

Your hair sticks up.

One hand up to smooth . . . Lovely.

Mostly I drew cows, see . . . riffling through pages to show that she can follow directions.

I should be flattered, hum. That you would think me worthy of that sort of attention.

You don't think it's good.

Mr. Gilbert . . . the vicar, when excited, creates a whistling sound through his teeth.

Yes, John . . . Gilbert turns but leaves two fingers on her sketch-pad to mark his place.

There's a yellow wagtail just above that second tree, do you see?

So there is, you're perfectly right, John . . . now to her . . . My opinion on good or not good is not the issue . . . now to the German . . . Piers, flip that sheet of paper over. You're getting distracted.

But sir, it's becoming something—

We're anti-something.

Piers turns to a fresh sheet of paper.

Back to her . . . You'd do well to take a page from young Thérèse there, swift marks, lack of hesitation. I could point out your capacity for detail or these marks which are gentle but convey a sort of urgency.

Those are the cows. What about my portrait of you?

I think we should move on to a different setting. I sense the others—

That time you did my portrait.

Yes yes.

Did you shove me behind the wardrobe with the blue woman?

Certainly not.

So it's not some kind of collection, then, of—

What are you driving at?

I don't know. I don't know what I'm driving at.

Shall we move on then? . . . turning away, rubbing his stomach . . . Piers, Vicar?

I'm getting at something here, Mr. Gilbert.

We'll wait then, Mrs. Ingle. No hurry . . . he turns back to her.

You get nervous.

Rubbish.   About what?

Me drawing you or—

You're exasperating me . . . leaning forward across her . . . Losing steam, Thérèse? Just a few minutes while Mrs. Ingle finishes.

Sorry to hold everyone up, just want one to feel proud of.

But when you paint me, I'm supposed to love it . . . watching Inred bend to her paper . . . You don't listen, really, to what I'm saying.

Catrine . . . Gilbert looks at her, she looks out to the cows.

You think I'm not as good as you. You think I—

Not true. Not true.

And another thing . . . turning get him square in the eye . . . Mothers are not replaceable.

What? What are you thinking?

Neither are Rosies.

I know that. What's wrong? What's different? . . . he takes his gaze to his left toward something she cannot see, then softly . . . Well, I suppose everything's different.

There was a moth.

Sorry?

Last night. In the bedroom. It kept me up, kept banging against the light.

You kept the lamp on?

No.

How odd.

Mr. Gilbert . . . Inred closes her sketch pad . . . I've about had it for these wretched beasts.

Hooking down to her, Gilbert whispers . . . Please don't do this, Catrine.

And the party goes forward to draw trees, meadows of sheep. The afternoon shifts, becomes colder, they draw quickly and move on, to keep the blood moving, keep themselves warm. She will walk beside dull Thérèse, *So, you are a bourdeur?* and so on until the girl vents her fascination for the more gruesome aspects of Inred's trade. The difference between mignon and tartare, wellington, brisket, the dotted cuts. At which point she falls behind.

It was a silent ride the rest of the way, on to Newquay. She did not know then that he called his mother Giddy. Nary a comment on broken radios or dangerous drivers. Passing headlights caught his profile now and then. But mostly they drove in black. Between them, her chips remained uneaten on the handbrake. His Fiat will hold the smell of those chips for months but she is not to know that. And then the moth banging against the light along with that feeling, that feeling like with Paul, that not knowing until it happened what it was that would be.

Sealed on the top floor, attic enveloping her in its triangles, hands on the cover, slept like a corpse. Woke to an abrupt light, yanked curtains, him silhouetted against the morning, one hand arranging the curtains, teacup in the other.

Sleep well, he asked as she sat up lying, Yes because the moth was gone. And sitting on the moquette, he stared at the teacup until she said, Is that for me, to bring him back. In the doorway, the same doorway it took him so long to leave the night before, he watched her fuss with the hot cup, bringing it carefully to her mouth. He said, Catrine. Couldn't he see how busy she was with her tea. Are you alright? After all, she didn't want to spill on the white coverlet or on her own knees. She answered about the tea, there didn't seem much point in talking about moths. It's so sweet. Too sweet? It's fine.

They continue toward more sheep. Next to Piers detailing the differences between education systems around the world, German, English, the term he spent in Maryland, conclusions formulated regarding America. She tells Piers that everything to know about that country is not found in Maryland but he will not be swayed. What will you do when you finish your degree, she asks, not caring in the least. The idea is never to finish, not while they're paying me, Piers picks at his lips, a chapped patch, Ah, to stay a student forever.

Vicar wants to point out birds, name them for her. And trees. Here's a chestnut not that I can draw it for the life of me. I'm only good at the figure. An eye for the ladies my wife says but I can do a man nearly as well. My trees. My trees always come out sickly. There you go.

Gilbert does a jig of hurry to establish space between the two of them and the other four.

A collection . . . he laughs not a real laugh and a sidelong look at her . . . That's not what you really think.

I think a lot of things, different things.

Contradictions you mean.

I suppose.

And in the morning after a long night with the moth, after his wake-up tea but before the kedgeree, Giddy's Men of Harlech reverberated up to her bath, even underwater. This is her body, her arms, her stomach. Tightness in her chest, rolling over on one side, a blanket of water, a bedtub.

Too hot, she slumped over the edge. Head lolling, nose cold against the porcelain. Shot in the bath and left for dead. Blood unfurling across the tiles. She glanced up.

He stood in the doorway.

Mr. Gilbert—

Like The Death of Marat.

Could you excuse me please. I'm in the bath.

So I see. There's a painting, David—

I don't care about the painting, Mr. Gilbert.

Well . . . as he went . . . Mind out. You're dripping into the drawing room.

Gilbert stands on a stile bench to address them. This will be our last sketch for today. Tomorrow is a day off and we'll spend Wednesday on watercolors. Beginning at the cliffs and ending at the church for a short discussion on methodology which is not as boring as it sounds. But today, during our last hour, take these sheep by storm, make bold, assertive mistakes. Good luck.

Capital . . . Vicar in a voice involving teeth . . . We have erred and strayed from thy ways like lost sheep. We have followed too much the devices and desires of our own heart.

I'm sure that's true, Vicar.

We have done those things which we ought not to have done . . . Vicar, on a roll, nothing will stop the falsetto, his teeth, the prayer, it will go on and on and on a bus rolling east toward the water the color of it the color of a coin on a day they should have been in school. In a town they'd never seen, headed toward a store at the edge of water. A ding as they went in, a ding as they bought the sugar cigarettes. And standing on a wall made of stones looking out over the metal water, she said, I'm not over it, Isabelle. I'm not over pretending that apple trees are horses. Twelve isn't too old for that sort of thing. Although since she had not yet been to England, it was fairly unlikely she said anything like *that sort of thing*. Whatever she said, it made Isabelle shake out the last cigarette like an old farmhand, regard the horizon, the folly of past mistakes found there. After a long silence, Isabelle said, I'm going to camp. To ride real horses. The wind picked up off the water. Let's try the hill, she said, walking away from Isabelle. The road they followed curved like an ear. Them in the drum. How long will you be gone? Nothing's definite, Catrine, after all. The way Isabelle said After all to her as if she were a child. Into the woods because Isabelle said, Men kill girls who walk along roads. Halfway down the hill they broke through to a clearing, the traffic clearly visible below. Let's throw something. Who said it, was it Isabelle, her face thinning with excitement, dried sugar dotting her mouth, or did she say it, as always mindless of the consequences.

They are not strong enough to reach the road with the rocks and sticks they find. They give up to walk home. Leaving, Isabelle trips. There in the dirt, half-hidden, the tire. Absurd but plausible. Isabelle brushes off the worms and on a count there's the traffic two cars a bus white van with red lettering and One should we take a run up Two it will go faster if we do Three and bursting from their grasp who knew Isabelle was that strong arms flailing high in the aftertow to the wind no stopping it a black rubber streak down the hill staring from car to plunging tire back and forth tire to car cause to effect finally dawning what was impossible to project when the tire sat in leaves, that a hurtling object shaped so weighing so set at such a course of this degree and that velocity might act—

Like a bullet . . . Isabelle whispers . . . Or something.

Back and forth road tire road tire and the tire bounced to miss a speeding mercedes before SMASH off the front wheel of the motorcycle the figure catapulting stomachs twisting sickly over handlebars landing in dense grass on the side of the road.

There is no health in us.

Turning, there's Vicar and his womanly cows, sheep as odalisque, finishing his prayer for them all.

What do you mean?

Ah now girlie girl . . . is he supposed to be Jamaican . . . Everyone's done those things which we ought not to have done . . . or is it more like Scottish . . . Is all I meant.

Gilbert passes, he smiles at Vicar, moves his eyes to her, teases Vicar about sheep doing things they ought not to have done and there is no health in his stomach.

No health in her. Both led and saved. Gilbert watches her as Vicar stories away in his elusive patois. A reverence or is it only the vicar's proximity.

Back at the sheep, her hand betrays her. The day painting mudscapes, a time when He Smelled Nice. Was nice. The coats of the sheep ruffle in the picking-up breeze. Whatever might happen to all of them, she and Isabelle in their far-flung worlds, Vicar, Gilbert or even the man, dead, alive, legless, she would never.

This man then.

After dinner, a dinner where Giddy made sausages. It was supposed to be toad-in-the-hole but the pudding burned almost black and Giddy had to pick the toads out of the hole and mix up some Smash so they could have a vegetable. Then Brussels sprouts were found in the freezer, four each, so Gilbert could say A regular feast. Not much talking until Gilbert's voice began squeaking out the day, painting, cows, butcher, cigarettes and sheep. She left him and Giddy, Cornwall, for her first day at Monstead.

In their hotel room, Father by a tiny light sewing name tags into her uniform as she slept. On and off that night she woke to see his hunched form jabbing to find the eye. On the way to the train the next morning, he said how often they would see each other, weekends, holidays. How he understood that all this was happening at such a furious pace. The platform, slick with a drying rain, smelled of metal, piss, of coal. Bags at her feet, watching Father waiting at the ticket counter. Something cut through her. He seemed so small. An approximation of the man she remembered. Making his way back to her through streams of Londoners leaving home or coming home, neither of which applied to her, coat overarm, hands full, a cheery strain. The cold on its way into her bones again, to stay there for weeks. She was still. Father, handing her the ticket. He was still. London on its way somewhere else. Even after six months alone, they were polite. A garbled announcement. Swahili, he said. Her train. A porter carried her cases on board, they could see him through the window stacking them by the door. A hug. He was small, she was fine. She moved to go. He said, I have these for you. Turning back, it was a box of chocolates, a sampler for a grandmother. Father pushed them. She watched her hand take the box, it was an unfamiliar hand. He said, Perhaps there'll be others from Monstead returning from the weekend. You'll have something to offer. The boxtop spelled *Chocolates* in cross-stitched lettering. For an odd moment she wondered if he had sewn it. She was fine she was fine. Thank you Father, she said. Da. Then she climbed the steps. The porter tried to help, made it more difficult. There was a moment before the train moved away. Father, he was her father. She wouldn't look out the window to see if he waved for she was fine and didn't need last minute waves. The train breezed through Wandsworth, Wimbledon, Kingston, Haslemere. People came on got off sat next to her then left.

Outside, on platforms, arrivers were greeted with hollow burps of pleasure. Sun came out from clouds or went in, rose or set. Sagging tights webbed like the foot of a duck. In new uniform, yes new despite all efforts, she sat like a good girl, chocolates on her knees, her mannish shoes below, staring at the box as if it held secrets along with marzipan, as if it might tell her why it affected her. On the way to Father's school, a good-bye to the plastic London kitchen. Father would begin the search for a new house. Yet the chocolates, his hasty offer, as if they were colluding. In the hurtling train, a woman across the way gave her a treacly smile. Well she didn't look up for a long while after that. No it wasn't school or mother, coal or piss or the weather that broke her.

This man then.

On the stairway, the rising blister of Giddy's television, Gilbert stops her on the final flight. The chocolate box stayed in the locker next to her bed. She never ate nor offered a single one. Finally, fearing ants, she threw away the chocolates but kept the stitchy box for letters, pebbles. Isabelle's, before they stopped and a shell she found in her orange squash one day. She leans against the wall, he is below, one foot on her stair, hands in pockets, leaning against the same wall.

You haven't been your usual chatty self. Giddy will think I've been telling fibs.

I don't talk that much.

What have I done, Catrine.

I was thinking about other things.

This man then, your poor man on his motorcycle.

What about him?

Well . . . Gilbert wipes his mouth with a hand . . . It deserves a longer conversation at some point, do you think?

Yes, sir.

You're not going to tell me what's got you all quiet, are you?

She shakes her head.

You'll slay me too, will you?

She moves to go.

I didn't mean that . . . he reaches out . . . Come back.

She stops . . . Am I an experiment?

Don't be absurd . . . Gilbert takes her hand from its wallpaper play, traces the remaining purfle of eczema . . . Poor Punchinello.

I don't care about it. It's mostly gone.

Eyes on her, he raises her hand to his mouth.

Giddy's voice floats up from downstairs . . . Are you coming to watch with me, Michael?

Without removing hand or eyes, he calls . . . Just drawing a bath for Catrine. Down in a moment.

I had a bath this morning.

Never have too many . . . pulling her up the stairs and down the corridor . . . You'll sleep better for it.

In the bathroom Gilbert rolls up his sleeve to rattle the drain. On his thumb, blue, a small bruise, smudged ink. The water runs. He gauges the temperature.

There's no collection behind my cupboard, Catrine.

So you said . . . closing the toilet lid, she sits on it.

Do you know for certain that the motorcyclist died? . . . Gilbert reaches up to dry his hand on a towel.

I feel it. In my bones.

In your pretty bones. Well, bones have been wrong before, haven't they? Perhaps he only broke his hip, jaw . . . sitting on the side of the tub they are knee to knee . . . The man was wearing a helmet?

Yes.

There you go. I'm sure he survived. Deep down, you're a pessimist, hum?

He went up so high.

Garish in the bathroom against the chortle of running water. Gilbert knows about probability, there's mathematics in chemistry for god's sake. Father in the train station with his granny chocolates, giving them so she could have something to offer but it never seemed a likely survival. An offer of as much as he had, certainly it often came down to chocolates in the end. And a helmet.

I want to help you . . . with one finger Gilbert presses her knee, the help button . . . To give you things, to make it better.

What things?

I want you to like me . . . press press . . . Is that horribly wrong? Is that. I mean would Mr. Betts for example—

Mr. Betts?

Oh I know we left him in Chittock Leigh, well the Council on Proper Behavior then.

They have an office here . . . she watches water from the tap rush furiously.

Yes, in town, I saw it as we drove through . . . he designs a figure eight on her kneecap, behind him, the water . . . I struggle with understanding why I brought you here.

You mean not for the painting group?

The eight stops.

I'm not talented at all, am I? Not a Fauvist at all, just bad. You're laughing at me. Thinking what kind of person would paint a rock yellow?

Come now, I'm not some sort of charlatan. I'm serious when I speak of possibilities.

Then what do you mean, you struggle to understand?

I'm thirty-four years old, Catrine. You just turned fourteen. Why do you preoccupy my thoughts? . . . he touches again . . . You remind me—

Of Rosie.

Yes and of—

Don't say of yourself.

Of no one I've ever met. You're shiny or. Uncompromised. I tried to tell you while we were driving, Catrine. Your life's so unlived, the potential—

The bathwater reaches a dangerous level, she motions, he turns to address it, twisting the tap. He runs his fingers through his hair, looks at her as he did that day in February so long ago when he painted her. How young she was then. She had been in the country for six months, she was a child fresh from trees she saw as horses. Now, she can no sooner imagine straddling a tree, than see it take equine form and bear her away. Gilbert's fingers wrap his chin, his legs plaited at the side of the tub. Painting her. What did she want from him so long ago, she hardly knew him, had not yet heard that he figured as Hamlet in the death of a father. She wanted to sleep on his pillow as she had done once and why will her thoughts insist on returning to chocolates.

Does that make sense to you?

All I wanted was for you to lift me up.

Everyone else feels old and dull to me . . . he leans toward her.

She leans away.

You're right. There doesn't seem anywhere to go . . . he stands, the mirror fogs, he runs his hand through his hair again.

I feel so dead.

He looks down at her, his hair is stuck. Sitting down again suddenly on the edge of the tub, Gilbert presses her hand to his mouth.

Stop . . . she pulls away.

Tell me you wanted—

No.

I thought—

I didn't want that. I wanted you to lift me up.

Please stop saying that Catrine, I don't know what it means. We were by the car, eating chips, yesterday evening. The sky is so purple, I thought. I said so and as I said it I looked at you, your concern with your vinegar-sodden chips, head bowed over them as though you prayed and I thought, Now there's a sky a Fauvist would love, I thought I love you, I thought you are my Fauvist and I love you. It overcame me. I wanted to eat you or grab you or have you. I didn't want anyone to get you, to spoil you.

So you did instead.

I thought that I was there as your protector and I would protect you always, watch over your bowed little head matted with sleep. I kissed you, you understand I had to, I had no choice, I had to touch your face, your mouth, I had to have what those chips had, your lips. And you kissed me back, Catrine. Didn't you. You kissed me back?

I don't know what I did. I've never kissed a boy.

Now come on, we both know this is something you wanted. We came into the house, I brought you upstairs, you took my hand.

I wanted to hold your hand. I wanted to smell you. I didn't want that.

How was I to know? You act so old.

Well I'm not.

You led me to believe—

I wanted the hair at the back of your neck, the shaven part and your scar and the way you hold your waist with your fingers pinching. I thought maybe you would hold my waist like that. I wanted to hear your horrible squeaky voice and see your teeth stick out like fangs when you can't stop laughing. I wanted to make you laugh. I wanted there to be no one else for you not Nessa or Fi or Dido, but I didn't want that.

All those times, in the snow in front of the school, and when you look at me that way.

Mr. Gilbert.

But I stopped I stopped tell me I stopped. I stopped.

You didn't.

He looks at her a look of fear his eyes move over her his hand he falls to his knees the water is so still he buries his head in her knees. It's true.

A movement. A sound. The door opens. Giddy.

6

Of course. The mountain. In stages of exhaustion. Behind her, still struggling up the final ascent, Vicar on the brink. At least the yodeling's stopped which was funny in concept only. And Piers with his damp matches unable to light a cigarette in one stopping to concentrate on the strikes yapping his most interesting or is it simply most frequent question, Why Am I Here which is not philosophical inquiry but a boredom with the whole enterprise.

Yes, she is first up. Butcher has done some evening reading in medical dictionaries, wants to spend the morning unloading gastric insight on Gilbert. First to take in the extraordinary swell of grassy meadow, the outcropping of cliff. Across a ravine, the rock has faces, folds of skin, a cragginess of age. Salt, she can smell it even here. Pervades. The bread of sincerity, the bread of truth. A deep breath.

Down for breakfast in her tunic. It was a uniform sort of dress but Father liked it. One large kickpleat in the front. A kickpleat, to say the word was worth the dress seeming uniform. You're climbing cliffs today, Giddy said, spinning a bowl of porridge in front of her, Is that appropriate for climbing? A dress? With a mouthful of porridge she turned sideways and kicked out a foot to show Giddy that she wore not her new Gilbert shoes but her squashers, exceptional for climbing mountains or kicking any pleats. Gilbert came in then fixing his collar saying, It's not the matterhorn, Giddy, she'll be alright. Over her spoon and for some reason her mouthfuls were extra large this morning so she could chew for minutes without reloading, she was interested in the space Giddy kept between them. A gift for you Catrine, Gilbert said disappearing into the corridor, Look what I have for you.

And here, first on the scene, a detective. The craggy faces hers for five minutes, hers alone. Resting both hands on top of the crook. You make a fine shepherd, he said when he gave it. I know how much you like sheep. Although, turning to Giddy, I tell you her handling of cows on Monday was expert indeed.

A sun plays on the rocks, takes them nearly white. Gilbert has the paints, what will she mix with white to find that camel color. The brown Gilbert owns is too yellow. Yellow belonged to another time. No yellows today. As if she needed him to name her. Fauvist. My name is for my friends. She is no wild beast. She has a kickpleat and a belted waist. Nothing out of place. Shortly to follow, a tidy mind. The canvas bag belonged to Father when he was a bicyclist. She found it at Felmar, wanted the bag because it appeared to have survived war. Strapped across her for her special brushes and a pear. The Gilbert original and a letter she found on the road this morning while Gilbert and Vicar changed the flat on the Deux Chevaux. The letter was impossible to read from water damage but had a Spanish stamp.

Piers and Thérèse arrive. A breeze raises goosebumps. Thérèse wears the red cardigan because she nearly cried about it. Giving it to Thérèse, she said, Watch out for Piers. Watch out for those motivations.

Well . . . Piers sets down his rucksack, takes out a cigarette, lights it to say . . . Not bad.

A valley in the distance holds the sun in a bowl. Now Vicar appears, no longer yodeling, in fact panting alarmingly. Thérèse lies down on the grass, looking up to the sky.

I have a leak somewhere . . . Piers folds down next to her cross-legged . . . Everything of mine is sopping.

Very blue at the same time containing every color like white. This vast, this infinite. This is where she is.

My . . . Vicar breathes . . . I can think of only one word for this.

Thérèse takes in Piers, his bag . . . Do you have a canteen in there as well?

Majestic.

Not funny . . . Piers begins taking out pencils, a book—

I usually sit on rocks will that be alright for all of you? . . . she doesn't move at the sound of his voice.

That's fine for me, Mr. Gilbert . . . Butcher's voice . . . Still young enough to rough it.

Folding her arms against the chill, the strap of her bicycling bag, some land alright.

Brought my own . . . the sound of Vicar arranging? pulling off?

his rucksack, the light tinny sound of metal or steel . . . Brand new, made of poly—

Super. Let's begin. Catrine?

Yes, Mr. Gilbert . . . now she turns to face him.

I have your paper and paints . . . his shirt open a few buttons, faintly perspiring holding by a long strap the bag at his feet . . . Give me a hand won't you?

Taking in the landscape one final time, no longer a private one, she goes to him . . . Are you still sweating from the tire? . . . she touches his forearm . . . Why are you so hot?

Gilbert kneels to the bag, draws out her paints . . . Butcher's been terrifying me with all the possible diseases I might have. Gastroenteritis, appendicitis.

But it doesn't hurt anymore. You said so this morning . . . kneeling next to him, kickpleat pleating, she takes up her paint tin, a loan for the trip.

Well Mrs. Ingle informs me that cancer pains can come and go.

Opening the tin then closing it . . . *Cancer?*

What now?

What do you mean, cancer?

Gilbert still bowed over bottled water and dirty cloths . . . Mrs. Ingle thinks it terribly funny I'm—Oh . . . he looks up . . . What was I thinking? I don't know what's happening, Catrine, my mind has gone to mush.

I don't want you to die, Mr. Gilbert . . . and taking the tin, she leaves him.

Thérèse and Piers have claimed a rock. Vicar, legs in a triangle, stands at his space-age easel. Choosing a place next to Butcher, she brings out her special brushes from Father's bag.

Over the porridge, and she ate two bowls, her hair dripped on the table. Giddy had shouted up to her that Gilbert might like one too. From the bath she did not call back, because the kickpleat tunic awaited and she was a pleasant tunic girl, No one knows your son's bathing habits better than I, and I agree, a few more baths would not go amiss. Instead she stepped out wet into slippers to take a blue towel to her hair and back, rubbing vigorously. Knowing Gilbert likely awaited, she brushed combed smoothed her hair straight straight straight, squeezing out any stubborn water. Rummaging in the medicine cabinet she chose baby oil and combed it into her hair thinking it might keep tame. At breakfast the oil dripped on to the table forcing her to furtively wipe it with her sleeve every time Giddy looked away.

As Gilbert drew his bath upstairs, she sipped her tea, waited for the porridge she would eat two bowls of, and tried to make conversation with this ungiddy mother. Nothing provoked more than one word answers until she said, I was sorry to hear about your illness last month. At that very moment Gilbert swung in looking for salt to put in his bath. He stood at the cabinet with his back to her, salt in one outstretched hand. She was thinking it was peculiar to see a teacher in his dressing gown so it took a moment to register Giddy's answer. In fact it was only after Gilbert left with his salt that she heard. *Haven't been ill in two years*. O Treachery O Treason.

Butcher leans across for an assessment . . . You're doing it so dark, love. Is there a storm approaching I'm not seeing?

O perfidious man. Haven't been ill in two years. There was a surprise for you. You who didn't think there'd be one. Then there was the gift of the shepherd stick. When Vicar honked from outside they walked down the rock path to the faulty car though they did not yet know the tire would puncture. And Gilbert only said Catrine. Her name like that as if that meant Forgive Me without having to say anything else. When the Deux Chevaux became an Un Cheval and she scoured nearby and found the letter, she looked over to the two men. Gilbert's newly bathed self becoming, even at that prebutcher point, sweaty at the back. Giddy's answer did not surprise her even as it did. Knowing and not knowing. When the new tire was secure, Vicar climbed in the driver seat as she and Gilbert put the flat in the boot. Gilbert said to her, Remember at Harrington when I showed you how to translate what you see instead of what you know? Yes, she said. Well, he said, shoving at the tire. Sometimes you have to rely on what you know to be true instead of believing what seems apparent. She wanted to answer, I'll Bear That In Mind. But with her tunic she tried for better. I see, she said. I see. He was, after all, showing her how.

Choosing where the sky gets pierced by two grassy peaks, between them, a blear of distant rocks. Blurred due to the demands of distance.

Penny for them.

Not Gilbert in the night, asking the wheel, the road darkening those moments before they ate haddock, but Butcher.

They're not worth a penny.

Some artists don't believe in green from a tube . . . Butcher judges her mountain . . . They think it should be mixed from primaries.

Checking her borrowed tin . . . I have green.

Ingle takes the paint . . . I'm sure your thoughts are worth quite a bit more than a penny.

I was thinking, am I petulant.

Petulant? Who called you petulant?

I looked it up in the dictionary . . . wiping her brush . . . Isn't that pathetic? I didn't know how I was being insulted.

Was it a teacher or—

It means unreasonably ill tempered, peevish.

But if you have reason to be ill tempered, would that make you not so much petulant as . . . Butcher squeezes out an ugly blue . . . Angry?

A thin brush to define mountain against sky perhaps she is a landscapist, a Constable, a Cole. He will call her dull a wash of what she can't stop herself the side of the mountain cries out for red is there any logic to it.

Something in her has lifted, yes it has, She never needed him to lift her up. A rock by her foot. She has been weathered day-in day-out or does weathering imply some sort of negative effect, in which case perhaps she has metamorphized. After all, she has felt heat, she has felt pressure. Scraping the rock against her hand. The mountain, squeezing the mountain she holds in her hand.

There he was her first day at Monstead under the arch. She remembered the wall from her visit with Father. Gilbert stood hands pocketed head bent to a short teacher as if he were hard of hearing. Here she was sweating from the train with her tabby and chocolates not knowing where or what the taxi driver near expiration with the weight of her things this frivolous lady with too many hatboxes. When she arrived the halls were empty. Middle of the day middle of lessons the cement rang with her dropped suitcase. Gilbert was not hard of hearing for he jolted saw her and her cases her distress over the shoulder of his anonymous colleague. Pushing the man aside Gilbert rushed to help to say You can't possibly manage that. Then told a passing someone Will you alert the POD a new pupil's arrived. When she said to him as they bent to rezip her bursting case having paid the exasperated cabbie big bright bills all caught up in her moneybelt zip said to him What's a Pod? He grunted with the zip That's the Person On Duty let's hope he's a stronger man than I. It was Mr. Betts. It was Mr. Betts who came to fix the zip and organize her cases and trunks. Everything so new and obvious she wanted to kick it but that would have been kicking Father. It was Mr. Betts who made a funny joke who asked her if she knew a woman he met at a party who lived near Missoula. When she said Missoula Missoula I've never been west of the Mississippi river but remembering manners politely added Though I would certainly like to go someday. Those were the days when she often said certainly because it sounded polite but it was a lie to say you were certain if you were not so she stopped the habit only a few weeks later. It was Mr. Betts who said I'm sure you will visit many places both in America as well as in our own country which I hope will please you. It was Mr. Betts who smiled at her even when he had other worries thin hair unkempt from the flights to her dorm from cuffing Owen Wharton it was Owen it was Owen and some other boy who helped Mr. Betts carry her many American cases up the five flights. And when she went to her first English lesson Mr. Betts made excuses of jet lag when she couldn't find Missoula on the map. Laughed when she said But this is Boston because she knew where Boston was. It was Betts who said softly You may sit down now Miss Evans when their eyes met across her trembling pointing finger. The same man who called her pornographic the same man who looked forward to seeing the results of a day spent in such academic vein. How could that be. It was not Mr. Betts her first day in Chemistry who said We have an American in our midst who asked her to stand and say an American phrase so the class could hear the accent who said Let's not blame nuclear threat on our new student hum. Almost giving them the idea to do so. It was not Mr. Betts who arranged a meeting in the library then never appeared due to Misunderstanding. How did it all unravel from her first days. Was it simply perspective. Surely what one sees provides what one knows. Surely those two things are not completely unrelated. The perspective for example on Gilbert's head that first day as he struggled with her zip was never again the same detached view. When she leaned to shove at a piece of shirt which Gilbert couldn't see but which was impinging his zipping efforts he watched her as he waited for the improvements.

Pretty.

He blocks the sun. She drops the rock, picks up the painting again. Gilbert squats down beside her, elbow against her back, then looks across to Butcher.

The cliffs, I trust, are holding still for you, Mrs. Ingle?

Better than cows, Mr. Gilbert any day. How's Vicar?

Finding odalisques I'm sure. And you, Miss Evans, may I? . . . Gilbert reaches for her half painting, propping it on one knee so they can both mull it over.

In the style of Thomas Cole . . . she tells him.

Ah.

Of the Hudson Valley group.

I'm aware which Cole you mean.

He's one of my favorites. They have a painting of his in Oxbow.

A lovely oil of a river. At the university museum. You took me there once, remember?

Dryly . . . Yes I haven't developed amnesia along with my stomach pains, Catrine. Lovely. Lovely work . . . passing the painting back, he stands abruptly . . . Carry on . . . almost militarily . . . Cole will inspire, no doubt.

Beside her, Butcher absorbed in color ratio. A moment. Gilbert stares down at her. Out of the sun she can see very well the creases carved by his mouth. Not laugh lines at all, more like frown. He looks over to Piers and Thérèse. A hesitation.

Compared to Fauvists, I mean . . . watching him . . . Cole is so much quieter.

I didn't know you went for quiet.

I don't think I have so much in common with wild beasts.

Ah yes . . . he smiles to Butcher as if they share a joke but Butcher mixes, oblivious . . . Thomas Cole . . . nearly spitting . . . What a visionary. What a passionate painter. Only thrilled your aspirations are aimed so high.

Rinsing her brush . . . I like him.

Do you. I prefer your earlier efforts. Since you recall that day in the Oxbow museum so well, perhaps you also recall my saying that the exact does not convey—

Truth. I remember.

Yet, this Cole fascination, newfound that it is—

I liked him that day. You convinced me it wasn't the right opinion.

I was guiding you.

Maybe I don't think Cole painted things exactly . . . lifting her painting to smooth the kickpleat . . . Or maybe I can't recognize truth.

Gilbert smiles at his shoes and over at Butcher who seems only aware of mountain, grass, cliffs, birds.

I mean . . . selecting a boring brown . . . Maybe that day in Oxbow, I was a new girl, I didn't know what I was seeing. But that's what you always meant to teach me, right? From the beginning you said that you would teach me how to see.

You have learned that have you. Well my job is done then.

I think so.

Gilbert hesitates, he has been vacillating between going and not going these last five minutes. Clearly he is thinking of a way to separate her from Mrs. Ingle, so he can lean down and say Don't do this Catrine so he can whisper in her hair the reminders of their times, sweet cinemas, clandestine castles. But now Butcher mumbles some damnation about a pencil sharpener, trips off toward Vicar and his naughty rocks.

I suppose you think . . . Gilbert watches Butcher's retreat . . . That you're bringing up your percentage with this farce. In fact you're spiraling toward failure.

I've been thinking about Mr. Betts.

Gilbert takes Butcher's place, doesn't pull his trousers at the knees, the sit is more collapse . . . What about him?

The first week he left me alone when I couldn't find Missoula on the map.

Did he.

You say that when you're not listening.

Well what does that mean, Catrine, Betts left you alone? . . . Gilbert picks up her rock . . . I don't understand you anymore. Was I supposed to leave you alone?

I don't know.

Gilbert passes the rock from hand to hand . . . Catrine . . . he tries to give it to her, but she has not asked for it . . . I have transgressed some—Let me begin again. I want it to be the way it used to be between us. The way it was before.

Before what? Before you lied about the library and your mother?

I was protecting you. Sometimes we protect each other with white lies. I made a mistake.

Which one?

On the drive up. When we had fish and chips. I misunderstood . . . his hand on top of hers his smell has not changed, a squeeze . . . Tell me what you want . . . he puts his arm around her shoulders as if she is very small, a petulant child with a scraped knee.

You can't protect me from yourself, Mr. Gilbert.

Help . . . Vicar, out of breath though he can not have traveled more than a few yards . . . The little girl . . . wheezing . . . Come quickly.

Gilbert drops his arm at the Interruption, and rushes away stuffing the rock into his pocket apparently forgetting it is a rock. She follows, leaving the bad Cole behind.

Piers is standing by a clump of gorse smoking at his paintbrush. Thérèse sits cross-legged on Piers' coat, holding her head in her hands. Butcher thrums comfort, arm around the girl.

What is it? . . . Gilbert kneels on the coat, taking Thérèse's hands away from her face . . . Mrs. Ingle, tell me what's happened.

Vicar and I were having an all-out search for this expensive pencil sharpener we invested in not two—

Yes yes.

Suddenly I realized the girl was crying. Well I went over to her and—

It's in my eye . . . still Thérèse does not look up.

What is . . . a gentle secret . . . What's in your eye?

My pencil lead . . . Piers, back and agitated . . . I struck the paper with force, the pencil point rebounded. I was upset it was so ugly, my drawing—

You're not supposed to be drawing at all . . . Gilbert pets Thérèse, soothing.

I was providing an outline.

I've been doing that as well, Mr. Gilbert . . . Butcher worries . . . Is it against the rules?

The child has lead in her eye, can we all keep our heads. Vicar?

Yes Mr.—

Pass me your water jug and the palette, there.

Gilbert moves swiftly quietly, cleaning the palette, filling a hollow with water, We're going to flush your eye We're going to flush your eye. Thérèse moans and Butcher says, After this course I should go back to nursing with all the casualties on any given day.

Standing by Piers, looking out on rocks. Way up on the next peak, a dot of white. Clump of edelweiss if they were Swiss. If they were in France, it would be a likelihood. But they are in Cornwall. So it is perhaps a colony of gulls, or covey, mutton stranded on a moutonnée.

I have blinded her, Piers says lighting a cigarette, I never expected the lead to bounce like it did. I was annoyed at my drawing, I was annoyed I was making no progress and I found the scenery, here he gestures with his cigarette, Boring. A stream of smoke dissipates into air. Behind them, the commotion of flushing and Vicar's new accents for Thérèse's amusement. They assess the same cliffs, she and Piers. She has no special vantage. A pause. Smoke. Piers? Mm, a draw on the cigarette. Well it seems we are looking at the same landscape, you and I, these cliffs, mountains, the blue sky and that clump of gulls or somesuch, well, this landscape you choose to call boring, the boredom of which you break your pencil point over, the boredom for which you blind a girl, I don't find so boring at all. I take offense. I think it's. Majestic.

A clicking like a key in a latch, back and forth. Yesterday, free day, no painting, morning after the day of cows and sheep but the morning before porridge, walking stick, the lie. Yes, it is the morning after the evening Giddy opens the bathroom door, proving to Gilbert that there can be such a thing as one bath too many. You must take Catrine to show her Penzance, Giddy, fingers drumming, The town after so much country. You must show her everything Cornwall has to offer.

On the boardwalk, before the games, the arcade and the shoes. Thin clouds, cirrus clouds suggested no rain. Two mornings after the night of the moth. His stomach persisted on this day too, the shoe day, in an on again off again fashion. But he brought her to the water, to the ocean which she hadn't seen in a year. And they sat down next to a great steerhorn for rope sat down the two of them below the railing designed to prevent sitting. He said, Welcome to the Atlantic the very same water as yours back home.

Staring at the ocean, Gilbert gave insight on ablutions, how Bonnard frequently painted women bathing because his wife never stopped, how she never gave him affection of any kind.

Maybe he was repulsive.

On the contrary, he was very handsome.

Maybe he wouldn't take her swimming.

Enough. Enough.

Maybe he was mean to her.

Shall we switch the topic?

Did he expect her to cry for the last time she had ocean, reminded of Mother, Maine. She wouldn't. They sat close together side by side after the moth but before the lie, they looked down at the brine and laughed about Vicar and old Inred, Piers' state of German angst, they smelled the sea together and pointed out a gull or turtle which on closer inspection always became rubbish. Nothing mattered. They looked down upon their remarkably similar shoes swinging off the boardwalk together the leather lace-ups excellent for squashing. Gilbert took her hand when he pointed to a man whose hat was blowing away. And she pulled her hand back as she drew his attention to a faraway ship. Instead of looking to where she pointed, he looked to where she replaced her hand, to her lap, then down to her squashers which is when he said, Time For New Shoes.

What she said she protested she nearly became angry because there was reason for it at least in her book but he insisted leaping up in his short-trousered way babbling about the sky's appearance for rain. They rollicked down the boardwalk screaming, scattering gulls because he tried to take her hand again so she made it a game. Breathing vicarlike up the hilly little town streets past the buttery the odd shop for bonnets or lace until they found a shop displaying winklepickers and sheepskin slippers.

Here we are, Gilbert swung in, leaving her outside pointing to the skinny shoes saying, Well I'm not wearing those. The rain began gently while they were inside. The clerk switched on a light, they were the only customers. Warm in lamplight. Gilbert walked the perimeter, hum, hum, pulling out a red shoe, high heel, an odd assortment. The clerk measured her foot using a metal slide rule. When the man disappeared she said, Mr. Gilbert I can't wear a shoe with a heel like that, I'll tip over. They stared at each other over a disembodied foot pierced by a rod. Sunday service requires a smarter shoe surely. Then the foot came into focus whereupon she laughed, not only because of the cut-off foot but because he sounded so serious. A smarter shoe. She laughed and laughed. Gilbert picked up a galosh, We can experiment at the very least. No harm in experimenting is there?

This one too loud, that one too small. She wavered in the pair with the heel. They came off with a suck. The clerk said, She's got a pair. A pair of what? Oh nothing, said the clerk, nothing at all. Careful mate, Gilbert told him, She's got a temper. Mate, like that like he was better friends with the clerk. I don't like that pair, she said, yes yes perhaps a tad petulant though there was reason enough in her book. Really? Gilbert said, I quite like them. Folding her arms against the best mates in cahoots against the far wall, she said, I find those shoes to be the ugliest in the shop. But as she summed up the sallow clerk in his pathetic frayed elbows, she saw them. Mr. Gilbert, she pointed. Mr. Gilbert.

Mate's name was Steve. Steve went to get them in a five, green shoes with a darker green circle embossed on the front. Timid heel, but she could still run. If she had to. Gilbert said, What's the circle for it looks like someone's dropped a penny on her foot. It's decoration, Steve said. Just for fun.

It's just for fun, Mr. Gilbert. For fun.

You like those?

You don't.

Not as much. I like whichever you choose. I want your happiness.

I'm happy with these.

The dropped penny shoes.

Pennies aren't green.

Well squashed pea then . . . Gilbert reached to pay . . . Are you wearing them?

Of course she was wearing them though first she ensured that Steve had a box for her old shoes, the ones Father bought for her. Of course she was wearing them. Coming out of the store into rain with no umbrella, they darted from doorway to shop awning on down the hill. Gilbert held her shoebox under arm, guiding her always with a hand to her back down the hill down the hill on to the boardwalk on to the arcade. Of course she was wearing them, they made her socks pink by the laundry appear intentionally pink.

Turning her foot as they went inside to wipe off the rain . . . Mr. Gilbert.

I'm buying us tokens.

Mr. Gilbert.

Which games do you like?

Over machines and whistles, sirens and the thwack of paddles, he couldn't hear so she pulled him down to say in his ear . . . Do they really look like mushy peas?

And he laughed his fangish laugh yes your honor the ugly one that breaks her heart, Of course not and lifted her shoe as if he were a blacksmith, pronounced them the most elegant he'd ever seen and had he succeeded in the tiniest way in making her happy? Saying it all into her ear somewhat too loudly for comfort but remembering a time when the smell of him and his sweater but that was in the past and what was the point in thinking about that. The present was now or at least it was then and she said into his ear, Thank you Mr. Gilbert. For my new shoes.

A scream. She turns with Piers who throws his cigarette to the ground leaving her to stomp it. They abandon the boring scenery and run back, nearly knocking over the vicar's metallic easel.

What is it . . . Piers hovers over Thérèse . . . Why is she screaming like that?

Gilbert glances up . . . She'll be alright. It's painful.

Piers picks at his lip and pulls out another cigarette.

Elsewhere if you don't mind . . . Butcher says to him taking the
palette from Thérèse and examining it. She passes it to Gilbert . . .
Think we got it.

Yes . . . he pats Thérèse . . . It's out. You'll be fine.

Thérèse doesn't move . . . I can still feel it.

Likely you've scratched your cornea . . . Butcher pulls back
Thérèse's hair . . . Like with a splinter, you think it's still there. But we
have the evidence. May I see your eye?

Hurts to open it.

Only for a moment, then you can have a nice sleep.

Thérèse opens her eyes looks straight at Catrine then turns for
Butcher's examination. Vicar's comments on cleavers don't emerge.
Butcher looks into corners pulls at the flesh around the girl's eyes mut-
ters a need for the torch she left in the car. I can't see, Thérèse says.
We're fine, Butcher says. No. Everything's blurred, please. I can't see,
Mrs. Ingle.

Close them . . . Butcher pets the coat on the ground . . . Have a
little rest.

Thérèse lies down closes her eyes. They move away.

Gilbert says to Piers, Didn't think I had to give a lecture on safety.
Seems I should have.

Vicar says to Butcher, Now I recall I left the sharpener at home.
Didn't want to risk losing it.

Butcher says to Gilbert, Don't be too hard on the lad. Everyone's
capable of mistakes.

Vicar says to her, Seems you and I are the lucky ones as far as ail-
ments go.

Butcher says to Vicar, What's the point in buying it if we're not
going to use it?

Gilbert says to Butcher, Never thought I was ringmaster of catastrophe.

Vicar says to Gilbert, Now that's apiece dramatic wouldn't you say?

She says to Gilbert, Is that what happens when a splinter comes out? You still feel it?

Piers says to them all, I wish I'd never done it and what's the likelihood of her regaining sight?

They played games for hours, skittles where you threw a ball down a wooden ramp and a game which required you to maneuver a gripper over a host of ugly toys. Her favorite was shooting chickens with a rifle, she won a stuffed frog. He excelled at throwing balls into a basket but never managed five consecutively. And throughout they took turns the two of them to comment on her shoes and what round green thing she had dropped thereon. When she won her frog Gilbert said, It's a frog baby you dropped which was so patently stupid it made the Lilt she was drinking come out her nose and onto the sidewalk. They were on the way home, it was beginning to go dark, it was the last time she laughed that evening. The next day she would discover the lie. In Giddy's lane, they stood together watching a pinkish sunset, the clouds had spun away as they played. When Gilbert said, Another Fauvist sky, she went on walking. At the door, he said, Why not put your other shoes back on, we'll save these to surprise Giddy with some other time. A special occasion perhaps. Sure, she said. Okay by me. He bent to help, she leaned against the windowsill, stockinged foot balanced on the bootscraper. Watching the top of Gilbert's head as he guided her foot back into Father's shoe. He was beginning to thin at the crown.

Is it fear of blindness that has them all hesitant to resume. They hover, some smoke, some reflect. Piers says, Travelers used to go through the alps blindfolded because mountain scenery drove them mad. And Vicar says meanly, Ah was that the plan then with the girl? Gilbert busies himself to not notice the pall the accident has left on his group. And then it becomes impossible, even for a resolute man, not to notice Inred's idle flicking back and forth of her sketches, or Vicar's consumption with his easel's efficiency. The mountain the mountain. And the edelweiss or gulls or is it some chalky patch like the white cliffs of dover or that horse in the hill. Difficult to tell, it seems closer.

Right then . . . Gilbert claps his hands, they turn from the mountain to face him . . . I was planning to address this later this afternoon, after a full day of painting. Over tea in the church hall. But while Thérèse rests, this seems a good time. Vicar, may I? . . . Gilbert borrows Vicar's easel and sets it in front of the group . . . Can you all see? . . . aiming it to Piers who watches Thérèse sleep.

Piers has one final look at his work, sits on the rocks next to Butcher. Gilbert pulls a large sheaf of sketches from his bag. These are his own. He lays them on the ground, chooses one and places it on the easel. A girl in red. The same red now pillowed beneath Thérèse's blind head. Yes for he is saying, One sleepless night he is saying, I painted it from memory. A girl sitting hands across lap eyes downcast. What is she sitting on, a settee, a chair, the seat of a car? He speaks of acrylics which await the group in days to come, he speaks of tone of harmony and scale. He does not mention truth.

On to the next, the red sleeves pushed up, the girl's arms folded, eyes no longer downcast but staring out, reproachful. Likely she makes that very face now. Butcher is saying something, I wish my nights of insomnia were only half so fruitful and Vicar, Girl resembles Catrine here, Vicar is laughing. Vicar is sticking out his teeth and bobbling his stupid head. Calling a vicar stupid might bring down some wrath but the hell with it. To hell with petulance. Gilbert can make her up from pigment, can take her apart by tone and light.

He came upstairs to carry the shoebox. Giddy was out the lights were out and the house needed lights for they had both seen the sun go down had noted the flavorful sunset. It was the night before she discovered he lied a white lie. A small act the kiss, determined. It was the night before the morning Giddy asked her not to wear the tunic and the house was dark except for one light in the kitchen, obese Mouser bumping against them Gilbert saying, Well her car's not here adjusting the shoebox she didn't need him to carry. He sat on the moquette, she brought out the new shoes, they looked on them, he was so pleased. He looked at her. But a sweep of lights across the far wall had him hurrying out to light up the corridor and his bedroom downstairs. She remained in the dark holding the shoes. That night, the night before the lie, it was clear she would never wear them again.

My homage to David . . . Gilbert picks up a new drawing.

And there she is slumped over in the bath, back up like a cat, looking out at them all with reproach or was it rebuke. It was the Re-'s she failed in Betts' test.

You know about Bonnard of course . . . her voice rings out, high, unusual.

Sorry, Catrine? . . . he looks up, a finger tracing light along her painted shoulder.

He forced his wife into baths all the time . . . oh this is strange . . . Made his wife scrub herself bloody she repulsed him so.

Gilbert presses his lips to stop himself.

When she met him she was a sweet girl from a village in Flanders where her family raised sheep and sold them at market or made sweaters from the wool. In the spring she helped her father shave them up . . . turning from them, Butcher's amusement to the mountain yes that white is definitely closer now it looks like a figure but she is forever finding things where they are not . . . She met Bonnard his name was and he convinced her that she was so dirty she should always take a bath . . . turning back . . . In fact it was his greatest wish in life that she never wear any clothes at all.

The story I'm familiar with suggests that she hated him.

Maybe she did but not at first. Maybe she got tired of having prunes for fingers.

Well, Catrine, this is all very amusing. You're amusing us greatly but the others in the group are paying for—

Your great wisdom—

Just—

On how to see.

Alright—

What you know might be different from what you see, have you told them that?

Sit down, Evans, this is no longer amusing, your dramatics are getting very very stale. And very silly.

They're paying for your opinion on whether they are or are not wild beasts.

I said sit down . . . Gilbert snaps.

Butcher looks up at her, mystified.

But you haven't even asked us, we could go around the circle, Mr. Gilbert, we could all tell about our own experiences with things like perspective. We could describe what it means to have an eye, Vicar could show us how the nude can be a mountain and Butcher could . . . now she's crying in front of all of them, it's not in control . . . Butcher could—

Gilbert is by her has his arms around her, the others are bewildered in her watery focus, Vicar beetles an eyebrow, she is crying. Gilbert says, What an unusual day for girls, is it the moon, a planet's retrograde path. She lets him stroke her hair, how could he put her up on an easel as if she were a tree. In the bath. When he knew how happy she was about the new red cardigan, the one she hates because right before he did it he said I rarely see you in color. And then he did it kissed her with his tongue like that.

Gilbert says, How do you feel about calling it a day. The white gone, it was a gull. It's a day, says Vicar and the others move away to pack up the paints and Gilbert's hand moving in the soothing now his mouth in her hair now.

Gilbert pulls away sharply. She wipes her face looks at him. His face is distorted. She looks where he does but cannot make sense of it. Gilbert says, What On Earth. Vicar and Butcher huddled over sketches together on the rocks, Piers prostrate at the feet of Thérèse, but now the figure of a man emerges at the crest of the hill transforming from a white spot into the figure of an amateur botanist, booming as he approaches, I THOUGHT AS MUCH.

Mr. Betts?

Miss Evans. Mr. Gilbert . . . Betts before them in the clearing, rucksacked, rugged, alpine wonder. Neatly combed, what there is of it, unflustered. It sounds a contrivance, how can it be, but you see the teacher has been there all along.

Gilbert takes his hands to his hips, whitening, lips go thin . . . Now you can hardly tell me this is some sort of coincidence.

No no. Wouldn't attempt to convince you of that . . . Betts takes her in, a deputized air to him . . . Miss Evans?

She looks back to the mountain, where did he—

Has this man harmed you in any way?

How did . . . Gilbert is shaking . . . Did you *follow* us?

Catrine Evans, answer my question.

That day on the balcony . . . Gilbert jabs his finger.

Has he?

Patrick . . . Gilbert barks . . . Listen to me . . . Betts looks over . . . That was no coincidence either was it? Harrington?

Coincidence is in the eye of the beholder . . . Betts swivels back to her . . . Wouldn't you say?

What's this all about . . . Gilbert glances over at Vicar and Ingle who have taken the distraction as an opportunity to pilfer a cigarette from Piers and share a smoke. Gilbert flashes her a strained smile, rolling his eyes to say, who would've believed it of old Betts.

This, Mr. Gilbert, and in no way do I wish to embarrass you . . . Betts takes down his rucksack . . . Is about your abduction of the American girl.

Abduction?

He didn't abduct me.

And who's to say you know what abduction is, hm? . . . Betts folds his arm . . . That day I found you with him on the balcony I gave some thought to my prior accusations of your character.

Calling me pornographic, you mean.

Yes. And in the heat of that moment on the playing fields . . . he pauses . . . As well as several times thereafter, it seemed a logical . . . searching . . . Conclusion to draw no pun intended or perhaps it was, I'm not certain.

Patrick—

Holding up a hand for silence, Betts out-herods Herod . . . The day I came upon you two at Harrington, engaged as it were in art, I gave quite a bit of thought to complicity and the idea of being led astray. We thought, I hope you won't feel I've been indiscreet, Evans, I spoke with Madame Araigny about it at length, and together we thought, how can a child, a girl, come across such notions on her own?

She has her own.

We surmised that the fault therefore must lie in the elder. A responsibility. The adult. He with the wisdom of age at his disposal.

Patrick, this is ludicrous, you jumping out of the trees like a cuckold in a bedroom farce—

An interesting analogy, Mr. Gilbert, to say the least.

—formulating the most appalling theories. I am teaching Catrine. This is a painting trip.

Teaching what, I'd like to know.

Don't be obscene.

Mr. Gilbert I have just come upon you with the girl in your arms.

The child is here staying with my mother.

I needn't remind you, you said it yourself. A child.

Yes, if you wouldn't mind keeping your voice down, that is a Man of God over there, I'm sure he has no wish to overhear your disgusting speculations.

I think we should ask the girl.

Are you so unhappy with your own life, Patrick, that you seek to meddle—

I have a cousin in Truro I thought, why not pop down—

Shouldn't you be in France?

French trip ended on Saturday. I'm surprised you've forgotten since you were scheduled to go. But then, you canceled, didn't you? Coincidentally, soon after it was apparent the American girl wouldn't be going . . . chomping the scenery . . . I was responsible for your father denying permission. I thought it wasn't wise for—

Wise for what exactly, Patrick?

Betts strolls over to Gilbert . . . For you to get the poor child sloshed on cheap wine so as—

For Christ's sake. Does she look unhappy to you? Is she bolting down the mountainside at the first sign of help? You're a sorry man. With perverted delusions. Go home. Go back to Chittock Leigh, put your feet up and enjoy the rest of the Easter holidays. And leave me to finish teaching.

At Harrington, you told me that teaching meant giving of oneself. Is this what you had in mind?

And what is *this*? Go on ask her . . . Gilbert takes the rock from his pocket tosses it up then catches it . . . Catrine, say something.

Betts reaches out for the rock . . . That's a nice piece of shale mind if I—? . . . he examines it, licks it . . . May I keep this?

This is all in a day's work to you, is it?

I rang the father . . . Betts says mildly, tugging at his rucksack.

What? . . . she has never heard him shout . . . What? . . . Vicar starts from the perch he shares with Butcher . . . You've done what? . . . even Piers raises his head from Thérèse's feet . . . How dare you you . . . they are all mad, broken, a party of explorers off the rails . . . Are you . . . spluttering . . . Some kind of lunatic. You've really lost your mind haven't you. Nothing's happened, Betts, you'll upset her father for nothing, the man entrusted—

And now the man's entrusted me with bringing his daughter back safely.

Catrine . . . Gilbert puts his hands on his waist hip jutting leg contrapposto you can smell him your first weeks in Chemistry you can smell his hydrogen his helium. That nap on his pillow when he compressed you. When he leaned to your forehead. When all you wanted was. Well it's time to know.

Butcher and Vicar appear, eager in their rucksacks to join the tableau. Betts asks what happened to Thérèse. A point went in her eye. Gilbert whispers, Please Catrine. He will have to speak up if they are to hear him in the back. Please tell the truth. You will remember that as the equation between what you see and what you know. He was the one who said I would have liked your mother, her democratic paintings but who also found ill mothers fit for lies. Who took away the chips. Who stayed. Who would have thunk it, Vicar would say who would have thunk he'd need her like this.

She takes the painted handkerchief from the bag strapped across her chest. Holds the cloth cold, hard in places where the paint has dried. Her Gilbert original. He smiles at her, he knows what she will say, she will make it alright because she is a girl who can see consequences. A girl with a sense of timing. Comic. After all this time, she has finally learned. Who would have thunk it would take as long as it did. No one can protect you in the end. She smooths her tunic.

He kissed me.

Silence.

With his tongue and lied. He put his hands . . . folding the handkerchief into a neat grid . . . Where I didn't want them.

Her voice sings out, clear in the air above the muddle of the others.

Gilbert's face fails . . . Oh no . . . he squeaks . . . What have you done?

You see . . . Betts trumpets, placing his arm around her . . . I knew he wasn't to be trusted.

She pulls away. Butcher's head swivels from Catrine to Betts to Gilbert while Vicar's gaze remains on her, as if her speech bears no relation to her mouth.

Who are you? . . . Butcher asks Betts.

Mr. Betts extends a hand to Mrs. Ingle . . . Colleague of Mr. Gilbert's . . . to Vicar . . . I had some worries about the girl, her well-being. I took it upon myself, I have a cousin in Truro, do you know a Kelley, um. So I drove down to see for myself.

See what for yourself? . . . Vicar croaks out . . . Is there some sort of problem? Mr. Gilbert?

Vicar, Mr. Betts belongs to a higher order of moral authority than you or I. He has convinced himself that my intentions toward Miss Evans are immoral.

Well you heard the girl yourself. She said you kissed her.

Is that what you were saying . . . Vicar looks at her . . . I couldn't make it out.

Catrine . . . Butcher at child level, hands on knees . . . Is what you say true? Did Mr. Gilbert kiss you?

With his tongue?

Ingle shoots Mr. Betts a look.

Mr. Gilbert looks away to the mountain, hands still on hips. He looks down at his cuffs his shoes. He bought a pair for her only yesterday, they laughed about the green circles, about stupid things like frogs, how pennies weren't green. Such a distance. An insignificant height.

He thought it's what I wanted.

Nonsense . . . Butcher straightens . . . You're fourteen. You don't know what you want. You barely have a mind of your own.

Lucy . . . Gilbert protests . . . That's hardly fair. You've spent time with the girl. Listen to the way she speaks. She has her own ideas. She's not entirely innocent here.

Mrs. Ingle walks over to Gilbert his hands at his sides dejected shoulders she dejected him what did she do does she have a mind of her own. Butcher stands in front of Gilbert Butcher raises back her hand and smacks Gilbert hard across the face.

Even Betts seems sorry for that. Vicar looks bewildered but makes no comment on cleavers. Then Ingle leans in and they all hear her say . . . If there was more to it than that, I'll kill you.

Don't. Don't hurt him . . . taking Butcher by the wrist to pull her away from Gilbert . . . Don't kill him.

Gilbert puts no hand to his cheek, allows it to redden in full view.

A brief interval. Buy some chocolates, stretch the legs.

Gilbert breaks the silence . . . She is fourteen, not ten.

Betts takes a step away . . . I wouldn't be surprised if ten year—

No . . . Gilbert interrupts . . . This is rapidly becoming absurd. It was a mistake, it was in some—moment. Vicar. I hardly brought the girl up here for evil intentions, Patrick. Mrs. Ingle, you've known me for how many years?

Suddenly it doesn't seem like very many.

You shouldn't be entrusted with the well-being of children.

Patrick, I have more interest and concern for my pupils than—

Well it's the type of interest that's the concern.

I don't have to put up with this . . . calling . . . Piers, Thérèse, we're going back down, collect your things.

I'll see to it that you won't return to teaching.

He turns to her . . . Wasn't I decent to you?

You were obsessed with her . . . Betts suggests.

I thought about her, she filled my thoughts. Don't make a monster of me.

She looks at him his hair trying to get him exactly right to capture him in the light of the mountains, the green behind him, new grass, too-short cuffs.

I lost my head, it was a moment of weakness. I love her like a—

A sister, like Rosie?

No, I love you like yourself, like my very own Punchinello. I never made you into something you weren't, into some replacement, some—

Analogy.

Catrine, tell me I helped you. Tell me I gave an accumulation of moments, however small. No one else gave you such love, not the school, not your father.

Well this is all very sentimental . . . Betts hoists up his rucksack . . . But we should be moving on. Get the girl's things. I promised her father I'd get her home by tonight.

No . . . Gilbert puts up a hand . . . I want to explain myself.

I think your desires have been indulged quite enough as it is.

Perhaps we should let him have a moment with her before we go . . . Butcher stops . . . What do you think, Vicar?

Vicar has spent this time mostly in a state of preventative asthma, mouth open, eyes agoggle . . . I'm not following any of this.

Alright . . . Betts walks away . . . But we're to watch from a short distance and he's not to touch her.

Fair enough.

Vicar puts his arm through Butcher's as they walk away mumbles, Is it the girl, has she, trailing away and Betts turns back once as he follows Butcher and Vicar to where Piers has been taking so long to help Thérèse put on his coat and open her eyes.

7

There you have it, a real drama. In the car reverse of only three days ago days of sheep shoes tunic mornings of kedgeree and lies nights of moth bathtub and moquette. Unto the place whence these rivers come thither they return. Telegraph poles bob and fall as the Amateur Botanist winds up the window with jerks face reflected in the glass when we come into a tunnel. I turn away. The window of a triumph turns you grotesque. Warped. And on through the county of mirrors where mothers draw only curtains and baths and maybe the odd conclusion. Who'd a thunk it. Vicar in the hallway his teeth more protrusive than ever who'd a thunk it from the teacher always thought him a man after my heart man of God etcetera but you never can tell what brews beneath the surface. Driving Inred in his Deux Chevaux why only this morning Lucy the man ruined a shirt helping me change my flat who'd a thunk he could mistake a girl for a man on a horse cantering next to the car for half a field but the sky darkens he should get back lest his horse trap a fetlock in a foxhole. We must forgive him he knows not. Well John I think he knows very well what he does I'm in no mood at this point on and on through counties of worried mothers of horsey mothers. Country where a mother stood next to a car as it plumed exhaust into a winter morning and said That's a coat suited more for fall than winter. At the top of the stairs so that looking up she ends at the knees and you know only her hem. Please do not leave me here on my knees. Sun burns down the sky into a haze of yellow like gassed nothing so wild anymore. Past houses off the main road into a town past the founder's statue gaggle of boys kicking at a ball or dog now parking for a dairy milk. I'll wait for you. I'll wait for you here. And Betts returns with an armload and a grin with chocolates as there are only chocolates in the end. No Lilt. Should have asked. Or he should have known just by looking that a Lilt was in order. You came at me full force like a train but perhaps because they are in a tunnel that occurs first. Why won't it rain when a scene demands rain. The forest dances heavy with music. Body up again first light again. Libraries never hold what they should. Once her yellow hair danced a bauble in the candleflame. There's an emptiness don't guess what it is when you haven't the foggiest. The yellow miasma shrouding towns with ham at the end on the table past smokestacks putting their own thoughts into the evening into the setting of a hazy sun. I am leaving you. I am racing away speechless for you have taken my tongue I had to give you something why do I need to ever speak again if that's what a tongue is capable of then blast all tongues. I will never speak again except to say I want to say I only had distant knowledge of him. Oh that's all wrong as usual. For the defense I feel still the pang of a despisèd love. That's my final word. Except to say What's it all for. Maltesers Benny would say Dairy Milk. No one here knows Benny and no one here can tell me whether that merited an eighty-five or a ninety-two. Something fairly high surely. Yes surely. I will say only that they will not pry it from me no matter the pressure applied no pliers no wheedling. Foods of foreign and exotic origin placed before me in efforts to cajole. I will only belch out Surely. That is my final word on the matter. This wasn't how it was supposed to be. This isn't how I began it. Surely I could have done it some other way. Surely it could have resolved itself differently. We could live on a cliff by the sea we could no you see no no there is no point in you have not learned anything. Please it was all my fault. I never saw you coming. Give the next man some warning. Hum. Flash of highbeams. You are the same fool you began. Orgon. You took the mask for the face. Cows lying in a field it will rain no time to stop for a sit and a chat devonshire cows might up and carry you away. Abduct you and you only want sleep. He has a photograph of a boy sleeping against a cow it hangs in the kitchen next to a cupboard he bought along with old old medical dictionaries but that is really all I'm willing to say on it. Yes yes your tongue flapping in your head American let it go Lavinia what story can you possibly have that might interest a faction of us. Your tongue loosed in your mouth like a ferret among rabbits like a clapper in a bell as well as well. No one listens not even you it is simply to chime out the hour to hear it ring every half and on. Better not to speak at all. As you promised only moments ago. Better to sit quietly hands in tunic lap bereft of art. The very ecstasy of love. She has her own ideas he said as though it were a curse. Least of all this darkening country wants to know your wild ideas. The console lit up like a plane's. Single engine over northern africa. Scattering gazelles in four directions as they come down for a landing. Father waiting at Felmar. Getting out from the triumph tunic still neat kickpleat with a kick to it. He'll see his old bicycling bag slung across her aren't you clever to have put it to such a use he'll say what have you got in there only my very special brushes which were a gift only a pear bruised beyond recognition with a thumbish cut in it what happened to your tongue you're speaking so strangely It was bitten off in a freakish accident I used to have art papa in my or your special bag it was an original given to me by an artist who made his trade by the profession of science but I gave it back for it stopped pleasing me. My that old bag of mine has seen some interesting sights. Oh yes Father oh yes racing madly around the house like a dog fresh from the car like a child screeching Let's fix up the pool Let's play the piano. Father will stand next to the triumph postponing the moment to speak of the automobile's handling capacity. He will wear wool with a press down the center of each leg. He will place his hands behind his back one cupped in the other as if to approach a nervous horse. The driver stuffed with chocolate staving off pins and needles in his right leg. What about the potting shed I promised you a place to paint. Oh Father I must be the one to tell you. It's a sad case but I have no eye. If you have the passion for it what matter if you are not so talented. Passion? Father? For art? Art is the least passionate subject I can imagine. I have more interest in war. Oh there are wars of all sorts roses worlds or wars lasting only seven days. Wars in Arabia where mercy might be passion or simply good manners. You have learned so much in such a short time. Yes but my knowledge cannot be trusted for I also learned that at fourteen I barely have a mind of my own. She could have taken her cleaver to him could have cleaved him in two old Ingle as the sky was cleaved by far-off trees. She had only distant knowledge of him for as a butcher she is better acquainted with cuts of meat with her old friend the vicar with whom she may or may not have shared more than a pencil sharpener. They may for example they may have holed up together in some inn at Land's End to escape the prying eyes of Vicar's wife. And like those famous sheep well gone astray. In the top room with sloped ceilings featuring a smell they discuss in their nervous adulterating undressing as camphor or death. Lying largely pink and naked in the drafty bed in a pool of light from a wonky desk lamp Vicar exploring the inglenook Butcher saying Stop the accents John just for the weekend for it seems I'm to be the one to inform you how annoying they are. Who'd a thunk—Vicar says before he can stop himself luckily Butcher shuts him up by clamping her mouth on his. And they roll and roll on and on past a pub disco spelled out in forlorn lights past a white place selling chicken. You will go in you will say good night to Father wearing the nightgown his gift for the trip. Or is that wise the lace collar might provoke nasty associations of executions in one or the other of you. No. Downstairs in the old pyjamas downstairs for hot milk with golden syrup because you hear it may cure sleeplessness which might plague you or might not but sounds delicious nonetheless. You will not want to discuss it tonight he will not press the topic he will follow you into the kitchen and ask if he might not have some hot milk too just when it's coming to a boil so you have to add more and wait. In his smart creased trousers he will sit on the counter to bong his heels as he always did in Maine. A distant aunt in Cheshire wants to take you into her home. He says this as he picks up the Lyles and says What's this for. Well what's it all for. You will take the green tin from him and set it down gently you will inform him it is to put in the milk as it will taste good that way. You will make Father a croque monsieur without him asking and when you press down the sandwich to make it sputter you will say I am alright Father. You will say I do not want to go live in Cheshire with whomever she is because I have friends at Monstead. They went to France. And Brickie brought back a postcard for me. He didn't know the address. Look he said It's all going to be different between us this term. I ask did he have a marzipan cake upon his return and what shape did it take. I say We have shared things you and I Brickie. You thought I'd be one of the lucky ones. But they'll get us all. Doubt not. Pieces in their games go chess we will next year become rook knight Bishop of St. Lieven the King of Athens but still only choose black or white squares. Oh Brickie is it really so bad. Through the arch heat from the laundry on a winter day a full plate of chips no need for bread the smell of autumn the promise of spring. No I'm an optimist. I know. The vaguery. Waking at night to see my jumble my grey lying on the chair tuck key aglint from some caught moonlight the breathing of the other eight to think This is my world my entire world a world without end. I am this Catrine so small I could evaporate. I wanted boaters not fires Brickie. I never expected you to see my life ebb and flow in the waffle of these shoes but if you are bound hand by foot to your own bed tell me that the welts disappear. Tell me that your stomach will quell for now it rises up where bed used to be a pleasure albeit a horsehair one now it is a fright but that too will pass and you will trust in sleep again. But this is all petty. I portray myself as shallow. What am I asking you who reveal nothing you who taunted me for weeks over some slight of my father's. Should he have taken the gun and aimed for a leg? Brickie let's not let this come between us Brickie come here with your cold eyes pull back your hair let some light in you see it's not so bad I know I know it took me a long time to realize. We drive toward summer when the tuck shop sells ice cream. I wanted you to say nice things I wanted you to tell me what you found in the crystal ball of my shoe. We had the shop girl and the glue we had your father and his padded fingers we had Paul. We both knew. I watched you as you watched me did you really think those times your black bastard eyes sought out mine that mine rested elsewhere. He bought me new green shoes but in the end those squashed as well. Over a bridge dark water rushing underneath boys with their poles in the water now the last of the light and Father will wait the house all dark but one light in the bedroom for he's caught up in reading. He'll want to know about the horsepower and ask the Botanist in for a drink. Now gasoline and finally a can of Lilt off again because there are Miles to Go. Do something do something. I wanted judgment conclusion I wanted morality to *ariiise* from my wild bestial plane. But I was always doomed for down. You have choice in the matter dear girl there's always a choice dear girl. Car speeds north leaving what little spring we had. Cornwall. Head against the metal door your face will hold wrinkles. Elasticity winnowing out. Skin and nails shedding. Leaving little bits of yourself on settees and trains. Stretching away until you die. Apologize to Bea say I'm sorry I never really heard when you spoke of him singling me out I was more entranced by the word than the meaning I'm sorry I never paid much attention to motivations which I took to be the bastard cousin of my enemy consequences. And you were there with Stokes visiting the same inn as Vicar and Butcher in Land's End with old Cyclops on sabbatical from his wife you came down to Cornwall you fancied a sherry he made up for not understanding why a girl sets a fire by pouring you an extra large one in glasses brought all the way from Chittock Leigh wrapped in his undershorts by holding open the door to the Indian restaurant he demonstrated it very well. And that night even more so. I'm sorry Bea forgive me Bea I'm a girl in a car a girl in a car. I am this Catrine. I was beginning Bea I was beginning to see how paths were laid down I was beginning to understand it was all up to me. I wanted to admit myself to the clutch saying You Are This. Am I petulant am I a beast don't I care for others at all? Why take refuge in him. Days pass hours pass with the cars rushing past I am in Maine a girl seldom alone I am here always alone I am in France eating madeleines with you I am a girl without her tire. Without Isabelle. The man got up and walked away. The man got up brushed off his knees looked once up the hill then back to where the tire landed he shook his head once he shook his head again *Well that's an anomaly in these parts*. The man took a piece of paper which had attached itself to his hip threw it back to the ground. He straightened his helmet righted his motorcycle. He was off again before you knew it. His face set against the road the scarce traffic. Sky could not be any clearer. We will arrive back at Felmar safely and recognize it is not Maine or Cornwall or Chittock Leigh. Not London where a man bends in half-light to sew. I do not look out this window into rain. Asleep I dream I drive I am a woman who complains in shops the woman who sighs the queue is too long the chops too fatty. The streets are not safe. Lock up your children. Hello I say Welcome to my lecture. I won't be hidden I won't be nude. I won't clack out from discreet doors. Well what's the point of showing a book of art in a museum full of it. The answer's so obvious. So one will know what one sees. Not everyone lives in a precarious balance for consequences they can barely fathom. They want to know this will happen C if you add A to B. Not like you poor girl raging from one moment to the next. A tsunami of consequence. Hello I say, Welcome to my lecture. I post it on the door. Wild beasts cannot be allowed to roam our heaths at will. At night untold damage has been done to flowering grasses in their natural state. Do not fight over the squish each boy will get his own if he does his best for England. If not I'm afraid you live by the sword you die by the sword. What one knows one must know with a sword in one's hand. No running on wet floors. Let me go please let me go. She will be there when you return the first the rest come tumbling running out of School House they will pile on each other frisking like puppies barking to know the adventures you had on the cliffs but she will stand off to one side while they tell you the troubles they had with abstract nouns. And when they shut up and you are still quiet she will shoo them away to have a word. Oh this is what I dragged you up for this debauchery? You forget ma'am you are not my mother. Well could it be you need a replacement? It will never be you. And she will perch on her enormous desk strewn with papers in her hideous stockings the color of mushrooms you cannot help yourself you imagine her underthings the straps the heavy material war remnants strong enough for missiles and similar in shape. Can it be your father is not doing his job as a parent? You leap from your chair she has thrown down the gauntlet. You Maggone have insulted my honor. Sit child sit we are not serving in the French legion away with these dramas of yours. At some point perhaps at that moment she rises to press her matronly self against your neck. And you leave the flat for a cliff in Cornwall. To say. Mrs. Ingle I understand you wear red for slapping. Thank you for all manner of advice. But I won't grow old. Won't catch me stopping long enough. I want a tunic for every day. I can be different even as I am the same. Even as we wake in uniform. I am thewy. This driver gave me the word. Motorway lights flash from the opposite path we keep moving Father awaits. Tomorrow he will make us a pancake in the shape of a mousehead the ears will run into the side of the pan and fold but you will know it for a mouse because it is always a mouse. He will sit across from you expectantly wonder when you learned to drink all that tea it can't be good for you but then so few things are. Let's fix up the pool Let's paint the walls that's the only sort of painting I want. Sort he'll say sort. You are getting some sort of accent is what sort. And you'll bite a bite that should be an ear but it's an accordion for your delight. I don't need to be American any more those white patches we left behind I've forgotten it all you'll say for his alarm then laugh then sip some orange juice which you actually hate. Good pancake mouse right? Smile as you pour more syrup. What will he do. What is he doing right this moment staring into his embering fire. Running water for another bath. He will want to feel clean for he has been made to feel so dirty. Asking the fire what went wrong what were his intentions I mean she has a mind of her own and anyone can tell you fourteen is not ten. Down at his foot encased in a slipper playing with the sash to his dressing gown. He is in Cornwall she is between them I love you I love you my Punch my sugar water you saturate. Please don't evanesce my anomaly my Marxist you held your waist as if you wanted mine but we never danced staring down at the robe in his hands he fixed your skin made it cover you back up as was originally intended. He will say no to dinner tired of toads but yes to cocoa which helps him feel it's all been a skinned knee. Look back in anger. There will be a tribunal. You have been paying her unwanted attentions not true not true the line down the middle not true not true the yellow line. They were wanted. Some of them. Most of them. You return from circumnavigating the globe on a motorcycle you walk into the lab with your hair in control. He sets down the book he's reading aloud to another form another year another ten years of that looks at you over them he finally bought glasses couldn't see the board about a year ago. Well hello he'll say and his trousers hit the same spot they did the day you left you are as tall as he no you are taller he wants to take you to lunch in the dining hall for yellow salad cream and custard. The class waits for your answer there you are in the last row the girl with a hunch in her back she wishes she could disappear evident in the part of her she can never make straight her back or shins or hair evident in what she sees in him. And lunch. You must decline you have been to escoffier but you will take a turn around those playing fields for odd time's sake. There's the spot you were with the boys there's the spot of the old pavilion. He greys. Remember old Aurora Dyer you say she burned the pavilion down to toast whatever happened to her. Who knows my memory these days my memory works like a sieve. And no matter how you describe Aurora the wild days with chemicals he can't remember. But it is not Monstead at all not if our Botanist has anything to do with it. Who knows if you will find him again who knows if it won't all just flame out once and die. But we have seen worse things than kisses in our day French or otherwise. When it snowed and he was kind enough to let her stay she slept on his pillow slept as she hadn't in a month yes she discovered paintings. No she didn't need to be told they were of Fi Hammond. They were like enough. The moment she saw them together in Bath. But there were times he marveled yes she saw it in his eyes What Goes Through This Mind it meant something it meant something. Like Piers I am leaking. Like Thérèse I am blind. There was a poinsettia design painted on wood Mother hated Father loved the old refrigerator you covered with stickers. I can't remember any of it. I have the disease the one in the movies a blow to the head. You recalled Father sitting on that counter heels slamming. Try. The bevel to the flatware a chunk out of the lintel the swing the stairs took weeding the hump in the middle of the driveway gravel sticking to your knees turning to see why she called from the porch how you couldn't see her for the sun. Father's first steps toward having enough. The kitchen the tile. Mother looked down said What good is this apron I have a postage stamp tied around my waist. And she stopped wearing aprons which was a pity because she had such a collection. The lace the jokes the see-through the plaid. That was the kitchen. It was where she heard war by radio and undercooked the meat. They had to put it back in halfway through. Waiting with empty plates forks upright and Nixon. The table was wood not plastic pitted and gouged not cracked with rivers. Buildings the outskirts of London they are rushing home take longer last longer I don't know what to tell my father. The driver asks about Easter. You are not a man I can tell. I have sentenced myself to Lovely to Marvelous to details on table settings or preparations for lamb noting concoctions of jelly or arrangements of flowers so as to have something to say in a moment like this. It was lovely we went to a family a friend of my father's they are a family I love so much by the name of Mitchells. Details girl a lie is known by the lack of details. They have a dog a shepherd I think. Or is it retriever or collie or mix. Details details. They have a house. Oh she fails she sinks it's obvious by his silence. And now you know what you will do from now on you cannot tell the truth you are obviously a miserable liar so you question you interrogate you frown with concentration giggle when it's appropriate you jolly you prod you cajole you simper pull the story from him whichever one it is he really wants to tell. And so it is France he talks about Araigny the food and the views well they were magnifique he will confide because he's feeling so fine he has it in mind to ask for divorce. It took a special talent on your part to extricate that. His jolly French vacances. Anything to switch off his voice offer God your eternal soul. Take me back turn the car around this has all been a dreadful mistake. It was never anything. I want to tell authentic stories I want to tell jokes to bring up my score. I want to be silly but I will go back back to her gripping my wrist wrenching my hands from my pockets I will return to her stares. I had that man's tongue in my mouth his hands in places his. And he took out my tongue he took out my tongue. There is no one there for you anymore. No one will take you to art. He fixed my skin. And now you are crying and pressing your face into the cold dark window as if you could float out into the night. He's there outside the window for you as he was in the beginning as he was that first day struggling over your suitcase. And after Paul he was kind he said Paul is a bad apple only he failed to mention that he was one too. Yes I'm fine I'm fine coming down with something. Let it go girl let it go. Lilt gone can crushed into a sticky pineapple smell underfoot with the purple foil. Do not leave me here on my knees. There it was spinning away from me like this road caught in the headlights then pass passing how did I know the Botanist would appear like that come crashing out with accusations. Because of foresight you say extrapolation. Well it all got away from me. I couldn't see them yes the consequences I'm always on about. I'm sorry forgive me. I wanted it to stop I wanted to catch my breath I didn't want everything taken away. Open the window a crack for air the hot blast of the heater suffocates. Oh I'm quite alright upset stomach yes a bit a bit I need the window open I need an end to politeness and matching towels I need to go back to the way it was between us when it was alright when we bicycled when you thought about wearing clips the first time we saw Courbet together or on the balcony when you rested your chin on your hand and suggested We and We Alone Are Significant. Back to the cinema because you love a train station good-bye good-bye. They left us alone at Giddy's but not in the bedroom. I said good-bye to the moquette on my own when I went to get the suitcase. In the drawing room you plinked a key you said this is the famous piano from the days of Rosie. And I sat down next to you as I had done so many times it seemed like a thousand times it seemed like my whole life or at least the very best part of it we sat side by side leg to leg they were in the kitchen admiring Giddy's collection of wedgwood you went down on your knees to look in my eyes you said no matter what Punchinello this was never your fault I made some stupid mistakes it could be I ruined your life it could be I'm a very bad man I have perhaps I have passions I shouldn't have I hurt you I hurt you I said yes you did but you were the only one who cared about me you started to cry my knees were all wet you said there are many people who care about you we've all just got such fucked-up ways of showing it. I had never heard you swear so that was a treat but I was sobbing too I said I'm never going to see you again it's all different and different in a bad way you said you never know we are optimists you and I all things will come out in the wash wash what wash I put my hand out to your hair but I had never touched you like that you wrapped your arms around my knees you said All Betts are off aren't they? I leaned over you couldn't see me take one final smell the place where your hair gets so short I touched your hair even though the promise of no touching had been made I can't keep a promise I said I never could he said you've kept all the ones you made to me you came when you promised. I said what happened that day you said Oh Catrine I knew even then it was all wrong I knew even then this was a downhill track to nowhere fast so I tried to stop no that's a lie I forgot I forgot we had a plan you didn't matter to me at all I cared not a whit no that's a lie too it was Fi and Dido we were having a threesome no it's untrue it's fibs and stories all of it. It never happened. You said will you be happy here in our country. I wanted to be petulant though anyone would agree there was reason enough for anger but you knew it would break him so you got hold of some of that famous strength you're certain you have and you said Yes I will Squeak. I will be happy here. He looked up at you all wet a mess to be frank he said I'm glad for that then after a silence he said Did you call me Squeak? Squeak? How could you? then he laughed and laughed even though you didn't say it to be funny then he said for that you get a one hundred percent. That's inflation I said which I'm learning in maths. Is that because there's no further opportunity for advancement like that I said it like I was Miss Maggone. Yes he said. Sadly enough that's the case. In that case I said I got up to go we could hear them getting nervous outside I want to tell you that you always rated one hundred in my book. Oh God you said like you were going to cry but you put your hand on top of my head like I was a teapot you led me outside. And off the motorway to the final small roads to Felmar where hot milk awaits. Father comes out in slippers and scarf he puts his hand on your shoulder as if the two of you stand in a painting. You say to no one not your driver or your father but to yourself you say I Am Not A Science Girl. You say I am made from grief from chocolate and air not from atoms not from paint. Dear Father I want to have character I don't want to be compromised. I am not harmonious my legs have wills of their own they grow at different rates and one likes north the other west. My neck can collapse will drop my head at the slightest provocation. It will roll off to land in the gutter or on a doily. I watch my wrist the line it forms with my thumb and pen. Watch as I ratchet my shoelaces to keep my feet attached to their ankles tighten my moneybelt to keep my halves together. This collection of spares. But the tunic the kickpleat the outline suggest a plan for harmony. You led me outside the pacing stopped. Vicar looked at me finally he understood. You smiled at everyone because it was a Misunderstanding. Giddy leaned in a doorframe she wouldn't look at me but told Butcher to come by later and she'd show her the crocus. Butcher said have you had your good-bye yes you said yes we've said good-bye. At some point crossing the parlor and out the door you managed to smooth your hair so as not to appear untidy. The Amateur Botanist said it will all be over soon and you said you only had the girl's best interests at heart. He wouldn't answer he wanted to help me into my coat he wanted to take my little case we all take up so much room in the corridor coatrack overflowing with all the company. No hard feelings you said your hand out to him he shook it without looking at you wouldn't look at me so I watched your hand on the doorknob behind you turning white as you gripped it camouflaging your scar. I am trying to tell you one thing I am trying to tell you well what if that night the night of the moth the night you sat on the bed the night you closed the door forever what if well. Couldn't we have ourselves back. Why did we. I wish we had never stopped for chips I wish the sunset had been pink and light not purple not red I wish it had never led you to Fauvism. He took me out to his car his hand still on my shoulder I wouldn't take my eyes off you no matter how impolite it was when Vicar and Mrs. Ingle were saying good-bye. You said how long have you been driving this machine Patrick it's not the one we see you with at school. Oh this I use for scaring around the countryside. It was his triumph we knew it would be. The one he drives toward Araigny to ask for her hand. I got in the car I still had Father's bag strapped around me I wouldn't wear my coat what was the point I opened the door I looked back and saw you off to one side Giddy in the cautious doorway so as not to let in the draft you held one arm crooked in the other a breeze disturbed your hair my knees buckled I wanted to be strong I wanted to be thewy God help me have thews I ran back up the steps I pulled open my bag you looked confused I took the pear by mistake my thumb cut the soft skin left some meat under my nail I pushed it aside to find what I wanted the driver climbing out to pull us apart I was aware the expression I had was severe my eyebrows drawn up as if you were going over the edge of a cliff I was throwing you a rope but all I had was the handkerchief I balled it into your palm you took it you knew what it was you said You Know I said Yes or maybe I only thought it but I meant to say it I meant to say Yes you are my one hundred. Pick up the fruit and nut the purple foil because you like to have something to squeeze. There were penguins from a machine. And you had them again the day of the mudscape. He had machines explode on him in bus stations but he protected you. He said you are a wild beast you have a talent for color and off color. You said this isn't much of a landscape where's the green and he tried to show you some. You couldn't find it which might make you a cynic. I'm sorry I'm sorry. I would find it today I would find it now. He wrapped his arms around you he lifted you up he lifted you up he said One muddle doesn't mean betrayal. He made it alright to cry. But was it only a road to moquette. Betts interrupts wants a Penny for them. You say They're worth so much more than that. Well I've only got a fiver. Not even for that. We'll be there soon he says too bad we've run out of chocolates but you're off again leaving traveling in the opposite direction with the volvo the peugeot the honda a truck. He says Your father but you aren't listening.